THE OTTOMAN EMPIRE
THE GREEK WAR OF
INDEPENDENCE

S0-BZV-279

0   MILES   200

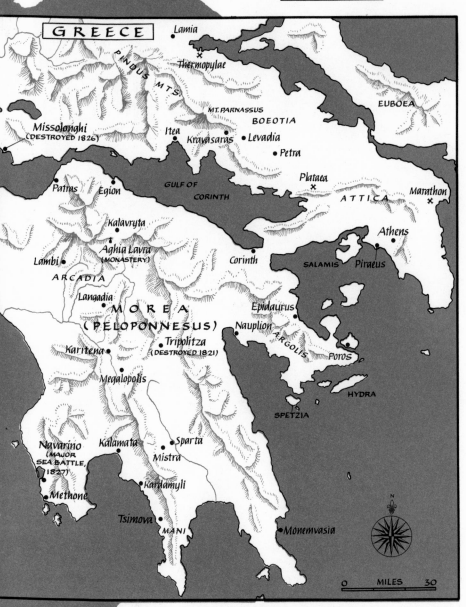

GREECE

S S I A

SEA OF AZOV

CRIMEA

Lamia

PINDUS MTS

Thermopylae

MT. PARNASSUS

BOEOTIA

EUBOEA

Missolonghi
(DESTROYED 1826)

Itea

Kravasaras

Levadia

Petra

Plataea

Marathon

Patras

Egion

GULF OF
CORINTH

ATTICA

Kalavryta

Athens

Aghia Lavra
(MONASTERY)

Lambi

Corinth

SALAMIS

Piraeus

ARCADIA

Langadia

M O R E A

Epidaurus

Nauplion

ARGOLIS

(PELOPONNESUS)

Karitena

Tripolitza
(DESTROYED 1821)

Poros

Megalopolis

HYDRA

Navarino
(MAJOR
SEA BATTLE,
1827)

Kalamata

Sparta

SPETZIA

Mistra

Methone

Kardamyli

N

Tsimova

MANI

Monemvasia

0   MILES   30

THE HOUR
OF THE BELL

Harry Mark Petrakis

A NOVEL
OF THE 1821 GREEK WAR
OF INDEPENDENCE
AGAINST THE TURKS.

DOUBLEDAY & COMPANY, INC.
GARDEN CITY, NEW YORK
1976

ISBN: 0-385-04877-7
LIBRARY OF CONGRESS CATALOG CARD NUMBER 75-40738
Copyright © 1976 by HARRY MARK PETRAKIS
First Edition

FOR MY FATHER,
REV. MARK EMMANUEL PETRAKIS,
WHO GAVE ME A MEMORY
OF HIS BELOVED CRETE,
AND FOR MY MOTHER,
PRESBYTERA STELLA PETRAKIS,
WHO GAVE ME A FRAGMENT
OF HER MIGHTY HEART.

CONTENTS

PRINCIPAL CHARACTERS

FATHER MARKOS	Priest of Kravasaras
AHMED BAJAKI	Wealthy Turkish farmer of Kravasaras
HASSAN	His son
KOSTAS MAKRYDIS	Agent of Society of Friends and captain of Greek forces
CLEON STARKAS	Second-in-command to Makrydis
MANOLIS KITSOS	Youth of Kravasaras who joins klepht band
EPHROSENE KITSOS	Mother of Manolis
PAPALIKOS	Renegade monk-soldier
VOROGRIVAS	Leader of klepht band on Parnassus
GHIOURIS	Second-in-command to Vorogrivas
BOUKOUVALAS	Legendary old warrior from Suli
LASCARINA	Woman fighter of the klepht band
LEONIDAS KONTOS	Sea captain of Psara
ASPASIA KONTOS	His wife
SKYLOS YARKAS	First mate to Kontos
KONSTANTINE KANARIS	Sea captain of Psara
DEMETRIOS PAPANIKOLIS	Sea captain of Psara

HADJI YANNAROS	Chief magistrate of Psara
YAKOUMAKIS TOMBAZIS	Admiral of the Greek fleet
PETROBEY MAVROMICHALIS	Prince of the Mani
KATERINA MAVROMICHALIS	His wife
ELIAS MAVROMICHALIS	Their eldest son
KYRIAKULIS MAVROMICHALIS	Brother to Petrobey
THEODOROS KOLOKOTRONIS	Revolutionary leader returned from exile to the war
ANAGNOSTARAS	Revolutionary leader
NIKETARAS	Revolutionary leader
XANTHOS	Historian from Zante and scribe to Kolokotronis
FATHER VERGANIS	Priest of the Mani
BALALAS	Veteran Maniat campaigner with Kolokotronis
ANDREAS MAKRAKIS	Youth of Crete
KYRIAKOS MAKRAKIS	His father and Cretan captain
GIANOULA	Sister of Andreas
BARBA SIMOS	Uncle of Andreas
VOULA PSYCHOUNDAKIS	Young girl of Villandredou
COSMATOS	Cretan captain from Sphakia
FARANDAKIS	Cretan captain from Sphakia
KRINGAS	Artillery officer and veteran of Napoleonic Wars
LAMBROS KASANDONIS	Cretan captain
PRINCE ALEXANDER IPSILANTIS	Commander of forces invading Moldavia and Walachia
PRINCE DEMETRIOS IPSILANTIS	His brother, Commander of Greek armies before Tripolitza
ARCHBISHOP GERMANOS	Metropolitan of Patras, commander of one of the armies before Tripolitza
ALEXANDER MAVROKORDATOS	Phanariot who became first Provisional President of Greece

ATHANASIOS DIAKOS   Greek captain, spitted and burned by the Turks in April 1821

BOUBOULINA   Famed Greek woman privateer

MEHEMET SELIK   Commander of Turkish forces at Tripolitza

ELMAS BEY   Captain of Albanian mercenaries at Tripolitza

ALI PASHA   Ruler of Jannina who revolted against Sultan Mahmud in 1820

KHURSHID PASHA   Military commander of Sultan Mahmud's forces besieging Ali Pasha in Jannina

BROTHER APOSTOLOS   Monk at the monastery of Aghios Vasilios

CALENDAR OF THE GREEK
WAR OF INDEPENDENCE

1821

FEBRUARY: Prince Alexander Ipsilantis invades the Danubian provinces and proclaims the revolution.

MARCH: Meeting of archons and clerics under Metropolitan Germanos at the monastery of Aghia Lavra.

MARCH: Revolt breaks out across Greece.

APRIL: Fall of Kalamata to Petrobey Mavromichalis.

APRIL: Hanging of Greek patriarch in Constantinople and massacre of Christians in Asia Minor.

MAY: Islands of Spetzia, Psara and Hydra join the revolt.

AUGUST: Surrender of Monemvasia.

AUGUST: Surrender of Navarino and massacre of Turks.

SEPTEMBER: Destruction and massacre of Turks at Tripolitza.

DECEMBER: Meeting of the First National Assembly at Epidaurus.

1822

MARCH: Destruction and massacre of Greeks at Chios.

OCTOBER: Firing of the Turkish flagship off Tenedos by the fireship of Konstantine Kanaris of Psara.

1823

MAY: Election of Theodoros Kolokotronis as Vice-President of the Executive Committee.

AUGUST: Raid by Markos Botsaris against the tents of the pashas. Death of Botsaris.

AUGUST: Lord Byron joins the Greeks at Missolonghi.

SEPTEMBER: First civil war breaks out in Greece.

1824

APRIL: Lord Byron dies at Missolonghi.

JUNE: Destruction and massacre of Greeks at Psara.

JULY: Second civil war in Greece. Kolokotronis imprisoned on Hydra.

1825

FEBRUARY: First landing of Egyptians under Ibrahim Pasha at Methone.

MAY: Surrender of Navarino to Ibrahim Pasha.

JUNE: Release of Kolokotronis from prison to lead the Greek forces against Ibrahim Pasha.

JUNE: Capture of Kalamata by Ibrahim Pasha.

DECEMBER: Armies of Ibrahim Pasha join the Turks besieging Missolonghi.

1826

APRIL: Fall of the city and massacre of Greeks at Missolonghi.

JULY: Attempted invasion of Samos by the Turks foiled by the Greek fleet.

JULY: Victory of the Maniats against Ibrahim Pasha at Politsaravon.

1827

JUNE: Signing in London of an agreement between England, France and Russia on the Greek question.

OCTOBER: Naval battle of Navarino, where units of English, French and Russian fleets sank Egyptian-Turkish fleet of seventy to eighty ships.

1828

JANUARY: Arrival of Ioannes Kapodistrias as President of Greece.

APRIL: Declaration of war by Russia on Turkey.

AUGUST: Landing of French troops in the Morea to evacuate Egyptian-Turkish forces.

1829

MARCH: Signing of an agreement between England and France fixing the frontiers of the proposed Greek state and its independence from the Sultan.

SEPTEMBER: Victory of the Greeks against the Turkish forces at Petra in Boeotia. Last battle of the Greek Revolution.

1831

FEBRUARY: Revolt of the Maniats against the government of Kapodistrias.

JULY: Firing of ships of the Greek national fleet at Poros by the Greek admiral Andreas Miaoulis.

OCTOBER: Assassination of Ioannes Kapodistrias.

1832

JULY: Signing by Russia, France and England of the final treaty on the establishment of the Greek state.

1833

FEBRUARY: Prince Otho, son of King Ludwig of Bavaria, installed as King of Greece.

The isles of Greece, the isles of Greece!
　Where burning Sappho loved and sung,
Where grew the arts of war and peace,—
　Where Delos rose and Phoebus sprung!
Eternal summer gilds them yet,
But all, except their sun, is set.

The mountains look on Marathon—
　And Marathon looks on the sea;
And musing there an hour alone,
　I dream'd that Greece might still be free;
For standing on the Persian's grave,
I could not deem myself a slave.

'Tis something in the death of fame,
　Though link'd among a fetter'd race,
To feel at least a patriot's shame,
　Even as I sing, suffuse my face;
For what is left the poet here?
For Greeks a blush—for Greece a tear.

Must we but weep o'er days more blest?
　Must we but blush?—Our fathers bled.
Earth! render back from out thy breast
　A remnant of our Spartan dead!
Of the three hundred grant but three
To make a new Thermopylae.

LORD BYRON

THE HOUR OF THE BELL

Part One

GREECE

AUTUMN

1820

CHAPTER
ONE

The village of Kravasaras was situated on a plain dominated by the towering peaks of the ancient, holy mountain, Parnassus, separated from Attica by rock-ribbed ranges and divided from the Peloponnesus to the south by the Gulf of Corinth.

A village like many other villages in Greece at that time, Kravasaras consisted of about fifty houses and nearly two hundred and fifty inhabitants. The majority were Christian Greeks except for a dozen Turkish families whose Moslem parents and grandparents had occupied the same land for generations. The houses varied from reed and straw huts, windowless and unheated against the severe winter, to some dual-level stone dwellings belonging to the affluent Turks and a few prosperous Greeks.

The road running through the village was pitted with ruts, hard and dusty in summer, muddy during the season of rain. Along this road, which came from Biskeni Agha, a town a dozen miles away, and which ran south to the Gulf, the farmers and shepherds of the village drove their donkeys, goats, sheep and carts to and from their fields. A few mulberry trees lined this street, flourishing because of the good water table, and, in spring and summer, spreading a dark green foliage across the brown and orange vistas of the land.

The center of the village was the Agora, a marketplace containing small shops selling produce, notions and fabrics. There was also the kafeneion, where after a day's work in the warmer seasons and all day in winter, when there was little work to do, the men gathered to talk, play cards, drink coffee and ouzo.

Once a year the Moslem tax collectors from Lamia, a major city to the north, rode into the village escorted by mounted Turkish troopers and summoned the citizens to the Agora. At that time, every Christian man, woman and child was required to pay the Kharaj, the tax that was the sacred obligation of every non-Moslem subject of the Sultan. For this payment a Christian was given a receipt granting the right to retain one's head for the ensuing year.

The two largest buildings in the village were the mosque and the church. The mosque stood at the northern end of Kravasaras, the tall spires of its minarets visible for miles. In the richly carpeted interior, shoeless and kneeling toward Mecca, the Turks of the village prayed five times a day, at sunrise, midmorning, noon, midafternoon, and at sundown, confessing their belief in Allah as the one and only God and Mohammed as His Prophet.

At the southern end of the village, beneath a cluster of tall cypresses standing like sentinels against the shadow of the minarets, was the church of Saint Athanasius, constructed of fieldstone a hundred years before. Separating the sanctuary from the uncarpeted and bare interior of the church, a row of faded icons hung mantled in the shadows. The only other decorations were roughly drawn paintings on the stone walls. There was the figure of Christ entering Jerusalem on a donkey, the sorrowful visage of the Blessed Virgin Mary, the unyielding, all-powerful hand of God. At dawn and in the evening, on Sundays and during the Holy

Days, the Christians of Kravasaras assembled to worship according to their own faith.

In 1710, the previous church in Kravasaras, built during
the reign of the last Byzantine Emperor, Constantine
Palaeologus, eroded by time and weakened by earthquakes,
finally collapsed. The villagers petitioned the pasha of the
province to allow them to build a new church. Unable to
reject their request because the policy of the Sultans in Constantinople granted the Christians the right to practice their
religion, the pasha interpreted this indulgence guilefully. He
granted the villagers a dispensation to erect their church, re-
stricting the work, however, to a total of five hours a week
and those hours to be confined to darkness so the eyes of the
true believers might not be shamed by the impious handi-
work of the rayahs.

The men, women and children of Kravasaras gathered by
moonlight and candlelight to construct their church. For ten
years the church formed slowly, fitfully, the old people
grieving when their time came to die because they had not
lived to see it completed. Finally finished, the last stone
mortared in the autumn of 1720, the Greeks of the village
with crowds of Christians from neighboring villages and
towns joined in a solemn thanksgiving, hundreds weeping
gratefully for the end of their labor and the church blessed
as a monument to God.

Then the pasha issued the final provision of his dispensation. Although a bell tower had been erected on the
church and a magnificent bell brought by ship from the
shops of artisans in Italy, the pasha ordered the bell buried
in the Christian cemetery of Kravasaras. There it would toll,
he ruled somberly, "for the bones of the infidels so they
might be reminded of the benevolence of their masters even
unto death."

For a hundred years the bell had been buried in the cemetery. Yet there were those villagers who swore they heard it
ring. Stories from grandmothers and grandfathers, hoarded

and recalled and whispered to children, told of hearing the bell tolling mournfully on those nights when the wind wailed from the mountains across the plains.

In the autumn of 1820, the priest of the church of Saint Athanasius, in Kravasaras, was Father Markos. His grandfather, Demetrius, and his father, Elias, had both been priests in the village. His grandfather had been among the builders of the church. The bones of these good and dedicated men were buried in the cemetery beside the bell that had never rung for them in life.

Father Markos had married as a young man and lost his wife of illness after just a few years. They had been childless and he grieved because he did not have a son to continue serving the spiritual needs of the village. Reconciled to being the last of his line, he sought to perform his duties conscientiously. Unable to exist on his meager earnings (true of his grandfather and father, as well) he was also a farmer, raising his seasonal crop of wheat, cotton and tobacco, maintaining a small vine-patch of grapes to provide him a ration of wine.

As he had grown older, beset by rheumatism that settled painfully in his shoulders and back, he could no longer farm his land. He had leased his stremata to younger villagers in return for a slim percentage of the worth of the crop. He cultivated a vegetable garden, looked after his donkey and his goat.

Now, nearing his seventieth year, a little labor in his garden for more than a few hours sufficient to set his back to aching, he anticipated those moments in late afternoon when the light began to falter, the landscape about the village realigned with shadows. The tall cypresses about the church gleamed black against the haze rising from the foothills of the sacred mountain, its wild crags and peaks accepting the merciful night.

He sat on the bench outside his small dwelling, separated

from the church by the cemetery, resting and breathing in the scent of lemons and figs. A few crop-headed boys ran shrieking up the street, a dog chasing them, barking in their wake. After they had passed, the ghostly sound of goat-bells carried across the twilight and a goat, finding his way home alone, appeared like a specter in the violet light.

A man, woman and a donkey came down the road, returning from the fields: the man walking beside the donkey, the woman with a hoe on her shoulder, trailing a few feet behind.

"Good evening, Sotiri, Despina," the priest called.

"Good evening, Father," the man replied, the woman echoing his greeting, neither of them pausing or breaking a step.

People have their rhythm, the priest thought as they passed on, measured and purposeful despite the leisurely pace. No one rushes along the road or paths of the village and only children were ever seen running. The pace seemed set by the walk of a donkey or a goat. The villagers took the strides they needed to accompany these animals and carried those spare movements into their homes. Women cooked and baked without haste. Men loaded a cart without wasted movement, yet rejecting unseemly speed. He was sure that was the way it had been in the village when his father and grandfather had lived, establishing a comforting continuity in his life.

In houses that had windows, the glow of candles and oil lamps appeared, the women preparing supper for their men returning from working on the tobacco seedbed frames. Father Markos could smell the scents of food and with a tremor of expectation in his stomach, considered his own supper. There would be a plate of green herbs from his garden, soaked in lemon and oil, some chunks of dark, wheaten bread and a glass of wine from the grapes he had pruned and crushed himself.

As the shadows darkened, he considered entering the

house to light his own candle and to eat. But he did not
wish to relinquish the serene twilight. These moments were
precious to him. In a few hours, sleep, casting her blandish-
ments more artfully every year, would rehearse him for the
embrace of her sister, death. That was the way the rhapsode
Hesiod defined the passage from life to death. When men
died, the earth received them back into her womb so they
might nourish the plants and crops to begin the cycle once
more. Such was the wise design conceived in the heart of
God.

Sometimes he wished, with a twinge of shame, that his
end would come soon. A selfish and cowardly thought, he
knew, but one prompted by his weariness and his fear.

The days were full of unhappy omens. Across the Gulf of
Corinth, a devastating earthquake had struck the Peloponnesus. Travelers in Macedonia told of seeing a horde of
lepers, a profane host with eroded noses and missing fingers,
extending their stumps in fearful entreaty. In the area of
their own village, the wolves howled on Parnassus, while
crows and blackbirds screeched above the cliffs and crags.
And in the dark of the confessional, women whispered to
him of strange apparitions in their dreams.

Father Markos had been eighteen in 1770, the time of the
last major rebellion against the Turks, when Prince Orlov
landed in the Peloponnesus under the banner of the Russian
Empress Catherine. From the Aegean islands, from Sphakia
in Crete, from towns and villages across Greece, volunteers
flocked to Orlov's pennants, singing the praises of Mother
Russia, who would help them achieve their liberation. Taking the Turkish garrisons by surprise, the Greeks and Russians were able to overrun most of the Peloponnesus in a
few weeks. Then the Turks sent in the terrible Albanian
mercenaries, who crushed the rebellion. Orlov fled by sea
with the ragtail of his army and the Greeks were left to their
fate. For ten dreadful years the Albanians plundered the
Peloponnesus and central Greece, burning houses and crops,

assaulting and raping hundreds of women and children. The scars of that bloody incursion were still upon the land.

Now there were rumors of the Russians coming to liberate Greece once more, people forgetting how they had once been abandoned by the Muscovites. Ali Pasha, the butcher of Jannina, swollen with his riches and made reckless by ambition, had challenged the might and supremacy of Sultan Mahmud II and now was besieged by the Sultan's armies. With the major Turkish garrisons in Greece providing soldiers for the siege, there were many who whispered the time was favorable for revolt. But were the times ever opportune for bloodshed and death?

Barely visible in the last tracings of twilight, Kronos, the idiot boy who tended sheep, passed along the road, shuffling in his broken gait. Father Markos called him a blessing. The boy paused, listening as if he could not be sure where the voice had come from, then resumed his disjointed walk.

Freedom or the lack of freedom does not trouble him, the priest thought sadly. Within the infirmities of his body, only death could make him free.

Yet the proddings and hunger for freedom did not pose a panacea for Father Markos. He had learned many years before that whether Mussulman or Greek, there was little difference between their avarice and cruelty. There were Christians he would not trust under his roof a single night, fearing they would cut his throat for a few coppers. And there were Turks like his dear friend Ahmed Bajaki, who lived in the big house near the mosque, a man he would have trusted with his life. Some who agitated for the overthrow of the Turkish rulers were disgruntled creatures who would not have been happy in Paradise. There were other men so eaten by envy for the possessions of others, they sought any upheaval that might improve their own fortunes.

The priest had captured rumblings among the villagers that he had grown old, the blood congealing in his veins, his loins curdled by fear for his worthless bones and by his friendship with Ahmed Bajaki. A few ingrates even referred to him contemptuously as "an uncircumcised Turk."

He was not unaware of the blessings of freedom. Sometimes when he woke in the morning, a strange dream of unparalleled sweetness carried into his day, a memory of some halcyon time when their land had belonged to them, before the wicked encroachment of Venetians, Franks and Turks. If they could regain that liberation, they would drink in freedom as the parched earth of a drought-stricken land drank in the rain.

Meanwhile, there had always been resistance to the oppressors. Men from their own village slipped away at night to join the klepht band led by Vorogrivas that lived on the crests and in the caves of Parnassus, as similar bands dwelt on the mountains of Olympus and the Pindus. From these citadels they raided the Turkish garrisons and towns, harassing the convoys and tax collectors of the pashas. They were the only free men in all of Greece.

Those men Father Markos feared for most were the ones who could not live in bondage, men who would sit staring silently for hours at the eagles wheeling above the shining cliffs. If they had wives and children they feared to leave as hostages for their flight, these men languished and sickened and died untouched by any recognizable illness or wound. He had witnessed that fearful decline a number of times. Walking in the cemetery on days he prayed for the dead, he would linger at the graves of these men, for while the earth above them remained in bondage, he imagined their spirits tormented even in death.

Yet their village had been fortunate in being spared the terror that existed in other villages. There had not been any incident in Kravasaras in years of Turks abusing the Christians, assaulting them or plundering their possessions. And only once, a long time before, had an earlier pasha issued an embargo on education. Even then the means were found to circumvent that restriction, the children attending secret

classes at night in a monastery on the slopes of the mountain. He had conducted some of these classes, his heart
pounding with fear, while the children sang softly.

> My little bright moon
> Light me in my walk
> For going to school
> To learn my letters
> God's good things . . .

Yes, he was grateful that the Turkish inhabitants in
Kravasaras dwelt peacefully with their Christian neighbors,
guided by the stern, fair strictures of Ahmed Bajaki, who
was respected by Greek and Turk.

Soothed by the thought that the peacefulness might continue, he rose from the bench and breathed in the scent of
the evening. The last traces of summer still lingered among
the leaves, resisting the sortie of winter and cold. On the
hidden branches of a nearby tree, a dove called, and another
bird crooned pleasantly in answer.

Inside his house, Father Markos lit a candle, the pangs of
hunger rumbling in his stomach. His dwelling was a windowless room, containing an old pair of chairs and a table,
on which he ate and, afterwards, wrote the notes for his special sermons. There was a stone fireplace, where he cooked
and heated his evening meals and from which, in the coldest
part of winter, he sought some warmth. His bed was a pallet
placed across a base of reeds and wooden planks. Beside the
bed was a shelf with his treasure of books, the copies of the
Old and New Testaments inherited from his father, the Lives
of the Church Fathers, the History of the Saints, a hand-
copied manuscript of the Psalms, and his beloved Hesiod's
Works and Days.

Placing the two logs in his fireplace in the form of a V so
only the points burned, he heated a tin with greens over the
frail flame, snuffing the logs out quickly since wood was pre-

cious and had to be conserved. He ate his greens and wheaten bread and drank a glass of wine. For the final portion of his meal he slowly chewed a spoonful of honey and sesame seeds a parishioner had given him. He had planned to save the delicacy for Sunday, but weakened, relishing the sweetness seeping into the pockets of his cheeks and across his tongue. Afterward, he leaned back in his chair, a satisfying ripple of gas passing his vitals. He felt his eyelids grow heavy and looked with longing at his bed. But he had to carry communion and a prayer to a farmer who had broken his leg in a fall. Then, before the hour grew too late, he planned to call on his friend Ahmed Bajaki, an event he looked forward to with greater anticipation than he would have liked to admit to his Christian brothers and sisters.

The farmer, Kalkanis, sat slumped on a chair, his bound leg extended like a stump, and raised his mouth for communion while several of his children huddled around him. The man's aged mother, living with them, glared at the priest as if he and God were mutually responsible for her son's broken limb. Father Markos was pleased to escape the house, hurrying through the darkness for the visit to his friend.

Ahmed Bajaki, the wealthiest inhabitant in the village, dwelt within a compound adjoining the mosque, an area enclosed by a stone wall and gate. The enclosure held several storage sheds, a grove of lemon trees and a grand marble fountain. The house, a fine two-story building with numerous rooms, was the most elegant dwelling in Kravasaras.

After removing his shoes and being ushered into the salon by Abdullah, Ahmed Bajaki's servant, Father Markos marveled, as always, at the luxurious interior. A stone floor was covered by plush rugs from Persia, a long divan ran from one wall to another, and the circular table was covered with a cloth as finely spun as the web of a spider. In addition, each room contained enough treasures of rare china and antique silver to provide a hundred dowries.

Father Markos knew the house even had an interior latrine! He had never dared muster the courage to use it, but had once looked with awe on that regal, sculptured throne set on a floor of mosaic.

As he breathed in the opulence surrounding him, his friend entered. Ahmed Bajaki was a swarthy, handsome man in his sixties with the powerful arms and shoulders of a farmer. He wore an embroidered jacket of white wool, and a long blue robe. His beard was pitch black and pointed like the tip of a Damascus sword and a silver earring hung from his right ear. He greeted the priest by passing his hand quickly from his chest to his lips and forehead and the two of them embraced. Ahmed Bajaki motioned the priest to sit down and Father Markos sank into the warm splendor of the divan. He stared up at the chandelier of a dozen glass globes suspended from the ceiling in the center of the room, each globe filled with oil, its protruding wick aflame. In the glare of that light he became conscious of his ragged, stockinged feet and drew them back under his cassock.

Ahmed Bajaki sat down in an armchair facing him.

"My good and devoted Father Markos," he said, a gentle banter in his voice. "Have you come this evening to discuss your conversion to the true faith?"

"My dear friend, Ahmed," Father Markos said. "I have come to inform you once again that, at your convenience, I will be pleased to receive you for the rites of baptism."

Ahmed Bajaki smiled, a flashing of strong, white teeth in his bearded face.

"There are merits to both positions," he said patiently. "Of course, one of the more significant differences is that we believers in the True Faith seldom ask Allah for favors. We limit our prayers to thanksgiving and adoration. You Christians are perpetually begging . . ."

"Since we are the subjects of your esteemed and benevolent monarch," Father Markos said, "we have a considerable need to pray."

Ahmed Bajaki nodded, a sparkle in his eyes affirming the effectiveness of the priest's response. They discussed their religions as a debate, with the scoring of points more important than conversion. They respected one another and Father Markos was especially fond of the Mussulman he knew as a deeply religious man and a loyal friend.

"According to Moslem teaching"—Ahmed Bajaki clasped his hands over his lean stomach—"Allah has provided men successive revelations through His prophets. Man consistently falls away from these prophets and the merciful Allah sends new ones. Mohammed, may His name be forever blessed, is the last, the divine messenger of Allah, who is transcendent, almighty, just, loving, merciful and good. When the world falls away from Allah, the end will come."

"A fine summing up of your position," Father Markos said. "Unfortunately you do not consider the Old and New Testaments before, if you'll forgive my bluntness, you perverted the text."

Ahmed Bajaki raised his hands in dismay.

"We perverted the text! My dear Father Markos, if any perversion exists, it is the result, if you'll now forgive me, of Greek connivance."

Father Markos stretched his feet out, settling himself more comfortably in the divan, forgetting his ragged stockings as he warmed to the argument.

"It is written in Proverbs," he said slowly, "that a word fitly spoken is like apples of gold in pitchers of silver. Yet it is also written that when a man is wise only in arrogance, then his mouth shall be filled with gravel."

Ahmed Bajaki's beard quivered as he leaned forward.

"It is also written in the teachings of the poets that if a man sees an ass, shall he not call it an ass?"

"It is always an honor for a man to speak with wisdom,"

Father Markos said loudly, "but a fool's mouth is his destruction!"

"A dullard!" Ahmed Bajaki blew the word like a wind between his lips. "Though his foot may rest in the flame, he will not suffer it to be moved!"

They hung poised, eyes sparkling, spirits enlivened for the fray. Ahmed Bajaki was the first to smile and sit back with a sigh.

"Iron sharpeneth iron," he said gently. "So a man sharpeneth the heart and spirit of his friend."

Father Markos nodded in approval. "Better is a friend who will rebuke you than an enemy who will flatter you."

They laughed together. At that moment the curtains at one end of the salon parted and Abdullah appeared carrying a silver tray with glasses of scarlet liqueur and tiny cups of fragrant coffee. Behind him entered Hassan, the youngest son of Ahmed Bajaki, and the only one of his numerous children living with him in the village. Dressed in a velvet jacket and small, flared pantaloons, he was a graceful-limbed boy of about ten years, olive-skinned with large black eyes and lustrous dark hair. Ahmed Bajaki's face softened with adoration and pride.

"Greet the good Father Markos, my son."

"Good evening, Father," the boy spoke the words solemnly.

"Good evening, Hassan," Father Markos answered gravely.

Abdullah had placed the liqueur and coffee before each man and left the room. Hassan watched his father, waiting for a sign, and then Ahmed Bajaki motioned the boy to him. With a shy delight the boy slipped into his father's arms. They came together as if they were halves of a single heart. The priest was swept with a tremor of remorse at his own barren fold.

Ahmed Bajaki stroked the fragile flesh of the boy's throat.

"Have you read your lessons?" Ahmed Bajaki asked.

"For two hours, Baba," the boy said eagerly. "Since evening prayers."

Ahmed Bajaki nodded in approval. "Now then it is time for bed."

The boy pulled reluctantly but obediently from his father's embrace. He bowed slightly toward the priest and then started from the salon, pausing before the division in the curtains to cast a final mischievous and endearing glance at his father, a look affirming the inestimable secrets only the two of them shared.

After the boy had gone, they sipped their liqueur and coffee in silence, the priest eased and warmed in the presence of his friend.

"Ahmed, what is happening around us?" he asked softly.

"I hear rumors." Ahmed Bajaki stared gravely at the priest. "But I have been hearing rumors of Christian revolt for as long as I have lived."

"There is a difference now," the priest said, and could not keep his voice from trembling. "There are omens. Old Sachtouris has been on the verge of death for a month. When he seems about to breathe his last, something sustains him. The old women whisper that Death is occupied with mighty plans and cannot bother with a helpless old man." He made a troubled gesture with his fingers. "I do not believe in such foolishness, but . . ."

"Perhaps the time has come for changes in this land," Ahmed Bajaki spoke quietly. "We have had our way for generations and have not shown by our wisdom or benevolence that we deserve to rule."

They were silent for several moments.

"I should worry about all of the country," the priest said, "but that concern requires at least an Archbishop. I can only worry about my people here in the village. I worry about you and Hassan, Tuju Effendi and his family, Bekir and his daughters, and, God help me, about my own worthless carcass."

"If Allah in his incomparable wisdom and mercy decrees our positions be reversed," Ahmed Bajaki said, "we may still go on living in this village together. You as the masters, I hope, will be wiser than we have been."

"I am not interested in being anyone's master!" the priest said fervently. "After nearly seventy years of life I am still having trouble mastering the priest of Kravasaras."

"Not all your Christians here feel the way you do," Ahmed Bajaki said. "There are those I pass on the road whose eyes hurl like daggers into my back."

From an adjoining room came the laughter of Hassan, a vibrant outburst of joy. A fleeting shadow crossed Ahmed Bajaki's face.

Understanding his friend's concern, the priest sought to reassure him.

"No harm could possibly come to the child!" Father Markos cried earnestly. "He is loved by everyone in the village. I pledge we will protect him. Besides, if any trouble comes, it will probably be confined to garrisons and soldiers."

"My old friend." Ahmed Bajaki smiled. "I marvel sometimes at your charitable innocence. You would have made one of your saintly prophets. When an earthquake splits the ground, the chasm engulfs all."

"Then why don't you move to Constantinople for a while? Or at least send Hassan there to be with his mother and sisters."

"I have considered that prospect," Ahmed Bajaki sighed. "But, the truth is that I cannot endure my days without him . . . merely to look at him from time to time is sufficient to provide me an undeserved but incomparable joy."

A reverence entered Ahmed Bajaki's voice.

"There are sages who speak of the most wonderful sight on earth being the nakedness of a woman one loves, or a plumed army moving to battle, or a great-masted ship riding a wild sea . . . but, for me, none of these can match the beauty of Hassan, the love in his cheeks and eyes when he looks at me."

He paused, looking up at the flames flickering in the globes above their heads. Light and shadow streamed across his face.

"Yet neither can I consider leaving this village just to take him away," he said. "Like yours, my grandfather and father sowed and reaped this land. Like yours, my grandfather and father fought Venetians and Franks, endured the earthquakes and the storms. If I had to leave, could I tear the tiles from the roof of this house and take them with me? Could I uproot the trees and flowers in my garden and be assured they would grow and provide the fragrance and shade they offer me here? And what windows would I find anywhere on earth that would allow me to look out upon our mountain, those great and luminous peaks like suns burning into the lids of my eyes? That is a holy sight my ancestors bequeathed to me that I will never relinquish."

He moved his hands restlessly from his chest to his knees, rubbing the cloth of his robe slowly with his fingers.

"No, I will not leave," Ahmed Bajaki said, "and I will not send Hassan away from me." A resignation, unlike anything the priest had ever heard from his friend's lips before, shaded his words. "Abu-Hāmid al-Ghazali prescribes that when a man is in his grave, complete, body and soul, he must then answer the questions 'Who is thy Lord and what is thy religion and who is thy prophet?'" He paused. "Whatever befalls us is not as important as that we must live and die so that we are able to answer those questions and accept the judgment upon our bodies and our souls as Allah wills . . ."

The following Sunday morning, Father Markos rose before dawn, shivering in the early chill, dressing hurriedly, brushing his beard and gingerly sprinkling his eyes with a few drops of water. He left his house, walking through the enclosure of the cemetery, the markers and crosses white and spectral in the shadows, to the entrance of the church. As he looked beyond the desolate, empty bell tower, he saw, in the distance, the first faint light of day shimmering above the crags and peaks of the mountain.

He pushed open the creaking door and entered the dark interior of the church, the mustiness mingling with the scents of wax and incense. He made his way along the walls, once rough-hewn stone worn smooth by the devotions of countless hands, until he came to the low railing separating the nave of the church from the sanctuary. In a row of glistening icons, the saints contemplated ghostly suppers and words spoken in haunted gardens. Above the altar, in the frail flame of the cresset, the faces of the Blessed Virgin Mary and the Christ-child shone pensive and tender.

For a moment he did not move. In this sanctified cloister the seasons and years were an eternal and unmeasured flow, the turmoil and anxieties of life banished, his spirit fused indivisibly with the spirit of God.

He lit a circle of candles and the church warmed and brightened in their glow. He began breaking bread and pouring wine for the chalice of communion. By the time he had slipped into his vestments, through the narrow solitary window high in the rear of the church, he saw the light disperse the final traces of darkness. At that hour he mourned there was no bell to summon the faithful to their prayers. Yet, even without a bell, the villagers came.

The old women dressed from head to toe in black garments shuffled in to lurk like crows or ravens against the white stone of the walls. All the juices of kindness long drained from their bodies, they crossed themselves gloomily, rejecting friendship, love, laughter and hope. He never saw them gather without the fear he might have felt at a coven of witches.

The church elders entered, a quartet of patriarchal old rams, booted and tight-collared, clutching their caps stiffly at their bellies. Tall and wiry like aged, still strong trees, they stood like sentries against the wall to his right. Father Markos drew comfort from their stern, unsmiling vigil.

Then the younger farmers and shepherds entered the church leading their families. The men were black-haired with their moustaches trimmed and their chins shaven. The women were handsome in clean headcloths. There were babies cradled in their arms, children with scrubbed faces clutching at their skirts. Boys whose bodies were bursting to their adolescence and slim, pretty green-budded girls with their long black hair in braids.

Father Markos swung the brass censer at the end of the clanking chains toward them, scattering clouds of incense about their bowed heads.

He saw their poor and shabby clothing, ragged and mismatched jackets and pants, dresses patched and mended and washed so many times they faded into the same sooty, neutral colors. He recognized their suffering, the melancholy like thorns about their heads. Yet, in that strange, prophetic moment, he saw something more.

They held no grievance against God. They came to church to worship, not to complain, to give thanks for what they had, not to condemn. From their hard and constant labor, the sorrow of living and the bitterness of enslavement, they had grown lean and strong. In spite of the harsh race holding their bodies in bondage, the eyes of children, women and men blazed with life.

Divining himself as a part of their strength and spirit, he joined his heart to their hearts, loved them so much in that moment that he turned to the altar, raised his hands in prayer, and cried his joy at the apocalyptic vision that they were the land and the land was theirs . . .

CHAPTER
TWO

For several days a fierce storm had battered the village, driving rain intensified by hard lashings of wind. Into the hours of darkness, the wind wailed across the houses, sweeping icy gusts beneath the doors.

On the first day of the storm, Father Markos tried to make his regular parish visits. After suffering the wind biting his cheeks and tearing at his cassock, seeing the tall cypresses thrashing as if they were frail saplings, he stabled his donkey and goat with Ahmed Bajaki's animals and retreated into his house.

When he was not in his bed, he sat huddled before his fireplace, a blanket draped across his shoulders, absorbing what meager warmth he could from the burning log as the wind rocked against his door.

On the third evening of the storm, lying on his pallet unable to sleep, he was startled by the door being hurled open. A cold torrent blew into the room, and the fire flared an explosion of sparks. Thinking first it was the wind, Father Markos cried out at the sight of a giant shadow that entered. The figure turned and slammed the door closed and it was not until he had stepped into the firelight that Father Markos recognized the tall monk, Papalikos, who lived in the monastery of St. Paulos, on the other side of Biskeni Agha.

"In God's name, Brother!" Father Markos sat up and made his cross. "You almost caused my wretched heart to stop! Why are you wandering in this tempest?"

"A good night to travel, Father," the monk said, and his voice was still as mocking and gruff as the priest remembered. "The roads are empty of Turkish pigs." He crossed to the fireplace with a single, long stride, stripping off his shaggy capote, lowering the cowl of his cassock, extending his long fingers almost into the flames. "I am on a journey"— he spoke with his back to the priest—"an extended journey . . . and I am wet, cold and thirsty." He laughed harshly again and twisted to look at the priest. "I stopped by to exchange blessings in Christ with the good Father Markos of Kravasaras."

"Delighted, Brother." Father Markos tried heartily to suggest a friendliness he did not feel. He fumbled at the blankets and struggled up from the bed. "Warm yourself and I'll get some wine and cheese and bread."

They sat before the fire, to which Father Markos, with a twinge of remorse, added another log. He had cut what remained of a gourd of cheese, bringing that and half a loaf of dark, rough bread to his visitor. The monk tore free chunks of bread and cheese that he popped avidly into his mouth. Father Markos could feel the crust being rent and torn by his strong, big teeth.

"A little more wine, Brother?" He poured from a wineskin into the monk's cup.

"You are very kind, Father." In the firelight the monk's lips curled in a parody of courtesy. Before swallowing the wine he swilled it around in his cheeks, sucking to loosen the particles of bread and cheese that lingered between his teeth.

Seated across from the monk, stealing glances at him

eating and drinking, Father Markos prayed for the Lord's indulgence because he disliked the Brother, was uneasy around him, sensing a cruelty and irreverence that was alien to the cloister and the cloth.

A swooping of wind battered the house, sending a quiver down the walls. Father Markos looked apprehensively at the ceiling, wondering if the roof might blow off. Papalikos continued to eat and drink, undistracted by the storm.

With his totally bald head, eyes sharp and barbed as nettles, black brows running in rough thickets to the tangle of his thick beard, the monk resembled a Mongol or a Hun. His brown cassock, shiny with stains, looking as if it had not been washed in weeks, smelled of garlic and rancid oil. His huge toes with long black nails, protruded from the tips of his sandals.

"Are you traveling far, Brother?" Father Markos asked to break the uneasy silence.

The monk stared into the flames. "Far enough, Father, far enough."

He finished the wine in his cup and without a pause in motion extended it from his lips toward the priest. Father Markos raised the wineskin and filled the cup once more. The monk tossed back his head and drank several deep draughts. When he lowered the cup, the wine dribbled down his beard.

"The tribes are gathering." An acrid joy rumbled in his voice. "Men are digging up their weapons, sharpening their knives . . . the smell of blood is in the wind . . ." He raised his head and, as if he were scenting some spoor the priest could not smell, he grimaced in pleasure.

"What is going to happen?" the priest whispered.

"Revolution and war!" the monk spit into the fire, a nub of steam hissing in the flames. "Judgment and vengeance!"

"Has it started?" The priest's voice shook.

"Soon now," the monk said. "Very soon! When the first blows are struck, the Turkish scum will know! And the master of pigs across the Bosporus will feel the shock in his balls!"

He threw back his head and bolted the wine remaining in his cup. Extending the cup once more toward the priest, he wiped his chin with the back of his other hand, the black strands of his beard wet and matted. The priest raised the wineskin numbly and filled his cup once more.

"I've left the cloisters," the monk said in a low, bitter voice. "Let the sheep-loined Brothers kneel and mumble their useless prayers. Prayers will not drive the Turk away. There have been four hundred years of futile Christian prayers!" He tugged the loose fold of the cassock against his waist and Father Markos saw a long, curved knife outlined beneath the cloth. "Only this dagger at their throats will teach them the word of God!"

The priest shivered.

"You are frightened, Father," the monk laughed. "Like my revered Brothers back in the cells, you don't understand the mission for killing . . . the joy of placing a knife against an infidel's throat and cutting through flesh and bone till the blood spurts. That is good for the teeth, the jaws, the mouth, the brain, the stomach . . . all of a man's body springs alive when he kills, curing fever, melancholy, the lunacy of love." He stared mockingly at the priest. "Don't you agree, Father?"

"No, no!" the priest said. "The commandment is, 'Thou shalt not kill.'"

"That is a verse for children," the monk grunted. "In this time, our innards eaten by the bloody oppressors, our children stolen, our women ravished, now a new commandment is needed." He stared at the fire, his eyes reflecting the flames. "Learn to love the fire," he said. "Fire is purifying, to cauterize by fire, to sacrifice by fire . . ."

"Fire destroys," the priest said helplessly.

"Amen!" the monk cried, and tore his gaze reluctantly

from the flames as another surge of wind battered the house. "Before one can build again, one must first destroy by fire! The wicked must be consigned to fire!" He raised his hand, pointing his long, dark fingers at the priest. "The new commandment must be, 'Learn to love the fire.' By that rule we will destroy every Turk in Greece!"

"The children, too?" the priest asked. "What about the innocent Turkish children?"

"Children grow up to become adults," the monk snarled. "The best time to kill them is when they are young, like a nest of baby snakes before their poison matures."

"I am an old man, Brother," the priest said quietly. "If I am fortunate I will die and not have to witness this purgatory of fire."

"If men are too old or too fainthearted to help in the battle for freedom," the monk said with contempt, "they might as well die. If I cannot be useful to our holy purpose, I am ready to die!"

He stretched across the distance that separated them, grasping the wineskin in his fingers, taking it from the priest to raise swiftly to his mouth.

At that moment there was a knock on the door. The monk wrenched the wineskin from his lips, gasping for breath, the wine dribbling down his beard onto the cloth of his cassock. His hand slipped to the knife at his waist.

"A Turk would not knock," the priest whispered. He started toward the door. When he opened it, a blast of wind drove the daughter of one of his neighbors into the room, a cloaked, pretty teen-age girl clutching a wrapped bowl in her hands.

The priest helped tug her out of the path of the storm. Straining with effort, he pressed against the door to close it, but the wind defied his strength. Suddenly the tall figure of the monk appeared at his side. He was startled how swiftly the man had crossed the room.

"Let me help you, Father," the monk said, a charade of concern in his voice. With a lunge of his powerful shoulder against the wood, he slammed the door. He turned back and looked down at the girl. A solicitous smile curled his lips but his eyes stared boldly at the cleft in the cloak that revealed the bare flesh of her throat. The girl flushed slightly and looked quickly toward the priest.

"I'm sorry to disturb you, Father," she said timidly. "Mama thought you'd like some hot soup."

"That was kind of your mama," the priest said, "and courageous of you, Dena, to bring it to me through the storm." He took the bowl from her fingers. "This is Brother Papalikos, my child, a refugee from this dreadful storm who is spending the night with me."

The girl looked uneasily at the monk.

"I have to get home. Mama will be worried."

She took a step toward the door and the monk moved to block her path.

"Why don't you keep us company for a while, my child?" the monk spoke softly. "We poor Brothers of the cloth, immersed as we are in God's work, don't often get a chance to visit with such pretty young women." He raised his big hand slowly, the sleeve of his cassock falling away from his long-boned wrist, and caught the cord at her throat. "Take off your cloak and share our fire . . ."

The girl shrank away.

"I have to go," she pleaded, and there was fear in her voice. She started around him for the door.

"Be careful, my child!" the monk cried. "The wind may knock you down!" He clasped her about the waist and with his other hand reached for the latch. When he opened the door, the force of the wind drove her slender form against his body. He held her tightly for a moment as she gasped, struggling to break free. When he finally released her, she pulled the cloak around her head and hurried out the door.

The monk closed the door slowly, relishing the wind

whipping against his body, staring at the darkness where the girl had disappeared.

"God, how young and juicy!" he said, turning back to the fire. "Won't be long before they sing her marriage song and hang the sheet with her virgin's blood out the window."

"She's only fifteen." Father Markos was embarrassed at the monk's words.

"Old enough," the monk said. He walked back to the fire, bent again and extended his hands, squeezing his fingers as if there were something in his palms he sought to crush.

"You village priests are lucky," he said bitterly. "You have sweet young fruit like that girl around. The abbot has prohibited my saying mass in any village. He fears I might contaminate the piety of the common people."

He brooded for a moment.

"It is getting late, Brother," the priest said. The sooner they went to bed and slept, the quicker the monk would be gone. "You are welcome to my bed."

"I'll sleep here by the fire," the monk said. "This is better than I usually have." He raised his arms, stretching his great height toward the ceiling, his fingers touching the beams. Then he lowered himself to the floor in a lithe, flowing motion and drew his capote up over his legs.

They lay in silence for a while, the priest on his pallet, the monk before the dying fire. From time to time a surge of wind swept the house. Then the few embers remaining cast up sparks that swiftly flickered out. The monk breathed heavily, the room surfeited with the scent of wine. The priest wondered if he had fallen asleep.

"Shall I tell you, little Father, how I wish sometimes I might die?" The monk's voice came slurred and weary through the darkness. "If we had lived in a different time, when our mission was not holy war, I would have wanted to die as an Assyrian king once died. He built an enormous pyre in his palace, heaped upon it all his gold and silver and then, gathering his concubines and eunuchs in the pyre around him, he consigned them and himself to the flames."

Father Markos shivered and twisted on his side, turning his face away from the fire to the wall. He drew the blanket over his head, fashioning a frail refuge against the storm and against the monk's terrible visions.

In the weeks that followed that night, the priest reassured himself many times that the monk was a benighted creature, tormented by aberrant longings. He led no band, lacked any partisans for his demonic cause.

The men and women in the village went about their tasks as they had done them for years, confirming the priest's belief in an existence sustained by faith and the needs of animals and humans. Shepherds continued to go out daily. Men returned from foraging on the slopes of the mountain with game for the larder of their families. The women planted the tobacco seeds in the frames the men had built. At night the men gathered in the kafeneion, talking and arguing while smoking their long chibouks. Late at night the dogs guarding the goat pens barked at the moon.

He buried old Chrisoula, the great-grandmother of them all, who, when she died at ninety-three, could still thread a needle. In her place a child was born, a lusty, vigorous boy shrieking like a new cub.

The feast day of the village was celebrated that month and several lambs were slaughtered and roasted. Father Markos made a new wineskin from the hide of one of them, sewing together the holes of its severed limbs with a heavy needle and a long gut thread, drawing the skin through the aperture where the neck had been, hair inside and the fleshy portion on the surface. Immersed in the rhythm of his work and days, he almost forgot the rantings of the monk.

Early in November, on an afternoon when he worked outside his house, mending some vines which had fallen in his grape patch, Kostas Makrydis and Cleon Starkas approached him.

"Good day, Kostas," Father Markos said. "Good day to you too, Cleon." Makrydis returned his greeting but Starkas made no response, warily watching the road from the village.

"Just a quick message, Father." Makrydis spoke in a low voice. "Tonight a group of our men go to join him." He motioned his head in the direction of the mountain. "They will be given the oath before they depart. We want you there for a liturgy to bless their hearts and their arms."

Starkas turned from the road, his face a knot of mistrust.

"Be careful how much you tell him." He spit the words out harshly.

"Close your foolish mouth," Makrydis said sharply. "I would trust my life and my son's life to this priest." He turned back to the priest. "Tonight, Father, about midnight in my storeroom."

The priest tried to control the tremor in his voice.

"Kostas, is this wise? Won't the men be missed? What about reprisals?"

"We must take that chance, Father," Makrydis said firmly. "I can't say more now. Will you be there?"

"I will be there." The priest nodded slowly. As Makrydis turned to leave, Father Markos asked, "Do I know the men, Kostas?"

Starkas grunted a warning but Makrydis looked at him sternly.

"There is Fanaris," Makrydis said. "Voulos, Saliris and Kofteros from Biskeni Agha, Manolis Kitsos . . ."

"Manolis!" The priest was shocked. "He is only a boy, no more than sixteen . . ."

"Old enough to shoot a gun and kill a bloody Turk!" Starkas said.

"He wishes to go," Makrydis said. "That is his right." He

started away once more. "At midnight, Father, and be careful."

As Father Markos waited for midnight, he sat in his chair, staring at the small candle burning on the table. A cold seeped into his bones and he was not sure whether it came from the night chill or from fear. He considered starting a fire but after the logs he had used during the storm, he was reluctant to deplete his slim supply. He spread a blanket across his shoulders and hunched over his Bible, trying to read a few verses by the flickering candle.

Men had gone from the village before to join Vorogrivas and his band of klephts on Parnassus, but never more than one or two at a time. Even those disappearances produced questioning by the police and once, even a visit from a Turkish constable in Lamia. He had interrogated the priest as if he suspected him to be the ringleader. What would the devil say about the disappearance of a half-dozen men? A new spasm of trembling pinched his flesh.

Shortly before midnight, fortified by a cup of pungent ouzo, he slipped nervously from the house and crept along the rear path toward the storeroom of Makrydis. Trying to walk quietly, his cassock tangled about his ankles and he nearly fell. He decided against stealth. If he were seen he would say he had stomach cramps and could not sleep. Just a week before, Widow Liakouris had brewed him some mountain herbs for just such a disorder. She would confirm his disability.

As he passed behind one of the darkened houses, a figure disengaged itself from the gloom. He stifled a cry of fear and shock. As the figure came closer and he braced himself for an attack, he recognized Ephrosene Kitsos, the mother of the youth Manolis. She came close to him, her grief and terror joined to his own.

"Father," she whispered. "Father, I know where you are going . . ."

"Hush, woman!" the priest cried softly, looking at the shadows in panic. "Have you lost your senses? Hush and get back into your house!"

"Father, I know my Manolis will be there." Her strong fingers dug into his arm like the talons of a bird. "He is too young, Father. He is only a child and all I have in this world!"

"There are other youths his age in the mountains," the priest whispered hurriedly. "They may be safer there than we are here. Now, in God's name, get back into your house!"

"Father, help me!" the woman pleaded. "Help me, Jesus!"

"I will speak to Manolis!" The priest imagined their voices carrying like claps of thunder across the silence. "Now, go inside or we'll all lose our heads! Go and pray and I will speak to him!"

He tore free from her grasp and without looking back to see if she obeyed him, he lowered his head and hurried on.

The storeroom of Makrydis, a separate building behind his house, was a windowless stone enclosure with an earthen floor, used for storing wine barrels, kegs of olive oil, tobacco seed and flour. The pall of the dark was broken only by the flame of a single large candle placed upon a table covered with a dark cloth. Beside the candle lay a skull, thigh bone and cross.

When Starkas let Father Markos enter the storeroom and he saw the altar holding those artifacts, he crossed himself quickly three times. He knew those emblems were the insignia of the Society of Friends, the secret revolutionary society formed in Odessa years before and sworn to the liberation of Greece. The organization was rumored to have thousands of members all over Greece and Anatolia, among all classes of people. The knowledge that a cell existed even in their small, insignificant village filled him with awe.

As a cluster of men knelt before the altar-table, Makrydis, standing across from them, spoke gravely.

"Before the face of the indivisible and omnipresent true God, who in His essence is just, the avenger of transgression, the chastiser of evil; by the law of the Society of Friends and by the authority which its leaders have entrusted to me, I receive you, as I was myself received, into their bosom."

He raised the cross and the skull and held them above the heads of the kneeling men.

"Now, repeat after me . . . I swear that I will not enter into any other society, or bond of obligation, but that my body and my heart and whatever else I may possess in the world, I will hold as nothing compared to the Society . . ."

Makrydis paused and the halting voices of the men echoed the words. Father Markos watched the face of the boy Manolis, pale in the sparse light.

"I swear that I will nourish in my heart everlasting hatred against the tyrants who enslave my country, their followers and their favorers. I will exert every means for their injury and for their destruction . . ."

The voices of the men repeated his words. Fear was so rampant in the airless, musty room, the priest could taste it on his tongue. But there was hate in the room, as well. Fear and hate mixing rancorous poisons around them.

"Last of all I swear by thee, my sacred and suffering country, I swear by the long endured tortures, I swear by the bitter tears which for so many centuries have been shed by our enslaved people . . ." Makrydis paused, as if the words had snarled in his throat. "I swear by my own tears, which I pour out at this moment . . ."

His words, driven through tears, scourged the priest for his terror and his weakness. I have not understood how they are suffering, he thought. I have lived among them for so many years and have not understood how fierce is their longing for freedom. I have been their priest, so old and useless, a stranger might have served them better.

The men's voices faded slowly. Makrydis turned toward the shadows where the priest stood.

"Father, bless us," he said quietly.

The priest moved forward. He raised the cross that shook in his hand and held it suspended over the bowed heads of the men.

"In the name of the Father and of the Son and of the Holy Ghost," he whispered. "Now and forever . . ." Even as he spoke the words, he thought them an inadequate prayer, a blessing spoken too many times before, made more ungainly by the shrouded figures of the courageous men.

The men rose from their knees and came to kiss the priest's hand and receive his embrace.

"Father, look after my old woman," Fanaris said. "She isn't much, but I wouldn't want harm to come to the old warthog because of me."

"I promise, Fanaris." Father Markos hugged the burly farmer's shoulders. "Go with God."

"Father." Voulos, another stalwart in his middle thirties gripped the priest's hand in his calloused palm. "If my father needs help with his wheat, see that he is given that help."

"I will, Janco," the priest said. "I promise you that. Go with God."

The touch of their lips chilling his hand, he had the conviction he would never see any of them again. They were surrendering families and friends for the barren life of the mountains, for wounds and battles, perhaps death. He wanted to cry out as if he were a woman mourning their departure.

When he thought the last of them had passed, he saw the youth Manolis. As if the boy had known of his mother's admonition to the priest, he hung back in the shadows.

"Manolis, come here," the priest said.

The youth moved slowly into the light of the candle. Despite that inadequate illumination, the boy's stunning handsomeness struck the priest with a curious impact, renewed each time he saw him. His flesh was olive-tinted and flawless, his eyes dark and large, their surfaces bright as moons, his black and curly hair thick about his temples.

"I promised your mother I would speak to you," the priest said. He paused, knowing the pleas would be useless, that the oath once taken could not be withdrawn.

"I can run, jump and shoot as well as anyone in the village, Father," Manolis said. "What I lack in experience will come soon enough. I have thought about this decision for weeks . . . since that Sunday morning in the early autumn when the warriors from the mountain came to the church. Remember, Father, the way he stood in church like God himself?"

"Don't blaspheme, my son," the priest said. "No mortal is God, not even a mighty captain like Vorogrivas." He paused, his thoughts returning to that astonishing Sunday when a dozen klephts appeared in the church, armed and bandoliered with cartridge belts and muskets, great yataghans dangling from their belts, the scabbards and hilts of their weapons scrolled and garlanded with silver and golden serpents and eagles.

They had ridden from the mountain, posting lookouts on the roads and sentries around the village. In the midst of the awed and silent villagers, Father Markos had given each of the warriors the holy sacrament. When Vorogrivas, the legendary chieftain of Parnassus, slayer of numerous Turks, knelt to accept the body and blood of Christ, the priest felt a ripple of some inordinate force along the metal of the spoon, coming from the lips of the captain, through the chalice. For a moment, swept by a sense of some divine and dedicated force, he had an impulse to kneel before the captain, as one would render obeisance to an Archbishop or a King.

"I remember," he said slowly to Manolis. "I remember . . ."

"I want to share the great hour with them," Manolis said, an excitement stinging his voice. "On the day they drive the

Turk from our land, I want to be with them. And the moment is coming, Father, when every castle will be attacked, fire put to every arsenal, those flames the beacon to tell the world our battle for freedom has begun."

"I will try to console your mother," the priest said.

The storeroom door opened and the harsh voice of Starkas assaulted the shadows.

"In the name of Jesus! Are you blessing or baptizing? They're waiting to leave!"

Manolis started quickly toward the door and then turned back.

"I have told my mother to plant a carnation and a rose in our garden," he said, an effort at gaiety in his voice. "As long as they bloom, you will know I am well. If the carnation and rose wither, then you will know I am dead, and say a last sweet mass for my soul."

The storeroom door opened and closed and the boy was gone, an indefinable fragrance lingering in his wake.

In the middle hours of that night, unable to sleep, the priest walked the short distance to the church. The night was clear and cold, stars glowing in a crystal band. The scent of lemon and jasmine drifted across the stalks of slumbering flowers. From grasses and weeds came the short, shrill chirps of crickets. A dog barked, an eerie echo answering.

He entered the enclosure of the cemetery and walked among the stones. He stood beside the markers above the graves of his father and his grandfather, the plots beside them where his mother and wife lay, the space that would someday receive his own bones, near the inert and mournful bell.

He could not evade the grim truth any longer. The omens were to be fulfilled. A storm of blood was moving upon them all, upon Makrydis, weeping as he spoke the oath to the kneeling men, upon Manolis, whose soul dwelt in the carnation and the rose, upon Ahmed Bajaki, who loved his son and his land, upon the monk Papalikos, preaching that men must learn to love the fire, upon the captain Vorogrivas, armed with his strength and his faith, upon the villagers, young and old, and upon an aged priest, in terror of what lay ahead. He felt a resigned and sorrowful alliance with them all.

He stared up at the black shape of the mountain. Even as he watched, a tiny spark burst on a ridge. The spark became a sliver of flame stretching into the sky. Almost at once, on another peak, a second beacon flared.

Help me, he whispered to the night and to the stars, to the mountain and to the dead sleeping beneath him, help me to know what I must do and give me the faith and strength to do it . . .

CHAPTER
THREE

Early that morning snow had fallen. Vorogrivas had been wakened before dawn by a wet fluttering upon his cheeks. Carrying from his dreams a chaste kiss that touched his lips, when he opened his eyes, he tasted the flakes on his tongue.

He pushed aside the goatskin cape and rose from his bed of boughs, staring up at the milky sky visible between the darker crags of the mountain. From the hidden peaks, the hushed snow fell.

During the winter many of his men sought caves or shelters built beneath the trees. He preferred the open sky, joined in the embrace of God that included sun and moon, mountain and stars.

He walked quietly from the encampment, wary of waking the others, retaining snow, silence and the first light for himself. At the boundary of the camp he saw one of the night sentries on a ledge in the distance. Moving away from the post, Vorogrivas began his descent to a lower plateau of the mountain, passing a sheepfold, the ewes nestled together for warmth, the abutment of an ancient battlement, a zone of fragrant fir trees. He caught glimpses of a badger and squirrels, heard the song of the thrush and on a crag above him caught the flash of a lynx. Suddenly the snow ceased and he entered a terrain of moist, cool air, the dawn of the breaking day.

Moving more swiftly, leaping from rock to rock, he began to run, great draughts of the fresh, brisk air inhaled into his lungs.

Coming to stand on the precipice of a bluff, he gazed at the snow-crested peaks above him, then looked down at the landscape of the earth. Thousands of feet beneath him lay a maze of miniature fields and forests, scrubby settlements of villages and towns, the misted, unimpressive sea and, on the horizon, the scatter of puny islands.

In that sorrowing and enslaved underworld, everything obstructed the eye and impeded the spirit, a tree or a house, a church or a mosque, the tumult of haggling traders, the babble of fretful voices. The faith of the mountains was impossible in the plains.

As the sun rose, the russet glow turning the crags and peaks golden, shining through the tendrils and foliage of the beeches and firs on the slopes above him, he stripped off his clothing and exposed his naked body to the holy light.

The warmth of the sun streamed over his shoulders, ran down his arms, seeping into every artery, absorbed into his blood. He felt a buoyant heat take possession of his soul.

Unable to contain his jubilation he did a swift, whirling dance on the edge of the precipice, careening on the edge of the rock, the earth spinning below him. Yet he did not fear that he might fall. He felt his arms enclosed the power of colossal wings, that if he extended them to their full, vibrant span, he would swoop aloft, soaring to marvelous heights, trailing the eagle to its inaccessible lair.

To prove worthy of these moments of sacred union with the mountain and the sun, he had hardened and tempered his body, relinquished the shallow, sensual delights of his companions, the feasting and the drinking, the scented, guileful bodies of women. All these pleasures of the flesh he regarded as Stymphalian birds, those demonic flocks with feathers like arrows that wounded and devoured men. His soul was the bronze rattle, made by Hephaestus at his forge and given to Heracles, with which the creatures were frightened away.

As a youth of twenty, almost twenty years before, he had sworn an oath that only when all of Greece was free as the bands in the mountains, would he consider the pleasures of men. He had sternly kept that oath, preparing for the revolt that would unshackle their sorrowing land. That moment was drawing closer. A wind had risen, born in the mountains, bred in the hearts of the klephts, a wind fanning a hurricane.

He screamed then, wild and exultant because he was primed and arrayed like an army for his role in that sacred struggle, a scream that assaulted the peaks, echoing in the gorges and ravines. And, God be praised, he felt the mountain rumble and reverberate beneath him!

When Vorogrivas returned to the camp, not a trace of the snow that had fallen earlier remained on the ground. He had the conviction that it had appeared for him alone, a good omen for the raid they planned later in the day.

The camp was awake, men washing with cold water flowing out of a rock into a hollowed log, milking goats, squatting beside fires, cooking and eating, ribald laughter and harsh jests rising with the trails of smoke. A few of the klephts who would be going with him on the raid were cleaning and oiling their weapons. Horses and mules grazed at the edge of the site, hungrily cropping the scant winter grasses.

Men fell silent as his shadow fanned across them, looking up to nod or murmur a respectful greeting. Their spirits and well-being were important to him, yet he discouraged familiarity, cultivating an aura of reserve, sharing their camaraderie without relinquishing his distance.

His lieutenant, Ghiouris, hurried over when he saw him, clothing askew on his strong, stocky body, his eyelids still puffed from sleep.

"Off by yourself again, Captain, without a sword or a gun!" Ghiouris said plaintively. "I beg you to let me or a few boys go with you. You never know if when you start down, you'll meet a troop of Mussulmen regulars on their way up."

"Don't worry, Ghiouris," Vorogrivas said gravely. "If they corner me I'll leap off a precipice and dare them to follow."

Ghiouris squinted at him silently.

"If you say so, Captain," he said.

Kapsakis, a lean, wasp-waisted man with a flaming thatch of red hair, brought him a small pitcher of milk.

"Here you are, Captain," Kapsakis said politely. "Still warm from the udders of the ewe."

Vorogrivas took the pitcher, feeling the milk's warmth against his palm.

A burst of strident hooting and raucous laughter rolled across the encampment. A tall, bearded klepht, Panagouris, had entered the rim of the fires, carrying capote, sword and boots, his demeanor weary and chagrined. Walking brazenly a few steps behind him was the woman Lascarina.

She was tall and broad as most men, her hair a dark, tangled forest, her black eyes curved like scimitars. Striding forward, her blouse unbuttoned to her navel, she revealed the palisades of her massive breasts.

"Hey, Panagouris!" one of the men called. "I'm surprised you can still walk."

"Did the fortress fall?" a second man asked.

"Better ask if the cypress fell!" a third man cried.

Panagouris snarled at them and dropped his boots and sword near a fire. He squatted heavily on his haunches and extended his hands toward the flames.

Lascarina walked through the groups of men, shaking away their pinching and pawing, ignoring their sneers and grunts. She came to stand in the center of the encampment, hands at her waist with the thumbs hooked into the heavy, ornamented leather belt around her hips that held the jeweled hilt of a long bone knife. She stared scornfully about her.

"Never mind taunting Panagouris!" she cried. "Who among you has done any better?" She spit with derision. "Strutting rabbits used to peeing in patches of carrots! Trembling whelps and spit-baked sheep!"

A few of the men laughed or sneered, some stared at her with anger.

"Bitch!"

"Goat-whore!"

"I've had enough!" An older klepht named Sachtouris with iron gray hair drew his dagger from his belt. "I'll cut the bitch's throat!"

As he moved toward her, Lascarina swiftly drew her own knife. A low, expectant growl carried across the camp. For a second they stood poised, Lascarina contemptuous and unafraid, Sachtouris staring at her with hate.

"Enough," Vorogrivas said quietly.

Sachtouris looked at him and cursed softly under his breath. He replaced the knife in his belt and turned angrily away.

Lascarina sheathed her own knife and laughed harshly.

"Who will play war with me tonight?" she said. "How about two of you, or even three?" She looked tauntingly at Ghiouris. "What about you, Rumeliot?" she asked. "Try a dive tonight into the Sea of Lascarina?"

"I'd rather fight a brigade of Turks," Ghiouris grumbled. He lowered his voice. "Give that woman a kiss and you leave your mouth in ruins."

Vorogrivas looked at the scornful woman holding them defiantly at bay. He did not send her away because she could fight and shoot as well as the best of them but he expected she would kill or be killed by the insane rages she fostered. She goaded men into her arms, burning with lust and hate, intent on destroying what she wanted.

Sometimes when Vorogrivas was near one of the shy, demure and slender village girls, he felt a softening of his spirit, a faltering of his resolve that he quickly repressed. He could understand a man being drawn to one of those flowers, but he could not fathom the attraction in Lascarina's bawdy and spiteful flesh.

As if she sensed his revulsion, he felt her staring at him suddenly, not a mocking, challenging gaze as she used with the others, but curious and wondering, with an enigmatic sadness.

Restless under the intensity of her eyes, he turned away and carried the pitcher of milk toward a shelter of boughs and goat hair capes built around a pair of cedars and boulders. He pushed aside a hanging cape that formed an entrance and, bending slightly, stepped into the dark interior.

Moving forward to a bed of boughs, he stood above the great, sprawled hulk of the old captain, Boukouvalas.

"Father," Vorogrivas said.

The figure stirred, uttering the growl of a lion roused from sleep and dreams of ancient, triumphant hunts.

"I brought you some milk," Vorogrivas said. "Warm and sweet."

Pushing aside the coverings around him, an imposing arm rose from the tangle.

"Lift aside those capes there," the voice rumbled. "Let some of God's light into this bloody grave."

Vorogrivas obeyed, raising several of the capes that provided the walls, a current of light and air streaming into the enclosure. He observed with affection and awe the magnificent head of the old klepht, the white-maned crown of a venerable king, a luxuriant growth descending into a majestic white beard. Indeed, his face resembled the mountain, a snow-peaked summit, the eyes ravines, the nose a crag, the beard the forests on the slopes.

When Vorogrivas first joined the band in the mountains, they had been led by the famous Suliot klepht Boukouvalas. He was not sure he could have survived if it had not been for the captain who made him his son.

Born and bred to the mountains and to war, Boukouvalas had counseled and guided him, helped him endure the desolate rocks and crags, the solitary nights, the cold winter winds that raged for days. From his vast lore, Boukouvalas had taught him the arts of war, the lightning strike leaving the enemy disorganized and uncertain where the next blow would fall, as if they were matched against ghosts. Above all, the old klepht had shown him the wisdom of accepting the mountains as home and country, family and friend.

In the last ten years, when the chieftain had grown too old and rent with wounds to lead his palikars in battle, Vorogrivas had taken command of the band. But the old warrior's wisdom was still heeded.

Vorogrivas knelt and put the pitcher of milk to the old man's lips. The klepht sucked noisily, trickles of fluid running down his chin, vanishing into his beard. He stopped once to catch his breath.

"Like I am at my mother's breast once more," he said with a sigh. "I suckled as a babe and, as a withered, dying old man, I suckle again."

"Withered and dying indeed!" Vorogrivas scoffed. "You will die, as we all must die. Meanwhile, I pity the Turks who might stumble in here prematurely."

The old man laughed and, struggling, raised himself to a sitting position. He stared toward the camp of men and stroked the tangle of his beard.

"The palikars are getting ready . . ." he said.

"We'll start down by noon," Vorogrivas said. "That should bring us to the Three Forks by twilight."

"How many ride?"

"About twenty, with Ghiouris."

"Holy God, how I wish I could ride with you!" Boukou-valas cried. "A curse on my rotting bones! I should have been killed in battle, my blood leaping and hot! Instead, I am dying drop by wretched drop, already buried in this grave above the ground!"

"Yes, come with us!" Vorogrivas said. "We will mount and strap you on your horse. And when the first Turk sees the leonine head of Boukouvalas, every garrison between here and Olympus will be alerted. A dozen beys will whirl like dervishes praying they might send your severed crown across the Bosporus." He waved at the old man in reassurance. "Rest and plan our strategy for the war that is coming. More men are coming to join us as they are joining bands in mountains all over Greece. We will have fighters enough, what we need are leaders to counsel where and how it is best to do battle."

"Honeyed words to soothe an old man's grief," Bou-kouvalas spit through his gums. "Sly words to make a poultice for my wounded spirit."

"I'll muster a few of the palikars to sing you a lament," Vorogrivas jeered. "Poor old Captain Boukouvalas! Having killed only a thousand Turks, having spread terror from Suli to Thrace, the old man moans the gods have been unkind. Give others a chance, will you? There are young men in our band who have not yet drawn Turkish blood! Would you hog all the glory forever?"

The old man scattered the capes around him. One huge hand snapped out and caught at a crook beside him, a thick rod made from the branch of a wild olive tree, the head carved in the shape of a serpent devouring a dog. He swung the crook in a swift assault. Vorogrivas leaped aside barely in time to evade the singing wood.

"Almost got you!" Boukouvalas cried gleefully. "Impudent donkey! If I'd been a shade quicker, you'd have danced out of here!"

"Bloody old wolf!" Vorogrivas cried, delighted at the old

man's resurgence of spirit. "Playing on my sympathy and pity! I would sooner pity a bear or a snake!" He burst into laughter and Boukouvalas joined him, rumbling with mirth. Then the old klepht's laughter became coughing, his body slipping heavily back against the boughs.

"Stay quiet now for a while," Vorogrivas said more gently when the fit of coughing had passed. "After the sun is higher and warmer, come out and sit for a while. Holler and the boys will help you."

"Send me Lascarina." The old man managed a weak growl. "With her buoyant breast I'll soar like a bird."

As Vorogrivas emerged from the shelter, Ghiouris waited for him with a half-dozen men dressed in the shabby, nondescript clothing of villagers, their caps held stiffly and respectfully in their hands.

"Captain Vorogrivas," Ghiouris said crisply. "These are new men come to join our band. Makrydis brought them, traveling all night to reach us."

"We are pleased to have you with us," Vorogrivas said gravely. "What village are you from?"

Each man waited for another to answer, until a stocky man with the strong, calloused hands of a farmer spoke.

"From Kravasaras and Biskeni Agha, your honor."

"There are no titles here," Vorogrivas said. He motioned the man closer. "What is your name?"

"Stefanos Fanaris."

"Welcome, Fanaris," Vorogrivas embraced the man lightly and then clasped his hands in both his own.

Ghiouris pushed another man forward.

"Janco Voulos," the man said.

"Welcome, Voulos," Vorogrivas said, once again drawing the man to his chest and squeezing his hands.

The last of the arrivals he met was a youth no older than sixteen. Standing before him, Vorogrivas had the strange feeling he had seen those luminous eyes, black as ripe elderberries, before.

"How old are you?" he asked.

"Seventeen," the youth said.

"Are you sure it isn't sixteen or even fifteen?"

The youth did not answer. There was something almost unearthly about his handsomeness, the harmony of forehead, cheeks and lips, his ragged clothing unable to conceal the grace and strength of his body.

"Your spirit is commendable, but I think you are too young," Vorogrivas said brusquely. "I do not tolerate any man in my band who cannot run and shoot with the best."

He felt the youth looking at him as if he understood, sensitively and surely, the anatomy of the captain's soul.

"I can run and shoot and fight," the youth said quietly.

"He is right." Makrydis had joined the group. He moved to greet Vorogrivas and the two men embraced vigorously and warmly.

"Believe me," Makrydis said, smiling at the youth. "I know him from the village. He can run like a young colt and can shoot better than I can."

Reassured and yet unable to dispel his unrest, Vorogrivas stared sharply at the youth. He was ashamed before the frankness and trust in the boy's clear gaze.

"What is your name?" he asked more kindly.

"Manolis Kitsos."

"Welcome, Manolis." He started to embrace him as he had embraced the others and faltered. Instead, he clasped the boy's strong, slender fingers in his own larger hands. As their palms touched, he felt a tremor deep within his blood.

He stepped back and spoke gruffly.

"Listen to Ghiouris here," he said. "He'll get you something to eat and weapons and clothing. After you have had a chance to rest, a veteran will be assigned to each one of you to teach you the way we live and fight. The mountains are not the plains and you will find life much harder here.

When we break bread together and fight side by side, a bond is formed that only death can break."

Manolis watched him, hanging on his words. To deny himself the pleasure of looking at the youth again, Vorogrivas turned away.

Afterward he sat with Makrydis under the shade of a great fir tree, the voices of the men floating in murmurs across the rocks that separated them from the camp. Makrydis pillowed his head against the root of the tree, staring wearily up at the cones and needles.

"We have had meetings with men from the bands on Olympus," Makrydis said. "They are ready and wait word like you."

"How soon will that word come?"

Makrydis shifted his body, leaning on his elbow. "There are many good auguries," he said, "reports from our agents all over Europe. They say an army is gathering in Russia to come to our aid. The Maniats in the South look toward Kalamata. The islands, rich with money and ships, wait to join. But"—a great sigh rose from his chest—"so many are frightened, waiting for others to begin, it may take months yet. You live here in the mountains among free men. But down there the political and church leaders are confused and in terror. They know revolution is in the air. On one side the people look to them to raise the revolt and on the other the Turks warn them to keep things quiet. In the middle, they fear for their heads."

"Give them a gun and a sword," Vorogrivas said. "Point them at the Turks."

"You have been free a long time," Makrydis said, a shadow darkening his cheeks. "Your spirit is mountain-sinewed. But I tell you, when a people has been enslaved as long as we have been, a worm of weakness grows at our core. How long can a country endure bondage before its will to revolt is broken?"

"Have faith, my friend," Vorogrivas said. "In my dreams I have seen an eagle with bloodied wings soaring to a great height. We will suffer but in the end we will win."

"We need money and arms for the men who join us," Makrydis murmured. "So many things must be looked after . . ."

"You can do nothing about them now," Vorogrivas said. "After climbing all night, you need to sleep. I will skewer two Turks for you on the raid and add the tax collector's gold to your coffers."

Makrydis slipped down to rest his head on the patches of needles around the base of the tree. A few more needles, loosened by a slight breeze, floated down upon his closed eyes.

Vorogrivas sat silently beside him. He did not know whether the things they had discussed caused the heaviness he felt at that moment. His concern suddenly was not about the coming of the revolt. He wondered what happened to men of war in times of peace, men who knew nothing of plowing the soil, harvesting the crops, planting terraces of flowers, raising their families? Peace, he thought with a curious melancholy, I have lived so long at war I know nothing of the ways of peace.

They rode from the camp at noon, a band of about twenty men, descending from the high trails and passes. The hooves of the horses rang sharply in the bright, clear air and the scabbards of the yataghans clanked against the bridles. The trees wore their winter raiment, except for pale remnants of summer, among the blue shadows of the trunks. Further down, the ruins of a small white chapel stood by a few cypresses. Mounds of stones surrounded the cloisters of what had once been a monastery where monks had taken a brief and futile refuge from the Venetians centuries before.

Riding the edge of a path beside a ravine, they passed the site of one of their own battles, when the Turks had sent a company of regulars against them. In testament to that bloody day, the stony slopes were still littered with skeletons, bleached bones shining in the sun.

They continued descending for several hours until they reached a stretch of plateau. From there the path ran more steeply and the horses grew skittish, sliding and slipping against the pebbles and the hard earth. They passed into a cluster of fir trees, the air aromatic around them.

"Winter, yet here it smells like spring," Vorogrivas said to Ghiouris. He breathed deeply to fill his lungs with the fresh fragrance.

When they finally reached the foothills of the mountain, twilight had fallen, a haze of purple shadows mustered along the plain. Vorogrivas looked back once at the towering peaks, darkening with the night. He thought an instant of the mountain as a mother to whose breast he prayed to return, and then pushed the longing away. At his signal, Ghiouris and two of the palikars spurred their horses forward, moving swiftly ahead of the band, deploying to locate the tax collector's convoy and secure their advance.

In the distance, Vorogrivas could see a few lights of the village of Kravasaras, where he and a few of his men had gone for communion on a Sunday morning some weeks before. Beyond that village, some additional miles away, was the larger town of Biskeni Agha, where a Turkish garrison was stationed. Any relief for the convoy they attacked would come from there.

As the twilight grew darker, he heard the sound of horses advancing at a gallop toward them, and reined the column to a halt, knowing it was their scouts returning. Ghiouris appeared out of the shadows, pulling his mount up sharply, close to the captain's horse.

"We caught sight of them about two miles from here," he said. "They're moving along in the dark, probably planning to stop in one of the villages or settlements for the night."

"How many?"

"Looked like two mounted men in front, the carriage, about twenty-five infantry and two more mounted troopers bringing up the rear."

"They'll pass the spring at Castelia?"

"Yes."

"We will wait for them there," Vorogrivas said. "The rocks and trees will provide us cover." He looked toward the sky, where a sliver of a crescent hung misted and low. "There will be just enough light."

Ghiouris motioned for the men who had scouted with him to pass the word to the others. He guided his horse beside the mount of Vorogrivas and the band began a gallop to Castelia.

At the spring, they dismounted. The horses were led far enough away so they would not be heard. The palikars, adept at blending into the terrain, concealed themselves behind rocks and trees.

"We must be quick," Vorogrivas said quietly to Ghiouris.

As Ghiouris slipped off to monitor the men, Vorogrivas stepped behind a large boulder. He rubbed the cold, hard grain of the surface with his fingers, reaffirming a bond running from the earth through the stone.

Around him the palikars waited, silent as graves. The sliver of pale moon glistened over the upper foliage of the trees and on the water of the spring. Slow and binding moments passed and then the faintest shiver rippled through the earth beneath their feet. Muskets were cocked and yataghans unsheathed.

Vorogrivas felt strong and alert, all of his energies concentrated on the coming battle, intent on overwhelming and destroying their enemies. Then something in him faltered, no more than a slight altering in the current of his blood, yet unlike anything he had ever experienced before. He knew suddenly, stunned and bewildered, for the first time in his life he feared that he might die.

The Turkish column appeared, mounted officers in the lead. Against the ashen night the shape of the horses loomed and grew larger as they came closer. Behind the horsemen rumbled the carriage, on either side the files of marching troopers.

Outraged at his body's betrayal, Vorogrivas leveled his musket at one of the mounted men, adjusting the sight to the rhythm of the horse's gait. At the moment when the animal came close enough so he could distinguish the rider's head, he pressed the trigger. The night was torn by the explosion of his gun. The Turk's hands sprang up as if they sought to flee from his body, the reins fell loose, and he catapulted to the ground.

A great bellow of war cries burst from the throats of the palikars, a savage chorus detonating their muskets. When that wave passed the night was rent by the moans and screams of wounded and startled Turks.

Holding yataghan and pistol in his hands, Vorogrivas led the palikars forward. They came from behind the rocks and trees as if they had sprung out of the earth, pounding down on the milling and panicked Turks. Out of the darkness the form of a Turkish trooper appeared, recoiling as Vorogrivas leaped upon him. The trooper struggled to raise his musket and Vorogrivas shot him through the heart.

Before the trooper struck the ground, he ran on, met another Turk and with a raging swing of the yataghan cleaved him from neck to chest. The nearly severed arm spun weirdly from the Turk's body, flopping back to dangle below his knees as a fearful scream burst from his lips.

His fury unsated, gripping his bloodied yataghan, Vorogrivas sought another foe. But the battle ended almost as quickly as it began, the ground strewn with dead and dying Turks, the palikars pursuing and butchering the few survivors trying to flee.

The ambush had been complete and successful, only a single palikar wounded in the thigh. They quickly collected the weapons and booty, slicing the throats of a few wounded Turks. The strongbox from the carriage was broken open, the gold transferred into the saddle pouches of the horses. The tax collector, a bulky, terrified Anatolian, they allowed to go free to carry word back to the pasha in Lamia. In less than half an hour after Vorogrivas had first fired his musket, the band was galloping back to the refuge of the mountain.

By midnight, returned to their camp, they piled brush upon the fires and in the leaping flames told and retold the details of the raid to the new men who had joined them earlier that day and to the envious comrades who had remained behind. They proudly exhibited the weapons they had captured, boasting of the Turks they had killed. Swollen with arrogance, they bragged and blustered how they would attack and demolish the garrison at Biskeni Agha.

Vorogrivas sat outside the circle of fires, divided in substance and spirit from the celebration. He stared up into the darkness that shrouded the crags and ravines above them, remembering with nostalgia as if it had taken place weeks before, the snow that had fallen on his cheeks in the morning, flakes like omens of triumph from those holy peaks.

There was a clatter at a corner of the encampment as the old captain, Boukouvalas, was carried from his shelter by a half-dozen men. His huge figure and head suspended between them, they labored to bring him before the largest fire, lowering him by a series of torturous lurchings to the ground, his back and shoulders braced against a rock. They moved away, leaving him sitting stiffly, holding the great carved crook like a scepter across his lap, the flames casting a scarlet glow across his white hair and white beard.

One of the younger palikars, sodden with drink that muddled his judgment, approached the old klepht.

"Tell me, Captain!" he cried. "Won't they someday sing of our exploits as they still sing of your deeds of daring?"

He stood swaying and grinning before the old man. For a moment Boukouvalas appeared to be sinking into his frame. Then he lashed out with the crook and slammed the young palikar across the ankles. The klepht howled with pain and began a leaping, disjointed stagger, falling finally to his knees. The men roared with laughter.

"You stupid, sniveling whelp!" Boukouvalas roared. "You dare compare the battles we fought with that game you played tonight?"

A safe distance from the old man's crook, the young palikar stroked his ankles fervently.

"I was only teasing, Captain," he protested, a whine disabling his voice. "I meant no disrespect, I swear." He pushed himself painfully to his feet, limping into the shadows to solace his humiliation and his pain.

For a few more minutes the old captain snorted and fumed, the crook weaving menacingly in his hand.

"All you young rams!" He glared around him. "Riding down to ambush a few troopers in the dark, rushing back here with your loot to swill and boast! That wasn't the kind of war we knew in Suli! Those weren't garrison soldiers we fought then, dull with wenches and bloated with food! We had Ali Pasha against us, the butcher of Jannina, curse his bowels with plague and fire! He did in Papathymo and Tsaras at the bridge of Pravi, a black day for all of Greece! I rode with Blachavas to relieve them and found their mutilated bodies on the ground. Their heads had been carried on the backs of mules to Jannina and cemented into a pyramid formed of the heads of Greeks the butcher had killed!"

The snapping and cracking of the flames waned before the fury of the old man's voice.

"Blachavas was wounded and captured soon after," Boukouvalas said, his body flinching as if he were reliving the anguish of that capture. "The butcher had him bound naked to a stake in the courtyard of the seraglio. When the devils began smashing his arms and legs with hammers, he never uttered a whimper. In the end they dragged the crushed, broken body of that last great chieftain of Thessaly through the streets of the city!"

For a moment, he struggled for breath, his chest heaving. The men sat sobered and silent. No one dared to move. Finally, Vorogrivas spoke.

"Tell us of Suli, Father," he said. "The battles you and your comrades fought against Ali Pasha."

The old klepht stared into the fire. He grimaced and rubbed his knees.

"An old man's fartings and belchings," he said. "You have heard all those stories before."

"Tell us again," Vorogrivas said. "There are new men with us tonight and those events should never be forgotten."

The old klepht raised his head and peered fiercely around the circle of firelight, daring any man to disagree. A cowed, respectful murmur of agreement rose from the palikars.

"We want to hear . . ."

"Tell us, Captain."

"Yes . . . Captain, please."

"All right," Boukouvalas said. "Only so these recollections can be preserved." He gripped the crook tightly.

"You've heard of the Spartans of Leonidas and the Macedonians of Alexander? None of them were any more hardy and heroic than the warriors of Suli. They could run all day, leap like goats from crag to crag, shoot like marksmen, and, with eyes like cats could see in the dark."

Almost in unison the fires seemed to be burning more slowly, no man moving to pile on more brush, light withdrawing from the figures sitting and sprawled upon the ground. A blue, misted haze crept in across them, bringing a chill Vorogrivas felt seeping into his bones.

"The butcher conquered and ruled provinces miles distant from Jannina," Boukouvalas said, "but as long as our bastion of Suli remained free, we were like a dagger at his throat. He tried bribery and treachery and for thirteen years, until 1803, he hurled one army after another against us. But always, enough of us survived to continue the battle." His hand rose, fumbled at his tunic, tearing it open to expose the dark, leathery flesh of his chest. "I was wounded here . . . cut here . . . a bullet still lodged here. Don't ask how I lived . . . by God's grace."

He paused and looked down into the fire once more. After a few moments of silence one man coughed and another lit his chibouk. A third man moved and the scabbard of his yataghan struck a boulder. The old man's head snapped up, redeemed by the clatter from his dreaming.

"He enlisted the armies of rich agas, promising them new dominions if they joined him in one final, great siege against Suli. For more than a year the butcher's noose tightened around us. The cowardly devil wouldn't venture into the stark ravines and dark gorges to attack our fortress, Kiafa, but waited for hunger to subdue us. Our women grew weak and the bellies of our children grew swollen. The babies sucking on the dry teats of their mother's breasts never ceased to cry. Finally, a shade from starving, we agreed to abandon Kiafa in return for safe conduct through his lines to Parga and a ship from there to Zante. We knew the bastard's promises were worthless but we thought it better to die fighting."

He looked up at the sky, shaking his head in bitterness.

"As soon as we gave up our fortress and began our descent, men, women and children marching together, we were attacked by his Albanians and Turks. One group fought its way to Parga, losing more than half its number. My own group, with most of the women and children, managed to reach the monastery below the mountain of Zalongos."

The mist grew thicker, obscuring the earth beyond the fires. A falcon passed overhead, trailing its throaty call across the rocks.

"For two days we held out," Boukouvalas said. "When

they finally smashed in the gates of the monastery, we men fought a rear-guard action while about sixty of our women and children, my wife and sons included, managed to scramble up the mountain. We were cut off from them and watched them climbing, fleet as young mountain goats, hurling rocks down on their pursuers. We saw their figures growing smaller, the Turks butchering those who lagged behind. The ones who kept going finally reached a ledge, as far as they could ascend, and the Turks raced to swallow them."

The old man's voice grew husky, the words harsh and labored from his lips.

"They knew they were lost, nothing left but slaughter or worse. I tell you what they did then . . . I swear by God I heard and saw it with my ears and eyes. The Turks and Albanians around us saw it too and for a few moments the fighting stopped. All of us looked up as the women trapped on that mountain began to sing, a song of Suli, and began to dance, dancing toward the precipice, where, yes, damn your rabbit boastings, holding their children in their arms, they hurled themselves to their deaths on the rocks below!"

The memory burned the old captain's body, the words torn in pain from his heart.

"They sang and danced and leaped to their deaths!" Boukouvalas cried. "Yet there was triumph and glory in their souls as they leaped because they knew what they were doing would be remembered and celebrated for generations . . . long after we are all dead and forgotten, people will tell of the women of Suli, of that last great dance on the mountain of Zalongos!"

His last reserve of strength expiring as he finished, the old klepht's head slumped forward, his shoulders sinking, his fingers loosening their clasp upon the crook.

For a long measure of time, no man moved or spoke. Finally, one by one, they rose to slip away from the fires, drifting into the darkness to shelters and caves. Several of the palikars went to raise the old klepht and carry him to his shelter. With a mustering of vigor, he raised his crook.

"Not into that grave!" he cried hoarsely. "I'll brain the first one who comes near me! I want to sleep out here tonight, under God's eyes!"

The men retreated and left the old warrior alone. He sat for a few more minutes staring into the embers of the dying fire. Then, his body swaying wearily, he braced himself on his arm and hand and lowered himself to the ground, sprawling finally on his back, his face turned toward the stars.

Vorogrivas sat without moving for a long time. The camp grew quiet, the noises of men submerged under the sounds of the night, cicadas shrilling in the trees, and on the distant peaks, the baying of wolves.

In the moment before turning to sleep, Vorogrivas saw the youth Manolis emerge from the shadows. Not having earned a place at the fire, he must have listened to the old klepht's story in the background. Now, in the sleeping camp, he came from the darkness and, quietly, without fear, he bent and gently covered the white-maned giant with his cape.

CHAPTER
FOUR

The bows of ships had a special place for Leonidas Kontos in the images of his childhood. He loved to sit for hours on the terrace of his father's house above the port of the island of Psara, watching the tiny specks of ships on the horizon grow into tall masts, graceful sails and sleek hulls.

From the ancient, leathery-skinned sea captains whose ships anchored in the island's harbor, he learned the history of the seas and the men and ships that sailed upon them. When poor landsmen reached the limits of their domains, the captains assured him gravely, life moved forward on the boundless sea.

With most of the earth's surface covered by water, the ripples from a stone he threw into the harbor might trace their way across the world, partaking of storms and currents. Surrounded by the sea and stirred by the stories of valiant men and stout ships, he came to believe with the Psalmist, 'They that go down to the sea in ships . . . see the works of the Lord and his wonders in the deep.'

When he was ten he made his first voyage on his father's ship *Miltiades,* visiting the ports of the Black Sea. For a terrifying yet exultant hour he was lashed to the mast during a gale, the wind stinging his cheeks and tearing at his clothing, the spars and rigging groaning above his head. While the ship drifted in a dead calm, he was taught the names of the parts of the vessel, tutored to mark the points of the compass. At night he learned the names and positions of the stars.

From the sailors in the forecastle, he discovered that ships are possessed of spirits that breathe into the canvas and wood at the time the vessels are built. They told him grim tales of ships that became ghosts, sometimes malign, maiming and killing the men who sailed upon them.

But mostly, the sailors reassured him, the spirits of a ship were beneficent ones that watched over the welfare of the men on board. If they treated her fairly and looked after her, she would answer her helm like a charm and skim across the waves. And if the seas were eternal, then ships had a certain immortality, sailing the waters as ghosts even after their hulls had gone to the bottom.

Between his tenth and his eighteenth year, he attended the island school in the morning and afterwards labored in his father's shipyard until dark. He began working in the saw pit, where the raw logs from the coastal forests of Asia Minor were turned into lengths of planking. When he first gripped the five-foot blade that sawed the logs, his palms blistered and he choked on the sawdust that filled his nose and throat. As he grew older and stronger, he moved to the hewing, wielding an ax to sever the chunks of wood between the scored lines on the huge trunks.

When the massive backbone, or keel, laid down on blocks on the slant of the shore was ready to be framed, and the stem or bow posts added, followed by the wishbone ribs, men all over the yard came to lend a hand. Those were the moments he cherished most.

For another year he worked on the planking gang, fitting each plank slowly and carefully against the frame, making sure each rib edge was gently curved. Finally, he joined in the caulking and scraping, driving in the tarred hemp and cotton to waterproof the hull. The sharp, ringing sound of the mallet against the hawsing irons startled the gulls that swooped and soared above their heads.

The final procedure before the launching was the application of paint to decorate the vessel and as a barrier between the hull and the destructive water. The colors were barn red and lampblack, sienna and yellow ocher, applied in several coats until the hull, bow and stern blazed in a splendid array. When the ship was ready, christened by the priest with a prayer and launched, Leonidas felt he shared an ancient, venerable ceremony of birth.

In his nineteenth year he journeyed to the university on the nearby island of Chios, remaining there for almost two years, until word was sent to him of the death of his father in a storm at sea. Leonidas grieved at the passing of that good man and the sailors who perished with him, yet he felt no bitterness against the sea. He wished at the end of his life he might die at sea rather than expiring slowly in some landlocked house.

He returned to Psara and took command of their fleet. In place of the ship that had been lost, he designed and supervised the construction of a beautifully modeled, light-rigged and swift brig. When the trim and lofty-masted ship was launched, he named it *Themistocles* after his father and captained the vessel himself.

For the following fifteen years he sailed the archipelago, his ships carrying rugs, carpets and linens from Damascus, taffeta from Persia, silk and cotton cloth from Iraq. His cargoes also included furs, flax, sesame rice and wheat that he delivered to the cities of Western Europe.

These hazardous voyages often endured attack from Algerian pirates in their swift vessels. Against these corsairs, Leonidas and the other island captains armed their ships with guns, drilling their seamen in the arts of gunnery and the skills of maneuvering for warfare on water against a wily foe.

Like the shipowners and captains of his island and of the islands of Hydra, Spetzia and Samos, Leonidas prospered, doubling and then tripling his father's wealth. He built a larger, more elegant addition to their family house, intricately louvered windows, and handsome ceilings of wood inlaid in strips by a craftsman from Venice. His ships which carried commodities to Western Europe, returned to Psara with fine French furniture, English porcelain and Murano glass, silk and damasks. In payment for a shipment of grain to a church in Barcelona, he brought home a magnificent chandelier that he hung from the ceiling in his spacious salon, a resplendent decoration casting more light through its prism of crystals than the flame from a hundred oil lamps.

In this period of prosperity, he also courted and married an island beauty, Aspasia Domestinis, the hazel-eyed, golden-haired daughter of another Psariot captain. They had three children, girls as fair and lovely as their mother. If there were times Leonidas regretted being denied a son who might assume command of his fleet of ships after he was gone, there was some consolation in the beauty and warmth of his daughters.

While they lived lives of luxury and ease, there was a temptation for the Psariots not to keep remembering they were in bondage. They knew that in all of conquered Greece, the islands were the most fortunate of the Sultan's dominions. Although they were obliged to provide sailors for the fleet of the Capitan-pasha, some silver for the Constantinople mint and grazing land for the Mussulman cavalry, there were no Turks living on the island. The government of Psara was democratic, all the citizens voting in the election of the magistrates and councillors.

In this atmosphere of democracy and affluence, every sailor was also a partner in the success of each voyage. After deducting the capital invested in purchasing the cargo, the price of provisions and a percentage for the treasury, everyone shared the remainder in equal portions. Even the cabin boys received a half-share.

Yet there were constant reminders of their bondage. Ragged, despairing refugees came in caïques from the mainland to Psara, recounting stories of massacres and murders, churches burned and looted, women and children carried off to be sold in the slave markets of Asia Minor.

These refugees were Christians and brother and sister Greeks and as they listened to the tales of calamity and horror, outrage and bitterness seethed in the Psariots. In addition, in the misery of the refugees, each Psariot foreshadowed what his own fate might be, his wife and children, everything he owned, arbitarily taken from him by an edict from a pasha.

The harsh truth was that as long as they existed in the suzerainty of the Sultan, regardless of their affluence, they were a subject people, their identity as Greeks obscured. Because they found this condition insufferable and demeaning, Leonidas and a number of other captains and shipowners had secretly become members of the Society of Friends, the organization dedicated to the freedom of all Greece.

These captains and shipowners of Psara agreed that an upheaval was imminent. Touching at ports from Salonika to Monemvasia and Navarino, they assessed the rumblings of revolution. Yet not all of the Psariots could agree on the action they would take when the revolt broke out. Men who had proven their courage at sea, dedicated to the cause of freedom, feared for Psara, a small island under the huge shadow of the Turkish mainland.

In that winter of 1820, as had been the custom on the island for years, the captains and shipowners gathered to eat, drink and dance. Although their wives sometimes joined them, after dinner, the women were banished from the salon, the dancing and drinking rigidly patriarchal. Lately, most of the time was spent arguing and discussing, dancing seeming frivolous before the coming storm.

On an evening when a group of shipowners and captains, who were also councillors, assembled in the lofty, carpeted salon of Leonidas, they sat on the ottomans and divans puffing gravely on their chibouks and cigars.

"All about us are unhappy omens," a grizzled old captain named Baltas said. "Imagine an experienced hand like Angelos catching his foot in a line and slipping in the rigging. That moment when he dangled until his foot tore loose and he fell was one of the most chilling of all my years at sea. I still see the poor devil in my dreams."

"Sometimes an old hand grows careless because he has climbed into the rigging so many times," another captain said.

"There are other omens," a councillor named Lazarou said. "The old women talk of finding the body of a disemboweled sheep, black with flies, looking as if it had been torn apart."

"A wolf or a wild dog."

"They say something bigger and fiercer than a dog or a wolf."

"What kind of animal would that be?"

"God knows . . ." a man said, and spit against the baleful spirits while several others crossed themselves.

"What about the *Despina*'s voyage?"

"Captain Rellis did not see the monster himself."

"His mate, Rombotsis, saw it! He told me a few hours west of Patmos, the great black creature with a square head and a fanned tail burst from the sea! And from the monster's mouth erupted a tongue of fire!"

"Rombotsis buried his head in a cask of wine before he saw that apparition!" a man scoffed.

"He swears he saw it! In port you might question his word, but at sea he has the eyesight of an eagle!"

An uneasy silence settled over the gathering.

"If we remain neutral, we may avoid the cursed omens," a shipowner said. "Let the mainlanders do what they wish."

"I agree with you!" a councillor named Desakis said fervently. "We would be insane to endanger our prosperity. We are under the Mussulman's shadow, a long way from the mountains of Rumelia and the Peloponnesus."

"If the revolution succeeds," another captain said, "we will gain our freedom. If the insurgents are bloodied and beaten, we will have been spared. Selfish, in a way, but we have so much more to lose than the peasants and farmers."

"Shame on you, Sefakis!" the grizzled captain, Baltas, said heatedly. "Would you have others fight to save your skin?"

"Are you calling me a coward?" Sefakis' face darkened with wrath.

"Let us remain calm, friends," Leonidas said, "and examine the alternatives. By remaining neutral, we may affect the outcome. If the blow to be struck at the beginning is not joined by the islands and the mainland together, we diminish the chances for victory."

"What word of Ipsilantis?" a man asked.

"Our friends in Odessa report he is gathering an army," another said.

"With the approval of the Tsar?"

"That is what Ipsilantis has pledged."

"Whatever he does affects the provinces only," Cambezis said. "He cannot prevent a single Turkish frigate from pointing its big guns at our warehouses, churches and homes."

"I observe you put the warehouses first," a man snickered.

"This is no joking matter!" Cambezis cried. "If you want to play the clown, go to the taverna!"

"I say we should let the Hydriotes begin the revolt if they wish," Despitas said. "They have idle ships in their harbors and disgruntled sailors drinking all day in the tavernas. Give the loafers something to do."

"You forget one thing, gentlemen," Kanaris said, and he spoke quietly but with a firm, resonant voice.

Konstantine Kanaris, a shipowner and captain of Psara, was about the same age as Leonidas, in his middle thirties, with a slender, wiry frame. Leonidas and Kanaris were the closest of friends, had sailed and fought Algerian pirates together. Better than any of the others, Leonidas understood the iron will and massive ability beneath his friend's quiet demeanor.

"Without the ships of our island," Kanaris said. "Without the ships of Hydra, Spetzia and Samos, the revolution cannot succeed. Our ships and seamen will determine victory or defeat."

"God forbid we have that responsibility!" Despitas said mournfully.

"Those are the facts," Kanaris said calmly. "Let us not fool ourselves that a war can be fought without us, or that lacking our fleets, they can possibly win."

"Kanaris! Kanaris!" Cambezis spoke in agitation. "Do you remember at Izmir, when we anchored almost under the shadow of the Capitan-pasha's flagship? Did we not agree we had never seen such a monster? Her tiers of decks studded with cannon, her double-layered hull, her keel of iron-hard teak, her bottom copper-sheathed. A leviathan of the seas! How can our light brigs fight against monsters like that?"

"At the Bay of Salamis," Kanaris said, "after the armies of Xerxes, the Persian, had captured Athens, he brought his great fleet from Egypt and Asia Minor to crush the lighter, outnumbered fleet of Themistocles. That could have been the end of Greece. But Themistocles destroyed the Persian Navy and won Athens a hundred years of supremacy on the seas."

"It is not fair to draw on ancient history, Kanaris!" Cambezis said indignantly. "Those battles were fought with galleys and her enemies had not yet learned to buttress their ships against the Athenian ram!"

"Our ships are lighter and smaller, but they are swifter,"

another of the younger captains, Papanikolis, said. "Our men are born and bred to the sea. The Turks are infantrymen under sail!" He spit in derision.

"We can put forty ships over a hundred tons apiece to sea!" Leonidas said excitedly. "Hydra could provide more than a hundred and fifteen ships, Spetzia another sixty. Do you know what a fleet that will make?"

"Who will command such a fleet?" Baltas asked harshly. "No Hydriote or Spetziot will tell me where to sail or how to fight!"

"What are we arguing about?" A thin-eared, stringy-haired captain said. "There are only rumors. Ipsilantis has not yet marched, fighting hasn't begun anywhere in Greece. The delay may last for years . . ."

The absurdity of that comment forced them to silence. They stared moodily at their knees, puffed deeply at their pipes. Finally, Leonidas turned to an old man who had not taken part in the discussion.

"What do you think, Hadji Yannaros?" he asked respectfully.

Hadji Yannaros was the chief magistrate of Psara, a revered retired captain in his eighties. The long years of voyages had purged all excess flesh from his lean frame, the ravages of sun, wind and water bleaching his face until the bones were faintly visible beneath the pearly skin of his cheeks. Wearing beaded slippers, and a waistcoat of scarlet with a collar of black astrakhan fur, he sat cross-legged, Turkish style, on the divan. While everyone waited for him to answer, he drew his chibouk slowly from his mouth and brought the long-stemmed pipe to rest across his lap.

"Young men dream and old men caution," Hadji Yannaros said gravely, "but all are prisoners of the whirlwind. I heard the voice of the Lord saying, 'Whom shall I send and who will go for me?'" His small, black eyes raked them all. "Then said I, shall I suffer others to do the work of the Lord in my place?"

The men murmured assent, a few of them nodding somberly. They waited for the old man to go on.

"When the storm comes, make no mistake, we will eat the bread of adversity and drink the water of affliction. The bones of our dead and the hulls of our ships will litter the bed of the sea. Our widows will wear black garments, but that will not end their grief. They shall be swept by the whirlwind, torn from their homes and their land. Their agony will cause the dead to mourn them."

Leonidas thought of Aspasia and his small daughters caught in that fury. The faces of the other captains, responding to that grave, prophetic voice, reflected the same vision of terror.

Hadji Yannaros let them suffer that apparition for several moments. In the tight silence one man coughed, another prayed softly, a third released a heartfelt sigh.

"Yet the souls of the righteous are in the hands of God," Hadji Yannaros said. "Chastised and cast down, in the end they shall be raised and rewarded. They shall bear witness when the Lord with his great and strong sword shall punish Leviathan, the crooked serpent . . ." His voice rose, billowing as a sail caught in a gust of wind. "In His name we shall slay the dragon and make the sea his eternal grave!"

A sardonic smile trembled the bloodless line of his lips.

"As for the possessions we shudder to lose," he said, "just as all men have one small entrance into life, so is there only a single, narrow exit. Even he who is a king must one day die and occupy the same portion of space on land or sea, as the poorest beggar of his realm."

After the captains and shipowners had departed, Leonidas sat alone for a while as trails of smoke lingered about the chandelier. When servants entered to clear away the glasses and extinguish the lights, Leonidas walked from the salon through the silent corridors of the house.

He quietly entered the bedroom where his daughters

slept. He was conscious, at once, of their vernal scents, aroma of fragile, fledgling buds. Then, in the mist of moonlight falling into the room, the faces of his sleeping daughters seemed strangely lifeless, static as subjects in a painting. With a flutter of fear he bent over each bed and kissed the children gently. The youngest, his four-year-old Nikki, stirred in her sleep at his kiss, raising her slender arms drowsily yet beguilingly as a miniature nymph. He knelt beside her bed and stroked her hair until she slipped easily back to sleep.

From their bedroom, he descended to another wing, containing the quarters where he and his wife slept. He undressed and washed in an anteroom and then, entering the bedchamber, he slipped quietly into the canopied bed. Aspasia moved beside him.

"Did I wake you, my darling? I'm sorry."

"I was dreaming a lovely dream," she said drowsily. "We were sitting in the garden, the children laughing and playing around us."

She pressed closer, her toes rubbing his legs, coming to rest against his ankle.

"Did you drink and dance?"

"We talked," he said. He felt his breath burdened in his chest.

They were silent for a moment.

"I have been thinking about you taking the children away," he said. "In three days Captain Maroukas sails the *Jason* to Marseilles. You might join him on that voyage and go from there to Paris. Fotini has a house where you could stay until we see the development back here."

"Only the most timid and easily frightened wives have left with their children so far," Aspasia said. "Will the family of Captain Kontos be counted among them?"

"It may not be safe for you to wait much longer," Leonidas said. "I think, tonight, everyone realized that the revolt is inevitable."

"I will not leave!"

"Aspasia, listen to me!"

"I have always listened to you!" she said defiantly. "But don't ask me to cross the sea to a foreign city where I will wait each day for a ship to bring me news that you are dead!"

"Knowing you and the children were safe would reassure me," Leonidas said.

"And if the island falls?"

"The sea would become our land," he said.

"I am the daughter of a sea captain," Aspasia said quietly. "The wife of a sea captain. I must not shame you or my father."

Even as he argued for her to take the children and leave, he admired and was grateful for her wish to remain.

The tracings of moonlight that had been visible in his daughter's bedroom streamed through the sheer curtains at the terrace doors. With the moonlight came a rustling of wind carrying the scent of lemon blossoms. Then the voices of a group of sailors emerging from one of the taverns in the town below floated in drunken clamor across the darkness. After a while their voices faded, the silence returned, until, sharp and clear, a ship's bell tolled the hour.

"I wish I were a tavern wench tonight," Aspasia said, her voice teasing in an effort to dispel the gloom. "I'd find a handsome sailor with a chest like a hull and arms like masts."

"Aspasia!" He feigned indignation. "You are a wicked woman!"

She laughed softly.

"Very wicked and fickle!" he said. "You have a hale and hearty Psariot captain in bed beside you. Why should you fancy other seafaring men?"

"Even Psariot captains grow bored with their wives after a while," she said. "Like fishing too long in the same channel or dropping anchor in the same port too many times. Perhaps we both need a change."

"I'll show you change, woman!" he cried. He swung his body above her and with one hand gathered her long, golden hair in his fingers, drawing her face up to him. Her eyes glowed as he pressed his lips on her lips, and he tasted and felt her tongue.

The quickened rhythm of her blood paced his own body and he slipped his hands slowly under the bodice of her gown to caress her breasts. She let out her breath in a fervent sigh.

Often, in their moments of love and secretly from Aspasia, he fashioned the fantasy they were embracing in the berth of his quarters at sea, the bed swaying slightly with the rolling of the ship. He assured himself he could hear the gulls crying above the peaks of the masts, the creaking of the spars and rigging, the snapping of the sails. By this vision he removed his spirit from the bondage of the land, from the shadow of beys and pashas. A free man, master of his ship, he was restored to an unfettered vigor as he thrust into his wife's sweet core.

After their lovemaking, Aspasia asleep once again, he lay restlessly in the darkness. He recalled the stories told by the captains, the old hand falling from the rigging to his death, the monster in the sea with the tongue of fire, the disemboweled sheep. In the old magistrate's prophecy of suffering and death, he saw their island plundered and despoiled, the balustrades broken, the mansions shuttered and empty. On the beaches lay the debris of wrecked and gutted ships, the wind blowing eerily through the tattered canvas.

He was still shaken by specters as dawn appeared at the windows, dispersing the shadows in the corners of the room. He heard the stirring of attendants in the courtyard of the house, the arrival of bakers who would be preparing hundreds of loaves of bread for the larders of ships, hard, brown-crusted loaves to be eaten with cheese and a ration of wine.

He slipped quietly from the bed and walked to stand outside the room on the terrace. The air smelled of thyme, the first light visible on the horizon. Below him, emerging from their shroudings of fog, were the dome of the church, the tiled roofs of the houses in the town. In the harbor lay half a hundred caïques and small fishing barks, while in the deeper water, a dozen brigs were anchored, sleek ships like jeweled wraiths in the ghostly light. Even as he watched, the harbinger of the sun flashed across the shoals in the distance, between the harbor and the outline of Andipsara.

Standing above that familiar panorama of stone, shells and gulls, houses, ships and the sea, he felt consoled and reinforced. This was his island, and the stalwarts who inhabited it were his people. A few generations earlier their forebears had been peasants and refugees. The grandsons of those ancestors had built a solid, enduring society, had conquered the archipelago, carrying the Mediterranean and Black Sea trade, resisting gales and storms and the assaults of Barbary pirates.

In that moment Leonidas saw the mission of the islanders clearly, the reason they had amassed their wealth and power. Not for personal gain but in order to help deliver all their people from the despotism and tyranny that had chained them for centuries. From Epirus to Rumelia, from Macedonia to the Peloponnesus, every man, woman and child was destined to attain the freedom a sailor felt on his ship, sailing the unemcumbered sea. A hundred captains who had charted their course by the stars would lead thousands into the constellation of independence so they might become a nation of giants once more.

CHAPTER
FIVE

For Katerina Mavromichalis, wife of Petrobey, the prince of the Mani, a constant scent of danger and misfortune lay across the rocky, barren land. Summer and autumn with their scant flowerings could not erase the smell, winter had not blown it away, and now, the faintest stirrings of winter's end coming to the almond, fig and carob trees, the odor still clung to her. She knew that it exuded from the hate and violence of men, emotions as natural to them as breathing.

As a child, her dominant memories were of war. Brothers, uncles and cousins crouched at the windows of the stone towers where they had taken refuge, their long guns poking from the slits, firing at an enemy unseen but there. All day and all night the guns exploded, banishing sleep, the flashes of light cracking the darkness. Even their hasty meals were tainted by the brackish taste of gunpowder in the food and water. The injured men groaned in the corners while women washed their wounds, trying to ease their pain. And when a man died, subduing all other sounds, the shrill wailing of women assailed her ears.

From the time of the laments of Hecuba and Andromache, it had been the cruel fate of women to mourn their sons and husbands lost in war. The only change over the centuries was that lances and arrows had been replaced by guns and cannon that wreaked more hideous wounds.

Married now for almost thirty-eight years, having borne eleven sons and three daughters, Katerina had mourned her father, three brothers and two of her sons, all of them killed in vendettas and wars. She recalled the long days and nights of vigil, washing their limbs, seeing life streaming from their eyes, leaving their skulls barren and dry. After their deaths, helping her mother and sisters wrap their bodies in the funeral shrouds, her sorrow turned to bitterness and rage. She came to believe that men craved war as they needed the body of a woman, to release the dark, venomous bile that seethed within them.

The periods of peace were fleeting, broken quickly by the eruption of fighting. When they were menaced from outside the Mani, for brief periods their guns pointed the same way. When there was not a common foe, the Maniats fought among themselves.

Perhaps the blazing light, the naked rock, the cactuses and unyielding earth, devoid of softness, were a breeding ground for war. Above the terrible mountain of Taygetus, so bleak that even eagles scorned its peaks, the sun burned across the immense palisades, reflecting like fire from the stones.

Hopeful that the endless vendettas and feuds would destroy the Maniats more effectively than an army, the Turks left them alone under the rule of a Maniat holding the power of a reigning prince and the title of bey. Since the first of these rulers, the pirate Liberakis Yerakaris, there had been eight princes of the Mani. Her husband, Petrobey, ascending to the chieftainship in 1808, had already proven himself the greatest of the beys. He had negotiated with Napoleon and reconciled the warring clans. A nominal yearly tribute was to be paid to the Sultan but it was rarely collected. Katerina had seen Petrobey derisively toss a petty coin to the Sultan's representative, flinging it down from the tip of his scimitar.

Katerina had been married to this man, descended from Skyloyanni Mavromichalis, "John the Dog," one of the great paladins who fought the Turks in the eighteenth century, at fifteen, awed that so regal and handsome a personage should want her. There was a legend in the Mani that the physical beauty of the Mavromichalis clan sprang from the marriage of one of their ancestors to a mermaid. In addition to his fine looks, her husband, Petrobey, had dignity, intelligence and courage. But, having lived with the man for almost four decades and borne his children, she knew he also boiled with a consuming ambition, was proud to the point of arrogance, and could be indescribably cruel to those who defied his edicts.

Swept from the innocence of girlhood into marriage and childbirth, she came to believe that the only function any woman served for a man was to provide a womb. After the birth of a son, there would be jubilation and rejoicing, each visitor laden with gifts, firing off his gun before entering their house, expressing the hope the male-child would gain renown in war. When a girl was born, there were neither gifts nor congratulations. Girls were useful only as breeders, drudges, dirge-singers. A sun was carved on the cradle of a baby boy, a moon on that of a girl.

Men were mourned at their death but women lived unmourned in life. They worked from dawn to dark in the fields and groves, often carrying the wooden cradles of babies slung from their shoulders. When the cisterns dried up in the desolate summer, they trudged for miles to fill kegs with water that trickled from apertures in the rocks near the sea. From childhood they were tormented by the males' sullen obsession with virginity. After marriage, an endless ritual of bearing children began, a cycle of blood and pain.

And when a male relative died, the young wives were required to relinquish any lightness or color from their dress, donning raiment of black for the rest of their lives.

Even the passage from death to burial was a burden in the Mani. The earth was full of stones and hacking trenches for the corpses was backbreaking labor. The dead person, swathed in shrouds since wood was too scarce to be used for coffins, was borne to the churchyard on a ceremonial bier; the corpse was lifted off the shoulders of the pallbearers and laid in the shallow grave that would be used over and over again as the bones were moved.

Only in their wild laments at these moments of interment, did the women push the dominant males aside. They wailed around the body by candle flame, the wails becoming screams as the corpse was lowered into the ground, the mourners gashing their cheeks with their nails and tearing at their hair.

Yet, Katerina believed, the women were not mourning for the dead alone, for shadows that would replace living flesh, for the memories of a few grudging endearments, but for the unbearable suffering of their lives.

As the men of the Mani had warred for centuries, another war was now pending, for freedom, they claimed, though certainly not the freedom of women. Vengeance, vendetta, insult, freedom, any pretext sufficed.

To see them bristling and armored was to confirm the absurdity of their martial preening. Dressed in baggy trousers, shirts gallooned with silver, they wore a webwork of belts to hold their arsenals. The pistols whose butts swelled into knobs, the curved yataghans and cross-hilted scimitars, powder horns and pouches of silver from Jannina. Their long-barreled guns, so heavy they could only be aimed when resting on a rock or the branch of a tree, they had the audacity to call karyophilia, the name for a flower!

But, even naked, they strutted as if all the lead and powder in their weapons were suddenly encased within the swollen, arrogant shafts they used to invade a woman's body, thrusting and battering as if to tear open the core of the earth.

When the first of Katerina's children had been born, she still hoped that gentleness and kindness might survive in their hearts if these qualities were instilled in them when they were young. But as her sons grew to manhood, their hearts hardened, they abolished compassion, came to revere the knife and the gun. They spoke with fanatic zeal of manhood, pride, honor, nobility, and, wary of slights, quivered with eagerness at any chance to fight and kill.

The pleasures she had been afforded in them as children were now provided by her grandchildren, whose mothers, her daughters and daughters-in-law, brought them to her quarters in the early afternoons. She cherished the small boys and girls, tanned by the sun to a gypsy darkness, their brown, slender legs marked by the scars of nettles and thorns, black, luminous eyes glistening at her in mischief and affection. They were the only things of any beauty left in the Mani.

Alone in her room after the children had departed, she sat before the wheel, her left hand pulling and twisting the thread from the hank of wool on the distaff she wore tucked into her apron, the gyrating spindle sinking downward from her forefinger and thumb, rising and falling, a slow, unchanging rhythm. In this same way her mother and grandmother had spun the thread, perhaps thinking the same thoughts with which she occupied her hours.

When twilight darkened her room she lit the lamps and placed a jug of water and a flask of ouzo on the table in preparation for the visit of her sons before the evening meal.

Tall, strong young men full of a swaggering roughness

they sought to harness in her presence, they swallowed the tumblers of ouzo quickly, proffering their filial obligation awkwardly, anxious to be on their way.

Only Elias, her favorite (though she did not confess that bond to anyone) did not hurry to leave. He was the handsomest of her sons, blending the tawny loveliness she had as a girl with the Mavromichalis strength and grace.

When he entered her room and bent to kiss her temple, she smelled the scents of pine and thyme and, in a flutter of nostalgia, remembered him as a small boy playing a haunting melody on a flute in a summer twilight.

"All your brothers have been here already today," she said. "If you are going to come later and later, perhaps you would prefer not bothering to come at all?"

"And miss my visit with my mother?" he said in a bantering voice. "Miss the ouzo and figs you always save for me?"

"No figs tonight!" She tried to make her voice convey a sternness she did not feel.

"Where are they?" he cried. "I'll turn the room upside down, tear apart every shred of cloth!"

"Leave that alone, you ruffian!" she cried, and could not resist laughing as he rummaged furiously in the piles of yarn and cloth. "The figs are in the cupboard!"

He walked to the cupboard and returned with the plate of figs. He poured a tumbler of ouzo. She watched him drinking and eating, his cheeks glowing in the flame of the lamps.

"They buried Kalouris in Yenetsari this morning," he said. "I went with Father and Gatsos. Phroso sang the lament."

"Old Phroso!" Katerina exclaimed. "Po! Po! Po! That poor old woman has grown so feeble she cannot remember from one minute to the next who is dead. Wasn't Antiope there?"

"She was attending a wake in Praxini," Elias said. "When she arrived too late for the funeral, you should have heard her complain. Kalouris dead and buried and she didn't say, 'God grant him rest,' but, 'The funeral was spoiled because I wasn't here to wail for him.'"

They laughed together and Katerina savored the warmth of the moment. Feeling tears coming into her eyes, she spoke brusquely to conceal her emotion.

"Zoe was here with your children today," she said. "Paulo is too thin. He is not eating enough."

"All right, Mama," he said. "We'll try to get more food into the boy to please you."

"If you want to please me, find someone to help Zoe," she said. "Don't be like the brutes that load their wives as if they were donkeys and goats."

"I will, Mama."

He rose suddenly, abruptly, to leave.

"You have just come!" she said in dismay.

"I can't stay any longer tonight, Mama," he said. "There is a special meeting of the Council."

"War, is it then?" she asked, the words falling grim and chilled from her lips.

Understanding better than any of the others the degree of her suffering and fear, he knelt and clasped her within the embrace of his strong hands.

"Not like the rest of the battles this time, Mama," he said quietly. "Not simply another vendetta or feud. It is for all of Greece that we will fight now, for our children and their children."

"I have heard that nonsense before," she said harshly. "Men always fight for honor, peace, manhood, pride and country . . . and for widows, orphans, famine, yes, and for wounds and for death!"

"Mama!" he said sharply, angrily. Looking at him she saw the stern, proud countenance of his father. Yes, she thought bitterly, the pleas of a mother's heart were helpless against the wiles of war's harlot. Father and son and the whole tribe of imperious and haughty males would have their way.

He bent and kissed her again and then he was gone, the room grown darker in his absence. She turned back to her spinning, more difficult by lamplight, twisting the thread peevishly, the rhythm broken by her fitful starts and stops.

In the next few weeks the barbarous leaders of war assembled in the Mani. Some came from mountains where they had been secluded and others returned from lands where they had been driven. The bloody Anagnostaras and the untamed Niketaras joined Petrobey in the Councils. And, just a few days later, the most infamous brigand of all, Kolokotronis, had landed at Kardamyli, returning secretly from his exile on Zante. The son of a famous klepht who had been a leader in the rising of 1770, Kolokotronis had been reared like a wolf on Rama in Messenia. When his family had been condemned to exile for offenses against the Turks, he had fled with them to the Ionian islands to serve in the English Army. He had returned now, drawn to the smells of danger and blood.

The aura of recklessness that surrounded the man served to excite her sons. In their visits to her room, they talked to her of the brigand with admiration, imitating his movements, the way he spoke, swaggered and laughed. All were eager to prove to him they were young Maniat hawks. Even Petrobey, normally assured of his primacy, seemed challenged by the brigand's presence.

The leaders met in Council for hours at a time, joined daily by the heads of clans from other parts of the Mani. She heard them arguing, threatening, blustering, each man determined to impose his will on the others. Over the multitude of voices, many of which she recognized, came the thundering voice of Kolokotronis, and she sensed that by sheer, primitive force, his will would prevail.

She had only caught a glimpse of him once or twice from a distance, but her impression was of a huge, clumsy-bodied man, an immense, shaggy head united to the brawny neck of a bull. She imagined him coarse and profane, a predator desiring to engrave his deeds on history with a sword dipped in blood. And the outrageous vanity of the man was evidenced by the great plumed helmet he wore in the Councils, a helmet of such ostentatious splendor it might have been worn by Alexander or Agamemnon!

The arrival of Kolokotronis not only excited her sons but produced a martial bellicosity in all the ludicrous creatures with hairy sacs suspended between their legs. Under the shade of the dingy eaves of the tavernas, worthless old louts, spitting through their toothless gums, loudly regaled one another and whoever chanced to pass with exaggerated recountings of battles they had fought, enemies they had killed, the booty they had amassed.

Children were caught up in the fever, hurling stones at dogs and pulling the tails and ears of cats. In church to light a candle and say a prayer, Katerina found the frenzy had spread even to the priest, Father Verganis, who was busily polishing a brace of pistols.

"Shame on you, Father!" she said indignantly. "You are a man of God and should be attending to souls!"

The priest had a florid, sharp-featured face, thick, oily black hair planted so low on his brow, it hung over his eyes like a cowl. He spoke with the ardor of a man disjoined from his senses.

"Praise be to God, I am attending to souls, Princess Katerina!" he cried. "The souls of infidels, and my mission, decreed by God, to dispatch them to Hades!"

"There is need for you here, Father," she said. "The poor must be cared for and the sick attended. There are many men able to go and fight, but your duty is here."

Father Verganis stared at her in outrage.

"This is the Mani, Princess Katerina!" he cried. "In the Mani, men, regardless of their occupations, do not shirk their responsibilities! I would be ashamed to face your revered husband, Prince Petrobey, if I neglected to serve

him now! My wife will attend the sick and the poor, with
God's help, who bids me join in this noble cause!"

"And your dozen children, Father?" she asked scathingly,
for he was a man who spent as much time swelling his wife's
belly as he did in saying prayers.

"God will look after them, as well!" the priest cried, and
turned away, flourishing his pistols with the joy of a child
holding his cherished playthings.

Among the retinue of men who had come to the Mani
with the brigand Kolokotronis, there was a slender, pale-
faced Zantiot, a quiet, reserved man whose lack of any
weapons on his person made him an incongruous figure
alongside the other men. Once, a week or so after their arrival, seeing him half hidden on a bench behind a plane
tree, reading a book, Katerina felt compelled to approach.

He rose quickly to his feet, flustered and awkward, as if
she had caught him in some mischief.

"Forgive me for disturbing you," she said, "but a book in
the hands of a man in the Mani is as extraordinary as a dove
in a flock of hawks. May I inquire what you are reading?"

"Certainly, Princess." He made a stiff, deferential bow. "I
am reading poetry . . . the verses of Appolonides."

She stared at him, her first encounter with any man who
read poetry. She noted the shabby cuffs of his jacket, the
threadbare fabric of his breeches. But she was drawn to his
eyes that reflected a sensitivity and sadness.

"And what part will the poetry play in the preparations
for war?"

He flushed, perhaps taking her words for censure.

"My regular duties are as scribe and adjutant to Captain
Kolokotronis," he said. "I understand the importance of
those duties and will not neglect them. I had a few spare
moments today and sat down here . . . to read a little . . ."

"A passion for poetry may be more timeless than a passion
for war," she said.

"Poetry can honor the heroic exploits of men in war," he said.

"I would rather that poetry concerned itself with peace and tolerance and love," she said. "Wouldn't you?"

He looked at her uneasily, as if uncertain whether she was testing him.

"What is your name?" she asked.

"Xanthos, Princess," he replied. "I am from Zante, and was a teacher."

"Well, Xanthos," she said. "When your duties permit you a few moments of leisure, would you be willing to come and read some poetry to me?"

"I would be happy to," he said, and smiled with a shyness curious in a man near fifty. That pleased her, as well, and she motioned for him to return to his book.

Intent on fanning the enthusiasm of the Maniats for the conflict to come, Petrobey ordered a feast in Tsimova to honor the chieftains Kolokotronis, Niketaras and Anagnostaras. Katerina attended the festivities because it was her husband's wish, but even as she dressed in a crimson jacket, brocaded oriental trousers and slippers adorned with gold braid, she felt her spirit clothed in darker raiment.

Several hundred Maniats, gallooned in their finery, armed as if on parade, their moustaches and hair waxed and oiled, gathered in the huge courtyard lit by the flames of a hundred torches. They strutted from table to table, shouting with bombast, forming in ragged lines to stamp and leap in drunken dances. Every so often one pointed a pistol into the air and fired, each detonation causing Katerina, sitting at a table with a group of the women, to wince.

In the course of the evening, Petrobey, magnificently attired in a short bolero decorated with as much bullion as a Spanish bullfighter's jacket, and trousers of green velvet, joined Kolokotronis, clad in a sparkling white and pleated fustanella, and a white, broad-sleeved blouse. He wore his great plumed helmet on his head.

The two men ascended opposite walls of the courtyard and from those vantage points directed the stationing of the men below on the flagstones that had been chalked into the squares of a chessboard. When the human pieces were assembled in their ranks, the chieftains began a game of chess, bellowing their commands, roaring with triumph at the capture of a piece that drove a man from the huge board. Along the perimeter of the courtyard, men milled about, shouting suggestions and support.

"Not the rook, Captain Kolokotronis, the bishop!"

"Protect the knight, Prince Petrobey . . . he is moving on the knight!"

"Attack the castle, Captain! Attack!"

As fresh flasks of wine were hoisted aloft to wet the throats of the players, made dry by shouting commands, both men grew drunker, teetering dangerously close to the edges of the walls. Katerina could no longer watch and turned away, thinking grimly that even in their games men had to play at war.

The table where she sat was reserved for the wives and daughters of leading Maniat families. Without joining their conversation, Katerina could hear the sardonic whispers of some of the younger, bolder women.

"Does the captain wear that kilt to bed?"

"Go ask him if you dare!"

"Easier than waiting while he pulls down his pants."

"Marisa!"

"I adore that helmet! A headpiece such as Apollo himself might wear!"

"Don't let your husband hear you."

"It would make a splendid trophy for my bedchamber."

"So would the captain!"

Listening to them giggling and clucking like addled hens, Katerina yearned for the serenity of her room, for the wheel that spun in rhythm with her thoughts. Looking away from the flames of the torches, she stared toward the sky, calculating the lateness of the hour even though there wasn't a single star visible in the blackness. A night for werewolves, she thought uneasily, and stringloparmeni, the witch-possessed ones. She began recasting the images she had seen in her dreams on the last few nights, unraveling omens the way she unraveled her wool. She remembered tasting cakes, a flavor of sweetness that foreshadowed bitterness. She also remembered seeing a house without a roof, and that portended an open grave.

Lost in her reveries, she did not hear the men approach the table. Only when a nervous animation stirred the women around her did Katerina look up, startled to see the brigand chieftain Kolokotronis standing before her. He held the regal helmet in the crook of his arm, his long black hair striated with gray, his complexion as dark as that of a Bedouin. Beside him stood her son Elias.

"Mama, I wanted you to meet Captain Kolokotronis," Elias said. "Captain, this is my mother, Princess Katerina."

Kolokotronis bowed with a courtly, formal gesture. When he straightened up, he spoke solemnly.

"My lady, I am an old soldier," he said, "more accustomed to the rough barter of the barracks than the courtesies of society, but I am honored to be presented to the Princess of the Mani."

"Thank you, Captain," Katerina said quietly. "My husband and sons are proud to have you with us."

Kolokotronis noticed the attentive, admiring women. He offered them a quick, gallant bow.

"Elias," he said, a trace of banter in his voice. "Why have I been wasting my time with soldiers who smell of powder and shot when here is a garden of flowers?"

"Sit in the garden for a while, Captain." Elias laughed. "I'll try to occupy the soldiers so they do not miss your presence."

Kolokotronis looked at Katerina, waiting for a sign that she did not object to his remaining. When Katerina nodded, Kolokotronis sat down, adjusting his sword and his scabbard, placing the helmet carefully on his knées, the plume rising almost to his chin.

Correcting her initial impression of him, Katerina was surprised that he was not nearly as big and clumsy as he had first appeared from a distance. He was of medium stature, with a strong, yet slender frame, and dark, piercing eyes to which his hooked nose lent a menacing and vigilant demeanor. She thought of an eagle perched on one of the crags of rock projecting from their mountain, Taygetus.

"I have met all your sons," Kolokotronis said. "The mother of such stalwart warriors must indeed be a proud lady."

"They are strong, good sons," Katerina said. "I wish for them what any mother would wish for her sons. A long, fruitful life."

Aware of the censure, he looked at her gravely and she was conscious suddenly of his glance, now wild, now soft and caressing, radiating a curious warmth through her blood.

"I too have sons," he said slowly. "In the years we lived in exile on Zante, I would take them to the peak of the castle hill and would point to the Peloponnesus and tell my sons those were the strongholds of their forefathers which they must someday make free again."

"Strongholds are not things a woman cares about," Katerina said. "A woman values healthy, living sons, grandchildren, and the passing of the seasons in peace."

While the women at the table murmured in awe at her audacity, Kolokotronis stared at her silently.

"I cannot deny a mother's heart," he said gently. "I can only speak of how it is for my sons and for me. If we die in battle against the enemies of our country, we will be greeted as comrades by the immortal dead, those warriors who gave their lives centuries ago to keep our land free. If we did less, we would shame their memory and shame ourselves."

She felt his passion, so vital and strong it bruised her spirit. Beneath his pompous, ceremonial attire, the rock of the man struck sparks. She had a sudden fearful vision of his mailed and savage destiny, the plumed helmet rising above the rubble of burning towns, in his wake the screams of the wounded and the laments for the dead.

As if sensing her fear and wishing to reassure her, he smiled with a warmth tinting his rough-hewn cheeks. She was startled again how so tender a glance could stem from such a harsh, bold visage, so primal and militant a nature.

"Kolokotronis." Petrobey approached the table, his handsome face flushed slightly with drink. "At this point we are stalled in the contest and the wagers cannot be paid. We must finish the game."

"In a few moments, Petrobey." Kolokotronis continued to smile at Katerina. "I am sitting here enjoying rare company for an old soldier, your wife and I discussing sons and battles."

Petrobey stared reprovingly at Katerina.

"My wife is a splendid woman," he said, "but her views on manhood and honor are those of a woman and should be discounted."

One of the younger women seated at the table, strong-faced, with gray, defiant eyes spoke up.

"Not all the women in the Mani feel as your wife does, Prince Petrobey," she said brusquely. She looked scornfully at Katerina. "But when a body grows old, I suppose the blood cools, as well."

Several of the older women shook reproachful fingers at the young woman. Kolokotronis stared at her sharply.

"If a man wants comrades in battle," he said loudly, "he will assemble other men. When he requires solace and affection, he will find a good, gentle woman." He paused, a sternness entering his voice. "Binding a cow's udders does not make the creature a bull."

The young woman bristled at the biting reprimand and then, unable to meet the chieftain's eyes, stared abjectly at the table. A few of the women mocked her in strident hissings. Katerina felt her cheeks flush while Petrobey stared stiffly at Kolokotronis, his pride seemingly piqued by the captain's spirited defense of his wife. Then, as if the implacable laws of hospitality required he divert his irritation, Petrobey sat down.

"Bring us wine," he called brusquely.

Several of the women rose quickly to answer his bidding. The two men sat in silence until the women returned with decanters of wine and filled their glasses. Kolokotronis raised his glass to Katerina.

"I drink to the miracle," he said gravely, "that allowed these rocks, cactuses and thorns to give birth to the most beautiful woman I have yet seen in the Mani."

Katerina felt her breath tightened in her breast, a rare, forgotten pleasure winging through her blood. Holy Mother Mary, she thought, I am a woman well into middle age who has borne fourteen children and yet I tingle under this strange man's eyes and words as if I were still a girl in her green-budded youth.

Petrobey swallowed his wine quickly and set the empty glass on the wood of the table with a loud bump. The women remaining seated around them rose hurriedly and scattered like nervous birds.

"Kolokotronis," Petrobey said, and he smiled a brittle curling of his lips. "Did you know that the Pasha of the Peloponnesus has called upon the leaders in the Mani to deliver up to him the person or the head of one Theodoros Kolokotronis? The bounty, I imagine, would be the ransom of a king."

In the tense silence that followed, Katerina heard the harsh and sodden voices of the men in the courtyard. Even their celebrations were overcast with obsessive pride, violence brooding in their blood. Looking uneasily at Kolokotronis she saw that all vestige of softness had disappeared from his eyes, his face an image hewn from granite.

"Petrobey," Kolokotronis said quietly. "Would any Maniat leader claim that ransom?"

"I mention it only that you may be on your guard," Petrobey said. "There are malicious and envious men everywhere . . . even in the Mani."

"Yes," Kolokotronis said. "Betrayals are not uncommon among our people, God help us. Even chiefs have been known to betray other chiefs."

Their eyes challenged and defied one another.

"If I thought it in the interests of my people to surrender any man, even a chief," Petrobey spoke in a resonant voice, "it would not be betrayal. I would announce it openly as a decision I made as Prince of the Mani, within my authority and by the power vested in me by the Senate of Elders."

"Authority and Senates mean nothing to me!" the words snapped from the captain's lips. "My mission must be fulfilled, and my freedom to accomplish that mission must be protected. If I were surrendered, I would deem it betrayal, and the man who authorized that betrayal would not breathe life more than an hour!"

Petrobey's face darkened and he placed his strong, long-fingered hands on the table and started angrily to rise.

"I have already been betrayed," Katerina spoke lightly and quickly. "You have both joined me here, driven the women away and sit growling of ransoms and betrayals." She shook her head chidingly at Kolokotronis. "My husband, after all, has been married to me for a long time and his consideration for me may have faltered. But I expected more from a valiant captain who has spent years in the company of the English and the French."

Kolokotronis stared at her, perplexed and taken back. Then a smile of appreciation lit his face.

"Forgive me, Princess," he said gravely. "You are quite right. We should both be ashamed." He looked across the table at Petrobey. "Prince Petrobey of the Mani," he said, "bearer of a noble name whose echo strikes fear into the hearts of agas and pashas from Epirus to Crete. I am sorry if anything I have said has given you offense."

"Not a word more, Captain!" Petrobey cried, spurred to contrition. "I was indulging a foolish, tasteless jest. You must know that every man in the Mani, Petrobey Mavromichalis first of all, would give his life to protect the valiant Lion of the Morea!"

Even the lion might feel slandered, Katerina thought wryly as she rose from the table, by the fickle posturings of men who could, in a moment, leap from the jagged edge of violence to flattery and praise.

"I forgive you both," she said. "Now I will say good night and leave you to finish your game."

Kolokotronis and Petrobey rose to their feet. The brigand bowed to her and when he raised his head, she fathomed again the dark, wild and cunning eyes. Once more she felt the man marked for some inexorable destiny, a fate, she understood sadly, that would leave countless women bereft of husbands, brothers and sons.

In the solitude of her room, she sat for a while before preparing for bed. The wine she had drunk in greater quantities than she was accustomed to drinking and the breezes through her windows carrying the first scents of spring, formed an unsteadiness in her blood.

She stood before the icon of the Blessed Mother with the small candle burning in oil. On a ledge near the candle were the white wreaths of her marriage crowns, fragments of that day in her girlhood so long ago when she began her life with Petrobey. She recalled the eagerness and frequency of his lovemaking in the beginning of their marriage, an ardency that declined slowly and steadily, so that in the last few years he rarely visited her room at night. She had not really regretted his absence since her age found her less sympathetic to endure the lungings of a man. Yet, in the strange restlessness that possessed her this evening, she wondered if he were taking younger women secretly into his arms.

She began to undress slowly, thinking again of the brigand captain, the tenderness that came so engagingly to his eyes. Intruding upon her reveries, there was a gentle, almost timorous knock on her door.

Thinking it might be one of her daughters or a woman come to gossip the events of the evening, she opened the door and was startled to see Petrobey. He stood a tall, imposing and flustered figure on the threshold. Noting the surprise on her face he made a mute gesture of entreaty, as if expecting to be rebuffed.

"Katerinaki . . ." He spoke the endearment of her name he had not used in years. She opened the door wider and he entered, staring at her silently.

"You looked very beautiful tonight," he said softly.

"You were, as always, the handsomest man at the celebration."

He flushed with pleasure and, emboldened, moved a step closer.

"All the younger women pale beside you," he said. "I swear you are still as beautiful as when we married." He paused, remorse entering his voice. "I'm sorry . . . you were right in reprimanding me tonight. I have not been attentive or considerate lately . . . the plans and the Councils of War, you know, have prevented me from spending more time with you . . ."

That is all right, my husband, she thought. She understood and accepted she was no longer as comely as she had once been. Now desire for her grew out of an occasional nostalgia or when his ownership was challenged, as it had been this evening, by the admiration of another man.

"I still love you, Katerinaki," he said softly, almost sadly.

He made an effort to stand straighter, as if fearing she might think an excess of wine had driven him to her room.

Tempered by a feeling of tenderness, she allowed him to take her into his arms. Over his shoulder she saw the wreaths of the marriage crowns, faded, withered garlands belonging to an ancient, irrecoverable time.

Yet, when they lay naked together in her bed, his strong arms embracing her, her breasts under the hard bony ridges of his ribs, she felt a bereavement enfeebling her limbs. Her desire faltered and a hard, demanding urgency against her body sought to pull her back. His gentleness had passed into the frantic, relentless drive of the male to gain entrance. She twisted her legs and thighs, dismayed by the burden of his frame, a weight she had forgotten during the months she slept alone. Managing to wrench her arm and shoulder free, she looked up at him and cried out. The visage that loomed above her was not her husband, but a strange and savage countenance, vindictive lusts within the eyes.

The lamps flickered and the room plunged into darkness. She sensed she lay imprisoned in a tomb filled with specters, ledges of rock hung with mosses under the wizened boughs of stunted trees. All the gloom was seamed with the tracks of snails and the webs of spiders.

In that terrible moment she understood it was Ares, assuming the form of her husband to deceive her, Ares, the god of war, spurred into the Mani by men preparing for violence and death, implanting a thorny and armored seed in her womb. From their union a gun would emerge, a male-child growing tall and strong so he could join eagerly with men in the carnage of battle.

She screamed then, in terror and despair, but her cry was lost, the tomb muffling and concealing the vengeful assault upon her body and her soul.

Part Two

GREECE

SPRING

1821

CHAPTER
SIX

The winter had been a cold, stormy and long season. At the beginning of March, the snow still crusted the lower slopes of Parnassus, and the frost would not relinquish its grip on the fields about the village of Kravasaras. Many farmers planted tobacco several times because the seedlings did not survive. Because of the shortage of wood, almost every house had someone ill, usually an old man or old woman, or a child suffering fever and chills. A few of the poorest families were saved from hunger by the provisions Father Markos obtained from Ahmed Bajaki, the wealthy Mussulman farmer, who donated a wagonload of flour and meal from his own storehouse.

Waiting for the winter to end, hopeful the first warm days of spring would loosen the painful knots in his shoulders and knees, Father Markos collapsed gratefully into his bed at night, huddling under his blankets to rest his aching bones. Beset by the distresses of his parish, he found it difficult to sleep and distracted himself by indulgent fantasies of bountiful meals before a roaring fire. In the gray, bleak dawn he rose, shivering and uncomfortable, because he had given the last of his winter's supply of logs to a widow with small children. Through the kindness of his neighbors, however, he had a hot bowl of soup or some broth to start his day.

In the middle of that unrelenting March, the news swept like a wind across all of Greece, reaching even to Kravasaras, that the Phanariot Prince Alexander Ipsilantis, with an army mobilized in Russia, had crossed the Prut River to invade the Danubian provinces of Moldavia and Walachia. In the reports of the fighting, accounts that became more extravagant with every passing day, it was proclaimed the invasion was the signal for revolt, that Ipsilantis' army, with the blessing of the Tsar, would march south to incite the insurrection in Greece.

Meanwhile the Turks spread word that Khurshid Pasha, commander of the forces besieging Ali Pasha before Jannina, was sending back a thousand Albanians to strengthen the garrisons at Lamia and Tripolitza. Within a week after the news was first heard, neither powder nor lead could be purchased from the bazaars in Kravasaras or Biskeni Agha. Mussulmen and Christians, even those who had lived for years as neighbors, watched one another with mistrust. Children were kept inside their houses and the doors were barred as soon as twilight fell.

In that tense, disquieting period, Father Markos was visited at the church by a traveling tinsmith who carried a letter to him from his wife's first cousin, Phaedra, in Kalavryta, a town across the Gulf of Corinth in the Peloponnesus.

My Treasured and Beloved Cousin:

I am saddened to report I have been struck severely ill with a high fever and dreadful pain. My good neighbors keep constant vigil at my bedside, waiting for the end. Before I depart this earth to join my cherished cousin, your blessed wife, I would like to carry to her some final message from you. In God's name, please

hurry, and I will exert all my strength to hold on to life
until you arrive!

Your devoted and rapidly failing,

Phaedra

For several fretful hours after reading the letter, Father
Markos considered ignoring the request. Not as a heartless
or unchristian act but because he knew, from grim experience, that his wife's cousin was a shrewish biddy who concealed the spirit of an adder behind a tongue dipped in the
honey of lies. On the pretext she wished only to look after
him, she had schemed for years to gain permanent residence
in his house. The summer before she had contrived to bring
him to Kalavryta by writing him she had discovered some
treasured mementos of his wife. When he had made the
journey and arrived at her house, she greeted him with a
chorus of lamentation, claiming the precious articles had
been destroyed by fire. Without evidence of any fire in her
house, she explained glibly she had given the treasures to a
neighbor for safekeeping and the neighbor had suffered the
fire.

Father Markos could hardly believe she would dare
deceive him so flagrantly again by pleading illness and impending death (a sacrilegious deception) but he knew the
woman would stop at nothing to get him into her clutches.
Yet, after he had wearied himself trying to resolve the problem of whether she was telling the truth, he knew he could
not risk the chance the harpy might actually be dying. He
prepared unhappily for the journey to Kalavryta.

He departed from Kravasaras riding his aging donkey,
Agathon, circling the foothills of the sacred temple at
Delphi, descending to a fishing settlement on the Gulf of
Corinth. Stabling Agathon with one of the fishermen, he
boarded one of the small fishing vessels to cross the twenty
nautical miles between the settlement and the port city of
Egion. On the journey, because of an unsteady sea, he be-

came seasick, hanging in misery over the bow of the boat, seeing his wretched face reflected in the water while the fishermen sat convulsed with laughter.

From Egion to Kalavryta, weak from his ordeal, he obtained a ride on a farmer's cart, perched gloomily in the midst of a brood of small children and assorted chickens, whose excretions were indistinguishable. By afternoon of the second day after his departure, and walking the last two miles on foot, he arrived in Kalavryta, the ancient Cynethus, a town of several hundred houses environed by mountains.

Assembling his spirit for a solemn vigil at the final hours of another human being, he was shocked to find Phaedra more hale and hearty than she had been in years.

"A miraculous recovery, blessed cousin Markos!" the old woman bellowed as she smothered him in an embrace that threatened to crack his ribs. "Knowing I have always been a good and devout Christian woman, the Lord, praised be His name, granted me some additional time. A miracle! Ask my neighbor, Lambrini. I tell you I was through death's door when the saints pulled me back!"

Exhausted from his arduous journey, assaulted by the sight of her stringy hair and ill-formed jaw like goat hide about her great teeth, his irritation passed into outrage and anger. Before he could assemble stern words of reproach, she surged past him into the yard, snatched up a hapless, skinny-fleshed chicken, and with a swift, skillful snap of her fingers broke the poor creature's neck. The priest sighed, resigned he would have to endure at least one meal under her roof.

Phaedra talked relentlessly during the meal, pausing only long enough to pop chunks of the fowl into her mouth, grinding it between her teeth, washing it down with swigs of wine before starting on him again.

"You have an unhealthy pallor, cousin, and look years older than you did last year! What if you fall ill? Must you depend upon the charity of strangers when the gentle, loving hand of a relative is available? Moving from here into your house to look after you would mean burdens and new miseries for me but I would accept them gladly for the sake of my cousin, your beloved wife, who said to me shortly before her untimely death, 'Phaedra, if anything should happen to me, I leave dear Markos in your care!'"

Two can play that crafty game, the priest thought grimly.

"It would be a blessing to have you near me, dear cousin," he said with fervor, "but I know how your neighbors and friends here treasure and revere you. I would be a poor, selfish priest if I denied them your presence!" He swallowed a final bite, the outrageous lie almost gagging him, and rose from the table. "I cannot in conscience, dear cousin, deflect you from your mission here, which is to bless your friends, enriching their lives with your Christian warmth!"

"But your beloved wife . . ." the old woman began to shout.

"Would understand and forgive you!" the priest cried. He took a deep breath. "Well, cousin, I am delighted to bear witness to your miraculous recovery. Look after yourself and, by all means, let me know at once should you suffer a relapse . . ."

The woman gaped at him in dismay.

"You can't consider leaving now, cousin Markos!" she cried. "No one travels after dark in these dangerous times. Just last week, not a mile outside town, thieves caught a traveler and cut his throat! You had best spend the night here with me!"

Father Markos shook his head, determined that whatever predators awaited him in the darkness were preferable to being locked in the small house with Phaedra through the night.

After a quick, final blessing, he hurried away. His last sight of Phaedra was her big, robust body filling the doorway, blocking out the glow of the lamp. When he was out of sight of the house he could still hear her shouting after him, promising ways she could service his decrepit old age. Spurred on by her voice, he did not pause in his flight until he had passed the last houses of the town.

From that point the road ran through a countryside that was desolate and ominously still. A full disk of moon illuminated a mist that crept eerily about his sandals. He recalled Phaedra's story of the thieves who cut the traveler's throat. Another one of her lies, most likely, but he could not be sure. For a nervous moment he considered turning back, perhaps knocking at one of the houses to ask lodging for the night. But he knew that doors were not opened as readily as they had been in the past and, peering anxiously back the way he had come, he suspected Phaedra might be trailing him to determine whether he planned such a stop.

The moon had slipped behind a cloud and the landscape darkened. He waited in the gloom, uncertain what to do. As the moon re-emerged once more, almost as if he were being provided a gleam of divine guidance, he remembered the monastery of Aghia Lavra, less than a half hour's walk from the town. He could obtain a bed there for the night and, at the same time, he would be safe from Phaedra.

He hurried along the road toward the monastery, apprehensive of each rustling or crackling in the fields about him. Crossing the bridge of Katzano, he felt the chill of the water like a cold wind across his ankles and he shivered, stumbling slightly in his haste.

When he entered the courtyard of the monastery, he made grateful thanks to God for his safe passage. He struck the great iron knocker against the heavy door, the sound echoing like a hammer on a forge in the stillness of the night.

Admitted by a young novitiate carrying a candle, Father Markos was taken to Brother Philomelis, a tall, thin monk with a pale, funereal face.

"Just a pallet for the night is all I need, Brother," Father

Markos said. "My thanks for your kindness and I will be on my way at dawn."

The monk gave him a tight, reproving look.

"You will, of course, Father, wish to join us in prayers before you sleep."

"Of course." Father Markos nodded quickly. He followed the monk along the corridor into the chapel, where a score of robed monks knelt at prayers while, before the altar, the abbot of the monastery performed the service.

Kneeling beside Brother Philomelis, his knees aching on the cold stone floor, the prayers droning in his ears, he was satisfied he had chosen the parish instead of the cloister. The fervor of monastic piety, the austerity and gloom, would have finished him. When the long prayers had ended, he could barely rise to his feet.

Afterwards, preceded by Brother Philomelis carrying a candle, he was led to a small, bare cell exuding an aroma of urine and the taint of mold. Throwing the wavering glow of the candle across the stone floor, Brother Philomelis revealed a pile of straw forming a flimsy pallet in the corner.

"You will not find the conveniences here you have at home, Father," the monk said somberly. "Our cloisters are arenas where we punish the weak, wicked shells that contain our souls."

"This will be fine, Brother," Father Markos said briskly. "I am grateful for your Christian hospitality." For a moment he considered asking the monk to leave the candle but the austere visage kept him silent. As the monk departed, leaving him in darkness, he comforted himself he had, at least, escaped from Phaedra.

He lowered himself stiffly to the straw pallet. He groaned as his shoulder struck the stone of the wall. Settled on his back, staring up into the darkness, he became conscious of a lighter square above his head, and perceived a narrow, barred window. Almost at once a gust of chilling wind came through it and swept down on him. He sighed and twisted on his side, drawing his feet beneath his cassock and cloak, curling his body into a tight, nestled ball.

He did not know how long he had been asleep when he wakened with a start. The reflection of torches, like leapings of lightning, flared across the ceiling of his cell. In a commotion and tumult rising through his window, he heard horses' hooves clumping upon the stones of the courtyard, laced with the shouts and cries of men. Dulled by sleep, Father Markos pushed himself clumsily to his feet. By gripping the ledge of the window with his fingers and, straining on his toes, he managed to peer down through the bars.

In the light of torches held by some monks, a disordered assemblage of men, horses and carriages was snarled in the courtyard. Dismounting from the horses and carriages were men who by the gilded trappings on their saddles and bridles appeared to be wealthy archons. There were also cassocked figures with the portly, confident manner of bishops. Most of them gathered about a carriage from which a white-bearded, white-haired prelate was emerging. His open cloak revealed him to be dressed in vestments so glittering and sumptuous he might have been the patriarch. The abbot of the monastery and a cluster of monks bowed and crossed themselves before him, bending in flurried genuflections to brush the back of his hand with their lips. Calling and motioning urgently to the bishops and archons, the imposing dignitary led them into the monastery. Several monks, trying desperately to hold the hem of his cloak from sweeping the ground, stumbled in his wake.

A moment after they had disappeared through the doorway, the courtyard rumbled with thunder, and a troop of horsemen galloped between the carriages, heedless of the grooms and monks scrambling to get out of their way. Fearing he would be trampled, a monk shrieked in terror, threw down his torch and ran.

The horsemen, about a dozen of them, reined to a halt before the monastery entrance and dismounted. The leader, astride a great bay stallion, was a familiar figure to Father Markos, but it was not until he saw the man's bald head gleaming wax-yellow in the flame of the torches that he recognized the monolithic figure of the monk, Papalikos, someone he had not seen since the night of the terrible winter storm.

Now, despite the laws forbidding Christians to carry arms publicly, Papalikos teemed with weapons. A pair of bandoliers crossed the chest of his woolen cassock, yataghan and pistol stuck into the sash about his waist, a long-barreled musket slung from his shoulder. Calling a strident command to his wild band of armed men, he entered the monastery with long, powerful strides. Several monks who stood in his path scurried aside like frightened children.

Father Markos slid his fingers from the ledge, lowering his heels to the floor. Staring at the ghostly images the reflection of the torches cast across the ceiling of the cell, he was conscious suddenly of the oiliness of sweat broken out across his body, an exudation of fear sharpened by his ignorance of what was happening. He considered remaining secluded where he was and then, rejecting his cowardice, he left the cell, walking slowly and carefully along the dark corridor. He descended a flight of stone steps to enter another corridor on the level below and found several of the young novitiates huddled excitedly beneath the flame of a torch.

"Forgive me, Brothers," Father Markos asked. "What is happening?"

The novitiates gathered him eagerly into their conclave.

"We must offer prayers to the Lord, Father!" one novitiate said with fervor.

"The moment to strike for freedom has come!" another cried.

"Praise God!" The third, a pale-cheeked youth with the limpid eyes of a fawn wept. "Praise God!"

"But what has happened?" the priest pleaded.

As the three young novitiates began speaking all at once, Brother Philomelis appeared in the corridor.

"Enough of your chatter!" he assailed them sternly. "Get to your duties and to your prayers!"

The young monks hastened away. As Brother Philomelis stared at Father Markos, the priest was surprised to see the monk's gloomy visage altered, all sadness and mournfulness dissipated, his cheeks and eyes burning as if he witnessed some redemptive vision.

"What is happening, Brother?" Father Markos asked earnestly. "I was wakened by the horsemen . . ."

"His Eminence, Metropolitan Germanos of Patras is here," Brother Philomelis whispered. "With the Bishop of Kernitza and the primates of Patras and Kalavryta, they were traveling to Tripolitza, answering the summons of the kaimakam, Mehemet Selik, when an angel appeared to lead them to our holy monastery. A miracle! A blessed miracle!"

He gathered the folds of his cassock into his fingers, tugged the cloth above his bare ankles and hurried off. The priest was left alone once more, the words of the novitiates and the monk scrambling in his ears. Freedom, visions, miracles! Did that mean the revolution had begun? He thought with remorse of his village. In the hour of the wolf, the shepherd was absent from his flock.

He started uncertainly in one direction, paused, then retraced his steps. At that moment a robed cleric in the finely tailored garments of an Archbishop's deacon, came along the corridor with the rapid, mincing steps of a bantam cock. He paused before Father Markos, looking him brusquely up and down, his thin nostrils quivering slightly as he noted the shabby cassock and mended sandals of a village priest.

"Who are you?"

"Father Markos of Kravasaras. I was returning from Kalavryta to my village and stopped . . ."

The deacon fluttered his manicured fingers.

"They are waiting for me in the meeting, Father." He

spoke as solemnly as a magistrate. "We are discussing matters of the gravest importance for all of Greece. Would you
be good enough to fetch His Grace, the Bishop of Kernitza,
a decanter of wine?"

"Wine!" Father Markos echoed, grateful to be allotted
even a minor role in the mysterious and significant events
taking place. "Yes, of course!"

Without knowing where to go to fulfill the request, he
started quickly in the direction Brother Philomelis had
taken. He passed several monks he considered asking about
the wine but the urgency of their missions was evident in
their haste and he hesitated to delay them.

The corridor led into the chapel, where he had first
prayed upon his arrival. The doors of the nave were open
and under the shadows of the columns he could see the
shrouded figures of monks in reverent and attentive silence.
Thinking a special liturgy might be in progress, Father
Markos slipped quietly into the chapel.

There wasn't a liturgy going on but what, at first sight,
appeared to be a play. Torches illumined the area before the
iconostasis and the sacristy as bright as the proscenium of a
stage. As if they were supporting players, a score of archons
and prelates stood in solemn assembly about the majestic
figure of the white-crowned Metropolitan of Patras, who sat
on the great episcopal throne, holding his ornate scepter of
office stiffly in his hand. For a bewildering moment it
seemed to the priest that the richly clad figures were
transfixed in a motionless tableau, as if posing for a painting
of the country's noble leaders in a moment of historic importance.

Then the priest realized they were not motionless, each
man involved in an exchange with someone near him, a
bishop waving a finger, an archon shaking his head. The
Metropolitan raised his scepter, pinpoints of light from the
torches lacing the extended sleeves of his vestments, and
struck the base against the stone floor, a ringing clatter

echoing throughout the chapel. As his tense voice flew clearly to the rear of the church, the priest noticed Brother Philomelis standing by a nearby column, staring entranced at the stage.

"Bishop Tsarellas," the Metropolitan said. "We have heard from Archon Asimakis. What do you advise?"

The portly cassocked figure of the bishop raised his hands in alarm.

"Dangerous and premature for us to follow the archon's advice!" the bishop said shrilly. "We are under orders to appear before the kaimakam in Tripolitza. Disobeying those orders will be construed as treason!"

"Once that devil has us inside the walls of the city," another man said, "he can jail us as hostages or even execute us!"

"I will vouch for Mehemet Selik!" Bishop Tsarellas cried. "He is a civilized man who wishes to consult with us on the best means of maintaining the peace."

"If that is true, your Grace, why does he still hold the Bishops of Corinth, Arcadia and Monemvasia? He holds them prisoners to guarantee the peace. And he will imprison us as well!"

The bishop appealed to the Metropolitan.

"Your Eminence, this unwonted delay has cost precious time. Word will be carried to Tripolitza that we are meeting here. We must not allow ourselves to be influenced by zealots!"

As the priest listened intently to the bickering, the tangle of angry, pleading, warning and imploring voices, he thought sadly, this then is the way noblemen and prelates argue. Not as he had always imagined, but in the same fashion as farmers and peddlers haranguing one another in the village market, each man seeking to overcome the other by shouting more loudly.

Suddenly, as if hurled into the gathering by some malignant wind, the monk Papalikos appeared in the midst of the assembly. The archons and prelates fell silent before his armed and imposing figure. For a moment the only sound in the church came from the flames crackling in the receptacles of the torches.

"Your Eminence, I will speak!" the monk's brazen voice resounded across the church.

A few of the dignitaries objected. When Papalikos turned his baleful gaze upon them, their voices fluttered and faded. Father Markos remembered the glowing, sinister power of the monk's eyes.

"We stand in a moment of destiny!" Papalikos cried. "Mother Russia is sending us an army that Prince Ipsilantis is leading through the provinces. All the slaves suffering under their yoke of bondage will rise to join him and fall upon the vile Turk! Are we less than Serbs and Bulgars? Must we wait for them to sound the clarion call for holy war?"

"Treason! Treason! Treason!" the furtive, frightened whispers came from the men around him.

"What this arrogant and misguided Brother forgets," Bishop Tsarellas said in an outraged voice, "is that once before Russia sent us an army, then betrayed us and fled. Let us not be deceived again." He extended his hands toward the Metropolitan. "Your Eminence, we are wasting still more time. We must resume our journey to Tripolitza at once . . . I implore you."

"I am one man but I have the power of ten!" Papalikos shouted. "Each of my men has the courage of ten because our mission is holy and just! When we strike we will shatter the Turkish beast! In Constantinople our agents stand ready to set fire to the palace and assassinate the Sultan!"

The archons and prelates recoiled in panic, retreating and pushing away to leave the monk alone in the center of a wide circle as if he embodied a dreaded ailment they feared would infect them. The priest felt something of their cold terror enfeeble his own flesh.

"He is mad!"

"Treason! Treason!"

"You go too far, Brother!" the Metropolitan spoke sternly. "I order you to be silent!"

A tall, handsome archon stepped forward, standing without fear beside the monk, confronting the Metropolitan.

"Your Eminence," he said quietly. "There is too much thirsting for blood in this monk's counsel to please me, but let us not discount all that he is saying. Petrobey and Kolokotronis hold loaded guns in the Mani. The islands are ready to sail with their fleets. The klephts of Parnassus, Olympus and the Pindus are armed and ready. If the decision to fight has already been made by our comrades, it would be dangerous for us to remain inert."

"No!" Bishop Tsarellas cried. "No! No! Release the demons of revolution and anarchy will reign. Even now the Church is under assault by those heretics who read foreign books and sip the poison of Voltaire and Rousseau. Nothing would please the Papacy more than to have our Church torn apart by a revolt we cannot control!"

"How long must our people, groaning under the yoke of centuries, wait for release?" the archon said sadly. "I, for one, vote to wait no longer. As a child I remember my father weeping as he taught me the hymn of our immortal Rigas Feraios. You will all remember those lines . . ." He began to chant the words.

> How long, my heroes, shall we live in bondage
> alone like lions, on ridges, on peaks,
> living in caves, seeing our children
> turned from the land to bitter enslavement . . .

The archon paused, his voice gathering passion and strength.

> Better an hour of life that is free,
> than forty years of wretched slavery . . .

In the silence that followed, the priest felt his blood wrenched with a curious longing.

"All of us were raised on those noble lines," Bishop Tsarellas said, "but we must be patient, plan and wait. As the troubles compound for the Mussulmen, our chances for compromise and negotiation of our grievances improve."

"The time is now!" Papalikos cried. "Fire and blood and the destruction of every cursed Turk on Greek soil!"

"Why should we listen to you?" Bishop Tsarellas shouted at the monk. "What right do you have to come here and speak? You are a common monk with no community or parish! We are the leaders of the Church and the state!"

"I am the voice of the people!" Papalikos roared. "I speak for the people!"

"How dare you make that claim!" Bishop Tsarellas fumed. "We speak for the people!"

Rattled and confused by the angry, shouting voices, the priest was certain of one thing. None of these venerable prelates, archons or the monk, represented the people. Swept by a surge of boldness, he considered hurrying forward. He was a village priest, shepherd of the poor people whose destiny was being debated. He would speak for them, act as their advocate, and, before his eloquence, even His Eminence, the Metropolitan, would sit silent with awe. Yet, at the thought of daring to speak, his legs grew weak, and he felt the blood becoming water in his veins. He knew before that august assembly he would be stricken dumb.

The Metropolitan rose, motioning with his scepter, bestirring the group to attention.

"We are all agreed that our people have suffered too long," he said slowly. "And we all remember the words Rigas Feraios bequeathed to us, and the final words he spoke on that black day when he was put to death, 'I have sown . . . others will reap.'"

He was silent for a moment.

"And we shall reap . . . with God's help, we shall reap. But after nearly four hundred years, a few more weeks or months are not unseemly. My decision is that one messenger will be sent to the Archbishop of Arta to ascertain the counsel of that wise, knowledgeable man. Another envoy will be sent to confer with Prince Ipsilantis in the provinces to determine the extent of his advance, and how soon the Tsar, the Orthodox Sovereign of the True Faith, will launch additional forces to aid us in our holy struggle. Meanwhile, it is best we return to our homes, sending on a message to the kaimakam in Tripolitza we have received secret warning we will be murdered en route by fanatics hoping to make our massacre the spark for revolution. In the interest of peace, we will use those threats as reason to turn back. Once more in our citadels, we will prepare our people and we will wait for the return of our envoys."

Murmurs of agreement and approval rose from most of the assembly but there were some dissenting, dissatisfied voices. The archon who had spoken so eloquently of freedom turned aside, shaking his head in disapproval.

"Now, Brother Papalikos," the Metropolitan addressed the monk in a tone of accommodation and entreaty, "we wish to dispatch you . . ."

"To Hell!" the monk roared, and in the stunned silence that followed his outburst, the priest felt waves of shock rattle his bones. The monk stood alone, a vengeful, angry apparition, raking them all with contempt.

"A few brave men might be found there who do not dribble pee down their flanks at the prospect of slicing a Turkish throat!" His arm rose like a sword, his long fingers aimed at the Metropolitan. "But you will not have your way! Our dead cry for redemption, and those who do not listen will be swallowed by the earth!"

"Brother Papalikos!" the Metropolitan cried shrilly. "I command you . . ."

But the monk did not wait for the Metropolitan's edict. He whirled and left the circle of men, moving swiftly through the church. As he entered the shadows where the priest and monks stood, his weapons clattering, his boots

striking the stone floor like iron upon a forge, a number of
the monks slipped quickly to their knees, crossing themselves, as if they had witnessed the passing of a saint.

Father Markos started on his journey home as the first
traces of pink dawn broke over the peaks of the mountains.
The monks gave him some hard brown bread and a flask
filled with water that flowed from a spring near an ancient
chestnut tree. The Metropolitan and the archons and prelates were preparing to leave, as well, to return to their
towns and houses. As the priest began to descend on the
road to Kalavryta, the first group of archons and their attendants spurred their horses past him, riding with a nervous urgency, scattering a storm of pebbles and dust in their
wake.

Looking back a final time at the dome and bell tower of
the monastery, the priest recalled the angry voices, the
noble words of the archon, the calm judgment of the Metropolitan. He felt a flurry of distress when he rememberd the
raging departure of the monk Papalikos, leading his band of
armed men in defiance of the decision of the assembly.
Thinking of the ways a fanatic could unleash violence that
might nullify the sober resolutions for delay, the priest
quickened his pace, anxious to return to his village, where
he would be among his neighbors and friends.

Yet, despite his mood of anxiety and haste, the morning
crested with a leisured, luminous beauty. Wildflowers
emerged from the shade of the lightening slopes, a bursting
of blossom after the somnolence of winter. In the distance a
grove of olive trees tangled dark forms in the blue mist of
dawn. The air was cool with a honey-sweet scent, and a
flock of small gray rooks cawed as they wheeled above his
head. In the midst of such serene and blessed florescence,
God would not permit the soul to linger on sorrows and terror.

Entering the outskirts of Kalavryta, the priest passed an

old man sitting on a stone under a plane tree, eating a cluster of grapes, his jaw thrashing with as much vigor as if he were masticating shreds of meat. When he saw the priest, he made his cross quickly as protection against bad luck and turned away.

"Thanks for the offer of some grapes, grandfather," the priest called in annoyance, "but I must keep to my journey."

Further on, in one of the narrow streets, a group of children played, a ball flashing back and forth between the girls with black hair coiled in braids and the boys with close-cropped heads. Father Markos paused an instant to watch them jumping and shrieking, the sight familiar and reassuring.

In the marketplace he spoke to several men loading carts with produce and when he found one going to Egion, asked him for a ride. The farmer, an old, weather-beaten Moreot with a face the sun had cured to a deep russet, motioned him to get on. The priest hiked up his cassock and cloak and pulled himself with some effort to the seat of the cart that was hitched to an aged and spavined horse.

As they left Kalavryta and turned on the road to Egion, the sun had risen across the plain. A group of women, their heads cowled, were already at work in the fields. A few sheep grazed beside the road, indifferent to the creaking passage of the cart. With each burdened, plodding step the ancient horse seemed on the verge of collapse. As if sensing the priest's thoughts about the animal, the farmer laughed.

"You wouldn't know to look at him now that he was once a champion, eh, Father? Quartered in the stables of a bey, rubbed down by grooms each night. In harness he wore a plume on his head and pulled the finest carriage in the Morea. But time passes, animals and humans grow old . . ."

For an instant the priest thought he heard the animal sigh in grievous assent.

"When will we arrive in Egion?"

"By early afternoon," the farmer said. "If you're lucky a

caïque might be crossing the Gulf. A good wind and you're home."

"I will be glad to get home," the priest said.

The farmer stared out across the fields.

"No home will be safe anymore," he said. "There is war coming, war that will tear apart the land. Lucky in a way we are old buzzards, eh, Father? If someone kills us, what's the loss?" He laughed raucously and jabbed his elbow into the ribs of the priest, who winced.

"I think the war may not come for a while yet," the priest said.

"No putting it off this time," the farmer said. "This time they'll fight and I'll tell you why they'll fight. Not for freedom or heroic songs and slogans, but because the wealthy Greeks own all the land they're permitted to own and no Turk can sell them any more. They hunger to own more land, grow richer and more powerful, and the Turks stand in their way . . . the problem is simple as that." He shrugged wryly. "Can't really blame them. If I were a rich landowner instead of a poor bastard grubbing for his bread, I might feel the same way."

From the road behind them came the thunder of hoofbeats. Both men looked back and saw the swirling dust cloud racing toward them. The farmer smacked the horse with his reins.

"Move, Mahomet!" he cried. "You drag-assed, sway-backed Mussulman eunuch! Move!"

The horse gasped and dragged the cart off to the side of the road. In a moment a band of a half-dozen men dashed past, wealthy archons with ornamented saddles, riding as if they were being pursued by the devil.

The priest coughed in the litter of smoke and dust as the horse heaved the cart back onto the road. The farmer spit several times, cursing under his breath.

"Archons from the meeting at the monastery of Aghia Lavra last night, I wager," the farmer said.

The priest looked at him startled.

"What meeting?" he asked warily.

The farmer grinned with the air of a man delighted to pass on a confidence.

"All Kalavryta was talking about it this morning," he said. "While you and I snoozed last night, Father, they had a meeting up on Aghia Lavra, all the wealthy archons and some bishops and the Metropolitan of Patras. They swore a sacred oath on the Holy Altar and the Metropolitan raised the banner to the freedom of Greece. That's what I was telling you. The war is coming now, for sure."

"But that can't be true!" the priest said. On the verge of telling the farmer he had been present at the meeting, he faltered, deciding to be cautious. "I mean, who brought word of that story to the town?"

"Foxes and birds." The farmer laughed. "One man tells another, who whispers to a relative, and the words spread all over town in an hour, every liar adding a little more to make the tale more exciting."

"But it may not be true!" the priest said in agitation. "They may have had a meeting simply to discuss various actions they might take."

"True or false, false or true, doesn't matter now," the farmer said. "Revolt has been in the air for months and any excuse will set it off. Oh, I suppose when the fighting begins I'll dig up my old gun and kill a few Turks just to share what's going on. In the end they'll probably kill me. No big matter either way. For us poor people, even if we become free, by God, we'll be as poor and have to work just as hard as we did before. Nothing on this earth will change that."

The farmer let Father Markos off at a crossroads where one of the roads led to the harbor at Egion, and continued with his cart of produce toward the market. The last glimpse the priest had of him was his lean, wiry figure slouched on the seat of the cart, his head and shoulders swaying to the burdened, uneven shuffle of the horse that had once drawn the carriage of a bey.

As the priest walked along the harbor, he felt a strangeness in the scene. The streets, stalls and tavernas of any port were places of spirited activity and clamor. But these environs were ominously still, sailors, peddlers and shopkeepers huddled in small groups, muttering in barely audible tones. As if they were suspicious of any stranger, even one dressed in the cassock of a priest, they fell silent as he appeared.

Several of the shops whose signs identified them as Turkish were canvased and barred. Before each one of them, sullen groups of Christians had gathered, motionless figures waiting, like barrels of gunpowder, the priest thought uneasily, needing only a spark.

At seaside, a dozen caïques bobbing in the water, Father Markos found an Albanian sailor about to cast off in one of them. Discovering he was sailing to Itea across the Gulf and would be willing to drop him at the fishing settlement for a copper, the priest settled into the boat.

As the Albanian pushed off with his oar, a disturbance broke out in one of the adjoining streets. There were hoarse shouts and a group of men ran by brandishing clubs and sticks. Somewhere a woman screamed, her cry whirling up like a wail of wind. The Albanian hoisted his sail swiftly to catch the breeze and slipped to the tiller. As the shore receded, a tendril of smoke rose from the port, joined in moments by a second, darker and thicker billow. The Albanian looked back for the first time and shook his head somberly.

"They're burning the Turkish shops," he said. "Probably break into the warehouses. God help any Turk they find in the streets today."

The priest stared back at the smoke beginning to rise higher into the clear, blue sky, like the signal fires of some pursuing host. His urgency to reach his village came over him like a fever.

They sailed into the bay of the fishing settlement in late afternoon, the sun setting a yellow cape across the water, casting shadows beneath the hulls of a few boats moored near the shore. The cluster of half a dozen houses seemed quiet but the Albanian would not go into the shallows, remaining adamant despite the priest's pleas. Finally, Father Markos tied his cassock under his arms, made a small bundle of his sandals and cloak, and rolled the legs of his trousers well above his knees. Mumbling a prayer, he climbed over the side of the boat into water that came to his chest. The Albanian did not wait to determine if he were going to make the shore, but the moment the priest was free of the boat, set sail once more.

"God show you the same kindness!" the priest cried after him. Then, gasping for breath, fearful he might lose his footing on the sandy bottom, the cold water soaking through his clothing, he waded desperately toward the shore.

On the beach, amid the rust-colored loops and canopies of drying nets, he sat on a piece of driftwood, rubbing his cold feet, shaking the water from his clothing as well as he could. Slipping on his sandals, he began walking quickly to the house of the fisherman where he had stabled Agathon.

The narrow street he plodded up from the beach into the midst of the houses was deserted and still. The doors of the houses were closed, the shutters fastened across the windows. He had the eerie feeling, however, that he was being watched, people peering at him from slits in the shutters. When he called several times, and even knocked on the door of one of the houses, the only answer was the cry of a gull.

In the yard of the fisherman's house, he found an old woman crouched on the ground, mixing meal with water in a battered skillet while a squatting hen watched her intently. Squeaking incoherent words and senseless phrases through her withered lips, she could tell him nothing. Anxious to be on his way, he led Agathon from the stable, haltered and mounted him, and started riding out of the settlement.

He rode the waning day over the hills toward Parnassus and Kravasaras. He would not reach his village until well after dark but he would have a full moon for the last hours of his journey. Because he was not too far from home, for the first time since leaving the monastery, he felt a relief.

He passed into a herd of sheep, Agathon picking his way between their shaggy bodies, coats of wool brushing the priest's legs. In the distance he saw the shepherd rounding up strays and, grateful for the presence of another human, called to him but lost his voice in the bleatings of the sheep.

At twilight he paused in an olive grove, dismounted to rest Agathon and to stretch his legs. A curious scarlet haze hung over the gnarled and twisted trunks of the old trees. Looking at the sky he saw with distress that the illuminated disk of the moon was crimson.

He rode on with his eyes lowered, his face averted from the sky, remembering stories of travelers incurring blindness or moon-madness in the glare of that scarlet light. Yet, even on the ground, boulders seemed to conceal the figures of crouching men and, as he passed under a tree, an owl took flight with a lizard dangling from its beak.

As he came down into the plain, skirting a familiar stone wall built by Venetians centuries before, he saw the sacred mountain looming in the distance and felt his heart expand.

At almost the same instant, a sickening odor came to him, a scorched, repugnant smell riding the waves of night from the direction of the village. With every measure of ground he covered, the stench grew stronger. He rode with foreboding, prodding Agathon with his heels until the poor creature reared his head and brayed in outrage.

When he entered the edge of the village and saw the minarets of the mosque and the houses apparently serene and undisturbed, he tried to moderate his fear. Yet the stench was stronger, covering the night like a pall. He dismounted before the gate to the courtyard of Ahmed Bajaki's house.

Walking into the garden he understood the reason for the omens. Everything was shattered and in ruins. The fragments of the fountain had been pushed off their pedestals, chipped splinters of marble and stone scattered across the ground. The trellises were broken, the vines torn down, and the flowers trampled and ripped out by the roots.

As he hurried to the entrance of his friend's house, a hunched figure scurried over the threshold, followed by a second, dark, stunted forms darting across the whiteness of the stone. He recognized them as black-garbed old women, scavenging like vultures for any scraps overlooked in the pillaging. He shouted at them furiously, but they slipped swiftly into the shadows.

Passing through the rooms of Ahmed Bajaki's house, he was appalled at the wanton destruction. What furnishings or decorations could not be torn loose and carted away had been smashed, the grand and elegant interiors reduced to the bare masonry of the walls. In none of the gutted rooms could he find a trace of the Mussulman or his son. He prayed they had fled.

He hurried from the house, sickened and embittered at this violation of the spirit and friendship of the village. The houses he passed were desolate and silent. Several times he called out the names of villagers, his voice, by turn, angry and pleading, frightened and indignant. The only response he received came from a chicken or a goat, raising its head warily at his noisy passage.

Then, from the direction of the church at the opposite end of the village, he heard a roar, a hoarse thunder of voices with something demonic about the sound. He recalled a winter years before when the snow had been heavy on the mountain and game was scarce. Maddened by hunger, the wolves of Parnassus had banded into a ravenous pack and descended to attack the sheep penned at the outskirts of the village. He had been hurled from sleep by their shrill, savage baying and was reminded now of that crazed and inhuman cry.

He rushed along the road leading through the village to the church and entered the marketplace, the shops dark and shuttered, the stench suffocating. In the center of the marketplace was a smoldering heap, tendrils of smoke rising from what he took to be rubbish or debris from the houses that had been looted. Walking past the pile, a wild moan leaped from his throat.

The mound was a funeral pyre of charred bodies, a pyramid of scorched heads and trunks, arms and legs, strewn in broken and blackened bundles. There were strips of half-burned skin like tattered rags, gaping wounds from which entrails hung, blood that was black by moonlight, skulls more naked than flesh. And the parched hands and feet emerging from bodies buried in the pile showed weird stalks of fingers and toes stripped to the bone by the flames.

Whimpering and moaning he circled the pyre and saw Ahmed Bajaki. The old Mussulman sprawled naked on his back, his charred face turned up toward the scarlet moon, one arm extended, palm up, the fingers cupped stiffly as if they held some unseen goblet. And, burrowed under his arm as if he had sought to shield the child to the end, was the body of Hassan, miraculously untouched by any fire, his face glowing and comely even in death.

The priest bent weeping to touch the pale, delicate cheek and saw the boy's throat had been cut, the blade gashing so deeply the frail, lovely head hung to the trunk by a thread of tendon.

Heavy with agony, he slipped to his knees before the bier of bodies and covered his face with his hands. This is not really my village, he thought as he mourned. I have lost my way by night and have entered some strange and terrible land.

"Father and Son," he whispered. "Blessed Mother Mary, let me die with them now."

He did not know how long he lay prostrate in the dirt before the pyre, but deep in the tomb of his grief, a sound intruded. He raised his head slowly and listened.

A bell pealed loud and clear across the night, ringing in the tower of the church, a bell that had been buried for a hundred years, a bell his grandfather and his father had never heard.

In that moment his body and spirit were no longer his own, but inhabited by the ghosts of his ancestors. Against his will they came to possess him, their haunted blood crying in his blood. So together they sorrowed and celebrated, mourned and exulted, grieved and rejoiced.

While through the moonstained darkness, the bell of the church of Kravasaras rang its winged and sweet litany of resurrection.

CHAPTER
SEVEN

For two stormy days the captains of the highland clans of central Crete sat in the house of Andreas' father, ranting and disputing, drinking casks of raki, smoking cones of uncured tobacco. Across the Sea of Crete, from the mainland of Greece, couriers had brought them word that a general or prince of some sort had crossed a northern river into the Danubian provinces, leading an army from Russia to liberate all of Greece. For days after that initial message, there wasn't any more news, only rumor feeding on rumor, crows and falcons whispering words into the ears of sleeping shepherds, who ran to pass their divinations to the people in the villages. In the space of ten days all of the citizens of the island joined in a fervor for battle. In the eastern and western regions, the councils met, obdurate and arguing, even as the one that gathered around his father's table.

For several hours at a time, Andreas would slip quietly into the room, sit in a shadowed corner listening to the men rumbling under a cloud of smoke. Besides his father, Kyriakos, there were Cosmatos and Farandakis, Sphakians from the warrior villages on the southern coast, and Kringas, a former artillery officer with the armies of Napoleon in Spain.

"I have said it before and I'll say it again!" Cosmatos cried. He was a swarthy, stocky man, ill tempered and forever snarling. "To hell with what the mainlanders do! We are Cretans and can decide for ourselves!"

"Let us not repeat the mistakes we have made so often," Kyriakos said. "If Crete rises alone against the Sultan, he will bring in a huge army and our graveyards will not be large enough to hold our dead women and children. Let us organize a council of the captains and wait for word and make plans to strike then."

"Our first task is to assemble cannon!" Kringas cried. He was a tall, lean man with sooty fingers and brows bleached by the stains of powder. "Time and again in Spain I saw cannon tear a breach in the enemy's ranks. We must raid the Turkish garrisons for their cannon . . ."

"The Sphakians must strike first," Farandakis rumbled. He was a burly, grizzled captain, his face scarred and brutal. Once hanged by the Turks he had miraculously survived and to cover the great, raw welt that remained around his throat, he had grown a tangled beard that hung to his chest. He seethed with a hatred of Turks and any who fell into his hands begged to be killed at once.

"We must strike together at the right moment," Kyriakos said. "It is not important which clan attacks first."

"You say to me it is not important!" Farandakis glared. "For a hundred years my clan has been in the vanguard of every revolt! Would you have us lag behind now?"

"I won't sit down in council with that Lasithian bastard Thrambulis!" Cosmatos cried. "Last year he tricked me out of a fine bay stallion!"

"We are not trading horses now!" Kyriakos said impatiently. "We are planning for war!"

"Fight!"

"Cannon!"

"Plan!"

By morning of the third day, the argument having raged

unabated through the night, the meeting was interrupted by a courier from Retimo, a man who had ridden madly from the harbor of the city.

"The news came from a brig that just anchored!" the messenger gasped. "Some bishop or bloody pope climbed off his holy rump and waved a flag to signal the beginning of the revolt! They're killing Turks all over the place!"

"Are you certain?" Kyriakos gripped his arms so hard the man groaned. "If this is forecastle gossip, I'll tear off your ears!"

"A dozen sailors and the mate swore it was true!" the courier cried. "And with my own eyes I saw loot from the Turkish shops!"

Cosmatos slammed his heavy fist on the table, rattling the wine jugs and cups. Farandakis growled with joy. Kringas leaped up and excitedly made his cross.

In the corner, Andreas cried out in delight. His father, solemn and composed in contrast to the others, turned and looked at him. He was a tall, erect man, with a strong, supple body despite his sixty years, clad in black Cretan breeches and boots, fringed headcloth around his thick gray hair.

Andreas understood how sacred and meaningful this moment was to his father, and not one to be spoiled by premature celebration. The history of their family was a crimson trail of sacrifice and suffering in the cause of Crete. Andreas' grandfather had fought and died in the revolt of Daskaloyiannis. Uncles and cousins had given their lives in the futile insurrections that broke out because Cretans could not endure their bondage tamely. On his father's body, Andreas had seen the scars of wounds made by Turkish swords, injuries that caused him to limp slightly when he walked, and, in his sleep, moan at the demons who came to remind him of the horrors he had shared.

"That's what we get for sitting here talking!" Cosmatos cried. "We have lost our chance to strike first! But I am through talking now and will ride to gather my kinsmen! We can be the first to attack in Crete!"

"Get food and wine from my daughter in the house adjoining the mill," Kyriakos said quietly to the courier. As the man left the room, Kyriakos turned to Cosmatos.

"What is your plan of battle, Cosmatos?" he asked gravely.

Cosmatos laughed boisterously.

"Who needs a plan of battle!" he cried harshly. "I am going to kill Turks!"

"That's all there is to it, eh?" Kyriakos said. "You'll lead your kinsmen like a whirlwind across Crete. Where you find a Turk, you will simply kill him."

"Yes, by God!" Cosmatos shouted. "I'll have their noses and ears in a sack at my belt! That's my plan!"

"You'll slaughter and swallow them, bones and all."

Cosmatos looked uneasily at Kyriakos, fumbling to divine the mockery.

"What the hell is this, Kyriakos? A monks' meeting? I am telling you all to gather your men and follow me!"

Farandakis spit out the black husks of tobacco he had been chewing, fragments littering his beard.

"My men and me follow no one," he said in a low, hoarse voice. "I lead and others follow."

The two Sphakian captains glared scornfully at one another.

"Whether you lead or follow, you need sense," Kyriakos said. "You will kill a few Turks, yes, but when their troopers have driven you back into the mountains, they and the Turkocretan rabble will take vengeance and reprisal. They'll rape women and butcher children, and burn villages to the ground. This is war now and we must fight with some strategy and plan!"

"Strategy! Plan!" Cosmatos said with contempt. "I'm goddam tired of hearing those women's words! I need no strategy to kill a pig-souled Turk! Give me my knife and a Mussulman's throat!"

Stamping his feet in frustration and fury, Cosmatos caught sight of Andreas in the corner.

"What about you, Andreas, my young hawk?" he bellowed. "Will you join your Sphakian comrades in battle? Get your gun, lad, and we'll wash our feet in Turkish blood!"

"That will be the first wash your feet have had in months," Kyriakos said wryly.

Farandakis bared his gums in a mocking laugh.

"Is that my thanks for coming to your council?" Cosmatos shouted indignantly. "I didn't come here, Kyriakos, to hear jokes! All I want to know is whether you ride with me for the glory of Sphakia and Crete?"

"I am for the glory of Crete and Sphakia," Kyriakos said quietly. "For killing Turks, as well. But none of my family will ride with you."

"Go to hell then!" Cosmatos cried. He twisted angrily and started for the door. "Take your coward's belly and go to hell!"

In stricken awareness that his imprudent mouth periled his life, the words froze on his lips. A strained silence gripped the room. Andreas saw his father's face darken in an effort to control his rage. Cosmatos turned to face him, his fingers trembling an inch from the butt of the pistol sheathed at his waist.

Andreas drew his own knife quickly. If his father were hurt, he would not let Cosmatos leave their house alive. Farandakis watched both men, the yellow husks of his teeth visible, nostrils sniffing gleefully at the prospect of blood.

Kringas raised his hands slowly, carefully. In the rigid scene, he was the only one that moved.

"Cretans . . ." he spoke softly, soothingly, "we must not fight among ourselves. Kyriakos, steady . . . think of Crete."

"You are a guest in my house." Kyriakos spoke to Cosmatos in a cold, hard voice. "For that reason I overlook your slur. Like a ram steaming in heat, you will ride to war. Well, go and kill Turks then and God forgive the suffering you will cause others."

Cosmatos, his small black eyes surly and defiant, hurled a final growl between his teeth and stalked from the house.

Farandakis grunted in disappointment and lurched to his feet, tugging roughly at his beard.

"You should have killed him!" he said harshly. "In the end the worthless bastard will betray us! I feel it in my bones, Sphakian or not, another traitor like Ephialtes, the betrayer of Candia!"

"Listen to me, Farandakis," Kyriakos pleaded. "Let us map some strategy. I have a plan I have discussed with the captains in the West. We join our forces to theirs and strike the garrison at Magalokastron. We'll have them trapped between us and outnumbered. With that bastion in our hands, we control the region."

Farandakis shook his head somberly.

"No time for that now," he said slowly. "The bones of my dead would be dishonored if that wild pig Cosmatos spills Turkish blood before me. I must go and prepare my men."

With a wave of his great arm in farewell, he lumbered to the door, his arsenal of weapons clanging and rattling.

Kringas rose and gripped Kyriakos by the arm, pressing his flesh in reassurance. "I am with you, friend," he said fervently. "You can count on this old campaigner. First, I must convince them to join me in capturing the cannons. Believe me, that is the only way. I'll be in touch with you soon."

He hurried from the house and they heard him calling after Farandakis, their voices fading into the clamor and hoofbeats of horses galloping away.

Kyriakos stared grimly at the table littered with scraps of bread and cheese, the pits of olives, the empty casks of wine strewn about the floor. As Andreas walked from the corner to join him, his father sighed.

"The agony of Crete," Kyriakos said sadly. "Men without the brains to match their courage."

He clenched his fists, then opened and closed his fingers as if to tear away his frustration.

"Well then, my son," he said, and his voice snapped with vigor. "We must look out for Crete . . . for Crete and for the family. Listen to me now, because time is important. Have Gorgios and Panfelios ride to alert your brothers at Alones. Have them bring their wives and children, the supplies and provisions we agreed upon, and meet us at Villandredou. They must be there by tomorrow evening. In a few days all of Crete will be at war."

Andreas felt an excitement and a fear.

"Is it the cave then, Father?"

His father nodded gravely.

"What do you want me to do?"

"You ride at once to Villandredou and tell our kinsmen there the war has begun and the council has failed. Uncle Simos will know what to do. Tell him by tomorrow we will all be there ready to start for the cave at dawn of the following day. Our kinsmen from Fangari will help me get ready here. We won't be far behind you."

Andreas walked to the fireplace and from the hook on the wall took down a pistol that he stuck into the sash at his waist, beside the scabbard of his knife.

"Remember what I spoke to Cosmatos," his father warned. "Go carefully now, by the upper trail, and if you see Turks, avoid them. There will be time enough for fighting later."

Andreas turned to leave. Something in his father's face held him, a sadness and melancholy in the way he stared about the room.

"Three times in my life I have rebuilt this house," his father said slowly. "Twice when your mother was still alive, once after her death, when you were only a child. I cleared the ground, brought together the stones and the mortar, rebuilt the walls and covered them with a roof. Three times I have made cupboards and the shrine in the corner for the icons and candles. When we return from the cave, if God wills, you will help me build it once more."

"I will, Father." Andreas made his cross.

He left the house, crossed to the stable and gave the message to Gorgios and Panfelios. The men saddled their horses and galloped off. Andreas led his own saddled mare to the cooking area, hens scurrying from the path of the horse's hooves. He crossed the threshold into the warm smells of leavened dough and fried sheep's kidneys. His sister, Gianoula, a small, pretty girl of sixteen, looked at him anxiously.

"What happened, Andreas?"

"The men have gone for Christos and the others. I am riding to Villandredou. We move into the cave."

Gianoula let out her breath in a tight, frightened whisper. Andreas smiled and patted her cheek in reassurance.

"Be a good girl and put a flask of water and some bread in my haversack," he said. "I'll say good-by to Giagia."

He walked into a dry, small room that absorbed the heat of the adjoining ovens. In the corner was an old iron-posted bed on which his great-grandmother lay perched among the pillows, swathed in a quilt. His eyes grown accustomed to the shadows, he made out the web of her face and her bony fleshless fingers like the rain-washed roots of an ancient tree. He knelt beside the bed and took her hand gently. Somewhere within her, voiceless and yet clear, he heard the whisper of his name.

In his childhood she had saved his life. The curse of an evil eye had been placed upon him and a fearful demon came to prick him in his sleep. His soul fled his body through the incision and he might never have wakened, his empty frame slipping into death. But, in her sleep, the old woman, who was gifted with prophetic and mystical insight, heard the cries of his lost and wandering soul. She had risen from her bed, came to rub his chest with warm oil, placed a white-handled knife in his palm, with which his soul cut entrance and re-entered his body.

Now, though she had grown ancient and frail, unable to move from her bed, he never entered her presence without feeling some of her durable, persevering strength pass into him. For a while yet her incandescent spirit and knowledge of sorcerous divinations would hold death at bay. Even after she died, she told him and he believed her, she would never forsake him. When he needed her, she would answer from the dark regions beneath the earth.

"I am leaving for a little while, Giagia," he said softly. "When you see me again, I'll bring you a sprig of basil from the mountain to place on your pillow." He kissed her fingers gently, feeling the flesh cold as stone. When he looked at her face he saw she was crying, two tears suspended on her cheeks as if a statue were weeping.

Spring came early to the mountains of Crete, the first glintings visible at the beginning of February. By the middle of March, the rocks and boulders, crags and peaks, were plumed by a rainbow of flashing bronzes, crimsons, golds and olive greens. The air was sweetened by the fragrance of flowers, scents of geraniums and marigolds, jasmine and daisies. Lemon petals drenched the trunks of trees and the tiny, starlike pimpernels blossomed in scarlet gardens across the slopes.

Andreas savored the spring but it was true that the grandeur of the island's massifs and ravines, forests of pine and fir, humbled every season. Upon first opening his eyes, his earliest memories were awe and joy in his surroundings. He could not imagine being born or living anyplace else in the world.

Riding the path between the huge boulders, emerging from the flankings of tall, stately pines, he could see in the distance the snow-crowned summit of Mount Ida, where cloud-thundering Zeus was born. No simple accident that in all of the Greek archipelago, the mountains of Crete had been selected for the deity's beginnings. The gods chose their domain for splendid events. In the time of the Cretan kings, Idomeneus led his fleet to the great war in Troy, joining Agamemnon and Odysseus to raze and burn that stronghold. When fire and earthquake leveled the great ancient cities of the island, the Cretans had always rebuilt. They would not be driven from their land and, over the centuries, farms grew in place of palaces, settlements in place of towns.

Drawn by the fertile and mysterious island, Saracen pirates, Venetian marauders, and Turkish predators engulfed Crete like outbreaks of pestilence. Yet each conqueror of the land could not understand his oppression was hopeless because slaves could not live among the towering mountains whose majestic peaks impaled the sky. The north wind rushed from the Aegean in winter and the hot livas of summer blew from the Libyan desert but the longing for freedom was a tempest that stormed unceasingly across Crete. For generations every family sacrificed lives in freedom's holy struggle. Now the time had come once more for the palikars of Crete, for Andreas and his brothers, to raise their arms and fight.

The spring of our war, he thought with jubilation, the war for which we have trained and waited, marking time through the lonely days and nights in the sheepfolds. And as they waited, fretful and impatient, feeding their passion and their envy, the indestructible old men recounted sagas of battles, massacres, deeds of valor. With the young men seated at their feet, they recited catechisms of courage, chanted heroic mantinades and predicted the destiny of the unproven warriors in the shoulder blades of sheep.

"What do you see about me in the bone, Grandfather?"

"You will fight bravely, my son, as long as God and the Blessed Virgin dwell in your heart."

"What else do you see in the bone, Grandfather?"

"Many things visible only to wise old eyes, my son. Someday, when you have honored Crete, you will be able to read the prophecies."

"When will I have my chance to fight for Crete, Grandfather?"

"Soon, my son, soon."

"When? When?"

"When the path of the moon sweeping the ridge of Selino crosses the shadow of the tallest pine on the slope of Lefkas."

In his dreams Andreas would hear the voices of the gnarled warriors intoning their auguries. He longed for battle, to prove his manhood, to be worthy of Crete. Each morning as he woke he said a prayer that the great struggle might be initiated on that day.

He paused and dismounted, resting his horse. From a hidden canyon somewhere above him he heard the gurgling descent of a mountain stream that in another few weeks would become a rushing torrent. He drank from his flask of water, poured some into his cupped palm for the mare, and resumed his journey.

Yet, his father had cautioned him many times, the war for freedom would be a long ordeal, not achieved through the success of a few forays or raids. Passion and courage were not enough—to fight on and to win, they needed to survive. For this survival, his father and the elders of the clan had devised a plan. When the war began, all the branches of the family—sons, brothers, uncles, cousins, their wives and children—would move into one of the huge caves in the recesses of the White Mountains. Once the clan was settled inside the cave that contained a small lake and ample grazing ground for the sheep, the regular entrance could be blocked by a landslide. Then the only entrances were through dense and narrow ravines, routes so precarious a small band of good men could hold them against an army. From that sanctuary, which they had been provisioning secretly for years, their women and children protected against reprisal, the men of the clan would strike at the Turks, joining their assaults with the efforts of families in eastern and western Crete.

Through the centuries many Cretans had lived and fought from the caves. The ballads and stories sung by the rhymadori told of caves at Nerada, in Messara, the Diktaian caverns and the mammoth caves near the village of Spilia that could hold more than four thousand people. Still another wonder provided by the island for the survival of its inhabitants.

Yet the cave was not a way of life Andreas favored. At his father's bidding, he had once spent a week alone in the cave of Mangada, to familiarize himself with that nocturnal existence. Denied the sight and warmth of the sun, he felt burrowed into the earth like a mole. As he struggled to adapt to that strange, unreal silence, collecting drinking water from the icicle-shaped stalactites, he endured a terror that he was buried alive. By the fourth or fifth day (without the sun he had lost track of time) he battled a hysterical impulse to flee. He suffered through the last days of his interment and when his brother, Christos, came to tell him the week was up, he stumbled out into the blinding sunlight, feeling he had been resurrected from some demonic underworld. Even as he boasted to his brothers and friends of how well he had adjusted to the cave, he pardoned his deception by assuring himself that when the time came for the clan to move into the cave, he would not be alone. The experience would be less hazardous and disturbing when it could be shared.

He had been riding for four to five hours, the sun descending, when he arrived below the peaks of Karpithi, the dozen houses of the small village of Villandredou on the mountain above him. Knowing a sentry would be posted, he reined his horse, cupped his hands about his mouth and shouted, the echoes of his voice ringing through the ravines.

He caught a glimpse of a startled ibex on the slope beyond, the animal rearing its head in fright before springing swiftly to disappear in a maze of boulders. After a moment, the strong voice of a highlander answered his call.

Impatient suddenly to deliver his news, and anxious to see Voula, he rode up quickly to a more level stretch of ground. On the crest of a huge boulder, a tall, young kinsman, Thanasi Cartsas, appeared, his musket slung in the crook of his arm.

"Giasou, Andreas!"

"Giasou, Thanasi!"

"What brings you to Villandredou?"

"Important news, Thanasi!" As he looked up, Andreas shielded his eyes against the sun. "The war has begun in Greece!"

With a jubilant cry, Cartsas raised his musket, pointing the muzzle toward the sky. The blast of the gun thundered across the rocky slopes. The mare, accustomed to gunshots, did not flinch, and Andreas patted her neck in approval. Cartsas sprang like a goat from the boulder, landing lightly on the ground before Andreas.

In a few moments, from the houses of the village, men and women appeared. Several men, carrying guns, ran toward them, young palikars in black, pleated breeches, black boots and headbands. They swarmed around Andreas, leaping and shouting in unrestrained glee. Several fired their muskets and pistols, the sound rolling like a cannonade across the peaks and through the ravines.

Andreas dismounted, and, leaving them rejoicing, walked toward the houses. A few older men and women had appeared. He saw his uncle, Barba Simos, a venerable old fighter with a nose like the beak of a hawk and a body lean and grained as a pine. They embraced and within the rough affection of the old man's arms, Andreas smelled the stringent scents of tobacco, resin and gunpowder.

"Look at your cousins!" His uncle scowled at the roistering young men. "Taken leave of their senses, leaping about like addled goats, wasting powder and shot!"

"But it's the war for freedom, uncle!" Andreas cried.

"War, yes," his uncle said, the same grave demeanor on his cheeks that Andreas recalled on his father's face when he first heard the news. "We will have to see about the freedom."

"Welcome, Andreas!" His aunt Sofia, small, bright eyes sparkling in the seamed circles of her face, hugged him brusquely in the folds of her apron. After a moment she pushed him away, looking him sternly up and down. "You have grown taller in the weeks since I saw you last but you are still too skinny. Kyriakos should let you stay with us for a while. I'd fatten you good!"

Behind her, a number of his kinfolk, men and women of the families Tsangarakis, Cartsas and Psychoundakis, reached out to greet him, smiling as they clasped his fingers and arms. They were strong and weathered, loyal and proud, the tanned men in knee boots and baggy breeches, the women in frocks of brown or black cloth, descendants of some noble lineage he was destined to protect. Seeing his youth and his strength reflected in their admiring glances, he felt himself swollen with martial importance, a young warrior bearing auspicious tidings. He looked toward the village with longing and impatience, anxious for Voula to share his reception.

"My father sends greetings to you all," Andreas said gravely. "I bring you the news of the beginning of the great war for freedom and to ask you to prepare for the cave."

A few of the women crossed themselves grimly, their lips murmuring prayers. The men muttered to one another, falling silent as they waited for Barba Simos to speak. That old patriarch looked at the slopes beyond the village, the peaks of the mountains hidden in a veiling of clouds.

"We will do what we must do," he said.

From the village a cluster of children came running. Having heard the guns they could not be held at their lessons and had burst free to join the tumult. Andreas looked over their bobbing heads to some older girls bringing up the rear and caught sight of the lithe, slender figure of Voula. Still separated by a considerable distance, he envisioned her dark, basaltic beauty.

The children hurtled by him shrieking, running toward the young men firing the guns, dogs racing and barking in their wake. After they had passed, Andreas saw that Voula, recognizing him, had paused, letting the other girls walk on alone. Shyly or coquettishly, he was not sure, she waited for him.

He slipped away from the gathering, frowning slightly as if he were examining the environs of land and houses, looking everywhere but toward the place where she waited. He felt the earth trembling beneath his feet.

His memory of Voula had no beginning. With his earliest awareness of life, he had secret knowledge of her, a haunted sense they had been nourished in the same womb. He recalled her as a child, a frisky, engaging creature several years younger than he, bounding in and out of his sight, taunting him with her beguiling smile. There was something, even then, marking her apart from other small girls, an innate grace beside their awkward stumblings.

For a time the two of them had been close as brother and sister, confiding and fighting in the way of siblings. As the years passed and he saw her only on feast days and holidays, he felt his feelings in transition, a curious excitement in her presence, an inability to refrain from staring at her. He hoped perhaps she had changed in her feelings toward him but he could not be sure. She was only sixteen and he could not expect her to respond to his love as if she were a mature woman.

A short distance from her, he paused to absorb her lissome loveliness, renewing his delight at her glowing cheeks and black eyes, her body in a plain, ankle-length frock unable to conceal a virgin's flame.

"Giasou, Voula."

"Giasou, Andreas."

"I have brought important news!" he cried. "The revolt has begun!"

She reached up to the kerchief that bound her hair, tugged it gently free, a gesture so measured and sensual it might almost have been some portion of her nakedness she was unveiling. Her glistening black hair cascaded down her shoulders, plaits as thick as a man's wrists, falling across her breasts. He felt desire for her sear his heart.

"I have some important news too," she said.

With a flaring of irritation, he felt his mission diminished.

"Your news can't be more important than the war!" he said sharply.

Resenting his reprimand, she looked away haughtily. He told himself she was not unflawed. In an accident of childhood she had severed the middle finger of one hand and, catching sight of that tiny stump, he expected to be repelled. Yet, in her stunning total beauty, that single flaw gave her a human quality she would not have otherwise possessed. As if the gods had decreed the only way to keep her among mortals, secure from their desire, was to mar her perfection.

Something of her divinity remained. He could not imagine her consigned to a life of labor like ordinary women, thumping and rinsing and spreading her husband's laundry on the boulders to dry or bending to toil in a stony field. She had to be revered as one would savor a princess.

He had never spoken of his love to Voula. Nor had he mentioned it to his father or to her family, but he took for granted they would be betrothed one day. He had sworn an oath that if he were rejected by her kinsmen, he would abduct her, forcing her marriage to him as the harsh custom of the highlanders decreed, scorning any vendetta that might result. If he preferred not to use violence, it wasn't because he feared her father and brothers but because he wanted to win her love without threat or force.

"Voula, I'm sorry," he said in remorse. "What is your news?"

She smiled, scuffing the tip of her shoe among a few fallen blossoms. He glimpsed the cinnamon shade of her bare ankle and when she looked up, catching him, he felt himself flushing. She laughed softly and secretly, as if savoring her power.

"I'll tell you my news later," she said.

She walked past him, motioning him to join her, the two of them moving together toward the gathering of men and women. He stole a final glance at her, jubilant with the knowledge that when the clans gathered in the cave, they would be together. And in place of the fear he had always accepted at the prospect of that descent into the bowels of the earth, he yearned to be secluded in the darkness beside her.

By early afternoon of the following day, his father, Kyriakos, his sister, Gianoula, his great-grandmother, his brothers, their wives and children and other kinsmen began to arrive in Villandredou.

They brought donkeys and carts laden with a few treasured belongings, icons decked with dried, faded flowers, the linen and laces of dowries. With the families of Villandredou they began packing the donkeys and carts with bricks of cheese, kilos of dark ambrosial honey, bags of flour and grain, casks of wine. The village took on the teeming color of a Gypsy encampment as people streamed in and out of houses, mills and stables. Hens, dogs and goats mingled their cackles, barks and bleats to the commotion. A band of shepherds who had formed the sheep into a single, large flock started driving them toward a grazing refuge high in the mountains. A group of horsemen led by Andreas' brother, Christos, rode off to replace the sentries who guarded the passes further down the mountain as protection against any Turkish attack.

Under the trees at the edge of the village, several aged warriors, veterans of all but forgotten battles, displayed their faded, tattered pennants to a cluster of eager children while regaling them with heroic tales.

"Those weren't Turks we fought then, children, they were gorgons, monsters who would cut a man's heart from his body and feed it to the pigs . . ."

"I remember Ali Tsaousis, a bloodthirsty Tartar, built like a Slavic bear, ravaging the villages of Spilia for months. We rode from the mountains to put an end to him and . . ."

"Anthoula, my little flower, all these grand stories have made me dry. Be a blessed child and slip over to your mother and ask her for a small gourd of raki . . . that's a good girl. God bless you, daughter, and someday favor you with a Cretan hero as a husband . . ."

The young men, caught up in the fever, felt their blood boiling and swaggered around the village, holding the butts of their guns, gazing at the girls with bold, challenging eyes. A few times Andreas caught sight of Voula, flying on tasks and errands with other young women, but he hadn't found another chance to talk to her since his arrival.

From sunrise he worked in his uncle's mill, his brothers joining him as they arrived, packing and loading grain into the carts. There were six boys in his family, including Christos, the eldest, who had gone to take charge of the sentries. All of them were strong, rough palikars, unabashedly delighted at the prospect of fighting, a glorious respite from the mundane chores of house and farm. As they worked they jested and taunted one another, punching and pummeling and tripping with glee.

"Damn your eyes, Elias! Stop fooling around!"

"Fix that strap, Thanos! If it breaks on the trip, the old man will eat you, bones and all!"

"Come on, kid." Mitsos, the brother nearest to Andreas in age and the only other one still unmarried, prodded him roughly. "Bring those bags to me over here."

"Get them yourself," Andreas said. "I have my own work to do."

"Listen to the snotty kid!" Elias cried.

"Pretty impudent for a pup!" Thanos said sternly. "Teach him a lesson, Mitsos! He's forgotten the last time you boxed his sassy ears!"

"I think I will!" Mitsos cried. He was not as tall as Andreas but was stockier and broader, with strong arms. "I'll give him one last chance. Boy, bring those bags to me here!"

"I'll bring you a boulder to shove up your ass!" Andreas grinned.

"Did you hear him?" Mitsos appealed to the others to bear witness. He glared ominously at Andreas. "You're really going to get a hiding now!"

As Mitsos came charging at him, Andreas spun quickly out of his way. Unable to stop his furious rush, Mitsos lost his balance, stumbled and landed on his knees with a groan.

"He's making a fool of you, Mitsos!"

"Get up, buffoon! Are you going to pray or fight?"

Andreas waited for Mitsos to rise and charge again, his blood leaping, his spirit reveling in the contest. He could already shoot, run and ride as well as if not better than any of his brothers, even the formidable Christos. He knew the time was near when none of them would match his skill in hand-to-hand fighting. He had taken their taunts and beatings for years, knowing the day would come when he would give them their measure in return, fulfilling the words he had heard his father telling his uncle, that Andreas was a born warrior who would someday gain great renown.

Flushed and angry under the barrage of jeers and hoots, Mitsos had regained his feet. Andreas could tell by the baleful glitter in his eyes that if Mitsos caught him, the punishment would be severe.

Once again Mitsos charged, flailing at Andreas with both fists. Ducking under his brother's swings, Andreas caught a blow on his cheek that landed with the force of a hammer. His vision blurred, and then, moving by instinct, he spun away swiftly before Mitsos could grab him in a bear hug.

"Stand and fight, you toad!" Mitsos bellowed.

"Give it to him, Mitsos!" Elias cried impatiently. "Stop fooling around and finish him off!"

Mitsos made a threatening gesture toward Andreas.

"I'll bash in your impudent teeth!" he cried.

"That's the way, Mitsos!" Thanos mocked him. "Worry him to death!"

Goaded by their taunts, Mitsos charged once more. Feinting as if he were going to dodge away again, Andreas turned suddenly to meet him. Catching his brother by surprise, Andreas drove his fist into Mitsos's belly and followed that blow with a hard, short punch to his head. Mitsos staggered backwards, his eyes glazed and his senses stunned, he feet tangling as he tried to remain standing. For a moment the sight of his brother's stricken face softened Andreas. Then he remembered the beatings he had suffered from his brothers for years, their taunts and jeers, and he swung a fierce, final blow to Mitsos's temple, tumbling his brother to sprawl like a lobster on the ground. He lay there breathing in short, pained gasps, a dribble of spittle and blood running from his mouth.

A roar of triumph burst from Andreas and he raised his arms over his head to herald his victory. Then he was hurled furiously aside. Barely catching his balance to remain on his feet, he looked into the stinging, raging face of his father.

"Are my sons clowns or louts to be horseplaying when others are working!" Kyriakos shouted wrathfully. "You kidney-brained clods!" He aimed a slap at Thanos, who was standing nearest to him, and Thanos dodged frantically aside. "God pity Crete if this is the way her sons prepare for war!"

The brothers stared sheepishly at one another. Andreas was ashamed and grieved at having offended and distressed his father. On the ground Mitsos struggled weakly to his knees.

"We were just testing the kid, Father," Elias said hesitantly. "Mitsos wanted to be sure he was ready for the fighting ahead."

Thanos and Apostolis nodded mutely in agreement. Kyriakos glared down at the battered, bloody Mitsos.

"Are you satisfied, moron?"

Mitsos blinked and nodded numbly.

"Help your brother up and see he washes his face," Kyriakos said sternly to Andreas, "so our kinsmen don't think the Turks have already attacked. Thank your patron saint, as well, that I have no time now to give you the beating you deserve!" He motioned brusquely to the others. "Bring those carts to the square! The women are waiting to load the bread! Move now, idiots! Betrayers!"

He started away, followed by Elias, Thanos and Apostolis. Elias looked back once and winked. Andreas bent ruefully to offer Mitsos his hand.

"You ruined me, kid," Mitsos said as he lurched heavily to his feet. "You about knocked me senseless."

"I'm sorry, brother," Andreas said. "I took advantage because I was faster."

"You beat me good," Mitsos said doggedly. "Fighting isn't a game with rules like church. Fight any way you can to win." He sighed. "For years we treat you like the runt of the litter and then, suddenly, you're full grown and bubbling with juice." He brushed the dust off his clothes, looking warily around to make sure they were alone.

"Now that you've become a man," he said in a low voice, "maybe it's time for you to make a visit with me at night to a woman I know in Capelas . . . she'll take all you have, I'll vouch for that."

Andreas felt his face flush.

"There's time enough for that," he said gruffly.

"I'm not so sure about that," Mitsos said. "The cave we're going into tomorrow has many dark corners, passages where two people can hide away for a while. It is best to have a girl and to know what to do with her." He smirked. "You might find yourself having to play in the dark with yourself."

"Shut your bloody mouth!" Andreas cried. "I'll lay you back on your ass!"

"All right, all right, wildcat!" Mitsos grinned. "I was just trying to help my little brother. Look after yourself for all I care." He shrugged, touched his lip gingerly, and walked unsteadily toward the well to wash his face.

To make amends to his father for fighting, Andreas worked steadily and vigorously for the balance of the day. Because of the imminence of the cave, he was conscious of the spring in a way he had never been before. The air smelled of flowers, rich and fragrant, even the buds perfumed, their aroma seeping into his nostrils.

As twilight fell, they gained a respite from their labors. The priest from Selino had been brought secretly up the mountain and held a special liturgy for them in the small chapel, dispensing communion and blessing their journey. Andreas saw his father kneeling beside Gianoula, his aunt Sofia beside his uncle Simos, his brothers and their wives, all served from the chalice. Feeling alone, he sought Voula, and saw her wearing a beaded frock of white wool. She seemed to float in the shadows as she knelt to take her place before the priest. Andreas pushed several young men aside in an effort to kneel as close to her as he could. Watching her mouth open slightly to receive the golden spoon and the shard of bread, he caught a glimmer of her crimson tongue.

As he raised his face toward the priest and the chalice, he had the sinful thought of kissing her moist, parted lips.

Afterward, everyone joined in eating the chickens and lamb that had been slaughtered and roasted and in drinking the oldest of the wine stored in the casks. He sought to approach Voula again, found her barricaded in the midst of her family, father, mother and brothers like a phalanx around her. He consoled his irritation by remembering that when they were in the cave he would speak to her often. Meanwhile, he determined to ask his father to discuss a betrothal with Voula's parents.

As the families of Villandredou prepared to sleep in the village for the last night, they took in some of the kinsmen from the other settlements. Gianoula and his great-grandmother were to spend the night in his uncle's house and his brothers' wives were dispersed into other houses. The men set their beds on branches and boughs under the stars. They lit fires and sat in circles, smoking and talking. From somewhere in the darkness a man sang a haunting ballad of the home he had left.

Andreas went to wish his great-grandmother good night and found Gianoula spooning the old lady some heated milk. The bumpy trip up the mountain had agitated her and between swallows of the warm milk, she uttered a series of shrill whimpers.

In an adjoining room, his aunt Sofia had some linens and belongings around her. She looked up as he entered, a melancholy on her cheeks.

"These linens are from my dowry, Andreas," she said slowly. "This little jeweled box was given to me by your blessed mother. This carved staff belonged to my koumbaros, a giant of a man murdered by the Turks outside the church at Gerandimos. This doll belonged to my first child, dead of the fever when she was three." She looked at him woefully. "How can I choose what is to be taken or what is to be forsaken?"

"Whatever you want to pack and leave behind, Aunt Sofia," Andreas said, "I'll hide in the morning on the mountain in a safe place."

"That's good of you, dear nephew," she said gratefully, and then sighed. "But what am I worrying about? The possessions will last but your old aunt may not."

A commotion came from outside the house, a clatter of horses and shouts of men. Andreas hurried to the door thinking perhaps Christos had returned. Crossing the threshold of the house, he saw a band of about a half-dozen horsemen dismounting, being received with enthusiasm and fervor by the villagers who crowded around them. They were Cretan palikars and Andreas recognized the tallest of them as Lambros Kasandonis, a celebrated resistance fighter against the Turks who carried a price on his head.

Andreas had first seen Kasandonis at a feast day gathering in Retimo a year before. Five or six years older than Andreas, there was an arrogant strength about him, incited perhaps by the rumor that he had been born of a union between a high-born Cretan warrior and a Venetian princess.

Kasandonis moved with sureness and confidence through the crowd, dressed in a fine beaded vest, a fringed headband, and an ornamented silken sash holding a brace of silver-handled pistols at his waist. He shook hands with Uncle Simos, who greeted him warmly. Moving on into the small garden before the house of Voula's family, he conducted a formal salutation with Voula's father and mother before they disappeared into the house.

Andreas returned to the room where his aunt sorted the items to be taken.

"Aunt Sofia," he said, an unrest he could not define bringing him a chill, "what is Lambros Kasandonis doing here?"

"He is coming with us tomorrow to the cave," his aunt said. "Your uncle Simos and the others are proud to have a chieftain of his stature with us."

"Why should he join the family? He isn't our kinsman."

"He will be a kinsman by marriage soon," Aunt Sofia said. "He is betrothed to a girl in our village."

"Who is the girl?" Even as he asked the question, his lips cold and his throat numb, he knew the answer.

"Voula Psychoundakis," his aunt said.

He did not trust himself to remain among humans. He turned abruptly, walking quickly from the room, hearing his great-grandmother whimper as he passed her bed. He left the house, fleeing the village and the men smoking and talking beside the fires, climbing the slope of the mountain, heedless of the nettles tearing at his hands and cheeks. He sat down, finally, beneath the boughs of a solitary pine, wanting to go on but dazed and exhausted, as if he had been the one beaten and humiliated earlier in the day.

In the darkness he heard the baleful cry of an animal at bay, a dark forewarning of blood and death. And in that wounded and mournful moment, he was uncertain whether the cry had not burst from his own soul.

CHAPTER
EIGHT

Through the winter, as Vorogrivas and his band waited word on the outbreak of the revolution, hard winds and stormy blizzards battered and chilled them. Most of the men took shelter in small caves or huts constructed of branches, boughs and boulders. Those hardy spirits who still slept outside huddled under greatcoats and cloaks piled in layers so thick and heavy, not a portion of their faces was visible.

During the day they practiced marksmanship, oiled and cleaned their weapons, groomed their horses, and trained the recruits who joined them from villages in the plains. To vent the energies fostered by their waiting, they wrestled to test quickness and strength and vaulted over the backs of horses set in a row.

During January and February of that year of 1821, Vorogrivas led his men in frequent forays, attacking Turkish caravans, raiding and burning Turkish settlements, pillaging the storehouses and granaries of beys. As quickly as they attacked, they would fall back, riding swiftly to the haven of the mountain, setting ambushes for any Turkish force foolish enough to follow them into the defiles and ravines.

Even as they gloated over small victories, Vorogrivas warned his men of the battles ahead.

"When we receive the signal to ride down into the plains," he told them, "a new kind of warfare awaits us. We will not be able to raid and run. We will be battling Turkish troops in the plains, assaulting fortified towns, joining other bands to make a Christian army."

In the gruff mutterings of approval from the men who remained confident of their ability to win any battle against the Turks, Vorogrivas noticed the calm, attentive face of the youth Manolis.

As Makrydis had told him the first day the youth had joined their band, Manolis proved he could outshoot and outride most of the men. He seemed to have matured years in a few months, learning quickly, and never complaining.

In the beginning, beset by a prodding fear the young man might be wounded or killed, Vorogrivas hovered close to him in battle. Concern with the welfare of the youth caused him to grow careless of his own safety and, once, almost cost him his life. By a slash of irony it was Manolis who saved him then, firing his pistol just in time to kill the Turk about to pierce Vorogrivas from behind. For a moment then, in the frenzy of the battle, their glances met in an unspoken and redemptive bond. Vorogrivas felt as if Manolis understood the reason for his captain's dereliction and, by the quickness of his own response, sought to reassure him.

Yet the curious, indefinable feelings toward the young man remained. He woke in the morning with delight at the prospect of seeing Manolis that day, watching him smile and sing, at work or in moments of repose. If several hours passed without Vorogrivas catching a glimpse of the youth, on some pretext or other, he went to find him.

That winter, as they waited for the beginning of the war, he came slowly and stunningly to accept the truth that he loved Manolis. But, he swore to himself, love in a way that was not carnal, something more, a longing in his lonely spirit to be united with an element in the youth he did not himself possess. He had never before understood the power of such friendship, blending their souls into the harmony of the bow and the lyre.

Yet he also had moments when he feared any deepening of the bond to Manolis might soften his own will and weaken his arm in battle. Love and war were forces in conflict, each striving to consume the other. In the grasp of that dread, he had days when he avoided any contact with the young man. Even this withdrawal Manolis accepted without sign of grievance or reproach.

In the early part of March, Makrydis brought them joyous word that a Russian army had crossed the Prut River into the provinces, the forerunner of a Russian fleet that would sail at the beginning of summer, both forces aimed at the liberation of Greece. Meanwhile, Makrydis told them, in every village and town the Christians were readying themselves to aid these invasions. A number of mills had ceased grinding corn and were secretly manufacturing gunpowder. Agents of the Society of Friends had been sent to other countries to purchase arms and ammunition and to meet with English and French societies that were sympathetic to the Greek cause.

"The world has not forgotten us!" Makrydis said. "Newspapers in France and England write daily of our plight and the suffering of our people. Meetings are called for the raising of funds and exhortations against the Turks. In England there is a poet named Lord Byron, whose verses, they say, on the tragedy of our great and noble people in chains, cut deeper than swords! I tell you, my friend, the hour is close!"

"And our own people?" Vorogrivas asked. "Are they united?"

"The people are ready!" Makrydis cried. "The only ones who hold back timidly are the cowardly and frightened archons and clerics, who, like rulers in other countries, fear any revolution that might upset their hold on power! But, by God, when the storm breaks they will have to take sides! We'll baptize the revolution in blood and there won't be any neutrals then! If they don't kill Turks, the bastard Turks will butcher them!"

The severe winter had been a tribulation to the aged Captain Boukouvalas, and in March he became seriously ill, feverish and rambling, refighting earlier battles as he tossed and heaved in his bed. Each day his decline grew more pronounced, his spirit detaching itself from the life of the camp. In more lucid intervals he spoke gloomily with Vorogrivas, who kept vigil for hours at a time beside the old man's bed.

"Don't grieve for me, my son," he said. "Even mountains come to misfortune in time. I am not ready but I must leave life soon. I enjoin you to bury my bones, clothed in the simple garments of a soldier, to be disinterred when God thinks fit to free our country and then to be reburied in the mountains of my birthplace. That much I pledge you to do."

"Don't be impatient, old warrior." Vorogrivas sought to console him. "You may last a long time yet."

"I know I am dying," the old man said in a rough, low voice. "I have lived and fought many years and it may now be time. The only cursed grievance is that I must die in bed, a disfigured and decaying carcass . . . God, what a joy to have died in battle!"

Vorogrivas, fearing the captain was about to breathe his last at any moment, brought a monk from a mountain monastery some miles away, to administer the last rites. Boukouvalas recovered sufficiently to unleash a tirade of obscenities on the Brother's head. The monk fled pale and shocked from the hut, mounting his donkey, his shaking limbs suggesting he had been called to render the final sacrament to a minion of the devil.

"There may be more life in the shaggy wolf than we realize," Vorogrivas said grimly to Ghiouris. "Bring half a dozen stout palikars and tell Lascarina to prepare the cupping tumblers."

"He'll erupt like a volcano," Ghiouris said. "Half a dozen of the boys may not be enough."

When the group entered the hut, Vorogrivas, Ghiouris and the palikars, and Lascarina carrying oil, wick and tumblers, the old man opened his eyes. His nostrils distended like those of an animal scenting mortal danger.

"What the hell is this?" he growled. "Can't you vultures wait until a man dies before sending in his gravediggers?" As Vorogrivas motioned the men to grasp his arms and legs, Boukouvalas struggled to push them away. "Damn your eyes, what are you doing? Get your hands off me, dogs!"

Despite the old man's fury, the palikars wrestled and tugged the massive old klepht over on his belly. Vorogrivas and Ghiouris pulled the clothing from his shoulders and arms, tearing away layer after layer until he was naked to the waist. The men muttered in awe before the rugged expanse of granite and rock running from his neck to his stern.

With the wick on fire, Lascarina heated a tumbler, and clapped it swiftly on the old man's back. As his flesh puffed and swelled into small, scarlet hills, the old klepht raged.

"Assassins! Traitors!" Boukouvalas roared. "Let me up and I'll butcher you all! My God, I'm on fire! Help!"

"The Lion of Parnassus!" Lascarina spit scornfully. "The legend who killed a hundred agas, howling like a babe at a little heat!"

The old man bellowed louder and shook furiously at the arms of the men who held him. Lascarina worked on his back with fiendish glee, pulling tumblers off and slapping others on, the hut exploding with the crack of popping flesh and the scorched scents of hair and skin.

After the cupping, Boukouvalas grew better. In the space of a week he was sufficiently recovered so he could be carried once more to join the men sitting about the fires at night, eating goat's cheese sizzled on the points of daggers and washing that down with draughts of pungent red wine. Yet even this eating he performed as if it were habit, taking no special joy in the life his body had salvaged from the dark dominions. As the klephts drank toast after toast to the battles before them, praying for the "good bullet" that would dispatch them cleanly into death, Vorogrivas saw the mournful yearning that swept the old klepht's bearded, pitted face.

There was a night later that month, when a rattle of musket fire sent men scrambling for their arms, tumbling from the shelters. With Vorogrivas leading them, several score klephts raced to the point. The sentries, trembling with excitement, pointed in the direction of the plains far below, near the village of Kravasaras, where a bright pillar of flame ascended into the sky.

"The signal, Captain!" Ghiouris shouted jubilantly.

While the men shouted and cheered, firing their muskets into the air, a second fire rose in the foothills of the mountain, confirming the first beacon by a message that they were to ride down to the village at once.

"All right, palikars!" Vorogrivas cried. "We can celebrate later! Now assemble your horses and arms!"

As the men surged around him, Vorogrivas saw Manolis' exultant face. They stared at one another in a gilded moment that excluded every other presence. Vorogrivas hesitated, wanting to clasp Manolis in that instant, in a sharing of joy and resolve. As if to spare him the decision, with a warm and flashing smile, Manolis broke into a run for the camp.

In the next hour the palikars prepared rapidly for departure. As each man came to take his place in the column, Ghiouris made a final swift check of his equipment and his horse.

"Son of a goat!" He punched one klepht wrathfully.

"Didn't I order you a week ago to get those rear hoofs reshod? For that blunder, you'll clean up the scraps!"

As each man reined his mount before Ghiouris, he clutched the horse deftly by the upper lip, stared down its throat, felt its chest muscles, and, running his fingers like spider's legs over its body, felt the knee joints, tapped the tendons and squeezed the bones above the fetlocks.

"Sound and strong!" he said. "Next!"

He checked horse after horse, determining by a glance and a stroke the animal's condition.

"Oaf! Ox!" he cried at another man after he had slid his hand beneath the saddlecloth. "I warned you to keep this cloth clean! A crumb will chafe the animal's back into a sore in a hour's ride!"

"I'm sorry, Ghiouris!" the man cried in remorse. "I'll shake the cloth till the colors fall off, I swear, only in God's name, don't leave me behind!"

As Ghiouris performed the final inspection, Vorogrivas walked to the old captain's hut. Despite the tumult and excitement in the camp, the snorting of the horses and the shouts of the men, Boukouvalas had not hollered for men to carry him from his hut. Vorogrivas thought that perhaps he chose to remain encased in the darkness of the shelter, sparing himself the sight of the band riding off to a war he could not join.

Inside the entrance, Vorogrivas heard the uneven hoarseness of the old man's breathing.

"Well, Father"—he tried to make his voice firm and hearty —"we have seen the signal from Makrydis. The holy struggle has begun and we ride down soon."

He waited for the old man to make some response but Boukouvalas remained silent.

"I will be leaving a detachment of guards to keep vigil over the camp. As I send men to replace them, they will bring you word of what is happening and carry back to us your counsel. Meanwhile, you will be well looked after."

Although his face was hidden in shadows, Vorogrivas felt the old man's eyes like knives.

"Take me with you!" Boukouvalas said harshly.

"No," Vorogrivas said.

"Take me, in the name of God!"

"No!" Vorogrivas said sharply. "We have discussed this before! You were the one who taught me the band's survival came before the welfare of any one man! If we need to move swiftly, you would hold us back! Protecting you, good fighters might be lost! Don't ask me to take you, Father! I cannot!"

"I don't ask that you drag me around for long!" Boukouvalas cried. "Just take me down with you and put me in the front rank of the first battle where the Turkish bullets can finish me! I would not ask that much except I cannot endure rotting away here, stinking like carrion, while men are fighting for freedom!" His voice, shorn of pride, came in a shaken plea from his throat. "If you refuse me now, then carry me to a ledge of the mountain and leave me to the hunger of the wolves! Even that death would serve more purpose than the one I wait for here!"

Vorogrivas stared down at the great shadowed bulk of the old klepht. From the camp came the clamor of men, jubilant shouts and joyous cries ringing in the gloom of the hut.

He was torn by sadness. Yet he was not thinking of the old captain, crippled and reeking, but of Manolis, the youth's comely grace and strength riven someday by the tides of time. He turned and stalked angrily to the entrance, pulling aside the cape that covered the doorway.

"Ghiouris!" he shouted. "Ghiouris!"

The lieutenant came running toward the shelter.

"Yes, Captain?"

"Ghiouris, fix up the big bay with the large saddle and the harness we use for men with broken limbs!" He motioned

brusquely inside the hut. "We are taking Captain Boukouvalas with us. When the horse is ready, send men to lift
and strap him on."

As Ghiouris moved briskly away, Vorogrivas looked back
toward the old klepht. Neither of them spoke but he heard
the altered rhythm of the aged captain's breathing, relief
and joy in place of despair.

They rode from the camp in a long column of horsemen,
almost a hundred palikars led by Vorogrivas, as the tracings
of dawn streaked the crags and the peaks. Each mounted
figure wore a bristly cloak, stiff as bark, the sleeves hanging
loose like a bishop's robes, the hoods raised against the wind
and the cold. Their long muskets were slung from their
shoulders, pistols, swords and the cords they used to bind
their captives dangling at their waists.

The initial jubilation had passed and the shouts and
laughter had been stilled. The men rode silently, from time
to time one of them looking back at the sanctuary of rocks
and canyons. A few crows wheeled overhead, wings black
against the sky, adding their shrill cawing to the snorting of
the horses and the jangling of the stirrups.

Several horses behind Vorogrivas, close enough so he
could keep an eye on him, the great frame of Boukouvalas
was strapped and lashed firmly on his horse. He rode stiffly
and awkwardly, each stride of the horse causing his body to
lurch against the heavy, creaking harness that bound him to
the saddle.

Dropping back to see how he was faring, Vorogrivas
could tell by the tight furrows in his face that the old klepht
was in pain. Yet nothing could dull his obvious delight in
the journey. His white-maned, unhooded head twisted from
side to side, his eyes staring with fervor at the blossoming
flowers and newly budded trees, his lips sucking the fresh,
crisp air.

"What are those bundles loaded on that donkey trailing behind you?" Vorogrivas asked.

"My silver knee plates and silver breastplate." Boukouvalas winked. "My pennants and the mighty jeweled sword with which I killed Kafta Aga. Would you expect me to ride to battle naked?"

"You are a rogue!" Vorogrivas said sternly. "All that nonsense about being left for the wolves. Even their tusks would not be sharp enough to rip your leathery and deceptive hide!"

Boukouvalas threw back his head and laughed boisterously.

"I feel reborn!" he cried to Vorogrivas. "The spirit moves me to sing a song!"

In a husky, trembling voice, he began to sing.

> "Mountain, what shall I say to thee?
> Blessed mountain, what shall I say?
> The klephts of Parnassus are leaving,
> Fleeing your temples and your peaks,
> Riding to war on the mean and wretched
> plains . . ."

He paused for a moment, laboring for breath, drawing air into his lungs.

> "Weep, beloved mountain, melt the snow,
> Melt the snow so that it roars
> Like a wild river to the plains,
> Show the way a mountain grieves
> And sorrows for her sons that leave . . ."

The band rode into the village of Kravasaras about noon, the dogs roused and barking at the heels of their horses, chickens dispersed before their clattering passage. As they passed the church, the bell in the tower began to ring and Vorogrivas was conscious of a clear, haunting clarity and richness in the sound unlike that of any church or monastery bell he had ever heard.

The villagers, men and women, boys and girls, ran forward to fling garlands of blossoms across their saddles, reverently touching their boots and the scabbards of their swords.

Makrydis and a small group of armed men waited for them in the square. Vorogrivas dismounted and the two men embraced fervently, tears on both their cheeks.

"Thanks to God we share this moment," Makrydis said.

All around them palikars leaped off their horses to be hugged and embraced by the villagers, the children shrieking and dashing in circles about them. The only one who remained untouched was the swaggering and weaponed Lascarina, no one daring to go near her. She stared about her with a haughty stiffness, challenging any man or woman to make a disparaging comment.

Then the crowd fell silent, watching in amazement and awe as a half-dozen men led by Ghiouris unharnessed the giant form of the old klepht Boukouvalas and lowered him slowly and heavily from his horse.

"Easy now, boys, easy!" Ghiouris said. "Watch the captain's legs!"

An old villager suddenly recognized the klepht and whispered his name. The whispers fanned and spread like a wind through the crowd. Carrying him in the throne of their arms, six men transported Boukouvalas toward one of the houses. Conscious of the men and women watching him, he held his leonine head and huge shoulders stiff and proud. Women at the outskirts of the crowd raised their small children high in their arms as if allowing them to witness the procession of a king.

"If the Turks discover he is here," Makrydis said grimly to Vorogrivas, "we'll need an army to hold them off."

"The Turks think they killed him years ago," Vorogrivas said.

"See that the palikars are given food and wine," Makrydis ordered his men. He clasped Vorogrivas by the arm and they started from the square. As they stepped on the threshold of Makrydis' house, Vorogrivas hesitated, uneasily entering the structure enclosed by ceiling and walls.

"I feel I'm entering a tomb," he said.

"For centuries all our houses have been tombs and our villages graveyards!" Makrydis said. "But that is over now!"

He paced the room excitedly.

"All over Greece our people are fighting with guns, when they have them, or scythes, pitchforks and clubs," Makrydis said. "Oh, there is a reaping of justice for the Mussulmen now! In our village and in other villages, the Turkish bodies were thrown on piles of offal and burned because no Christian will dig graves for them." He walked to a large, handdrawn map of Greece hanging on the wall.

"In some of the larger towns, the surviving Turks have taken refuge in the old Venetian and Frankish fortresses and our forces are laying siege to them. That popinjay Archbishop Germanos has finally attacked the citadel of Patras, and in the south of the Morea, Kolokotronis and Petrobey are planning for the siege of Kalamata if they have not struck already. In our own region here we know that Athanasios Diakos, with fifteen hundred men, mostly klephts from the Pindus, is on the move toward us."

Makrydis pointed to a location on the map.

"We have laid siege to Salona and Levadia, where Turks have taken refuge in the castle above the town. I told you that Diakos comes to join us, but we also have word that Pehlevan Pasha is on the march from Lamia with a strong force, maybe a thousand men, Turks and Albanian mercenaries. You know what those devils are like. They caught one of our scouts, broke in all his teeth and gouged out his eyes. When we found him the poor devil was still alive, begging to be killed!"

Anger choked off his words and he paused to calm himself.

"What we fear now," he said, "is that Pehlevan Pasha will attack our blockading forces from the rear unless we can delay him somewhere on his route long enough for Diakos and his men to arrive." He clasped Vorogrivas tightly by the arms. "That is your task, my comrade, why I signaled for you to come at once. Pehlevan Pasha must be stopped. He has ten times more men than you and many good palikars will die, I know. But we have no one else and every hour you buy for us is worth the lives of a hundred Greeks. If that bastard joins the Turks of Salona and Levadia, they will break free, and he has sworn not to leave a Christian man, woman or child alive in central Greece!"

"He will have to kill us first," Vorogrivas said quietly. "Where shall we confront him?"

"I think you will agree the best place will be the stone bridge across the Kifisos River that runs down the mountain from Lamia," Makrydis said. "He must cross there or march an additional forty miles, because we have burned the bridges to the west."

"Can he outflank the bridge by fording the river?"

"The stream is too rough now," Makrydis said. "The bridge is their only access to the other side and they can only try to cross a few men at a time. The terrain is rocky and you should be able to build a solid barricade for cover. See what you think after we have studied the maps. Meanwhile, your men can rest in the village tonight and you can ride out at dawn. We have scouts and snipers tracking Pehlevan Pasha, but even if they harass and delay him a little, his force will probably reach the bridge sometime tomorrow afternoon."

They spent several hours studying the maps. Later in the day they left the house. Ghiouris had been waiting under a nearby tree and he rose to meet them.

"I've got the men and horses settled, Captain," he said. "And I've posted sentries several miles from the village in all directions." He stared uneasily over the roofs of houses toward the mountains. "This level land makes me feel naked."

"We'll be moving out early in the morning," Vorogrivas said. "I'll go over the plans with you and the men later. How is Captain Boukouvalas?"

"Groaning and cursing," Ghiouris said grimly. "That ride down was hell for him. We got him into a house but he wouldn't let us put him in bed. We had to set a straw pallet for him on the floor." He looked anxiously at Vorogrivas. "Forgive me, Captain, but what are we going to do with him?"

"God only knows," Vorogrivas said.

"Let him stay here," Makrydis said. "We'll look after him. And by the way, my friend, the villagers want to throw a glendi for your men, let them eat and drink a little."

"I don't want them worn out and sodden for the morning," Vorogrivas said. He was silent for a moment, thinking of the battle ahead, and that many of them would never live to celebrate again. "All right," he said. "Let them have their glendi, but, Ghiouris, warn them."

"I'll keep a close eye on them, Captain," Ghiouris said. "It's not the drinking that worries me, but that many haven't seen a woman this close in years." He shrugged. "Not counting Lascarina, who has a horn herself."

As Ghiouris and Makrydis moved off to arrange the glendi, Vorogrivas noticed Manolis standing outside the door of a small stone house across the road.

"Captain," Manolis called to him. "This is my house. My mother is inside . . . would you honor us . . . ?"

Vorogrivas crossed the road and stepped into the garden.

"Our house is poor," Manolis said with a slight, apologetic smile. He handed Vorogrivas a sprig of basil. "From our garden," he said, and as Vorogrivas took the sprig, a faint tremor passed through his body. He rubbed it slowly between his fingers to release the tangy aroma that he carried over the threshold.

The house was a single-roomed dwelling with white-washed walls, sparsely furnished with some cane chairs and a table set with a fringed lace cloth on which a candle burned in a lamp.

A woman emerged from the shadows beyond the flame of the candle, a tall, handsome woman, dressed in black. Expecting a resemblance to her son, Vorogrivas was still startled at the likeness, her nose, cheeks and mouth curved the same as the face of Manolis. When she came closer he saw the image of the young man's eyes in her eyes that were equally dark and deep, but with less innocence, her glance darkened by a sterner assessment of life and men.

"You honor our house," she said, and without being certain, he defined a resentment in her voice.

"You honor me by inviting me in," he answered gravely.

"Manolis, bring the captain a chair."

"I told you the captain has many things to do, Mama," Manolis said. "He cannot stay to visit."

"He can sit for a moment," the mother said. Her tone reproved him as if he were still a boy.

Manolis brought him a chair and Vorogrivas sat down. For a few moments a comfortless silence lingered about them. He noticed things he had not seen when he first entered. A shirt of Manolis hanging on a peg, perhaps left there by the mother as a reminder of her son. On the ledge above the fireplace was a carved wooden figure of a shepherd that suggested the young man's hand. He longed suddenly to have it.

"I want my son to remain here with me," the mother said abruptly. "This is his house and there is work in the fields I cannot do alone."

"Mama!" Manolis said. "Mama, you promised!"

"I have a right to speak!" the mother said harshly.

"I will not stay to listen!" Manolis said bitterly. "And I ask the captain to leave with me!"

Vorogrivas raised his hand to calm him, indicating he would stay. After a moment Manolis turned and left the house.

Alone in the candlelit room with the woman, Vorogrivas felt her eyes burrowing to his soul, invading his secret yearnings.

"I understand your concern, mother." He tried to speak quietly. "But there isn't peace or a refuge anywhere in Greece now. A village can become a battlefield and men can die here as well as in the mountains."

He marked the baleful strength of her eyes again and understood with certitude they were enemies and rivals.

"The time has come for men to fight now," he said earnestly. "Wives, sisters and, yes, mothers must provide their men faith and courage. Manolis is the youngest of my palikars but he is among the best."

"Do you think I care about such things?" she asked in a low, scornful voice. "Do you think I gave birth to him in pain and blood so he could join your homeless band?"

"He is a warrior!" Vorogrivas said sharply. "You should be proud of him as I am proud to have him beside me!"

"If he dies, he adds to your fame!" she cried. "That is all he means to you!"

He flew wrathfully to his feet, the chair pushed backward to strike the floor. He stood above her, trembling with fury. She stared up at him, braced as if he might strike her, but defiant and unafraid. Realizing further words were useless, he started for the door.

"He is my son!" she cried, and followed him. "You have many men but he is all I have!"

He crossed the threshold and then turned to say something else. He noticed then in the garden of pale spring buds, a flaming red carnation and a snow-white rose, their full-bloomed splendor dwarfing and diminishing the thin, weak seedlings about them.

A chill wind from some spell-crafted and sorcerous region blew upon his spirit. He left the yard quickly, striding down the road. After passing several houses, he looked back. She remained standing in the doorway, her figure stiff and black. From the garden beside her he saw once again the red and white flowers hurled like arrows against his eyes.

A mass was held in the church of Kravasaras that evening, the white-haired old village priest administering communion to the men of the band. Afterwards, they flocked eagerly to a central gathering in the square, to eat and drink and dance. Soon the night resounded with revelry and the wail of lyres and flutes.

Vorogrivas did not join the celebration. He lingered outside the church at the edge of the cemetery, watching the lights of stars glimmering across the markers and stones. Several times he heard Ghiouris and others in the band calling his name, but he did not answer.

Living away from villages for so many years, he had no knowledge of the courtesies required in social contacts. He imagined his men swilling wine, growing maudlin, flaming when a woman brushed against them. He wondered uneasily if Manolis were still angry, and had joined the men. For an instant he regretted permitting the men the celebration.

The church door creaked open and the cassocked figure of the priest emerged, drawing the heavy wooden panel closed behind him. Walking the path that led by the cemetery, he saw the shadow of Vorogrivas.

"Who is it?" the priest asked in a frightened voice.

"One of the men in the captain's band," Vorogrivas said quietly.

"You are not joining in the glendi?"

"There isn't reason yet for celebration," Vorogrivas said. "Men who laugh tonight will die tomorrow."

An owl's plaintive cry sounded from the hidden branches of a tree. The priest sighed.

Vorogrivas had little experience or patience with monks and priests. They were the vessels by which God performed his rituals of worship on earth. A few were decent and capable of sacrifice but many were pious frauds preaching the blessings of poverty and denial while growing fat on the donations of their impoverished flocks. Yet he felt a burden of sorrow in this old priest.

They stood hidden from each other in the dark, sharing the scents and sounds of the night, the clamor of music and voices floating from the square. In those moments when the tumult diminished, the trilling of crickets rose from the grasses around the gravestones. Behind the church a dog raised a harsh, guttural howl as it caught a hare.

"When men are killed in battle," the priest said slowly, "how are they buried?"

"Fighting men don't worry about that," Vorogrivas said. "That is a question for a priest to ask at night in a cemetery."

"I am sorry, my son," the priest said in an apologetic voice. "I did not mean to offend you. We are at war now and I know nothing of the ways of war, the ways in which I might help my people . . ."

He turned to leave.

"Wait, Father," Vorogrivas said. As the priest paused, an eerie whistle of wind carried the scent of the mountains around their heads. "They are not buried the way you bury them down here. We do not bedeck them with flowers, put rings on their fingers or wreaths around their brows. We wash them, wrap them in a shroud, inter them deep in a cave or under rocks so our enemies won't find them and desecrate their bodies. We leave their graves marked only in our hearts."

"Forgive me," the priest said. "It is only because I know nothing of the ways of war." He moved uneasily. "The night chill is getting into my bones . . . I must go." He started along the path to the small house, his cassock rustling across the stony ground, a scent of incense trailing in his wake.

"God bless you, my son, and keep you safe," his voice carried back softly to Vorogrivas.

They departed from the village just before daybreak, riding past the houses emplaced gray and silent in the bleak light. A few women watched from doorways, crossing themselves mournfully as the men clattered by, weapons and stirrups jangling. A girl emerged from a yard, running alongside the horse of one of the palikars, reaching up to clutch his hand, a flurried whisper passing between them before she was left behind. A cock crowed, its raucous cry heralding the day. As that crowing faded, the church bell tolled, hallowing the stillness. Vorogrivas envisioned the rope of the bell being tugged by the old priest who knew nothing of the ways of war.

Makrydis waited for the band at the outskirts of the village. Vorogrivas reined in his horse and bent down to clasp the man's hand in a strong grip.

"The scouts will keep you posted on the advance of Diakos," Makrydis said. "God go with you, my friend."

Vorogrivas nodded.

"Look after the Captain Boukouvalas," he said. "Last night he seemed to steam with fever. I am afraid he is near the end."

"I'll tend to him," Makrydis said. He stepped aside and the column started forward, the men raising their hands to him in farewell.

"When we reach the Bosporus, we'll send word for you to join us!" a man called to him.

"We'll bring you some Turkish ears!" another said.

"Good-by . . . good-by . . ."

They cantered across the plain, skirting the foothills of the mountains, Vorogrivas staring with nostalgia at the snow-capped peaks. High among those sheltering crags, the spring torrents were beginning to rush down the ravines, the long-winged eagles soared against the sky, the wild, tangy figs grew swollen and sweet.

He twisted in his saddle, glimpsing the riders aligned in columns of fours behind him. The short, stocky Ghiouris slouched low on his mount. Manolis riding in a lithe easy rhythm, Lascarina appendaged with weapons across her formidable body, the red-haired Kapsakis, Panagouris, Stathis, Paulos, Nikos. All of them comrades with whom he had ridden and fought.

A breeze chilled his back and the sun which should have been visible in the east was obscured by a massing of dark clouds. A strip of lightning tore the overcast and thunder rumbled in the distance. The horses snorted and quickened their steps in an effort to bunch together.

By early afternoon, the masses of dark clouds pursuing them closely, they reached the Kifisos River and the bridge where they would make their stand, a stone structure built by Venetians centuries before. The water surged and eddied around the pillars of the base and then rapidly billowed on. Although it was not yet swollen to the full spring crest, as Makrydis had told him, the river was impossible for man or horse to cross. The palikars led their horses to drink at the water's edge, staring across the river toward the rocky slopes where Pehlevan Pasha would descend.

The horses were harnessed into teams of six and eight and the palikars used them to haul boulders toward the ramp of the bridge. After several hours of intense labor, they built a wall of stone, providing a dozen crevices for the muzzles of their muskets. They left an opening in the center only large enough for a single man and horse to enter or leave at a time. As the horses were driven back to be picketed in a grove and the men sat to eat a light ration of brown bread and cheese, the sky grew so dark it merged with the blackness of the rushing water.

"Ghiouris." Vorogrivas sat staring across the river at the slopes. "If we place about twenty men across the way, securing them behind boulders, we can delay them on that side for a while."

"Right, Captain!" Ghiouris said. "You'll need men over there who can race like goats from rock to rock, shooting on the jump."

"Let me fight over there!" Lascarina said harshly, her coal-black eyes glowering under the visor of her cap. "Give me a chance to kill one of the first bastards in sight."

"We need you at the barricade," Vorogrivas said.

"Let me take a group over there, Captain," Manolis said eagerly. "We'll fly around and sting them like wasps."

Staring at the young man's cherished face, Vorogrivas felt a quiver of fear.

"Ghiouris and I will take charge over there," he said brusquely. "We have done it before. Remember, Ghiouris, the pass at Vantidos?"

"Right, Captain!" Ghiouris chuckled. "We made them think thirty palikars were an army!"

For a moment it seemed Manolis would press him to be taken along and then the youth turned away.

As they gathered muskets and ammunition to carry across the bridge, lightning ripped the sky directly above them, thunder exploding and then re-echoing from the cliffs and passes across the river. Some of the men looked up fearfully and made their cross.

"What are you quaking for?" Vorogrivas cried. "The heavens are sending us a good omen! The god of war waits here with us for the Turks!"

The men broke into smiles, slapping one another on the

shoulders and backs. A few drew their swords and by wild gyrations and acrobatic leaps demonstrated the way they would terrorize the enemy with their ferocity and skill.

"God help me having to fight beside you squeaks!" Lascarina cried scornfully. "You battle like children full of boasts and air!"

As the men shouted her down, Vorogrivas thought, yes, there was something childlike and innocent about them. Despite being stalwart warriors, they entered battle as if it were some artless game. Staring at the fallen form of one of their comrades, mourning his death, they were unable to accept the possibility of their own deaths. As if each of the palikars, to the instant a bullet took his life, believed that he alone of all the band was immortal.

By the time Vorogrivas, Ghiouris and a score of palikars had crossed the bridge and hidden among the boulders on the other side, rain fell from the burdened clouds, deluging the river which consumed the downpour. Raising his head to peer at the vault of the sky, Vorogrivas felt the rain pelt his cheeks, running into the corners of his mouth, a fresh, chill trickle of water down the dry channel of his throat.

From an area of the slope hidden from sight, came the rattle of muskets, followed by triumphant shouts. Kapsakis appeared, his long, lean body balanced on the edge of a rock.

"Turkish scouts!" he called. "Both are dead!"

First blood has been drawn, Vorogrivas thought. They will know we are here but will not be sure how many they have to overcome.

They waited again. The sky cleared slightly, a few dark-blue streamers appearing among the blacker hues. A trace of sun flashed through a narrow crevice in the haze, disappearing quickly as if in haste to flee. As the thunder moved on and the wind died down, over the cascade of the river, they heard the shrill, agitated cries of birds.

Then, as if he had burst from the earth, a solitary horseman appeared along the crest of the slope, his figure silhouetted clearly against the sky. He reined his horse and stared
over the terrain of rocks and boulders running down to the
bridge.

Vorogrivas knew the man was an officer or chieftain.
Jewels glittered in his turban, a golden scabbard dangled at
his waist. He held himself arrogantly in the saddle, disdainful of concealment. His horse, scenting danger, whinnied
nervously, but the Turk scorned cover or retreat. Admiring
the man's boldness, feeling a twinge of regret because a
brave man, even one who was an enemy, had to die,
Vorogrivas raised his musket and took aim along the rock.

The Turk seemed to notice the barricade on the opposite
side of the bridge for the first time. He twisted eagerly in his
saddle, one hand on the pommel, the other arm raised in an
imperious signal to others not yet visible behind him. An instant later the first Turkish troops appeared, dark-cowled
men crouching low as they scurried over the ridge, muskets
ready in their hands. As the mounted Turk spurred his horse
to descend the slope, Vorogrivas fired, the shot booming
across the air.

The Turk seemed to lunge from his saddle, hung
crookedly as if about to fall, but by some feat of spirit held
fiercely to his mount. Until the horse, feeling a dead man on
his back, reared up with a wild snort of terror and plummeted the Turk to the ground.

From the cover of boulders, the palikars began firing in a
furious volley. Vorogrivas reloaded, aimed and fired again.
The Turks milled about confused, shouting vainly, then
turned and fled across the ridge. In the space of a few moments the slope was littered with wounded and dead. At the
barricade across the bridge, the palikars raised their voices
in a lusty cheer.

For the balance of that day, the battle raged on the slope,
groups of Turks charging the men hidden behind the boul-

ders, shrieking and waving their pistols and swords. One by one they located the palikars and by the weight of numbers overwhelmed them. Some died under the onslaught of Turkish swords, others darted to new positions behind other boulders. The Epirote, Stathis, racing gleefully from one rock to another, was struck by a Turkish shot, his body spinning weirdly in the air before sprawling on the ground.

As the Turks encircled rock after rock, the remaining palikars were driven down the slope. A bearded trooper appeared before Vorogrivas, firing at him almost point-blank. The bullet came so close the powder scorched his temple, burning his eye. In pain and fury he slashed at the bearded face, a savage blow that split the man's skull, a shattering of brains and bones.

Turning away, Vorogrivas saw the red-haired Kapsakis staggering about blindly, bellowing as he pawed at his bloody face. A volley of shots felled him, rolling his body over and over down the slope, his booted heels kicking a scatter of pebbles and earth in his wake.

The battle swirled from rock to rock, confused and disordered, men leaping, screaming, shooting and slashing. Racing to another rock Vorogrivas found a Turkish trooper there before him. Driving at the man with his sword, the blade entered at the chest, grating against bone. As he tugged it free, the man choked, seemed to shrivel, his dying face gray as ash.

At twilight, the handful of palikars who survived, led by Vorogrivas and Ghiouris, snatched up whatever wounded comrades they could carry and raced across the bridge. As they stumbled through the opening in the barricade, friends embraced them with hoarse and exultant shouts, taking the wounded and carrying them to a small grove.

Vorogrivas, his eye burning and swollen, sat exhausted against a tree. Manolis knelt beside him and gently bathed his face. Another palikar brought him tea sweetened with honey.

"Ghiouris!" he called harshly. "Ghiouris!"

The bulky figure of his lieutenant appeared in a haze before him. Vorogrivas shook his head to clear the mist from his vision.

"Here, Captain!" Ghiouris loomed above him. "Battered to hell but still alive!"

"How many palikars were lost?"

Ghiouris was silent for a moment.

"Maybe ten, Captain, counting the two wounded men we couldn't save." He shook his head grimly. "The poor devils would be better dead."

"All those good men . . ." Vorogrivas whispered. And the loss of each comrade added a scar to his heart.

In the darkness of that terrible night, the Turks carried the two wounded palikars to the water's edge. Over the sound of the river, the men of the band could hear them calling farewell, crying a last prayer to God. When the Turks began torturing them, their cries became screams.

"Butchers!" Ghiouris shook his fist wrathfully at the other shore. "Bloody butchers!"

After the screams were finally silenced, another agony was joined to the darkness. Roused by the scent of blood, wolves came down from the mountain, foraging in the dark for the corpses. As they set upon a body, the pack loosed a brutal and hideous howling.

When the first bleak daylight unfolded across the river and the slopes, the shadowed outlines of a dozen lances with shrouded crowns were silhouetted on the opposite ridge against the sky. As the dawn grew lighter, the crowns became visible as the severed heads of the palikars who had fallen in battle, raw, shattered skulls and drained, sightless eyes, hanging like blighted fruit from the Turkish lances.

The men of the band wailed in grief for their comrades,

raised their muskets and swords in vows of hate and vengeance, hungry for the battle to begin again.

All that day the Turks assaulted the bridge, charging
across in a dense horde, boots clattering on the stones,
shouting and waving pistols and swords. When men in the
front ranks tumbled under the shots of the palikars, the soldiers behind climbed over their bodies. As they reached the
barricade, the palikars clambered over the rocks to meet
them. At close quarters they hacked and chopped, the bodies of the dead rising in piles, blood forming puddles that
drained off the bridge into the churning water. When there
was no longer room to fight, a hasty truce prevailed as the
wounded and dead were carried away. Then the Turks
stormed the barricade once more, were driven back again,
yet each time leaving a few more dead palikars.

"How many are there?" one of the palikars cried shrilly.
"In God's name, how many?"

"Kill, don't count!" Lascarina cried savagely.

Vorogrivas fought until his musket and sword weighed
like anvils in his hands. In momentary lulls, he became confused what battle they were fighting. There was no way to
separate the stench of powder and blood, the carnage and
the screams, from so many battles he had fought before.

The row of wounded men carried from the bridge and
laid within the grove of trees, grew longer. Some bit on the
handles of their knives to stifle their shrieks of pain. In an
effort to help them, a few palikars mixed earth with powder,
chewed it into a sticky pulp and caked it over the raw,
bleeding wounds. Sometimes the wounded died and then a
few palikars dug desperately to excavate a grave under the
shadow of a large rock, hoping to secure the bodies from the
Turks.

After one of the assaults that had been repulsed, the
Turks retreated off the bridge to regroup. One of their
wounded crawled weakly after them on his hands and

knees. Several of the palikars fired at him from the barricade but he floundered on. Suddenly, slipping through the opening in the barricade, Lascarina sprinted toward the crawling soldier. Seeing her racing along the bridge, a group of Turks on the slope started quickly back to meet her.

"The bitch is crazy!" Ghiouris cried. He ran through the opening and a few palikars leaped to follow him.

Lascarina reached the wounded man. As if she were on a horse, she straddled his back, one hand clutching his hair to jerk back his head, the other hand raising her knife. With a swift, whipping motion, she cut his throat.

As she jumped off his body to start back, the Turks fell on her in fury. Still a distance away, Ghiouris shouted and the fleeter palikars raced past him in a furious sprint to aid her.

Under the Turkish assault, Lascarina was battered to her knees. A pair of Turks held her arms extended while a third raised his curved yataghan and slashed down across her breasts. She bellowed in rage and pain and he slashed her again across the belly. Then, as the palikars approached, the Turks fled.

On her knees, Lascarina moaned and swayed, her hands pawing feebly at her breasts and belly in a futile effort to press back the crimson coils of intestines that bubbled from her wounds. The palikars stood back in revulsion and fear.

When Ghiouris reached them, gasping for breath, he raised his pistol quickly and shot her in the heart. A final screech burst from her lips as her great, strong body pitched forward on the stone. Ghiouris shouted at the men to pick her up and when they did not move, he shoved them forward. Holding her clumsily by the arms and legs, they stumbled back to the barricade with her body, the bloody entrails dangling and dragging at their feet.

By afternoon of the second day after the battle began, only a score of the band remained and a half-dozen of those men were wounded. The powder and shot for their muskets and pistols had run out and their only defense was their swords.

Vorogrivas had a poultice in a patch over his injured eye and Ghiouris had his gashed left arm in a makeshift sling. The remaining men had assorted injuries, many of them bearing rags to stem the flow of blood. Only Manolis, as if his body bore some mysterious, impregnable power, remained unhurt.

With the Turks preparing for their final charge, an eerie silence settled over the earth. Even the rushing river seemed quieter, the cascade diminished to a sound like a horde of hissing snakes. The sun curved to the west trailing a scarlet streamer through the sky, sinking toward the twilight that hung like wedges of gray, plowed soil at the horizon.

The ragged remnants of the band that included the wounded who might still fight, waited in silence. Those few who might have wished to flee to save their lives did not speak of flight.

"Hey, Alexis," a palikar called to one of the wounded men struggling to rise to his knees. "What the hell can you do on your knees? Do you think the Turks will squat to oblige you?"

"I fight better on my knees than you do standing!" Alexis cried. "Come here and I'll show you!"

"You're both oafs," Ghiouris grumbled. "Kneeling or standing, it's a shame men like you are all we have left."

"Listen to the hero!" the palikar sneered. "I saw you running across the bridge when we tried to save poor Lascarina. You started twenty jumps ahead of me and I passed you like your ass was dragging a cart of stones!"

"That's right!" Alexis cried. "Ghiouris has to fight to the end of every battle because he couldn't outrun a one-legged Turk!"

Ghiouris glared at him and then couldn't restrain a sheepish smile at the accuracy of the barb. He began chuckling and the others joined in a hoarse mirth that rumbled into gales of laughter, made wilder because it was senseless, easing their tension, relieving their fear.

Hearing Manolis laughing with them, Vorogrivas felt his spirit lightened. He had contrived to save the young man's life by asking him to carry a message back to Kravasaras that their resistance was near the end. But the silent reproach in Manolis' face shamed Vorogrivas into rescinding the order. Manolis had fought as valiantly as any of them and had a right to remain with the band. They would fight and die together, perhaps the way it had been destined from that first instant when Manolis came to the camp, young and comely, long months and many battles ago. In gratefulness for their companionship, for the joy he had felt in the presence of the youth, Vorogrivas had retained a single ball in the pistol stuck in his belt. Before he'd let the young man be captured alive by the Turks, he'd send a shot into his heart.

The sun sank lower in the sky. From the camp hidden behind the ridge, they could hear the chanting of the muezzin at prayers. Afterward, over the sound of the river, they heard the exhortations of a dervish whipping the Turks into a religious frenzy. There was a massed roar of voices like the thunder before a storm and then the Turks appeared, hundreds of men advancing down the slope, chanting and shrieking, waving their muskets and yataghans, moving toward the bridge. In the midst of them, astride a great white horse adorned with jewelry and plumes, escorted by a dozen horsemen carrying the pennants and lances of his royal guard, rode Pehlevan Pasha.

"Our first sight of that bastard!" Ghiouris spit toward the river. "He's coming now for the kill."

They carried the wounded palikars to the barricade, propped them with their backs against boulders, placed swords in their hands. The standing men took up their positions.

The first troop of Turks stamped onto the bridge, the chanting and shrieking growing in volume until it muffled the rushing stridence of the river. Behind their barricade the palikars murmured prayers and farewells to one another.

Manolis extended his hand to Vorogrivas. As they clasped fingers, that spare touching of flesh binding their bodies and hearts so they would enter the world beyond as a single soul, both men smiled.

Suddenly there was a faltering among the ranks of Turks descending the slopes. Men paused to stare uncertainly over the pillars of the bridge. On their flanks officers with raised swords cried harshly for them to go on. Gesturing uneasily, a number of the men on higher ground pointed to something in the distance. Catching their unrest, the men already on the bridge shuffled to a halt. The royal guard closed ranks around the mounted figure of Pehlevan Pasha.

Vorogrivas swung up on the barricade and stared across the open plain behind them, for a fleeting, hopeful moment thinking it might be the force of Diakos. He saw only a solitary horseman spurring his mount toward them.

On the slopes the officers shouted once more at their men to move. Pehlevan Pasha pressed his mount impatiently against the horses of his guard. The ranks advanced a few burdened steps forward. The single horseman galloped closer.

When Vorogrivas saw the stunning white mane of hair on the rider's head flowing in the wind, the sun glinting on his armored breastplate, across his armored knee plates, turning man and horse into a whirlwind of racing flame, he loosed an incredulous cry.

"Boukouvalas!"

The palikars stared up at him in disbelief.

"Boukouvalas!" Vorogrivas shouted down at them. "Boukouvalas!"

The first rank of Turks beyond the barricade heard the name, whispered it hoarsely to the men behind them, until it rose in volume, leaping loudly from mouth to mouth. When a score of men cried the name to Pehlevan Pasha, he rose like a startled bird in his saddle, staring wildly over the heads of his men.

Almost at the bridge, the flying hooves seeming not to touch the ground, horse and rider swelled in size until they were the height and breadth of Titans. When Boukouvalas drew his sword, the jeweled sword with which he had slain Kafta Aga, the sun flashing and sparkling on the blade seemed to extend the tip to some summit in the sky.

The unsheathing of that sword in a demented charge against an army must have confirmed to Pehlevan Pasha that the horseman was not human but the legendary giant returned from the dead. With a shriek of terror, the Mussulman chieftain twisted his horse, frantic to flee. The royal guards cut a swath through the men packed around him and he spurred madly through their ranks. As he charged wildly up the slope, all about him men, catching his hysteria, threw down their weapons and raced to follow his retreat.

As the foam-flecked horse of Boukouvalas, sweat streaming from his flanks, reached the palikars, Vorogrivas caught a glimpse of the old captain's face glowing with a searing and unearthly force. Without breaking a stride, he rode onto the bridge, prodding the horse in a powerful lunge through the opening in the barricade.

Seeing the horse with the armored giant crossing the bridge in attack against them, fueled the terror of the retreating Turks and with cries of despair they clawed and stumbled up the slopes. Leading their scrambling rout, the white horse of Pehlevan Pasha, tail and mane flying, disappeared over the ridge.

Reaching the end of the bridge, the old klepht and his horse leaped up the stony slope, making for the peak in a furious, impossible ascent. Then the bay stumbled, legs crumpling beneath him, tumbling backwards in a screaming landslide of stones. The great armored giant, torn from the braces and harness that bound him to the saddle, was hurled like a catapult from its back.

When Vorogrivas and the others had crossed the bridge and gathered around his fallen body, they found the old warrior dead. The white mane of his hair spread like a mantle across the earth, his face of leather and bark strangely serene, the last rays of the sun glinting crimson homage on his majestic head.

The vanguard of Diakos found them there a short while later, keeping a silent, twilight vigil about the fallen body of Boukouvalas, kneeling as if they were mourning.

Yet, awed and mute as they were, Vorogrivas knew they were not mourners. They were witnesses to one more extraordinary event added to the legends of their past, another marvel that would be exalted and recounted for as long as generations lived on and drew faith from their sacred and haunted land.

CHAPTER
NINE

Xanthos, the teacher from the Ionian island of Zante, had traveled to the Mani with Kolokotronis in January of 1821, as scribe and adjutant to the famous chieftain. His avowed purpose, however, was to write a history of the impending revolution with a reverence for truth that would bequeath an accurate chronicle for future generations. He felt himself qualified for this grand task by his extensive readings in Homer, Herodotus, Thucydides and Xenophon, as well as the lesser historians. He believed there was a pattern in the web unrolled from the loom of time and a knowledge of the past was an invaluable prerequisite for understanding the impending conflict.

Unfortunately, others did not appreciate his sense of mission. From the beginning, in the harsh, bleak world of the Mani, a landscape of boulders, stones, ruined towers and the ugly, prickly ilex, so unlike the lush, verdant foliage of his native island, he was an outcast. In a society that measured a man by his capacity to shoot a gun or wield a yataghan, skill with pen and words was a useless art, levels below a woman's weaving. At least her warp and weft might produce a garment to be worn against the chill of the wind.

Among the rough and superstitious Maniats, he was

treated with a barely veiled contempt. Yet, though they sneered at him, nobody had actually harmed him, mostly, he supposed, because Kolokotronis was his patron. God forbid, even that might not be enough to save him if they discovered he also wrote some poetry.

Ancient Laconia had been a military state, hard and punitive in laws and rituals of conduct, but Herodotus and Thucydides recorded many instances of the nobility of its citizens. The Maniats, claiming descent from those Spartans, seemed more a tribe of barbarians, their dialect grating in the "bar-bar-bar" of some strange, guttural tongue. And despite the fancy clothing and affected courtesies of Prince Petrobey Mavromichalis and the other Maniat chieftains (at least those few who even bothered), their thin crust of restraint crumpled quickly. Then, in wild flarings of temper they shouted, argued, threatened, overwhelming less by appeals to reason than by the menace of force and fear. Searching for links between them and Greeks of the classical past was snatching at flecks of gold that turned out to be coarse grains of gravel.

Even the children seemed tainted by the virulent world of their elders. During his first week in the Mani, Xanthos had witnessed small boys tormenting live rock pigeons they had snared, stretching the birds' beaks open until they broke, squeezing the tiny, downy heads between their fingers until they had crushed them. Perhaps their cruelty was due as much to ignorance as to the brooding obsession with violence, since there was not a single school in the Mani at that time and only a small number of the adults could read and write.

Xanthos had suggested to Prince Petrobey that since his vocation on Zante had been that of teacher, he might undertake to set up some kind of elementary school for the children.

"There is no time for that now," Petrobey answered him brusquely. "Freedom comes before letters."

Xanthos knew they supposed, as an Ionian Greek, he was unable to understand the mesmerizing lure the mountains of the Peloponnesus held for Kolokotronis, or the way in which the Maniats acquired energy and purpose from their stone-littered and desolate terrain. Worse still was that his knowledge of war came from books rather than actual combat. "Asking a capon to assess a rooster's work," was the scathing way he had heard one of the Maniats describe him.

Yet, despite lacking first-hand experience of fighting, he had read comprehensively of war. How could anyone study the pages of fearful, bloody battles between Achaeans and Trojans that Homer described in the *Iliad*, explicit recountings of dreadful combat beneath the Trojan battlements and at the black ships, without coming to understand the terrible nature of war?

He did have one good and precious friend in the Mani, the Princess Katerina Mavromichalis, wife of Petrobey and mother of his great brood of children. Xanthos had come to know and greatly admire the remarkable woman with the stately bearing and consummate dignity of some authentic, royal line. In the few hours they managed from time to time to spend together, she enjoyed having him read poetry to her. These were moments he treasured as well.

O my dove, that art in the clefts of the rock, in the secret places of the stairs, let me see thy countenance, let me hear thy voice; for sweet is thy voice, and thy countenance is comely.

Take us the foxes, the little foxes, that spoil the vines: for our vines have tender grapes.

My beloved is mine, and I am his: he feedeth among the lilies.

Until the day break and the shadows flee away, turn, my beloved, and be thou like a roe or a young hart upon the mountains of Bether.

In those moments, seeing her face softened by a tremulous smile as if she were being drawn back by a remembrance of love, he marveled how beautiful she was. With nostalgia of his own awakened, he thought of the last weeks on Zante before leaving for the Mani, the young student Chryseis, a girl less than half his age with pale, reddish hair that shimmered like the mane of a pony, leading him into her bed as if she were a woman of maturity and he a green-dim youth. In the nights they spent together, his flaccid body and somber demeanor were made fruitful and joyous by her loveliness and grace.

"You have stopped reading, teacher."

"I am sorry, Princess." The sovereign dream dissolved swiftly. "Some thoughts of my island . . ."

His voice trailed away, his embarrassment evident. Yet in her knowing, compassionate glance, he had the feeling she reassured him and approved his secret delight.

Yet, if her response to love was tender and pliant, her feelings about men and war were stern and unsparing. Once, reading her some lines from Tyrtaeus, the martial poet of Sparta, part of a verse that went:

> The youth's fairest form is fairest when he dies.
> In death the boy is beautiful
> Because he perished on the battlefield . . .

he was interrupted by the princess raising her hand in a gesture of denunciation.

"No more of that nonsense, teacher, please!" she said in agitation. "Only a man and a fool could have written lines like that! Any woman, wife or mother, knows better."

"It is simply a poem of war," Xanthos said.

"A poem by an idiot for idiots," she said. "How can the wrenching of life from the body of a young man make him fair and beautiful?"

"Perhaps the poem is hyperbolic, Princess," Xanthos said. "I suggest the poet means a spiritual ennoblement. After all, war produces the valor of a Miltiades at Marathon and of a Leonidas at Thermopylae."

"War produces widows and orphans!" she said, and bitterness honed a raw edge to her voice. "War mocks God's commandment, violates women, aborts the sons they nourished to life, kills the innocent without mercy! War is man's ancient, ritual justification for murder!"

If, at times like these in the company of the princess, Xanthos found himself an apologist for conflict, he did not believe war justified ideals and honor being abandoned. A society enslaved for hundreds of years might not be able to produce a Miltiades or Leonidas, but the captains who had gathered in the Mani should aspire to the stature of those great men.

Another great Greek leader might rise from the ranks. Perhaps the Bey of the Mani himself, a regal, handsome man, vibrantly asserting authority. Yet he was impeded by vanity, a Maniat's temper, and a dislike of having his orders challenged. His brother, Kyriakulis and his eldest son, Elias, hardy and judicious warriors who would cause havoc among the Turks, were, somehow, followers rather than leaders. There was Niketaras, the nephew of Kolokotronis who had come with him from exile, a dark, sardonic man, clever and courageous, but lacking the magnetism to inspire others. There was the monk (if that were indeed his mission) Papalikos, from some shadowy region north of the Gulf of Corinth, a strange, brooding creature whose counsel always climaxed about the orgiastic joy of killing. Even some of the bloody-spirited Maniats found the monk too murderous for their tastes.

Of all the chiefs, Xanthos felt the most potential for greatness lay with Kolokotronis. Perhaps not as sophisticated in political administration as the prince, not as instinctive a fighter as Niketaras, he had a rudimentary force and wisdom. In addition to his ability to cleave decisively to the heart of an argument, he also understood the dimensions of the struggle beyond the scope of their own theater of action.

In a meeting of the central council where the captains had bickered for hours, debating methods and resolutions, feeling they had fallen to captious carping, Kolokotronis rose and struck the scabbard of his yataghan on the table, banging for silence. The captains succumbed reluctantly, frowning and muttering even as Kolokotronis began to speak.

"Nowhere on earth," Kolokotronis said gravely, "and at no other time in history has the issue between wrong and right, darkness and light, tyranny and freedom, been placed before the world more clearly than now, when we are about to rise up against our oppressors."

He stared from one captain to another, challenging them to quell their mutterings before he continued.

"Anyone but a Greek would consider our struggle hopeless. Not only do we have the Sultan's Empire against us but, fearful of revolution, the cabinets of Europe are opposed to aiding us. They maintain the divine right of kings but, to my judgment, the revolutions in France and in the distant land of America, ended that fallacy. People once thought that kings were gods upon the earth but those revolutions proved kings can be tumbled and deposed."

"Kolokotronis, we understand that," Petrobey began. "The problem we are discussing . . ."

"Forgive me, Prince Petrobey," Kolokotronis said brusquely. "Let me finish, if you please, and then we can start arguing again. For arguing, the saints help us, is in our nature. It has been truly said of us that where we are twelve soldiers, there we have thirteen captains. But I tell you now what cannot be disputed! We have all been baptized once with holy ointment; we shall be baptized again in blood for the freedom of our country! Let us argue if we must, but let us not forget that God has pledged his word for the liberty of Greece. If we do not falter or lose sight of the goal, He will lead us to the sweet embrace of freedom!"

In February, with the auguries suggesting the war was only a matter of weeks away, an English merchant ship landed at Tsimova and several ship's officers Kolokotronis had known when he was in the service of England on Zante, came ashore. A splendid dinner was arranged for them and afterwards, the air swirling wine-fumes and smoke, the captain, a ruddy Yorkshireman, urged upon Kolokotronis the course of convincing the other Greek captains to draft an appeal to the English Government so that, through England's mediation with the Turks, Greece might be constituted a principality, vassal to the Sultan.

"The Sultan knows war is threatening," the Englishman said. "For that reason perhaps more can be achieved by negotiation now, my dear fellow, than by fighting."

Kolokotronis did not answer for a moment. Xanthos watched the light of the candles flickering on his cheeks, his flesh glinting like the burnished bronze of armor.

"If I suggested such a course to the other captains now, my friend," Kolokotronis said quietly, "they might skewer me. I would not blame them. You see, Greece has never recognized the suzerainty of the Sultan."

The English captain looked puzzled.

"The Turk came upon us as a rapacious marauder," Kolokotronis said. "He put to death some of our people and made slaves of others, but when our King in Constantinople fell in battle, he made no treaty with the Turks but left a bequest bidding his people carry on the war. His garrison has never given up and his fortresses have never capitulated."

"Begging your pardon," the English captain said. "I don't understand . . . what are these fortresses and garrison you speak of?"

"The garrison of our country are the bands of klephts in the mountains," Kolokotronis said, and his eyes struck sparks.

"They have always been free! As for the fortresses that have never surrendered, they are the bastions of Mani and Suli!"

Yes, a complex, extraordinary man, Xanthos thought, and by candlelight each evening, he sought to record the leader's words, and the events of the day which he directed or shared. For if words and actions were not faithfully reproduced, they might appear to those who had not lived through them the play of chance and not the product of a leader's wisdom. Xanthos believed speech and action could form a kind of literature and there must have lived many a noble man before Agamemnon and Achilles who, having chanced no chronicler, remained forever forgotten, unpraised and unmourned.

Meanwhile, the flexions of spring heated the sun, sending warming rays across the stern rocks and the forbidding sea, heating the heather, thyme and sage so they filled the air with moist, heady scents. Suckled by the warmth, patches of red and yellow flowers opened in the spines of bushes. Growing stronger each day, the sun drove down across the cypresses and poplars, spilt into the groves of stunted, dwarfish olive trees that were all the poor, stony land could sustain.

In that month of March, the Maniats reinforced their camps which lay concealed on the opposite side of their mountain, Taygetus, from the plain of Kalamata. Into the camps each day, mules arrived bringing the grindings of powder from the mills in Kalyvia and Tsimova. The powder was stored in big panniers, covered over with charcoal or some country produce, taken off carefully and carried by men into the magazine.

The strategy of the chieftaians was to march down from Taygetus onto the Turkish city of Kalamata. The citadel of that capital of Messenia stood on rising ground about a mile from the harbor, but it was small, had only a single well and could not store water for a long siege. The Greeks would take possession swiftly of the lower, undefended town and blockade the citadel from that side. Other troops would cut off the harbor from the town and a select detachment of their best fighters would assault the citadel.

Men poured into the camps each day, drawn from Laconia, Argolis and the south of Arcadia, the number risen to almost five thousand by the middle of March. As the time for the assault came closer, scouts and sentries were posted along the passes from Kalamata into Sparta to prevent word being carried to Tripolitza of the preparations.

Xanthos moved with Kolokotronis and Niketaras from Tsimova to the main camp, riding in a troop of men bristling like porcupines with long-barreled guns, scimitars, yataghans and pistols embossed with silver. As they clattered through small villages, cats and mangy dogs scurried to take refuge.

The entries of Xanthos in his journal grew more terse as the movement toward war quickened. He had an unceasing series of duties to perform, dispatches to be sent, problems of supply to be handled. Their activities had to be carefully circumscribed to prevent fighting breaking out before they were fully prepared to move.

March 27, 1821

Today a courier brought word that the voivode of Kalamata, learning that bands of armed Greeks have assembled on the flanks of the mountains towards Messenia, has called together the wealthier Turkish residents, resolving to lead a cordon of them to Tripolitza. They plan to leave secretly by night, save themselves and alert the capital city to send troops to their aid. Papalikos and Niketaras have been sent to intercept them.

March 30, 1821

It has begun! The troops under Niketaras and Papalikos ambushed the Turkish column fleeing Kalamata, dispersed the Moslem guard protecting the nobles and killed several of them including Murad, one of the most influential Turks of the city. I think we will move on Kalamata now! A fever of excitement has spread across the camp!

April 3, 1821

Today marked the fall of the city! All our projections of fierce and prolonged fighting were in error. When the army of more than three thousand men led by Petrobey and Kolokotronis crossed the ranges of the Taygetus and surged down upon Kalamata, men, women and children, some still half-clad as they were awakened from their morning sleep, ran back and forth in panic and terror. Some sought to find refuge in the citadel and others fled to the harbor seeking escape by boat. The Greek army made its way up the narrow streets towards the citadel which surrendered almost without a shot needing to be fired! Solemn assurance has been given by the captains to the authorities in Kalamata that Turkish lives will be spared. Somehow, seeing the vengeful, merciless faces of the Maniats, I do not know how much value can be placed in the promises.

April 5, 1821

A sacred, memorable day, which I am thrilled to record! All the army, Maniats and their allies, sang their first thanks to God for their victory by the banks of the torrent that flows by the city. Twenty-four priests officiated and thousands of armed men stood round. The solemn service was celebrated with great fervor, hearts seeming to overflow with sincere devotion to heaven, with warm gratitude to Church and God. I witnessed patriotic tears pouring down the cheeks of gruff, uncouth warriors, and strong giants sobbing like children. Petrobey and Kolokotronis both wept and embraced one another, and all the captains (even Papalikos!) pledged unity and devotion to the cause.

April 9, 1821

The brief, euphoric respite of good feeling is over. The council of captains has once more become a cauldron of anger and shouting. Today Papalikos and Mourtzinos nearly drew swords against one another and if they were not held apart, blood would have flowed. The monk has taken a few of his scurrilous followers and has left Kalamata. I am glad to see him go but other serious divisions remain. Petrobey wishes to keep the army camped on the slopes of Taygetus, train and organize the new men, establish a civil administration capable of ruling and conducting order, and only then march north. Kolokotronis, wild with joy at the news of the invasion of the Danubian provinces and the fall of Kalavryta, endorses a strategy of taking the field at once. With two armies, one driving the Turks southward, the other northward, they would unite before the fortress of Tripolitza. Kolokotronis made an impassioned plea, swearing that while soldiers fought, he could not abide sitting in meetings drafting documents and epistles. Men listen and respect him but obey the will of Petrobey, who rules in the Mani.

April 11, 1821

Petrobey Mavromichalis has been appointed Commander-in-Chief of the first Greek army in the field and with a few archons and primates of the region has formed the Senate of Messenia. He has asked me to help him draft a proclamation to the powers of Europe.

I have asked Kolokotronis and he has agreed to allow me to aid the Prince.

April 14, 1821

After three days of endless argument, shouts and absurd phrases, it is finished and I am exhausted. It has been titled *Manifesto Addressed to Europe by Petros Mavromichalis, Commander-in-Chief of the Spartan Troops and the Messenian Senate, Sitting in Kalamata:*

The insupportable yoke of Ottoman tyranny hath weighed down for centuries the unhappy Greeks of Peloponnesus. So excessive has its rigor become, that its fainting victims had scarcely strength enough left to utter groans. In this state, deprived of all our rights, we have unanimously resolved to take up arms against our tyrants. All our intestine discord is plunged into oblivion as a fruit of oppression, and we breath the air of liberty. Our hands having burst their fetters, already signalize themselves against the barbarians. We no longer run about day and night to execute corvées imposed by a merciless taskmaster. Our mouths are opened; heretofore silent, or employed only in addressing useless supplications to our tormentors, they now celebrate a deliverance which we have sworn to accomplish or else to perish. We invoke therefore the aid of all the civilized nations of Europe, that we may the more promptly attain to the goal of a just and sacred enterprise, reconquer our rights, and regenerate our unfortunate people.

Greece, our mother, was the lamp that illuminated you! On this ground, she reckons on your active philanthropy. Arms, money and counsel are what she expects from you. We promise you her lively gratitude, which she will prove by deeds in more prosperous times.

(Signed) PETROS MAVROMICHALIS

Given at the headquarters
of Kalamata:

March 28
_____ 1821

April 12

Within a day after the issuance of the proclamation,
Kolokotronis told Xanthos to prepare for their departure.
Kalamata was taken, whatever small Turkish villages still
remained on the hillsides would soon be overrun. The serious fighting in Messenia was over. But to the north, in Arcadia, there were fortified Turkish towns which would have
to be subdued or rendered powerless to send help to
Tripolitza, when that principal bastion was finally assaulted.
Among these strongholds was Karitena, an entrenched town
situated on a precipitous hill above the gorge of the
Alpheus.

That was to be their target. With an army of volunteers
assembled from villages they marched through on their way
north, Kolokotronis would attack Karitena. The strategy
made sense, Xanthos thought, yet perhaps Kolokotronis
might also be anxious to leave Kalamata because he chafed
at the way in which Petrobey dominated events in Messenia.

The leave-taking was warm and amiable, all dissension
between the chieftains forgotten in the enthusiasm of departure. Petrobey wished them Godspeed and promised he
would join them with a Maniat army at the gates of
Tripolitza. In those last moments they also bade farewell to
the Princess Katerina Mavromichalis. As Xanthos bowed before her, he carried a fleeting glimpse of the mournful, enigmatic quality of her eyes.

"Good-bye, Princess," Xanthos said.

"Good-bye, teacher," Katerina said gravely. "Thank you for all the good hours we have shared together. Good luck in your task. And where you can, remind others of God's reward for gentleness and mercy."

"A hard thing in time of war."

"A hard thing for men anytime," she said quietly.

As she turned away, he noticed a slight swelling of her abdomen beneath the gown she wore. Strange, he thought, she had borne more than a dozen children and was no longer young, yet in that moment she appeared once again to be carrying a child.

Kolokotronis, Niketaras, Xanthos and about a dozen Maniats who had received permission from Petrobey to join the force, started out leading their horses where the mountain was sheer and steep, treading carefully between the sharp rocks and hazardous ravines. They had sent their baggage mules on ahead of them by a few hours. Above them the savage crags of Taygetus were still bound in snow, although lesser mountains had already succumbed to the lures of spring.

At twilight, camping in a village for the first night of their journey, Kolokotronis was greeted by the villagers with enthusiasm and fervor. As if he were a king returned from exile to lead them in their struggle, he was attended with reverence and devotion. Seated in the square of the village, he was brought the best food and drink they had in their larders, and women carried small children for him to sanctify by his touch.

"By God's grace, Captain, perhaps he will grow up to be as great a warrior as you."

"Mine too, Captain, put your hand on my Mihali!"

"Your blessing on my son, Captain."

"By the time they have grown to manhood," Kolokotronis said gravely, "our blessed land will be free. But, to achieve that liberation, I need their older brothers and fathers now."

Stirred by his eloquence and his presence, men flocked to his banner armed with whatever weapons they could muster, including sticks, hoes and scythes. Within the first few days of their march, compounding problems of movement and supply, the band had grown to almost a thousand men, stragglers spread across the countryside behind them for several miles. Still Kolokotronis was not satisfied.

"There were fifty able-bodied men in that last village," he told Niketaras in agitation. "Less than twenty have joined us. Why?"

"They have wives and families." Niketaras shrugged. "Fields and stock to tend. If others can be induced to do their fighting, why should they risk their lives?"

Kolokotronis pondered for a moment.

"Then I tell you what to do," he said slowly. "Pick out two or three of the most affluent farmers and property owners in the village and burn their houses. Burn them to the ground! Let word be spread that if a man of fighting age does not join us, his house will share the same fate!"

Seeing Xanthos watching him with a shocked expression, Kolokotronis smiled.

"You don't agree, teacher?"

"Forgive me, Captain," Xanthos said hesitantly. "It only seems . . . well, Xenophon has written that willing obedience is always superior to forced obedience."

"Xenophon is right, but I am right too," Kolokotronis said. "Imagine the fate of that village if Turks had passed instead of us. If a man has nothing to leave behind him, he departs more willingly. If he is bitter and a little angry over the way we have treated him, some of this anger may be unleashed against the Turks. You will see what I mean."

Perhaps he was right, Xanthos thought. Once in his command, men fell under the charisma of his presence. To watch him walk along the line of men, the plumed war helmet on his head, his aquiline visage radiating the strength of some warrior of old, was an inspiring sight. Men reached out to touch his arm, knowing his family had never accepted the domination of the Turks, that he had suffered and prepared himself in exile while lesser men bent their shackled heads. This legend of resistance, coupled with the victory at Kalamata, provided him an aura of invincibility and power. His voice, swing and color stiffened men's will and sparked their pulse. They sought to match his imperious walk, his frown and fulminating gaze.

Nor was the chieftain humbled by their devotion. "My army," Xanthos heard him call it proudly, almost as if it were a personal possession. He felt he had created it, drawn it together, would mold it into an extension of his arm and his vision. Toward that end, even as he supervised their training under the Maniat veterans who had come with him from the Mani, he tried constantly to make the men, who had rarely thought beyond their planting and herding, understand their role in the great drama being enacted.

"What we do does not belong to our small land alone." The chieftain spoke to several hundred men at a time, men sprawled or sitting in attentive silence about him. "When it is learned throughout the world that a handful of us moved against the might of the Sultan, it will cause the upheaval of nations and the overthrow of decaying dynasties. Do you understand? For generations to come, in countries across the world, where tyrants reign, men will remember what we are doing here and will strive to match our glory!"

More and more men came from villages and settlements to their camp. Rumors abounded that after the capture of Karitena, the army would march to overthrow Tripolitza, keep sweeping north until it had united with the army of Ipsilantis in the Danubian provinces, its ultimate goal to regain sacred Constantinople with the holy cathedral of Aghia Sophia.

From a thousand men the army grew to two thousand and then to three thousand. So much time was spent assimilating and training recruits, they slowed to a crawl. For hours every morning and afternoon, the Maniat veterans led by a burly campaigner named Balalas, a veteran of the fighting in Spain and Austria during the Napoleonic Wars, drove and prodded the men at their drills. Musket practice was finally discontinued because a score of men were injured by misdirected shots.

"Constantinople, is it!" Balalas chewed kernels of grain vigorously and spit out the husks. "This mob would have trouble subuding a Moslem sheepfold without stabbing or shooting one another in the confusion!"

Yet, for Xanthos, it became an inspiring experience, that massing of an army, something impossible to understand from books. Several thousand men in long marching columns, their voices raised in jubilant song that rolled in echoes from the canyons and defiles like the tumult of thunder. At twilight, the sound of goat-bells mingled with the clanging of muskets and swords, a teeming sibilance of voices in the gathering mist. And, at night, hundreds of campfires dotting the rocky slopes, the charred smell of sizzling entrails floating across the fire-flecked shadows. A family, Xanthos thought, more numerous than any clan he had ever known, secured by a bond stronger than blood, a common aim, a mutual goal. As he made the entries in his journal, he could not suppress his pride because he shared the grandeur of the experience.

Time and time again in those days of marching, the canny capacity of Kolokotronis to inspire confidence in his men was proven. Once, moving on his white horse beside a detachment of marching men, he heard some grumbling in the ranks. Pausing to assess the complaint, he listened to one of the men protesting.

"But there is an unfairness here! We are not on a level! You are riding on horseback while we are wearing ourselves out walking, carrying our weapons, as well!"

Without answering a word, Kolokotronis jumped down from his horse. He pushed the man who had complained, a long-faced farmer, from the ranks, took his weapons away from him and started forward on foot as fast as he could. With his own helmet and breastplate, it was arduous going, but he moved at a more rapid clip than anyone around him, urging those behind him to keep up with him, pressing those in front so he would not tread on their heels. After more than an hour, the other soldiers growing vexed at the relentless, driving pace the chieftain was setting, began cursing and throwing stones at the man who first complained. The man pleaded with Kolokotronis to give him back his weapons and his place and allow him to march in the ranks once more.

On the afternoon of the fifth day after leaving Kalamata, they arrived in Megalopolis, the ancient town in the center of the Arcadian plain, the peaks of Karitena visible in the distance. They found Megalopolis in the hands of insurgent Greeks who were in the midst of bitter wrangling over the division of the spoils they had taken from the Turks. A score of them crowded around Kolokotronis, crying and shouting their grievances.

"I fought twice as bravely as that pig Vafides!" one man cried wrathfully. "I deserve a larger share!"

"Your grandfather and father were liars! So are you!"

"I killed more Turks than either of these stinking goats, Captain!"

With an angry roar, Kolokotronis silenced them.

"Are you fish peddlers or soldiers! The Turks sit snugly inside their bastions while you quarrel over casks of wine and a few slaves! You should be ashamed!"

The men muttered and growled, not one of them exhibiting, Xanthos observed, a trace of that shame.

"You will observe the rules I have set for my own men," Kolokotronis went on sternly. "Half the booty captured or its equivalent value goes into the treasury for the expense of the war. The other half is to be divided among the men in equal shares."

As several of the men raised their voices to protest bitterly once more, Kolokotronis warned them to be still.

"Not another word! In any battle, all men risk their lives! All are comrades, therefore, and share what is to be shared!"

Afterward he came to slump wearily on a bench under a poplar tree, removing his helmet, smoothing his long hair. Niketaras, several of the other officers and Xanthos came to stand and sit around him.

"I sometimes think," the chieftain murmured, "that we face greater danger from ourselves than from our enemies, greater hazard from our greed than from our foe's swords."

He was silent a moment longer and then, as if he were making an effort to shake off the pall of gloom, he spoke loudly and brusquely.

"How far is Karitena?" he said to Niketaras.

"Four, five hours' march."

"The town is pregnable only from one side," Kolokotronis said, "but that road runs steeply up to the gate, parallel to the city wall. If we advance in daylight, they will be able to rake us with a broadside." He paused. "Is there any chance we might surprise them?"

"They must have word of our march," another of the captains said. "They will be expecting us."

"What's the difference?" a third captain said. "Perhaps like Kalamata, they will have no belly to fight."

"We can't count on that," Kolokotronis said. "Our best chance is to slip into place under cover of darkness, scout the situation at the walls and if the decision is made to attack, storm the town just before dawn."

"How soon do you want the men ready to move?" Niketaras asked.

"After they have eaten and rested a bit," Kolokotronis said. "We should arrive before Karitena sometime after midnight."

Niketaras and the captains moved off to alert and prepare the men, leaving Xanthos and the chieftain alone. For several moments Kolokotronis stared in silence at the town.

"Many years ago I was captain of armatoli here," he said. "The ruins of the theater are very close. I would like to see them again before we leave. This Megalopolis was founded by Epaminondas, wasn't it?"

"Yes," Xanthos said.

"Tell me something about him."

"He came of a poor but distinguished family," Xanthos said, "tracing its origin to dragon's teeth sown by King Cadmus a thousand years before. He was a quiet man, of whom it was said that no one talked less or knew more. He was modest, ascetic, devoted to his friends, prudent in counsel, courageous and yet self-restrained in action. He was admired and loved by all the Thebans."

Xanthos paused, wondering uneasily if he sounded too much the pedagogue, speaking as if he might have recited facts to a classroom of children. Kolokotronis nodded for him to go on.

"He did not love war," Xanthos said, "but he was convinced that no nation could lose its martial spirit and habits and yet maintain its freedom."

"Yes," Kolokotronis said. "Yes . . ." He lowered his head as if there were some weight pressing on his shoulders. "So many great men," he said quietly. "So many noble examples for us poor stumps who follow."

He stretched out on his back along the bench.

"Shall I have them bring you some nourishment, Captain?" Xanthos asked. "Some food or a little wine?"

"A little sleep, my Zantean Homer," Kolokotronis said, and he stared up into the branches and buds of the poplar. "An hour of blessed sleep, untroubled by dreams and fears."

They started from Megalopolis an hour after sunset, a long column of several thousand men moving briskly and fearlessly into the darkening night, advancing toward the hills and mountains that receded before them into a mist. Men chattered and laughed with their comrades, their spirits buoyant and cheerful. Their garrulous exchanges grew so loud, the captains rode along the line commanding them to silence.

Crossing the first range of hills between Megalopolis and the fortress of Karitena, they could see the watch fires on the ramparts of the castle like tiny beacons in the distance. At an order from Niketaras, a score of skirmishers and scouts rode off at a gallop to reconnoiter the ground before them.

Sometime after midnight, the forward detachments halted, waiting for the echelons in the rear to catch up. The captains gathered in a council with Kolokotronis. Some were for assaulting the town and fortress at once. Others advised setting up a siege line, awaiting the arrival in the days ahead of the other corps, Petrobey and his men from the Mani, Archbishop Germanos with his troops from Patras, the bands of klephts from the mountains.

"It might be more prudent to wait!" Kolokotronis' voice carried impatiently once to Xanthos, who stood a short distance away. "I understand that!"

Yet, as Kolokotronis left the council and made his rounds of the men sitting or kneeling in groups, Xanthos felt him restive and eager for action. He circulated with a brave and martial confidence. Men would rise from the ground when he neared them, crowding around him, their faces glowing with reverence and trust. Xanthos could see the magic working.

"Give us the signal, Captain! We'll tear down the walls before sunrise!"

"I've promised my wife a Turkish captain's ear! I don't want to disappoint her!"

"How soon are we going to attack, sir?"

"Give us the word to advance, in God's name, Captain!"

Kolokotronis was delighted at their eagerness.

"Patience, my eagles!" he told them. "We must make sure of the ground before us, the strength of the defenses of the lower town. But soon now we'll make a decision. Be patient!"

A few moments later Xanthos heard the chieftain exhorting Niketaras and the other captains.

"Have you ever witnessed such spirit? These men have blazing eyes and hot hearts! They would follow me anywhere, storm any obstacle to please me! An army is not guns alone but hard-rock spirit and will! What a pity if that edge were dulled through days of siege!"

Sitting with the veteran Balalas, Xanthos asked him what he thought they should do.

"I'm a common soldier, scribe," the bearded Balalas said. "Not my place to tell captains what to do. When they order me to fight, I'll fight like hell . . . kill or be killed, no problem there." He paused, staring toward the watch fires of Karitena. "But I don't like sitting here, down in this valley, waiting. We should have made camp back in the pine forest on the lower slopes of the mountain, decided what we are going to do from there."

Xanthos slept restlessly for a while, his head cradled against his arm. As weariness drew him further into the dark, he slipped into deeper sleep. He woke suddenly to see the first faint daybreak silhouetting the crests and crags in the distance. A few solitary cypresses, taller than any other tree, pointed like huge black swords into the sky. Against the unfolding light, the ramparts of Karitena were visible for the first time, ominous and cinder-gray. At the same moment he heard men whispering about him, muffled voices and a muted clatter of arms.

"Has the order been given?" a man near Xanthos asked.

"I didn't hear it," another answered.

"The Arcadians over there are moving!"

One of the captains slipped up to their group and the men crowded around him.

"The scouts have found the gates of the lower town open," the captain said in a low voice that quivered with excitement. "Kolokotronis has given the order to attack. Prepare to advance at once!"

The men started a cheer but Balalas appeared beside the captain and waved them sternly to silence.

"The games are over now!" he said. "Watch and listen and clamp your mouths!"

Making an effort to assemble quietly, the men shouldered their arms. Some started to advance toward the town and the fortress and others followed quickly as if fearing to be left behind. Soon it seemed the whole encampment was on the move.

Xanthos thought he caught a glimpse of Kolokotronis, rallying a portion of the army, the dim light glimmering upon his helmet. As he started in that direction, Balalas caught his arm.

"You are not a combatant, scribe," Balalas said in a low voice. "Better stay in the rear with the baggage animals so a stray bullet won't dry up your pen forever."

"I have a loaded pistol and I can shoot it!" Xanthos said with a trace of indignation. "Besides, I can't write of battle from a distance. I must be present to record the event when the army captures the town."

"Then stay close to me," Balalas said gruffly. "When I tell you it's time to crouch down behind a rock or a tree, don't play the hero with me or I'll knock you on your Zantean ass!"

The men advanced, slowly, their voices hushed now, the only noise the scrapings and rustlings of their boots across the stony, brush-rubbled ground. In the wavering shadows of that purple light, Xanthos noticed heads and bodies around him floating and swaying as if they were small boats on an open sea.

The jagged mountain of Karitena grew larger before them, the fortress at its peak looming like a battlemented castle suspended in the mist. A new sound was joined to the movement of the men, a hoarse hissing as if from a flock of birds. Feeling his palms moist, tension leaping between his groin and his heart, Xanthos sensed the hissing was excitement and fear exhaled from the parched throats of the men.

His knees beginning to tremble, his belly tossed by nausea, he looked anxiously for the figure of Balalas. He was reassured to see the veteran's bulky body plodding on slightly ahead of him, musket in his hand and a brace of pistols primed and ready in his belt. At that instant Balalas paused, listening intently, staring toward the ground. Xanthos stopped beside him.

"What is the matter, Balalas?" he whispered.

Other men passed them in the drifting, gloomy haze and one paused.

"Getting cold feet, Maniat?" a man taunted the veteran in a low, mocking voice. When Balalas ignored him, the man grunted and moved on.

"Something is wrong," Balalas said uneasily. He bent to his knees, laid aside his musket, and, braced on his palms, he placed his ear and cheek against the earth. He remained motionless for a moment and then rose swiftly. "God help us!" he said.

At that moment from the slopes of Karitena, a musket shot shattered the stillness. Before the thunder of that detonation had faded, a storm of blood-chilling shrieks joined its echo. Springing suddenly to life, every tree and boulder on the lower portion of the mountain disgorged hundreds of Moslem cavalry, charging down the incline, brandishing swords whose blades gleamed and flashed in the cold, blue dawn. As they charged they screamed their battle cry. "Bismillah . . . Bismillah!"

For a shocked instant the Greeks stood transfixed. Then men began to shout and point, rushing to cluster like frightened children. Some raised their muskets and fired, hasty, futile shots.

Balalas sprinted forward, bellowing and waving furiously for the men to scatter. On the right flank a small group of about a dozen mounted Greeks, a feeble phalanx against the approaching horde, galloped through the field of men toward the Turks.

Xanthos could feel the earth rumbling and recoiling under the pounding hooves. He was astonished how swiftly the Turkish cavalry vaulted the distance that separated them from the first Greeks. In a moment their forces had been joined, and from the saddles of rearing, snorting horses, the Turks whipped their swords from side to side, slashing and hacking at the heads and backs of the men on the ground. Those Greeks who were not trampled and rended in that first terrible assault threw away their weapons and rushed blindly on the ranks of men behind them, screeching and wailing, the Turkish horses raging at their heels.

As the rout reached Xanthos, he turned with them and ran. A narrow gully of rocks and brush loomed to one side and he fled toward it. Mad with fear, a Greek bolted across his path, battering him down. The hooves of a horse barely missed Xanthos, a fusillade of gravel and stones kicked at his head. From the ground he saw the fleeing Greek look back once, eyes swollen like moons, before tumbling under the hooves. The Turk wheeled his horse around and around, trampling the man's body. When he rode on, the battered bundle that remained twitched and jerked a few times and then lay still.

Bound to the earth like a beetle, crawling on his belly over the brush and stones that pricked his flesh, Xanthos reached the gully. He huddled in the cavity, whimpering and trembling.

In those moments of what he expected was the end of his life, he saw the huge horses pivoting around like black

whirlwinds, nostrils steaming and snorting. The earth
groaned as men were torn and killed upon it, their bodies
split like sheaves of corn by the Turkish steel. In surrender
or a plea, a Greek raised his arms high above his head. An
instant later both his hands had been severed at the wrists
by the whipping cut of a yataghan. He waved the stumps
that spouted blood, howling as he fell, thrashing and rolling
on the ground. Another Greek crawled toward the gully
where Xanthos lay, dragging a slashed leg, his trunk
lurching up and down in a weird, flapping frenzy to cover
ground. A Turk swooped upon him, sword cleaving down.
The Greek's head shattered under the blow, flaps of skin and
muscle, blood and splinters of bone hurled in all directions.

Xanthos closed his eyes then, twisted on his belly, and,
using his fingers like claws, sought to burrow into the earth.

He was not sure whether he fainted or slept in an anguished effort to block out the horror. He woke once to feel
a small lizard or snake crawling across his neck, again to
hear the shrill moaning of a man in pain. Finally, the wild
cawing and screeching of birds startled him and he twisted
from his belly to his back. He rubbed away the soil that
caked his eyelids.

While the ring of the sun was still at midpoint in the sky,
the plain before Karitena was shrouded by a scarlet haze. As
if the earth had uprooted a ghostly, bloody fog to conceal
the dead and dismembered bodies. From somewhere along
the edge of the plain, although he could not see them,
Xanthos could hear the frenzied cries as the wounded were
butchered, the sickening whack and crunch of swords splitting flesh, severing the heads for trophies.

Terror sent him to his feet, stumbling from the gully, a
reek of raw entrails trailing his path, a stench that made it
painful to breathe.

Within a patch of the plain where the mist had lifted
slightly, he looked upon a frightful landscape, countless

bodies sprawled in the ugly forms of death. One man lay on his back, arms outstretched so he appeared crucified on the earth. Another lay on his belly, one leg drawn awkwardly up, as if he were making a leap from the ground when he died. A third body seemed to have a black growth springing from its skull, until, coming closer, Xanthos saw a raven perched on the dead man's forehead. The bird pecked down sharply, raised its beak dangling part of a slimy, oozing eye that it ate in short, nimble swallows. With a low hoarse cry Xanthos drove it off, the bird taking flight in an angry flurry of dark wings.

He hurried toward the green woods of pine and fir trees that began at the foothills of the mountain. Looking back, fearful of pursuit, he ran across the final stretch of level land and plunged into the cool and fragrant woods with a prayer of gratitude.

After advancing only a short distance in the forest, he came upon a Greek soldier, wounded but still alive, a man he recognized as one of the Maniat veterans who had traveled with them from the Mani, a lean, grim fighter with the frosty, glinting eyes of a man who thrived on war.

He was sitting on the ground in a strangely bucolic bower overhung with green, leafy masses of firs, his back propped against a boulder, his capote bunched and held pressed against his belly. Around his groin and knees, his shirt and trousers were soaked with blood, scarlet streamlets running off into the cones and needles that cushioned the body.

"Oh dear God," Xanthos said, and he knelt beside him.

At the sound of his voice the Maniat opened his eyes and the pupils were glazed by an opaque and yellow veil. Xanthos bent closer to examine the wound, and the man hissed him away.

"Perhaps I can help you," Xanthos said.

The Maniat's eyes flickered.

Xanthos placed a flask gently to the man's purple, crusted

lips. His tongue came out slowly and feebly to suck at the trickles of water.

"Do you know what happened to Kolokotronis?"

The Maniat did not answer.

"Some of the army must have escaped," Xanthos said. "Have you seen any of them?"

He stopped, aware suddenly the Maniat could not hear his voice. The man hung a breath from death, his cheeks leprously white. Then he lifted his head toward a fragment of sky visible between the peaks of the tallest pines, the leafy spires that looked south in the direction of the ranges they had crossed on their way from Kalamata.

"Taygetus . . ." the man said, and he spoke the name of the mountains of the Mani in a wistful whisper. That last word flung like a feather into the track of the wind, his head slipped to the side, his temple coming to rest against the rough, gray boulder.

Xanthos crossed himself slowly, staring at the dead man's face. Somewhere in his body a lament began, burning from his heart to his eyes. Yet he was not mourning only the man dead before him, but all those others on the bloody field at Karitena. Those men mustered with hope and zeal from their villages and farms, husbands and fathers who would never herd or sow or reap again, never watch the morning star take its eternal western course across the mountains, or mark the moon cut the same silver path across the sea. And in that moment he understood that, for him, war had fled the pages of books and would forever after lodge in his heart like a wound.

He climbed on again, trudging the rough slope, through the forest, up the mountain. Weariness slowed the current of his blood, he coughed and sighed. When he sat down to rest and regain his breath, every movement and sound in the foliage, the darting of small, furry animals from the base of one tree to another, the startled cries of birds in the branches, above his head, frightened him to his feet.

In a leafy ravine he came upon a herd of sheep and the shepherd, a gnomelike man with cheeks the texture of bark, and a tall, wild-olive crook in his gnarled hand. He gave Xanthos a ladle of milk, still warm from the udders of a ewe, and pointed his crook in the direction of the crags above them, to a cluster of village houses built on the side of the mountain.

"Chrysovitzion," the shepherd said.

Xanthos resumed his ascent. The first winds of late afternoon rustled the foliage. He shivered and drew his collar about his throat. Gray areas of mist rose from the earth, the shape and form of trees grew charcoal-black. The first sliver of moon, a glistening Moslem crescent, hung at the corner of the sky. He heard the brawling refrain of crickets.

As the sun disappeared, leaving a lingering tail of crimson across the sky, he entered the path leading to the village. He hurried along toward the spire and bell tower of a church on the outskirts of Chrysovitzion. A half-dozen horses were tethered before the church, a few more in a pasture nearby. He made out the figures of men on benches outside the church. He waved to them and hastened his pace. Several of them rose and walked to meet him. One moved ahead of the others and came to clasp him in a strong embrace. Looking into the face of the Maniat veteran Balalas, Xanthos cried out in shock and relief.

"Don't say anything, scribe," Balalas said soothingly. "I am as surprised to see you as you must be to see me. Miracles, both of us." He pointed to the other men. "Damn few miracles on that bloody field."

"The captain?" Xanthos asked.

"A miracle for him too."

"Thank God!"

"Not by much," Balalas said grimly. "As if God could not quite make up his mind whether to save him."

"How was he . . . how were you saved?"

"When that Turkish cavalry from Tripolitza ambushed us in the open plain, veterans would have run, let alone green recruits. I shot a Turk off his horse and mounted in his place. A few of us escaped that way and gathered around the captain. We cut our way out and made it here." He paused, looking somberly in the direction of the church. "But he will never be the same. He's been in there since morning, won't eat or drink anything, won't speak to anyone."

"Let me go in to him," Xanthos said.

"How about some food and drink for yourself?"

Xanthos shook his head, clasping the veteran's hands warmly once again, and then walked to the church. A dozen ragged men slumped wearily outside, some swathed in bloodied bandages, silent and morose. One or two nodded but most were indifferent as he passed.

He pushed against the heavy wooden door, the hinges creaking as it opened. A square of light fell across his body into the darkness before him. As the door closed again he stood in the blind-black church, absorbing the chilled, damp mustiness of stone, scentings of incense and waxen candles. He began slowly to discern objects, candelabra, rafters, paintings, the holy altar. He made out the figure of the chieftain on his knees at the altar rail, a forlorn suppliant before an icon of the Blessed Virgin and infant Jesus.

A whispering came from the chieftain. Xanthos could not distinguish all the words but he was able to hear snatches of prayer and pleas for forgiveness, remorse for blunders and arrogance, repentance for vanities and folly. On and on in a furious ritual of exorcisation, the hissing, anguished whisper rising and falling beneath sparks from the candles that burst fanwise in the dark.

Xanthos lost track of the hours. When the chieftain finally fell silent, he heard the wind wailing in the bell tower and the piercing cry of a loon. Exhaustion drew his blood thin

and feeble, he thought of Chryseis, remembered the solace
of sleep beside her warm, young body. He wanted to find a
place to rest, yet could not leave the chieftain alone. In the
last hour before dawn he felt the night shifting, darkness
breaking into fragments before the incursion of light.

Sometime in that hour the chieftain rose from his knees
and started toward the door. Unable to conceal himself,
Xanthos waited. Even in the dim light, he saw an altered
man. Gone was the strut, the sparkle, his long hair unkempt,
a bandage binding his arm. Almost upon him, Kolokotronis
paused.

"Captain . . . it's Xanthos."

The chieftain did not evidence any surprise that he was
there or how he chanced to survive.

"I am glad you are here, teacher," Kolokotronis said, and
his voice was changed, as well, twined in the hard weeds of
despair. "There is a great deal for us to do."

He opened the door and left the church. Ready to follow,
Xanthos first walked to the altar to offer his devotions and
his own prayer. He made his cross before the icon of the
Blessed Virgin and bent to kiss it.

Something glistened and moved before his eyes. He
thought it the reflection of the candles, then with his lips almost upon the surface of the glass, he gasped and drew
back. On the cheeks of the Blessed Virgin, beneath the
infinite and imperishable eyes, two incandescent trails of
tears ran in slow, mournful streamlets down to the robes at
her throat.

In that frightening and awesome moment, Xanthos understood the terrible measure of the chieftain's grief and remorse, pain so black and fearful that before it, even the
Sorrowful Mother and Queen of Heaven could not restrain
her own tears.

Part Three

GREECE

SUMMER

1821

CHAPTER
TEN

In May the principal islands joined the war. Spetzia was the first to rise in revolt. Psara followed, hoisting the flag of independent Greece, the cross rising above the crescent, from her ships and public buildings. Almost at once a few captains bent on capturing early prizes, set sail, foraging up and down the coast of Asia Minor from Tenedos to Rhodes, snaring several Mussulman sloops and brigantines that could not run to safety under the guns of a port. Meanwhile, the primates of the most powerful of the islands, Hydra, resisted the fervor of her people to join the revolution. These leaders lamented the expense of fitting out their ships and paying wages from their own pockets for what could be an unprofitable and dangerous service. A popular uprising ended their timidity and the islanders proclaimed the independence of Hydra and its union with the new Greek state.

On Psara, many people were jubilant at the prospect of war against the Turks, but there was fear in the air, as well. They knew only a few miles separated them from the Turkish mainland. Feeding on their fear, charlatans peddled charms in the marketplace. Men and women visited fortunetellers and filled the churches, day and night, imploring the aid of God in the battles to come. A few even had the temerity to ask the Deity's assistance in assuring profits.

Adding to the confusion, from the loquacious captains of every brig and schooner that dropped anchor in the harbor of Psara, Leonidas Kontos and the shipowners of the island heard outlandish, often contradictory reports of the progress of the revolt. By filtering and gleaning and comparing one man's story against those of the others, they came to some general understanding of what was taking place. Even that was subject to revision with the arrival of another ship.

What seemed beyond dispute was that the initial invasion by Prince Ipsilantis across the Prut River into the Danubian provinces had gotten only as far as Bucharest. The general had mired down there, surrounding himself with a court of adventurers, conferring high military titles on his followers, captains of a hundred men made generals who responded by treating him with oriental servility. But for the assertion of Ipsilantis that his invasion had been authorized by Tsar Alexander, there were unconfirmed rumors that the Tsar had denounced the invasion as unlawful and unsanctioned and had dismissed Ipsilantis from the Russian service. If these assertions proved true, his venture, begun with such high hopes, was apparently doomed to expire in the provinces.

But whatever his fate, Ipsilantis had helped ignite a flame of revolt in Greece. Ships arriving in Psara from Nauplion and Piraeus carried word of the capture or siege of numerous Turkish towns and fortresses on the mainland. All across Greece, the Christians had risen in fury and killed Turks wherever they were found. Turkish shops and farms were leveled into piles of rubble and stone. Nor were women and children spared. One captain told of seeing a Greek soldier cut the throat of a Turkish baby. When he condemned the action, the man told him even baby snakes contained the poison and had to be prevented from growing larger.

Listening to the tales of slaughter, Leonidas recalled Homer's words that slavery robs man of one half of his humanity. The Turks were paying for that theft now, the moon devouring them in fulfillment of the grim prophecy.

Meanwhile, from refugees aboard ships fleeing Black Sea ports, they heard of Turkish reprisals, equally bloodthirsty, against Greeks living in Asia Minor. At Adrianople, the ex-patriarch Cyril, his protopapas, eight church leaders and twenty Christian merchants were hanged in a single day. In Smyrna, mobs roamed the streets of the city burning the Christian houses and shops, and murdering any Greek man, woman or child in their path. The Mussulmen Mollah and Ayan, magistrates presiding over the religious and civil tribunals, were cut to pieces by the mobs because they would not sanction the massacre of the Christians.

In Constantinople, the enraged Sultan Mahmud's retribution fell on the revered patriarch of the Orthodox Church, Gregorius. Dragged from his cathedral on the morning of Easter Sunday, the white-haired old cleric was hanged from the lintel of the gate at the patriarchate, a sentence of condemnation pinned to his breast. After leaving the body hanging on the gate for three days, it was given into the hands of the mob, who dragged it through the streets of the city to hurl finally into the Bosporus. But the Samian captain who told Leonidas and others the details of that fearful event, made his cross then and added a testament of resurrection. The body of Gregorius was retrieved at night from the Bosporus, the captain said, conveyed in an Ionian vessel to Odessa, where the Russians welcomed it as a holy relic which the waters cast up to strengthen the faith.

Most confusing was the news that various authorities on the mainland of Greece claimed to be directing the course of the war. Bishop Germanos and the notables of Patras had established an assembly known as the Directory of Achaia. Petrobey Mavromichalis, after his capture of Kalamata, had convened a Senate of Messenia that named him president. There were committees set up by primates and clerics in Corinth, Argos, Levadia, Athens, Athos and Missolonghi. There were captains like the famed klepht Theodoros Kolokotronis, besieging Tripolitza, scorning any of the committees. There was even the newly arrived Phanariot Demetrios Ipsilantis, elected representative of the Society of Friends, claiming command of the forces of Greece in the name of his brother, Prince Alexander. The result of all these political rivalries and disparate claims was that the islands kept their own council, agreeing only to form a unified sea force, an association that could founder any time on the shoals of jealousy and pride.

But there wasn't any divided leadership in Constantinople. All the captains who sailed to Psara agreed on that. Sultan Mahmud was moving the Empire in a solid force to crush the uprising. Levies were being collected, troops were being conscripted and trained. The first contingents of that army had begun their advance toward the Danube, planning to sweep down into Greece along the routes used by invaders from the time of the Persian Wars, passages on either side of the massive range of the Pindus Mountains. On the east through Larisa and Lamia, in the west by way of Jannina and Arta, their purpose to relieve the siege of their fortresses, recapturing the towns the Greeks had taken, restoring the Sultan's dominions.

Meanwhile, at ports in the Dardanelles, the Capitan-pasha's heavy frigates were loading and provisioning for what would be an expedition into the Aegean to help supply the land invasions, and crush the islands into submission.

To scatter and defeat this force before it could assault their shores, the three islands, Hydra, Spetzia and Psara, agreed to cease their independent foraging and put their combined fleet to sea. Despite the acrimonious bickering as to who should command this fleet, the more judicious captains and members of the Society of Friends, including the

Psariot admiral Apostolos, prevailed in getting all parties to agree on the Hydriote admiral Yakoumakis Tombazis.

When the first reports of the revolt on the mainland reached Psara, Leonidas had not been among the captains who hastily put to sea. He anticipated the war would be a long, arduous conflict and careful preparations had to be made. To that end he set carpenters and gunners to work on his flagship, the swift brig *Themistocles*. The sails were replaced, the rigging strengthened with additional hemp, the hull given a fresh coat of sealer and paint. The ship was equipped with sixteen four-pound and six-pound cannon mounted and two swivel guns. Not particularly imposing artillery against the heavy-gunned Turkish frigates but reasonably accurate at one hundred fifty and two hundred yards. The decks were reinforced to withstand the cannon's recoil and kegs of powder and grapeshot stored in a rebuilt magazine in the hull. The crew's quarters were enlarged to carry a greater number of men. Finally, casks of water and provisions, fruits, vegetables, hard bread and dried mutton were loaded on board.

Concerned with the best possible fighting crew, Leonidas sought to obtain a picked core of men. To help form them into a tightly disciplined force, he arranged with the chief magistrate, Hadji Yannaros, to have Skylos Yarkas pardoned from the island prison.

Skylos was six inches over six feet tall, supple as a snake, with skin as scaled and horny as the back of an armadillo. His right forearm was tattooed with an angel, his left forearm with a devil. There was little question which way Skylos inclined. Because of his penchant for privateering, raiding Greek as well as foreign ships, he had twice been captured and sentenced to death by hanging. Each time he had been pardoned because he was also a gunnery specialist who could shoot the wing from a hornet. He knew ships and the men who sailed them and his presence commanded respect and fear.

"Sign here," Skylos would say brusquely to each recruit he had approved. "If you cannot sign your name, mark your X."

"What do you mean, X?" one man answered indignantly. "Do you think I'm a Turkish landsman?"

"The usual share of the profits?" another sailor signing on asked Skylos.

"Man, this is war now!" Skylos cried. "Not a pirate expedition!" A few men snickered and quickly fell silent as Skylos glared at them. "Don't fill you head with fancy ideas about profits. If there are any, we may share them. If not, we will content ourselves to send Turkish vermin to the bottom of the sea."

Some of the men grumbled but signed on. Since the Napoleonic Wars, the sailors of the islands had grown accustomed to being hired on a co-operative basis, sharing the profits as well as the hazards of their expeditions to French-occupied European ports blockaded by the British. Now a seaman would have to risk his life without assurance of any profits. Skylos did not give them much time to ponder.

"Sign here!"

"Can I sign on my brother and cousin, Skylos? They are fishing today but they are good men who have sailed with Captain Kontos before and want to sail with him now."

"Sign on everyone but your wife," Skylos said.

"You're making a mistake, Skylos!" A man standing nearby guffawed. "Vasili's wife has a mouth more deadly than a cannon!"

"What about your wreck!" Vasili cried. "That woman is so ugly you should keep her head in a sack when you take her out!"

"Son of a pig!"

"Brother of a goat!"

As the two men waved their fists angrily at one another, Skylos bellowed for silence.

"What is this! A tavern brawl? Are we playing games here
or signing on a crew? Quiet down or I'll heave you both
over the side!"

Although Leonidas admired the island sailors as skilled
and resourceful seamen, he knew they were also independent, clannish and argumentative. If a sailor on ship-
board saw anything to be done, he would often do it without waiting for an order. If an order were given, a dozen
hands might argue vehemently as to who should do it. And
each sailor felt free to tell his captain what he thought,
where they should sail, the place to fight, when to remain at
sea and when to return to port.

"They'll be all right, Captain," Skylos told him when they
had the full ship's complement of nearly a hundred men
signed on. "Not all of them are the best of the Psariots since
every other captain is after those men first, as well, but none
of the taverna loafers either." He grinned. "I know every last
one of those warthogs, so one couldn't slip by me."

"I don't worry about them at the sails and rigging,"
Leonidas said, "but keep them at the guns, keep them practicing until they can load and be ready to fire in under a
minute."

"Aye, Captain," Skylos said.

During the final days of preparation before the departure
of the Psariot ships for their rendezvous with the ships of
Hydra and Spetzia, Hadji Yannaros visited Leonidas aboard
the *Themistocles*. As the long boat rowed by a dozen
seamen approached the hull of his ship, Leonidas recognized the old chief magistrate sitting rigid and upright in
the stern sheets.

"Careful!" Leonidas called loudly. "Steady the gunwales!"

"Toss your oars!" came the command from the mate in the
boat.

Helped by several burly seamen, the old chief magistrate
ascended the first rung of the heavy rope ladder hanging

over the side. He climbed slowly, raising one foot stiffly after another. As Hadji Yannaros neared the top rung, he trembled and both Leonidas and Skylos bent to stretch their arms, gripping the old man under the shoulders, and hauling him onto the ship. He breathed a deep, fervent sigh.

"Welcome aboard the *Themistocles*." Leonidas smiled and clasped the old man's hands warmly between his own palms.

"Good to stand on the deck of a living ship again," the old man murmured.

"Any sailor in Psara would be proud to sail with you again, your honor!" Skylos said smoothly. "Say the word and I'll get you the best crew in the archipelago!"

Hadji Yannaros gazed up at the tall seaman sternly.

"Don't waste your syrup on me, Skylos Yarkas," the old man said. "Remember what I told you when you were pardoned. I believe God has decreed that you end swinging from a yardarm. How soon depends on you."

"How could I forget, your honor!" Skylos said cheerfully. A slight trace of smile flickered about his lips. "Maybe I'll send so many Turks to hell first, God will wish me reprieved."

One of the men in the long boat had climbed the ladder and over the gunwale handed Hadji Yannaros a long, dark circular case. The old man gripped it tightly in his veined and bony fingers and began plodding toward the stern. Leonidas followed him to the quarterdeck, where Hadji Yannaros stood looking up toward the flag that hung above the stern, the folds lifting slightly and curling in the breeze.

"Sixty years I have been sailing the seas," the old man said softly. "Witnessed marvels I will never forget. Monsters that could swallow a ship, rainbows like the trade routes of paradise, pirate coves teeming with the treasure of kings, ebony women with the bewitchment of Circe in their bodies, volcanoes rising like Jupiter's forge from the sea." He looked at Leonidas, his small black eyes glinting between his webbed, bleached cheeks. "I would trade them all for one voyage under this flag."

"None of us is worth a bone of your frame," Leonidas said. "But give us your blessing and remember us in your prayers."

The old man gazed toward the wide waters beyond the harbor.

"Now the ships are anchored together," he said. "But once at sea, scattered to the winds, caught in a gale or becalmed with sails limp as shrouds, a captain and his ship are alone. He cannot ask or expect help from others."

Leonidas nodded slowly.

"Remember that although you are a Greek, you are also a Psariot," Hadji Yannaros said. "Remember also that Hydriotes and Spetziots are a different breed than us and Tombazis is a Hydriote. He is a judicious man, but deficient in decision, seeking and taking the advice of those who have less courage and knowledge than he possesses. He has never been able to comprehend that an imprudent measure, exercised with promptitude and vigor, is, in war, more effective than a wise measure feebly and slowly carried out."

"I will be on guard, Hadji Yannaros."

"Yet a strange feeling of futility gnaws at me," the old man went on. "I think our destiny and the success of this struggle is even now being decided in the councils of Europe. In the end, what they decide to do will determine what becomes of us."

"Those are matters of grand politics and strategy," Leonidas said. "I am only a sea captain. I will sail and fight Turkish ships and leave those imposing designs for others."

"You will have problems enough," Hadji Yannaros said. "Our men think discipline a scourge. They are good sailors but indulgent and unlicensed."

"Skylos and I will keep them busy."

"Take council as often as possible with Kanaris," the old man said. "He is made of flint and will find the way to master the Turkish frigates." He patted Leonidas reassuringly on the shoulder. "I do not slight your ability, my son, because you know my regard for you. I simply tell you what I think is true."

"Konstantine is my dearest friend," Leonidas said. "I am a good captain but if he commanded, I would follow him through the Dardanelles."

The old man nodded in approval, squinted toward the descending sun and handed Leonidas the long black case he carried.

"I brought this for you," he said. "It is my spyglass, the long one I carried with me on all my voyages. I am an old vessel and dull sailor now, my eyes can't see across the gunwales. The glass is useless with me. Take it."

Then the old man embraced him gently. Leonidas felt the wiry spars and canvas of the old man's frame, the scents of salt and foam.

"God go with you," the old magistrate whispered. He turned and began walking slowly toward the ladder where Skylos waited to help him descend to the long boat.

The evening before their departure, the families of the seamen came in boats from the shore, carrying garlands of fresh flowers to drape from the rigging and spars. The ship smelled like a garden, the water of the harbor glowing with colorful reflections of light.

Aboard the *Themistocles*, Leonidas greeted the throng that included his wife, Aspasia, and their daughters. He carried the girls about the ship, letting them stand on the quarterdeck, and touch the huge wheel with their tiny fingers. All about the ship, women and children clustered around the cannons while their proud, swaggering husbands and fathers boasted of the way they would send the Turkish frigates to the bottom of the sea.

With the girls cared for by friends, Leonidas and Aspasia descended to his cabin. Through the curved windows at the stern, the lights of the *Pericles* and *Heracles*, the brigs of Kanaris and Papanikolis, glistened off his bow. Aspasia walked slowly about the cramped quarters, touching his pipes, smoothing his clothing. She came into his arms then and he inhaled the fragrance of her body. A beguiling glitter shone in her eyes.

"Aspasia!" he spoke in delight and apprehension.

"Why not?" she said defiantly. "In that way you will feel my presence and my love all about you. You will not be able to sleep without remembering this last moment of love. Yes!"

He left her arms for a moment to bolt the door and then returned. While voices floated from the deck and shadows flitted across the water, to the sounds of laughter, the wail of a flute, the soft creaking of rigging and timbers, she undressed slowly. When she came finally into his arms, her body glistening and golden as the sun, he had the sense she had risen from the sea, a naked and bewitching nymph sent as a favorable omen for his voyage.

She left at dawn, in the last of the boats to return to shore. The children slept in tight, curled forms about her legs. Leonidas stood at the gunwales, a few sailors beside him, calling their final farewells. Aspasia rose suddenly, as if to call him back, standing above the seated women. Then the boat was lost, obscured in the mist, the clear, clipped sound of the oars dipping in and out of the water all that remained.

"Captain?"

Skylos stood at his side.

"A signal from the flagship. Admiral Apostolos wants us ready."

"Ready."

"Stand by the capstan. Hands aloft and loose topsails."

He watched with familiar delight the seamen surging up the shrouds and along the swaying yards, their bodies small and black against the sky. As canvas thundered loosely from the yards, the ship gave a long-drawn shudder.

From forward came the cry, "Anchor aweigh!"

The *Themistocles* tilted steeply to the wind, the headland sliding across her jibboom as with more and more canvas hardening from her yards, she paid off into the wind.

"Anchor secured, Captain."

Spray had soaked his face and clothing. He felt the jubilation he had experienced many times when they first got under way.

"From the flagship, Captain. Take station to windward."

Moments later with her courses and topsails filling to the morning breeze, the *Themistocles* glided swiftly past a few ships remaining behind, small craft bobbing astern in the frothing wake. For a moment, then, in final separation, the island rose from the water, slopes of terraced houses, shops along the wharves. He caught a glimpse of his house and then he could see nothing but the open sea, the silhouettes of the other ships, their fore-topsails filling to the wind, and, above the tips of their masts, the wild screeching of the gulls.

No matter how many times over the years he had set sail from the harbor of Psara into the Aegean, entering the expanse of clear, blue water, the rippling ocean floor visible through fathomless depths, the deck tilting under the press of canvas, the hull skimming the waves, he felt his soul burst free.

There wasn't a body of water anywhere in the world quite like their sea. Wherever they sailed in the Aegean, they were never out of sight of one of the islands, sometimes no more than a pillar of rock configured against the horizon, yet enough land to absorb the sun so that it never sank into the sea. Fair Psara, Chios, Samos, Ikaria, the islands of the Cyclades about sacred Delos, mystical Crete and Karpathos in the southern sea, islands formed, as the legends told, from the limbs of a god whose body was torn asunder as he fell from the sky. While on each island, small, whitewashed chapels to Saint Nicholas, patron of seafarers, kept a vigilant, benedictory spirit over the Greek ships that passed their shores.

Following the current which flowed from the Dardanelles along the coast of Asia Minor, their seven ships sailed in a westerly then in a southerly course, skirting the islands of Ikaria and Amorgos, awaiting their first glimpse of the ships of Hydra and Spetzia.

While they waited, the shortened sails of the other Psariot brigs visible in the distance to windward and leeward, on the *Themistocles*, under the bawling direction of Skylos, the sailors spent hours in practice at the guns.

Afterward Skylos came to the bridge, where Leonidas stood beside the helmsman.

"A minute ten seconds, Captain."

"Not tight enough," Leonidas said. "It must be done under a minute. Keep them practicing."

All that day and the following day, the strident whistle blew the seamen to their stations at the guns. Swiftly casting off the cannons' lashings, they hauled the guns inboard, removing the tampions from the muzzles. Raising the gun port one man leaned out to vigorously sponge the barrel. The instant he had withdrawn the rammer, powder cartridges and balls were shoved home, followed by rope yarn jammed solidly so no space existed between the powder, shot and wads.

Standing to windward the gun chiefs primed the touchholes with powder. With every man heaving on the tackle, the gun carriages were pushed forward until the muzzles extended well beyond the ports. Blowing on the slow-match, the chiefs ignited the powder in the base rings. With roars that were only seconds apart the balls hurled from the cannons, the force of the expulsions driving the guns backward against the heavy breeching ropes. As a series of explosions and geysers of spray marked the entry of the balls into the water about two hundred yards distant from the ship, a rousing cheer burst from the men.

"Hey, Skylos, did you see that last shot of mine take down her mainmast?"

"Mine dropped into her hatch!"

"The bloody Pasha-Pig caught my ball in his lap!"

"All right! All right!" Skylos snarled. "When there are Turkish frigates out there instead of empty seas, there won't be time for boasting. Get those sponges in now to extinguish any sparks before reloading."

By the end of the second day, the best of the crews could run out, prime, load, point and fire their cannon under a minute. Leonidas ordered an extra ration of brandy for the men.

As twilight fell across the water, he stood on the bridge listening to the voices of the men lounging beneath the sails, their palates tickled by the brandy, laughing and jesting in good spirits. He was filled suddenly with homesickness, wondering what Aspasia was doing at that moment, perhaps at dinner with his daughters, thinking of him even as his thoughts swept on the back of the winds to her.

Vasili and a group of the other sailors approached the bridge.

"Begging your pardon, Captain," Vasili said. "The boys and me were just having an argument. You know, about history, the Argonauts." He waved toward a man behind him. "Kleon here claims they were better seamen than we are."

"They were fine seamen," Leonidas said. "But you are fine seamen too."

Vasili nodded gravely.

"Begging your pardon, Captain, that's true. But I told Kleon we were better seamen and offered my proof."

"What is that proof, Vasili?"

"Why, Captain, they're all dead now and we're alive. If among them a man could be found to climb the mast faster than any of us or loose the headsail quicker or fight off an enemy more bravely, why none of that matters now. They're all dead and we're alive and that's why we're the best. The worst sailor alive is better than a dead admiral. Begging your pardon again, Captain."

"I think Vasili is right," Leonidas said, and smiled in the darkness. Vasili made a pleased sound with his lips. The men moved off and continued to argue more quietly, Vasili's voice confident and reinforced.

Yes, Leonidas thought as the men gathered under the sails once more, their voices floating across the darkness, the dead cannot solace us now. The mightiest warriors who had ever fought for Greece could not kill a single Turk or sink a single ship. That task was in the hands of the living whether they were the best or not.

On the morning of the third day their lookout descried sails on the western horizon, fragments of white accumulating until the full expanse of the westerly sea was dotted with the sails of brigs and sloops from Hydra and Spetzia. It was the first time Leonidas had seen such an aggregation of ships and he could not contain his excitement, hanging over the gunwales with the crew to witness the inspiring sight. When they had assembled and the Psariot admiral Apostolos had greeted them with a salute of cannons, there were more than thirty ships in their fleet. Leonidas wished suddenly that old Hadji Yannaros could have seen them, as well.

For the balance of that day the ships took their stations, the admirals meeting on the flagship of the Hydriote admiral, Yakoumakis Tombazis. With orders, finally, to sail, an absence of wind left them becalmed.

Lying in his bunk that night, wakeful and alert, Leonidas knew by the lantern's sluggish movement and the uneasy creak of timbers that the wind remained motionless. Later, he must have fallen asleep, for he opened his eyes with a start to daylight and the sounds of feet thudding on the deck, the shouts of Skylos sending men aloft. He leaped from his bed and hurried to the deck. The moment his head rose through the stairwell, he felt the fresh, strong gusts of wind whip his cheeks.

"A beautiful blow, Captain!" Skylos cried. Above their heads the men scampered up the shrouds and out along the swaying yards, and as canvas thundered free, the ship gave a mighty shudder of joy. Checking the compass, he looked up to see the *Pericles* of Kanaris, her masts already swinging across their stern, her fore-topsail billowing to the wind as she heeled over.

"Lay her on the larboard tack," he told Skylos. "We will get the courses on her and see if we can take the edge off the *Pericles*' lead."

Moments later, with her courses and topsail filling to the strong morning wind, the *Themistocles* leaped through the sea like a dolphin.

"By the gods, Captain!" Skylos cried, his hair whipping in the wind and his teeth bared in delight. "Is there any other life but this one?"

Yet, later that day, they were once again flattened by the perverse winds dying. The hands worked steadily to make or shorten sail, trimming the yards in the hope of catching the faintest breeze. Then, at sunset, they were struck by a sudden, violent squall, the wind roaring through a shower of foam and spray, the ship groaning and tossing in the troughs as they desperately sought to reef their sails. At dawn their fleet lay scattered and dispersed like children's toys, fragments of sail littering every horizon. Skylos stared across the water, his face wrathful and dark.

"Is there any other life but this one?" the tall privateer snarled. With a grimace, he spit to the leeward in disgust.

The fleet took nearly the whole of a day to reassemble before they could sail eastward once more. On the afternoon of the fourth day after they had gathered in the sea north of

Ikaria, the lookout's voice cried down from the crow's nest of the *Themistocles.*

"Ho, the deck! Sails on the starboard beam!"

At almost the same instant they received an identical signal from the *Pericles* running leeward of them. The men crowded along the starboard gunwales, a silence falling upon them as they peered intently toward the eastern horizon.

"Skylos," Leonidas said. "Send your sharpest-eyed man aloft with a glass."

"Aye, Captain," Skylos said. "I'll go myself."

With the glass stuck in his belt he raced to the weather shrouds, his long arms and legs covering the ascent swiftly and well.

Leonidas took the long spyglass of Hadji Yannaros and trained it toward the barely visible sail in the distance. Minutes passed and as the distant ship lifted on some large roller he saw her huge topgallant sails shining in the sunlight. She was clawing her way close-hauled on a converging course toward the Greek ships, her yards braced so tightly they were almost fore and aft.

"Ahoy, the deck!" Skylos' voice came from the lookout. "More sails on the starboard beam!"

"How many?" Leonidas cried up to him.

"Three, four, Captain! Big ones!" Skylos shouted down and after a moment. "Still more sails! Looks like the bloody Mussulman fleet!"

The men watching at the gunwales muttered and a few made their cross.

Steadying his legs against the motion of the deck, Leonidas leveled the spyglass once again and saw the many-masted sails hove into view. They were mammoth Turkish ships of the line, rising from the sea like mountains, their tiered decks swarming with men and scores of cannon protruding from the ports.

Skylos came leaping down from the shrouds.

"They're ships of the line, all right, Captain," he said. "One maybe a seventy-gun, by the look of her, the other a shade smaller. There are three big frigates and some sloops and brigs." He turned toward the men.

"All right!" he bellowed. "Man your gun stations!"

The men broke from the gunwales and scurried to their guns. The gun chiefs unlashed the cannon, primed and loaded them. When they were ready, the men standing about the guns, a silence descended over the ship, broken only by the creaking of the spars and rigging, and the screeching of a few gulls that wheeled in excited circles above their masts.

"Hornets against a bear," Skylos said, and he spoke so quietly only Leonidas heard him. A chill swept his blood and he prayed for a fresh, strong breeze that would let them tack swiftly and sail well.

While the Mussulman ships were still out of range of the nearest Greek brigs, their gunners fired eager broadsides, the sky rumbling with long peals of thunder, the ports of the ships obscured in clouds of smoke. Scores of balls falling into the expanse of water between the two fleets sent up showers of spray like schools of fish leaping in and out of the foam.

"Wasting their shot," Leonidas said.

"Turkish sailors," Skylos said scornfully.

As the ponderous ships of the line sought to close with the Greek brigs, the captains tacked swiftly out of range, sailing in circles to the bows and sterns of the bigger craft. One of the Turkish frigates seeking to tack quickly and follow the brig of one of the Greeks, ran afoul of the cannonade of one of the ships of the line that narrowly missed her bow.

"If we leave them alone, they'll sink their own ships!" Skylos grinned. "God's blessing those Turkish gunners keep aiming. If they close their eyes, we're in trouble."

For the remainder of that day's light, a curiously futile

and ineffectual skirmishing took place between the two fleets. As the Turkish ships of the line plodded forward, firing unending volleys, the swift Greek brigs skimmed just out of range, circling or running a zigzag course around the slower Turkish behemoths.

On one of the swift circles, the *Heracles* of Papanikolis, as if suddenly impatient, turned her bowsprit toward the Turkish ships, and under taut, full sail bore toward them.

"By the gods! What is he doing, Captain?" Skylos cried.

"Showing the Turks the way a ship can be sailed," Leonidas said. He leaned his hands on the gunwale to steady them, watching the stunning foray of the brig. He saw the gunports of the ships of the line quiver and send off a barrage. All around the racing brig the balls fell into the sea. Spray and foam obscured the sails and for a fearful instant Leonidas thought she had been hit. Then from the mist the brig emerged, sleek and unscathed, scornful of the shots falling all about her.

"She's going to ram!" Skylos cried.

"No! That isn't what he has in mind!" Leonidas said.

When it seemed inevitable that the *Heracles* would collide with one of the Turkish ships, she tacked violently, her hull rising from the waves as she spun, her sails refilling and hardening on the new tack. Sweeping along the side of one of the frigates, a salvo of cannon fire burst from the *Heracles*. With a mighty shattering of wood, the frigate's mast was struck, the great long topgallant sail collapsing. A great cheer went up from the decks of the Greek ships even as the stunned frigate sought desperately to retreat behind the cover of the other ships.

It had been a superbly timed and executed maneuver, a marvel of seamanship, plunging into the teeth of the Turkish ships, administering punishment and soaring away out of range. The sailors of the *Themistocles* jumped and danced about the deck in a paroxysm of delight.

"What a beauty!" Leonidas said, and he burned with intemperate pride for his Psariot friend.

Emboldened and challenged by the success of the *Heracles*, some of the Hydriote and Spetziot brigs sailed into range of the mammoths that fired at them in frantic, enraged cannonades. Once, as a Hydriote ship swept past a frigate, a row of seamen clambered onto the shrouds, turned their backs to the Turks and tugged down their trousers, waving a cluster of white, naked behinds at the furious Mussulman gunners.

"They're growing careless," Leonidas said anxiously, "So eager to show their bravado, they're abandoning good sense."

Almost as the words left his lips, one of the Hydriote brigs, racing closer to the ship of the line than any other Greek captain had dared to go, was struck. Her hull gave a violent shudder as the heavy salvo plowed into her. For a moment she was engulfed in smoke and then, as the smoke cleared, Leonidas saw that her main-topmast was gone, her sails ripped and punctured like rags in a gale.

The laughter and joy that prevailed on the other Greek ships turned suddenly to shocked silence. Men stood helpless at the gunwales watching the Turkish frigates closing in on the crippled brig. Firing almost at point-black range, the frigates emptied their cannon into her. As balls slammed into the lower hull, fragments of wood and limbs of men were blasted apart, tossed like scraps into the air.

In the space of a few moments, nothing was left of the twin-masted, square-rigged brig but a shattered hulk, the water around her littered with the wreckage of masts and shreds of torn canvas. A few survivors thrashed to stay afloat while from the shrouds of one of the frigates that hovered nearby, Turkish marksmen tried to pick them off.

Staring grimly and silently at the carnage, Leonidas turned angrily toward the men of his crew, who clustered in small, shaken and doleful groups.

"You have seen destruction and death at sea before!" Leonidas shouted sternly, "You will see it again! They have sunk one of our ships!" He motioned at the sails of the Greek fleet. "We still have our power! I pledge to you on the soul of my father, our turn will come!"

That night there was a meeting of the admirals of the three islands on the flagship of Tombazis, a gathering also attended by a few of the senior captains. Kanaris was there and afterwards he came in a cutter to the *Themistocles*, where Leonidas and Papanikolis, captain of the *Heracles*, waited for him. They lit their pipes in Leonidas' cabin, the air growing thick with the aroma of pungent tobacco.

"Did they speak of the destruction of that brig today?" Papanikolis said in a grave, troubled voice. "All afternoon and this evening, I have been thinking of the widows and orphans waiting at the dock in Hydra." He paused. "Did they speak of blaming me?"

"Demetrios, let it rest!" Leonidas said. "This is war and any brig might be hit and sunk."

"If I had not made that impetuous run," Papanikolis said with bitterness. "If the Hydriotes and Spetziots had not taken it as a challenge . . . perhaps that brig might still be afloat."

"Your run was magnificent, Demetrios," Kanaris said firmly. "Every man on our ships was heartened and cheered. But without the element of surprise, the brigs that tried to imitate your maneuver were foolhardy. Tempting providence on land or sea is not wise."

"You cannot blame them for becoming impatient," Leonidas said. "We sailed to fight. What kind of warfare is this? We cannot get close enough to those Turkish fortresses for our guns to damage them. All we can do is sail around them in circles proving we are better seamen."

"Once they get us in range," Kanaris said, "they are great beasts with formidable jaws. Tombazis and the others in the meeting tonight were of the opinion that if we must stay out of range, other methods of attack are necessary."

"How do we attack them?" Papanikolis asked.

"There were several suggestions, some outlandish ones as you can imagine," Kanaris said. "One was that we send a few men in a small boat to try and slip on board one of the frigates or ships of the line to explode her magazine. The most serious discussion was again about the brulots, the fire-ships."

"We have discussed them a number of times," Leonidas said. "The situation is not the same as it was in 1770, when the Russians used them against the Turkish fleet. The problems are massive. To sail up to the hull of a frigate or a ship of the line in the dark without detection, ram it solidly, set the train afire and then slip safely away in the small boat carried astern would require seamanship ten times more daring and precise than Demetrios displayed today."

Kanaris puffed on his long-stemmed pipe.

"I made the suggestion that we send at once back to Psara for them to prepare a couple of brigantines and have them daubed with pitch and sulfur and sailed back to us as quickly as possible." He sighed. "Some of the captains were too impatient to wait the time that course might require. Tombazis himself mentioned that John of Parga, you know, Patatuka, had been with the Russians at Tchesme and knew how to prepare a fire-ship. Theodosios offered to give up his vessel to be converted into a fire-ship that Patatuka will prepare."

"A patriotic gesture!" Leonidas said.

"Not that patriotic." Kanaris smiled. "He demands the payment of forty thousand piasters to be paid by the treasuries of the three islands. They agreed. But I have reservations whether all the preparations can be made adequately at sea. Believing you would support me, I have already sent the *Marathon* back to Psara for the fire-ships."

"I agree!" Papanikolis struck his big fist vehemently against the small table.

"How soon will Patatuka have the fire-ship ready?" Leonidas asked.

"He promises by tomorrow evening," Kanaris said. "If the wind is right, they may try a strike at twilight."

"Will they let us sail her in?" Papanikolis asked.

"I suggested that," Kanaris said, "but the Hydriotes and Spetziots are not anxious to allow a Psariot the first moment of glory. Patatuka himself may take her in." He looked at them gravely. "I am afraid the effort will be wasted. You know those northern merchantmen with their heavy tops and small topsails. Men like Patatuka who have gained their experience sailing ships like that lack nautical science."

For a long moment the three of them were silent. The flame of the lantern swaying above the table hissed softly. A ship's bell rang the hour and vibrated through the cabin.

Kanaris rose from his chair.

"We will have to wait," he said. "Wait and see."

He walked slowly toward the stern window. For a melancholy moment he stared out upon the dark, hidden sea.

"Meanwhile," he said softly, "let our comrades who sleep in the bed of the sea tonight find safe haven in God's port."

In the morning, a misted dawn settling across the hulls of the ships, drawing them slowly from shadows to frail light, the same futile, desultory battle began. The ships of the line launched thunderous and useless cannonades that plowed the open sea. The Greek brigs remained just out of range, cautious about any repetition of the previous day's disaster. Meanwhile, in a small cluster of ships some miles away, Leonidas knew they were preparing the fire-ship. By twilight, as Patatuka had promised, it was ready.

Word of the impending attack had spread to the crews of the Greek ships and now, on the *Themistocles*, they crowded the gunwales and clung from the shrouds, peering against the fading light until they saw the brig emerge from among the Greek ships. Like a dark-sailed phantom she bore a silent course directly toward the line of Turkish frigates.

"She stands too clear yet," Skylos said. "They should have waited for more darkness to conceal her masts and sail."

"Harder to locate the target in the dark," Leonidas said. He prayed for the brig's success even as he remembered the apprehension of Kanaris.

Suddenly one of the lookouts on the frigates spotted the ship skimming toward them. Within moments the frigate opened fire, the volleys bursting like flares. Like dogs joining the clamor, several of the other Turkish ships opened fire.

"They're not sure what course she's on!" Leonidas said. "Their confusion should help us."

As the volleys from the frigates and ships of the line dismembered the darkness, clouds of smoke swirling above the water, the fire-ship was lost. Then a great flaring flame leapt to the brig's sails as the train of the Greek ship was set afire. In the glow that spread across the sky, the men at the gunwales and on the shrouds cheered and shouted. For a jubilant moment Leonidas thought the brig might have struck her target, her bow rammed into the frigate's hull, her hooks entangled in its rigging. As he saw the burning fire-ship floating free, he realized bitterly the train had been set afire too soon, her crew too timid or frightened to wait, fleeing in panic to the boat they carried astern.

For an instant longer the brig blazed uselessly, separated by a broad expanse of water from the Turkish ships. When the powder casks in her hull exploded, the sky steamed with flying flame, reddening the untouched sails and rigging of the Turkish frigates, exposing the small boat with her crew rowing frantically for the refuge of the Greek ships. As the glowing chunks of spar and mast and sail fell into the sea, their fire extinguished with a hoarse, hissing like the bubbling of boiling springs. A few orange embers glistened on the surface of the water and then snuffed out. Tracking scents of smoke, burnt powder and brine, the darkness returned.

As the men on their ship groaned their dismay and Skylos unleashed a string of sea-dog's curses, Leonidas turned away. Now we wait for the fire-ships from Psara, he thought. And a coarse net of fear snared his body, not fear of death but of shame and failure as the fire-ship already launched had failed, her captain's cowardice exposed to the total Greek and Mussulman fleets.

Another morning. The sea was dark, waves rising and falling in choppy swells. The wreckage of the brig, like the remnants of a funeral pyre, floated in scraps of charred spar and canvas on the water. At the same time as the refuse became visible, the lookouts discerned activity among the Turkish ships, the hoisting of topgallant sails on the frigates and ships of the line, their broad yards swelling with canvas. For a while there was frantic signaling among the Greek ships, uncertain whether the Turks meant to breach their circle. It was not until they had received confirmation from several of the Hydriote ships leeward of the *Themistocles* that Leonidas understood the Turks were retreating, turning their bows back to their own ports.

"Could be a ruse, Captain," Skylos said.

"Why should they bother?" Leonidas said. He steadied himself against the helm-post and peered through the long spyglass at the mustering sails. "That fire-ship last night scared them. They were not damaged but that fire fanned fear in their bellies."

"Probably have to trail the bloody cowards all the way back to the Dardanelles," Skylos said. He shouted toward the deck. "Hands aloft and loose topsails!" As men leaped to ascend the shrouds, he turned to Leonidas. "We can stay on their tail, Captain," he said glumly, "but by the time the fire-ships from Psara arrive to join us, those bastards will be anchored in some Turkish port, their sailors swilling raki in some seaside tavern and boasting of their victory as they nestle between some harbor harlot's thighs!" He shook his fist after the retreating ships in mute, futile rage.

By afternoon, their brigs in swift pursuit and yet taking care to remain out of range of the powerful guns, it was evident the Mussulman fleet was headed for one of the Asia Minor ports. Frustrated and thwarted, Leonidas felt the days at sea wasted and barren. Was this the way all their vaunted battles would end? The same circling, nipping and retreating, cautiously pursuing, able to follow but not to impede.

"One frigate is falling behind, Captain," Skylos said. "That's the one Captain Papanikolis struck the other day. She's listing to port, may be having some trouble with her sails and rigging."

Almost at once Leonidas saw the *Pericles* of Kanaris tack to leeward and begin a series of rapid signals to their bridge. With a leaping excitement he understood what his friend was attempting.

"All hands to the braces!" he cried to Skylos. "Lay her on the larboard tack in the wake of the *Pericles!* The Turk is lagging and Kanaris will try to cut her off from the others!"

He watched the frigate limping in a trough of foam, men in her rigging struggling with her topgallant sails. Windward of her, fore-topsail filling as she heeled, the *Pericles* set a course to bring herself across the Turk's bow. In swift pursuit, more and more canvas thundering from her yards, Leonidas sent the *Themistocles* after her, as well. To leeward the *Heracles* of Papanikolis followed them.

By later in the afternoon, the Turkish ships and the Greek brigs under Tombazis that trailed them had become small bunts on the horizon. The frigate, slightly crippled, still posed a threat and time after time as one of the Greek brigs sailed too close to her port or starboard, she volleyed a broadside from her tier of gun decks that churned geysers of water into the air, spraying their bowsprits and hulls. Yet each time she sought to tack in the direction the remainder of the Turkish fleet had taken, like swift, cunning foxes they harried her, running across her bow, feinting and retreating, firing their smaller cannon in alternating volleys more to add to her confusion than because they could inflict any harm.

As the first trace of evening streaked the sky in shades of plum and purple, the Turkish captain, perhaps remembering the fire-ship that came with twilight the evening before, ceased all effort to change course or to fight, and fled for the island of Mytilene that lay ahead. The Greek brigs followed in her wake until the darkness and then they trailed her by starlight and the crescent of moon that shone in bright, rippling streamers across the water.

When dawn came, they were off the coast of Mytilene, and the frigate, like a great, exhausted bird, lay at anchor in the harbor of Erissos. As the *Pericles* sailed into the harbor entrance to probe her condition, she launched a furious broadside that forced Kanaris to tack swiftly and flee.

All day the lookouts on the brigs scanned the horizon anxiously for sails, hoping the fire-ships from Psara would find them. In the harbor, the sun sparkling on the tips of her tall masts, the frigate gleamed like a huge and bounteous prize that remained tauntingly just beyond their reach.

In a meeting on the *Themistocles* once again, Kanaris, Papanikolis and Leonidas agreed they could not chance waiting for the fire-ships any longer. The frigate might make her repairs, muster her courage and sail from the harbor to breach their siege. The Turkish ships of the line might return. They would have to prepare, as handily as they could, one of their brigs as a fireship.

"We have no other choice," Kanaris said. "That frigate has cost us two brigs and will cost us another. But the Turks fear fire now and if we manage to ignite and sink her, the blaze will provide us a victory we sorely need and strike terror throughout the Mussulman fleet."

They fell silent, each man considering, Leonidas knew, the possibility that his own ship might be the one sacrificed in the attack on the frigate.

"Whosoever ship is chosen," Kanaris said, "we will, of course, share the cost of a fine, new brig. Yet that will not console any one of us, I know, if we lose the old beauty we have sailed with for so long." He paused. "Shall we decide by the stones?"

Leonidas and Papanikolis looked at one another. Both men nodded.

The small, deep jug with the stones was brought and each man reached in to bring one out. For an instant they held them clenched in their fists. Kanaris was the first to open his fingers and reveal a white stone. Papanikolis opened his fingers slowly and he held a white stone, as well. Leonidas smiled wryly as he held up the black stone.

"I am ready," he said, trying to speak quietly to conceal his harsh sense of loss. "My ship knows my hand like a wife and she'd wish us to sail into that harbor together."

"So be it," Papanikolis said, "and I will sail with you to light the train." He motioned to Kanaris. "You are senior captain and can remain in charge of our ships."

"In God's eyes there are no senior and junior captains here now," Kanaris protested. "We are sailors and Psariots. Nothing else matters. I will sail with Leonidas."

"The stones again?" Papanikolis said.

A white and black stone were put back into the jug. When Kanaris opened his fingers, he held a white stone once more.

Kanaris sighed and embraced them both. "Like a woman then," he said quietly, "I will light a candle to Saint Nicholas and offer you my prayers."

All that day a hundred men labored swiftly to prepare the *Themistocles*. Everything of value was carried by long boats to the other brigs that anchored nearby, the sea trunks of Leonidas, the ship's provisions, supplies and shot. He wrote letters to be held by Kanaris for Aspasia and his children.

Stripped finally, and ready, his ship was daubed on the insides with a composition of pitch and sulfur and filled with whatever combustibles they could find on the brigs. New hatches were cut along the deck on either side and casks of powder placed beneath them. The rigging was soaked with turpentine and tar and the ends of the yards armed with great hooks to catch and entangle in the enemy's rigging. A train of powder was laid from the combustibles, running to the casks of powder in the hold to the stern of the ship, where a single boat was tied to effect their retreat. All the crew were moved to the other ships except for Skylos and twenty picked men, who remained with Leonidas and Papanikolis on the *Themistocles*.

"I want every man to know exactly what he must do," Leonidas said to Skylos. "When it is dark and the wind has risen, the signal will be given to send them aloft. On our run into the harbor, they must muster quickly at the stern to be ready to evacuate ship the moment the train is lit."

"I'll make sure they understand, Captain," Skylos said somberly. About to say something else, he held his silence. He descended from the bridge and motioned the men to the forward part of the ship.

Leonidas touched the helm-post gently, fingered the wheel, rested his palm upon the compass.

"All right, my beauty," he said softly. "It will be all right."

Never had mother night come with more sadness and grandeur, he thought as they waited. Across the waning day, a few clouds like lynxes with slate-gray haunches stalked the orange and scarlet-tailed peacocks of the sun. As they drove them into the sea, the stars came out to mourn. In the beginning only a score were visible but as the vault of the sky blackened, a fine-spun web of thousands of tiny keeners appeared, a fragment of moon, curved like a pearl shell, leading their grief. The North Star burned to leeward and the constellations of Orion and Pegasus harnessed their lament to a stout breeze.

At the first rise of the wind, the men on the *Themistocles* leaped like silent wraiths to the shrouds. At the helm, the deck tilting under the press of canvas, Leonidas watched the bowsprit swing toward the harbor, the jibboom surging toward the stars before plunging forward and down over the furrows and crests.

They sailed swiftly through the darkness, every sail full-bellied and drawn. He felt they scudded the trough of some uncharted sea, unearthly birds racing the peaks of their masts.

Faster and faster they soared, beset by the winds of north, south, east and west, of zenith and nadir. Beyond their port and starboard lurked the specter of phantom ships, doomed to sail forever. While from deep-fathomed graves, rising to the surface, bodies of bleached bone bobbed like buoys at their passage.

The spars and towering masts of the great frigate loomed suddenly before them, huger and more menacing than anything Leonidas had ever seen before. A startled cry failing at his lips, he saw Papanikolis waiting by the train of powder, the men around him rigid as statues, peering across the bulwarks. When it seemed the ship ahead of them was a silent and abandoned hulk, they heard the first shrill cries of alarm, the tiny figures of men scurrying along her gunwales, a rapid firing of muskets sending shells squealing into the deck.

Crossing the final stretch of water between them and the mountainous hull, the whistling of the sails was joined by a sound he never remembered hearing before, yet one he knew at once, a long-drawn ghostly wail rising from the core of his ship's timbers, a final, unearthly shriek that mariners had heard from the time of the ancient voyages. And in the moment before they struck, he knew it was the death cry of his ship.

The bow of the brig sheared into the hull of the frigate, planks torn to shreds, masts cracking like giant trees being shattered. As the wheel spun useless and broken in his hand and men cried out around him, he knew the ships were banded and linked as if they had been grafted together.

The men scrambled over the stern. On the deck Papanikolis calmly touched the train. A spark of flame sputtered across the deck, racing toward the hatches where the kegs of powder were heaped. Leonidas and Papanikolis tumbled over the gunwales, jumping the last rungs of the ladder into the boat. The moment their feet touched the planks, Skylos, standing at the stern sheet with a pole braced against the brig, heaved away.

Under a mighty, desperate surging of arms and oars, the boat skimmed the water. Looking back at the locked ships receding from them with every pitch and wave, Leonidas saw the pillars of fire leap from his ship's sails onto the rigging of the frigate, spreading a conflagration across the spars. An eerie apparition, three towering arrows of flame, the frigate glowed and seethed with fire.

The night erupted in an explosion of thunderblast and lightning. Hurled from the water, the ships blew apart, spars, masts, rigging, bodies, scattered into a thousand particles of flame. A whirlwind of blistering heat and light scorched and blinded their eyes.

Surging rollers tossed their boat in a massive upheaval. Oars torn from their hands, men flung to their knees wailed in terror as the boat rocked and spun. Leonidas cried and prayed, and a gull with charred and blackened wings plummeted past him into the sea.

As the darkness returned, there stirred in his blood fearful memories of fire. Torches in the hands of avengers, burning human victims, blazing and ravaged towns.

Yet in fire there was also life. Light and warmth in the chill, dark night, the triumphant and recurring phoenix, the primal sun. Perhaps, like these, their suffering land might rise regenerated and reborn from the sacred, dreadful flame they had kindled that night.

CHAPTER
ELEVEN

As a child Andreas remembered his mother telling him that the morning star kindled the sun's light, the evening star prepared its bed in the abyss of night. But growing up in the mountains under the beacon of the stars, he never imagined night could be as black as the wolf's belly of the cave. The nightingale's sonorous cry, the cricket's trilling, the warbling of birds, all were smothered within the musty passages and chambers of the labyrinth. In the spectral silence, and in the sparse light of torches and candles like the watchfires of some ghostly host, figures moved like apparitions in the gloom, voices carrying in hissing echoes.

He would never forget the first hours they entered the cave, descending through a jagged aperture into the tomb of the mountain. The long column of men, women and children groping over the strange terrain, flames from scores of torches lighting their passage between the scaled limestone walls. Burrowing deeper and deeper into the mountain, they crept nervously beneath glittering stalactites that hung like swords above their heads, the children crying, the blindfolded mules snorting and balking as muleteers drove them with curses and sticks. Following the markers of stones set by guides, the women clutched the hands of the tiniest children to prevent them straying into some chasm.

When the caravan reached the huge central chamber of the cave, a damp, barren vault, the men unloaded the packs and provisions and the women prepared the first meal. Even then, rows of torches holding back the dark, the babble of voices dispersing the silence, the roasting lamb a familiar scent, Andreas could not subdue his revulsion and fear.

In the days and nights that followed, separate compounds were established for the men and women. The men cleaned and oiled their weapons, milled and stored gunpowder, built clay ovens, and planned strategy for their forays. The women and girls gathered water from the clear, cold spring that flowed from apertures in the rocks, wove the wool sheared from the sheep into clothing and blankets, baked bread, made cheese and cooked. A few looked after the very old and infirm members of the clan like his great-grandmother. And all sought to comfort the small children, who, unable to understand the loss of sun and light, whimpered for hours at a time. Sometimes one of them began to scream. Then they were wrapped firmly in lamb's wool, watched carefully and prayed over for hours. Cave-madness, the old men called their blight, a fearful malady that might strike a victim at any age.

Andreas woke from brief periods of sleep confused whether it was day or night. Warming his chilled hands and feet at the small fire his brother Mitsos had built, he heard men around him emerging from their pallets of straw. For all the bravado many of them affected, he felt they secretly yearned as much as he did for the warmth of the sun. A few of them were permitted to leave the cave as sentries assigned posts on the mountain's surface or as ostlers and shepherds tending the horses and sheep. But veterans including his older brothers were chosen for these assignments. As the youngest son of Kyriakos, he could not seek any favor.

Since separation between the male and female compounds was strict, Andreas had not seen Voula since entering the cave. Even when the clan gathered for the communal meals, the swarm of people and the murky torchlight kept her hidden. Yet he felt her presence, a fleeting wraith that evoked rage because of her betrayal and longing because he still desired her.

If he did not see Voula, he could not avoid Lambros Kasandonis, the chieftain to whom she was betrothed. The man dominated every council, his loud, brash voice kneading authority over men who were easily cowed. He swaggered about the cave, the metallic jangling of his weapons deceiving the women and girls who did not know any better that he alone would protect them. Even Kyriakos succumbed to the man's bombast, emerging from the meetings of the Council of Elders to assure his sons that Kasandonis was "a great leader we are fortunate to have with us."

"Let's wait until he proves what he can do," Andreas muttered to Mitsos.

With his spirit solitary and somber, except for the companionship of Mitsos, Andreas kept to himself. When his tasks were done, he left the central chamber in which the clan lived, taking one of the ominous passages that led deeper into the mountain. In this way he laid siege to his panic and terror. When his legs weakened and he could go no further, he sat down with his back braced against the roughcast wall, knees drawn to his chest. Suspended in silence and darkness, he escaped the cave in chaste, large-hearted dreams.

In his fantasy he would be lying beside Voula on the surface of the mountain, the ground about them strewn with fragrant red and yellow blossoms. Along the slopes that slanted toward the sun, enormous beech trees formed a majestic stairwall, sunbeams shining through their masses of leaves. While in the sky high above their heads the graceful and unencumbered swallows soared and sailed and glided on the spirals of the wind.

Disrupting his dream, some loathsome creature of the cave, lizard or snake, crossed his knees and he cried out and leaped up.

Cave-madness, he wept as he stumbled back to the chamber where the others dwelt, cave-madness is growing in me and soon I will begin to scream like a child.

At the end of their day's labors and as a balm for their confinement, the clan assembled around the fires after dinner while the musicians played. Old Petros Zourbakis, a rhymadori descended from those poor, sometimes blind bards who wandered from village to village, singing and chanting stories, brought out his treasured santour. His feet shod in black, patched boots, his snow-white hair bound by a strip of blue cloth, he placed the instrument carefully on his knees, caressing it in a slow ritual of preparation. If a vagrant whisper rose from the circle of watchers, the old man's head snapped up in a glare of reproof. Only when there was total silence except for the crackling of fires would he begin.

The haunting tones of the santour would soar through the cave. Playing slowly in the beginning, each note separate and distinct, as the old man quickened the tempo one note flew so closely upon another they resounded like a single sustained bell peal. As the final echoes drifted to silence, the old man began to sing. Sometimes he told of the Sacrifice of Abraham, the love story of Erotokritos, the Revolt of Daskaloyiannis. In almost all of his tales of love, heroism and war, a central figure was Charos, the grim reaper, the ferryman who conducted souls across the river of the underworld.

> They wrestled on the iron threshing floor,
> And nine times the youth threw Charos,
> And Charos rose up again nine times,
> Grasped the youth's hair, forced him to his knees.

—Let go my hair, Charos, and take me by the arm,
Then I will show you what heroes are made of.
—I take all heroes just like this, Charos laughed.
I take beautiful girls and fighting men.
And I take little babies with their mothers.

The santour resounded again in a stern warning, a funereal reminder to all who listened that in the end Charos would have his way.

Why are the mountains black and filled with tears?
No wind assails them, nor rain beats them.
Only . . . Charos is passing, sweeping the dead.
Sweeping the young in front, the old behind
And dangling the poor babies like tiny hares on the
    saddle.

Then, to banish the chill of the old man's tales, the players of the three-stringed lyres would come forward, their short bows flashing in lilting melodies across the strings. Men and women, singly or in chorus, would raise their voices in song. They sang the songs of their roots, songs of journeys, songs of the table and the hearth. They sang old songs which had been sung by their fathers and grandfathers when they were still children and they made up new songs which had never existed in words or in music, songs which grew out of the fire and the cave, songs which still unborn children would someday sing long after those who had dwelled in the cave were gone.

Finally, at a time when Andreas crouched to drink water from one of the springs, a group of girls came to fill jugs for the cistern. Without seeing her he knew Voula was among them. His first impulse was to draw back further into the shadows, concealing himself till they had gone. Then, scorning his timidity, he called her name.

"Voula!"

She separated from the others, peering toward the shadows where he stood. One of the girls uttered a warning but Voula brushed her aside. The girls filled their jugs quickly and retreated, whispering nervously until their voices faded.

"Have you been avoiding me, Andreas?" Voula asked, her voice a cunning parody of innocence.

"Why shouldn't I avoid you?"

For a moment she was silent. He was grateful the shadows concealed the bewitchment of her eyes.

"What's the matter, Andreas? What have I done to you? It is foolish, isn't it, for you to be sulking when we are buried in this dreadful place. What have I done to distress you?"

He was outraged that she counted her betrayal of slight importance.

"We have always had an understanding that you belonged to me!" he said harshly.

Voula stepped forward, the oval of her face glistening and pale.

"Who said I belonged to you?"

"You have always belonged to me," he said doggedly. "From the time we were children and played together, that was taken for granted."

"You had no right to take it for granted!"

"It was always understood!"

"Stop saying that! Nothing was understood! You are a fool, Andreas, if you think a girl can be acquired like a cow or a sheep, claimed without her consent! I chose you as my friend! I do not belong to you! You have not bought me!"

"He bought you!"

"He did not! He did not!" She clenched her hands into tight, small fists, raised them as if she were going to strike him. "He did not! I accepted his proposal of marriage because he is a fine, brave man . . . and because I love him!"

He felt an unbearable pain that hardened like a stone in

his chest. As if she suddenly understood, Voula reached out and caught remorsefully at his arm.

"I don't mean to hurt you, Andreas," she said softly. "We have been dear friends for so many years. Perhaps there was a time when we were children and I too thought we might love each other in that way. Don't blame me for what has happened now. If you love me as a friend, have mercy, and try to understand."

"To hell with you!" Andreas cried. "Let Charos be your friend!"

Voula recoiled from him with a shrill cry. For a penitent moment he yearned for the strength to annul and waste the curse. Then a specter of Voula's naked body in the other man's arms brawled through his blood. He brushed roughly past her and hurried away.

The full fury of war came to Crete. The scouts and couriers of the clan came to the cave with the news that the Bishop of Kissamos and four hundred Christians of that population were slaughtered. In Megalokastron a mob of Turkocretans hanged priests and bishops. None knew whether the massacres were in reprisal for attacks by bands of Cretans on Turkish villages or whether, hearing of the outbreak of war in Greece, the Turks were striking. But ancient enmities scorned mercy. Villages were ravaged, men murdered, women and children carried off to be sold in the slave bazaars of Asia Minor.

In their own area, the sentries standing watch on the mountain reported pillars of smoke rising from the villages by day, pillars of fire glowing by night. The first ragged survivors who managed to escape up the mountain were brought into the cave by the sentries. They were embraced by the men and women of the clan, fed and given a chance to rest. Those who could, spoke of the horrors.

"In my village," one of the refugees said mournfully, "they

hanged forty men from the great plane tree in the square. Every branch held a naked Cretan body, eyes bulging and tongue hanging out. God should have blinded me before letting my eyes look on such a sight."

"Our village elder, Karnaros, sought to reason with the beasts," another of the refugees said. "They threw him to the ground and kicked the old man back and forth with their boots until he was a pulp his own wife could not recognize."

"In our settlement some young men barricaded themselves in a house," a man with a bloody bandage on his head spoke. "They killed half a dozen Turks before the house was set on fire and they perished in the blaze. Because the boys were dead and could not be tortured, they mutilated the burned bodies." The man began to weep quietly. Another man from the same settlement continued. "Two of those boys were his sons," he said.

Women whispered in pity and made their cross. The men of the clan muttered in fury, unsheathing their daggers as if to warm them with rage. In the glow of the fire, his face stern and vengeful, they waited for Kyriakos to speak.

"Who are the butchers that have done these things?" Kyriakos asked.

"They were Janizaries from the garrison town of Avrianna," one of the refugees said.

"Those beasts have forgotten the Janizaries Troulinos hung as a warning years ago," Kyriakos said. "Well, we will pay a visit to Avrianna and refresh their memories."

Men leaped to their feet, cheering lustily, eager to escape the cave and to fight. Andreas joined his voice to their shouts, an angry jubilation surging through his blood.

Lambros Kasandonis, tall and booted, a black kerchief bound about his hair, motioned for silence.

"My men and I are at your disposal, Kyriakos," he said. "Order us as you wish."

"You honor us by joining our force," Kyriakos said. He looked somberly at the clustered men. "I know all of you will wish to ride this first time," he said, "but a force must remain to guard the cave. My son Christos will remain here in charge of the defense. Fifty men will remain with him and fifty will ride to begin our raids. To determine who goes and who stays, we will draw lots."

The large crock of stones was brought to the center of the crowd. One by one the men shoved in their hands and pulled them out clutching one of the stones. They chortled in pleasure at a white stone, cursed with disappointment when a black stone in their palm decreed they would remain behind. Mitsos drew out a white stone and shouted with joy. Another brother, Elias, drew a black stone and walked off to brood.

Andreas could not endure the shame of remaining behind with the women and children since Kasandonis, his status as a chieftain not requiring that he draw a stone, would be riding into battle. When he drew his hand from the crock, he kept his fingers closed about the stone. As the men who had not yet drawn crowded in for their turn, he slipped into the shadows. Without examining the stone he threw it far out into the darkness. He stamped back to the others with an exultant stride.

"We ride together, Mitsos!" he cried.

As Mitsos cheered, one of the disappointed men stared suspiciously at Andreas.

"Where is your stone, Andreas?"

"I dropped it somewhere. I saw it first and it was white."

"That isn't fair," the man grumbled. "We have to see the stone." He turned to complain to Kyriakos and Andreas stepped into his path, gripping the man's arm.

"I tell you it was white," Andreas said quietly. "Are you calling me a liar and a cheat?"

The man stared at Andreas for a moment and then shook

his head. "If you want to go so much, then go," he mumbled.

The men armed themselves with muskets, pistols, swords and daggers, ample quantities of powder and shot stored in their pouches and belts. In their saddlebags they carried hard brown bread, coffee beans and some sugar. Uncle Simos led them in a prayer and afterward the men scattered to bid their families good-by.

Andreas hurried to the women's compound. He hugged his sister, Gianoula, and then knelt beside his great-grandmother's pallet, smelling the stale, sour odors that rose from her emaciated frame. Each day saw her slipping further into the shadow of death.

"Giagia, it's Andreas . . . Andreas."

For an instant she did not seem to recognize him and then, with a stiff thrust of her hand, she fastened her bony fingers about his wrist. He was startled at the strength of her grip. Wondering if her talismanic power envisioned he would not return, he felt a flutter of fear.

"Giagia, please!" he pleaded. "Let me go! They will leave without me!"

He struggled, gently at first, then urgently, until he had pried her fingers loose. He rose and a short, mournful cry from her lips followed him. As he hurried away, he caught a glimpse of Voula and Kasandonis. He averted his gaze quickly to avoid witnessing their farewell, his fear replaced by rage.

The men moved rapidly along one of the corridors into a chamber with rope ladders suspended from rocky ledges above. Strapping their muskets to their backs, they clambered up the ladders, taunting the heavier men who climbed slowly.

After weeks of being buried in the earth, emerging onto the surface of the mountain in the deepest hours of dark-

ness, none of them were prepared for the blinding power of
the stars. As they looked up they shielded their faces with
their hands and cried out in awe at the sky laced with fiery
flares that struck their eyes.

Mounting the horses which ostlers from the clan grazed in
a secret pasture, they rode down the mountain. Andreas
savored with deep breaths the fruity aroma of earth and
flowers. From the slopes and trees beyond the path of their
descent, came the howls, barks, screeches and hoots of animals and birds marking their passage. He felt the taint and
poison of the cave fall like leper's scales from his body.

They crossed the foothills of the mountain still mantled in
darkness, spurring their horses into a gallop for the Janizary
town of Avrianna. Their route led them through one of the
Christian villages the Janizaries had burned and looted.
Passing the rubble of razed houses, the ruins of a small
church, men held their kerchiefs pressed against their noses
at the putrefied stench of blood still clinging to the air. The
horses, snorting and tossing their manes in revulsion and terror, had to be held tightly to prevent their bolting. Mitsos
cursed in a low voice and Andreas made his cross for the
souls of those who had been murdered.

At the outskirts of the village they passed a narrow ravine
hastily converted into a shallow, mass grave to bury the
dead. Extending from the freshly turned earth like a ghostly
plant, a hand with wrist and fingers withered to parchment
beckoned, an eerie apparition pointing them along the path
to vengeance.

The first, feeble light of dawn misted the horizon as they
came in sight of Avrianna. Gathering in a grove still some
distance from the town, the men dismounted quietly.
Kyriakos would lead half the band to the east around an or-
chard and assault the barracks from the opposite side.

Kasadonis would lead the remaining men in a charge against the houses.

Andreas and Mitsos led their horses to join their father.

"Only one of you can ride with me," Kyriakos told them. "The other must stay with Kasandonis. That is only proper."

"I am older and I choose to go with Father." Mitsos grinned at the disappointed Andreas.

For a moment it appeared his father would say something to Andreas. Instead of speaking, he reached out and clasped his son's shoulder, his strong fingers pressing flesh, muscle and bone to convey reassurance and love. Afterward assembling their part of the band, his father and brother had mounted and gone.

Kasandonis gathered the others in the grove. Andreas could not see his face clearly but heard his arrogant voice.

"Remember this, my Cretans," Kasandonis said. "If a man is meant to die on land, he will not drown. If death on a battlefield is to be his lot, he will not die of sickness or old age. God's dispositions are fixed in our stars. Be brave and think of Crete."

I do not need to be reminded of Crete, Andreas thought resentfully, and turned abruptly away.

They waited for a while to allow his father time to reach the far side of the town. Finally, at a signal from Kasandonis, passed in whispers along the ranks, they mounted and began their advance toward the dark cluster of dwellings. In the distance a loon cried, the sound splitting the stillness. Above them a swirling mass of clouds revealed narrow patches of sky beginning to lighten.

They rode closer, the clatter of their horse's hooves on the rocky ground rumbling like thunder to Andreas. When they reached the boundary beyond the first houses, a volley of shots rang out from the area of the barracks. Then the night burst apart with percussion and flame.

Kasandonis shouted a command, waved his sword and

lashed his horse forward. They galloped into the town as men and women, hearing the fusillade from the barracks, stumbled drowsy and dazed from their houses into the street. Seeing the horsemen charging upon them, they scattered in panic. Those who dodged the first rank of attackers, scrambled into the path of other horses, fell screaming under the hooves.

Confused by the bedlam of moans, screams and the pounding horses, Andreas almost rode down a man and woman, jerking the reins of his horse to avoid them barely in time. The man lunged at Andreas, sword glinting in his hand, his mouth open in a bellow. Pulling his mount away quickly, Andreas raised his pistol and shot him, sent him sprawling to the street. The woman stared mutely at his body and then flung herself on her knees beside him.

The first man I have ever killed, Andreas thought. For an instant he felt the bite of remorse. The scream of a dying Cretan, tumbling from his horse with part of his temple shot away, inflamed his rage once more.

A volley of musket fire came from those Janizary officers and married men who had remained inside the houses. Bands of Cretans rode into the yards, leaped off their horses, pounded in the doors with the butts of their muskets and charged across the thresholds. They emerged dragging and kicking men and women before them.

A brawling phalanx of horsemen mowed the length of the street like reapers in a cornfield, slashing at the heads and arms of men and women in their path. After they passed, a new shambles of dead and dying littered the stones. Dogs raced and barked in maddened circles about them while frenzied chickens flailed their wings.

A barefooted child in a nightgown with long black hair streaming over her shoulders flew screaming from one of the houses into the street. A galloping Cretan horseman rode her down, the rider not bothering to look back.

Sickened by the small, shattered form that remained in

the street, Andreas spurred his horse toward the barracks. He found that courtyard full of half-dressed, shrieking Turks trying to muster a defense against the Cretans. A few had piled rocks in makeshift barricades, others crouched to fire muskets from behind the corpses of fallen comrades. A tall Janizary officer, shrieking at his men, was shot in the face. His head seemed to explode, his body tumbling backward to land in a weird sitting position against the barracks wall, a ghastly trunk without a head.

Searching for his father and Mitsos in the disorder of the fighting, Andreas did not see the Turk leaping at him until the man grabbed his leg, trying to get his teeth in the calf. Andreas lashed his horse forward, the Turk hanging on furiously, shrieking as his feet left the ground and he was hurled away. Nearby another Turk pulled a Cretan from his horse, and swiftly plunged a dagger into his heart. The startled animal reared its head in confusion at the sudden disappearance of its load.

The last pockets of defense crumpled as the Cretan horsemen narrowed the circle, scattering small enclaves of Turks, slaughtering them quickly. A huge, bearded Janizary braced against the barracks wall, his musket clutched like a war club in his great hands, swung it wildly as a half-dozen horsemen led by Mitsos circled him.

"Crawl, reptile!" Mitsos cried. "Beg for your life!"

The Turk spit with contempt and made an obscene gesture with his hand. Crying with fury the Cretans charged. Swinging his musket in a savage arc, the Turk caught one of the Cretans across the belly, hurled him like a catapulted stone from his horse to land with bone-breaking impact on the ground. Then Mitsos and the others rode the Turk down, slashing with their swords at his head and arms, bending from their saddles to chop at his body like woodsmen hacking at the bole of a massive tree.

Even Turkish beasts can die bravely, Andreas thought,

and suddenly the fever of killing drained from him and he felt chilled and weak.

They loaded arms, powder and whatever spoils they could carry onto their horses. Then they tied and dragged the bodies of the dead Janizaries into the houses and set them afire. In a few moments every dwelling in the town was burning, flames surging from the windows, a pall of black, noxious smoke rising into the sky. As the only survivors in Avrianna they left a bedraggled cluster of Janizary wives and children, misshapen and ugly with grief and hate. Riding past them on their way from the town, the Cretans called down disdainful jeers.

"No more Turkish bastards now, Fatima!"

"Don't forget us, sweetheart! Tell your scurvy Sultan we send regards!"

"If you ever need a man, ask for Sotiris!"

"Wash your face first, or a pig wouldn't touch you!"

Some of the women hugging the smallest of the children, wept and wailed, a few stood dazed and mute, while bolder ones cursed the Cretans in return.

"May your kidneys roast in hell!"

"Our turn will come!"

"Murderers! Assassins!"

Andreas rode past them in silence. One of the Cretans riding near him, a grizzled veteran named Kapenakis, fumbled at something he carried on his saddle and hurled it at the women. The object struck the ground, rolling over and over like a ball. As the women shrieked and stumbled from its path, Andreas saw it was the head of the huge Janizary in the courtyard, a grisly, bloody trophy with eyes swollen like great black olives. As the women howled, Kapenakis roared with delight.

A few miles from Avrianna, the troop paused at a crossroads by a small stream. About a dozen men bore wounds of varying severity and the more serious ones would have to be returned to the cave. To the dismay of Andreas, his father was among them, an ugly gash in his thigh made by the thrust of a Janizary sword. The wound had bled copiously while he rode, staining his breeches and running into his boot, leaving a patch of blood across the belly of his horse.

Despite the vehement protests of Kyriakos that the wound would heal quickly, the older Cretans pleaded and cajoled him to be sensible and lead the wounded men back to the cave. When his wound had healed, they would all be joined once again at Langada.

As Andreas and Mitsos went to bid their father good-by, they found him sitting propped against a rock while two men washed his wound and bound his leg. He embraced each of them, his face tight and pale with the effort to contain his pain.

"I'll be back with you as quickly as God and my good horse allow," he said. "Look after one another and, in my absence, offer Kasandonis the same loyalty and obedience you would give me." He stifled a groan. "Damn you, Harilaos! Are you trying to bind or geld me?"

"Sorry, Kyriakos." Harilaos winked at Andreas and Mitsos. "Those big ram's sacs of yours get in the way." He rose to his feet. "All right, boys, give a hand so we can hoist your father to his saddle."

"Keep your stonecutter's hands off me!" Kyriakos said harshly. "I'm not dead yet. Just bring me my horse."

A Cretan led over his big colt and, bracing himself against the rock, Kyriakos pushed himself to his feet. He rested his left hand lightly on the horse's withers, speaking to it in a soft, soothing voice. Then, gripping the pommel of the saddle, with a mighty, concerted heave he swung himself into the saddle, the shock draining the blood from his cheeks.

"Come on, then, you mangy wrecks and clumsy cripples!" he shouted. "Let's go!"

As the wounded men, slouched and bent low in their saddles, shuffled slowly by, the men remaining with the band cried farewells.

"Say hello to my wife, Stathis! Tell her I'm a hero!"

"She won't believe me! She knows you too well!"

"Don't worry, Yanni. When I feel better I'll comfort your Iliana for you!"

"Stay away from my wife!"

"Gorgio, tell my mother the Bible she gave me saved my life!"

"You must have been wearing it on your ass!"

"Ask my sister to light a candle for us!"

"Good-by . . . good-by . . ."

Leading the column, Kyriakos looked back one final time and waved a forlorn farewell. Watching them disappear into the foothills, feeling a chill at their separation, Andreas heard Kasandonis call for the men to mount and ride. They traveled in the opposite direction from the wounded men, leaving a clear trail to draw any pursuers away from Kyriakos. Before them the shadow of the earth's eastern rim vanished before the corona of the rising sun.

At noon they made camp in a wild, heavily bouldered canyon, sentries standing guard in the rocks above. Men spread their capes on the stony ground, molding themselves like lizards to the rough terrain. A few built small fires and crushed beans with the butts of their pistol to brew cups of strong, black coffee. Some sat in excited, chattering groups, proudly exhibiting their booty, ornamented daggers and guns scrolled with silver. Afterward, as men drifted off to sleep, the camp grew quiet.

Andreas found a solitary pine to shade himself from the sun and lay down on his cape. A shadow moved beside him and he saw Mitsos, disheveled and weary, slip to his knees. Spreading his cape beside Andreas, he lowered himself to the ground with a groan.

"Well, kid, how did you like your first battle?"

"Your group attacked soldiers in the garrison," Andreas said. "We assaulted the women and children. The great chieftain, Kasandonis, was his most valorous leading that charge."

"Andreas, are you forgetting the village we passed on our way to Avrianna?" Mitsos said. "Holy Jesus, they did the same or worse to our people. Don't forget that!"

"I'm not forgetting anything," Andreas said, and turned away from his brother, wanting to forsake talk and sleep.

They fell silent. Andreas closed his eyes. Around him he heard the grunts and snores of sleeping men, the contented neighing of horses that had been fed, the strident cawing of ravens. Into his nostrils seeped the soft scents of the blossoms of lemon trees.

For a wistful moment he thought he might sleep and wake cleansed and renewed. Perhaps the baptism of battle, the surfeit of death he had seen in just a few hours, had sated him. Before he slept, his lids pressing like stones against his eyes, he knew that was a child's illusion. The killing had not appeased his jealousy or his hate of Kasandonis.

In the weeks that followed, the band hid by day in canyons and small caves, emerging at dusk to ride in swift attacks against Turkish settlements and villages. Wreaking destruction, they disappeared like spirits, moving rapidly to span many miles before striking again.

"They will think we are Titans," Kasandonis told some of the men who grumbled that he was driving them too hard, "or that there are several bands of Cretans in this area of Crete instead of one."

"Father would have planned the same strategy," Andreas told Mitsos.

Yet, as word of their raids spread across central Crete, more of the Turkish and Janizary garrisons were alerted, troops searching the mountains for them. The battles became fiercer, good Cretans killed. To prevent the bodies being stripped and mutilated, they carried their dead away with them, burying them under rocks or deep in caverns, murmuring prayers above their unmarked graves, scattering flowers into the wind.

A reinforcement of men came from the cave to meet them at Langada, but Kyriakos was not among them. His wound had festered, the men told Andreas, leg and thigh grown dark and swollen. He reclined like a wrathful, disabled bear by the fire, relentlessly driving the old women into preparing one poultice after another to draw the poison from his wound. He sent word to Kasandonis that he would join them soon if he had to crawl down the mountain.

Andreas was disturbed by news of his father's slow healing and disappointed he could not join them. But the weeks of constant riding and fighting had gained him a power that did not depend upon anyone. His body was leaner and stronger than it had been, his flesh toughened by sun, rain and wind. From the hours spent peering into the trails of night, his senses had sharpened, eyes and ears closer to an animal's keenness and cunning. Like an animal, as well, his body acquired the odors of their assorted lairs, the caves, hollows and gorges where they camped. The grime and crust of clothing, slept and fought in for days at a time, formed a lamina like a second skin.

Yet in some perverse, indefinable way he felt the severest change in him was that he had grown more callous to the brutalities of war. He had lost his fervor for glory and his illusions about courage. He had seen enemies fight as bravely as any Cretan, die unrepentant, still convinced of their cause. He gave up trying to understand the meaning behind the way men fought and died. That could wait until Crete was free.

He spent hours watching Kasandonis, evaluating his leadership, eager for signs of weakness. Grudgingly he came to understand the chieftain was a hard, unflawed spirit. He was, as his father had told them, a leader who combined bravery with a masterful skill at war. As for the vanity and bombast he had seemed to show in the cave, at war Kasandonis did not swagger or boast. Finally, when there was a dangerous action to be taken, he led it himself, asking none of the men to do anything he would not do.

Once as Kasandonis demonstrated to some of the men including Mitsos and Andreas the most effective way to swing a sword, utilizing the full power of shoulder and arm he set an example by severing a thick tree limb with a single, stunning blow. The men murmured in admiration and approval.

Kasandonis, pleased at the way he had impressed them, motioned toward an equally thick-girthed bough.

"Now you men try," he said.

One by one the men slashed with their swords at the bough but none of them could match the feat. Mitsos failed and turned to Andreas.

"He's the only one can do it," Mitsos muttered.

Andreas looked at the bough gashed and chipped by the blows the men had struck. He turned away and selected an unmarked, even stouter shaft. While the men hooted and teased him for his bravado, he gripped the handle of his sword tightly, raised it and brought the blade down in a slashing, powerful fury that almost wrenched his arm from his shoulder. The severed bough spun free.

The surprised men burst into vigorous applause. Mitsos embraced him in pride and glee.

"Splendid, Andreas!" Kasandonis cried in tribute. "Your father would be proud of you as I am proud!"

Yet Andreas sensed an unrest in the chieftain's gaze that lingered on him, perhaps glimpsing for the first time an ominous challenge to his own supremacy.

The feat was soon forgotten, dismissed as a drill ground exercise that could not be duplicated in the turmoil of battle. That denial and the unremitting admiration the men displayed for Kasandonis rankled Andreas. In an effort to shadow the chieftain's light, he began taking wilder, more reckless chances in their attacks, boldly claiming a place in the forefront of every battle, ignoring his own safety. The acclaim of Mitsos and the younger of their comrades was a nectar he sought to replenish by still more daring. The older men began to regard him with a kind of fear, making their cross when he passed them in the camps.

On a night when Andreas, Mitsos and some of the men were cleaning their weapons by the fire, Kasandonis appeared. He touched Andreas on the shoulder, asked him to join him in walking a short distance away. Andreas rose and they walked beyond the circle of fire.

Kasandonis lowered himself lithely to the ground, clasped his arms about his knees, rocking slowly back and forth. Andreas waited for him to speak.

"You are still a young man, Andreas," Kasandonis told him quietly. "Brave and bold enough to become as great a warrior as your father. But the way you storm into each battle now, I am afraid you will not live very long."

"Are you ordering me to be more cautious?" Andreas could not keep a barb of scorn from his voice.

"I am only suggesting it is foolish to risk one's life needlessly," Kasandonis said patiently, "and to court wounds by being reckless. This war will go on, I think, for a long time. Crete will suffer for many years. Children who still run and play now will grow up und join our struggle. Young men fighting today must become leaders for them in the future."

"I cannot think of the future," Andreas said. "I am concerned with killing Turks now."

"Kill Turks, yes!" Kasandonis said. "But use judgment, as well. I have some reputation for bravery but I tell you I am a cautious man. If retreat seems wise, I retreat. If the enemy fire is heavy, I crouch behind a boulder and wait for their volleys to pass and for their guns to overheat. Kasandonis enjoys killing Turks as much as you, believe me, but in order to do so he needs to stay alive."

"I am not Kasandonis," Andreas said.

"We are more alike than you know." Kasandonis smiled faintly. "Perhaps that's why I feel the demon in you. When I was your age, the old men also called me 'possessed.'"

They were silent for a moment, Andreas staring up into the branches of a tree.

"I understand why you might resent me," Kasandonis went on gravely. "Young men often feel they should lead and not have to follow. That will come for you soon enough. You are the son of a chieftain and you will become a chieftain. Meanwhile, I offer you my pledge of friendship and will gratefully accept any confidence you wish to share."

Andreas felt his jealousy wavering before the man's effort at kindness. Then the absurdity of comradeship or friendship between them hardened his spirit. As long as both of them desired Voula, they were rivals and bitter enemies.

"There is nothing to confide, Captain," he said, "nothing to explain." He walked slowly, gloomily, back to the fire.

There was a night not long after they had spoken when Kasandonis set a cunning ambush for a Turkish convoy carrying wagons with guns and powder for the garrison in Retimo. He struck it first with a small force, allowing himself to be driven off, the major portion of Turkish troops in hot pursuit. Circling around he joined the segment of the clan that had been held back and together they struck the convoy. Before the pursuers who had set off after them could reassemble in defense, they had carried off sufficient weapons and ammunition to last them for months. Entrenched back in one of their camps, the passes leading to it secured by sentries, the men celebrated by drinking abundant quantities of raki from two large casks they had also liberated from the Turks that night.

They danced and sang by firelight, their noisy, leaping bodies throwing long, tempestuous shadows across rocks and trees, the darkness ringing with their shouts.

Sitting in a circle of men around the fire, Kasandonis accepted the plaudits and tributes of the clan, the frequent toasts to his valor and wisdom, his growing legend and fame.

Andreas did not join the dancing or singing. He drank raki steadily, the hot liquid burning his throat, kindling a fire in his belly. After a while drink and misery gutted him like a burned and ravaged house. The intolerable irony, it raged in his thoughts, was that every victory Andreas fought for added to the chieftain's fame, driving still another wedge between himself and Voula.

He stared dejectedly into the fire. As a surge of tears stung his eyes, he angrily wiped them away.

Mitsos came to him, a flask dangling from his fingers.

"Drink up, brother!" Mitsos shouted drunkenly. "More victories like the one tonight and we'll drive the last bloody oppressors from our island!"

"Yes, by God!" Andreas cried. "Crete for the Cretans! Turks, Franks, Venetians and their cursed offspring can leave our land!"

He was conscious of the night slashed to silence. The voices wavered and died, the dancers stopped, the revelry extinguished. In a circle of frozen men, he saw Kasandonis watching him.

"My mother was a Venetian, Andreas," Kasandonis said quietly. "Perhaps you did not know."

"I knew," Andreas said.

Gruff mutterings of disapproval rose from the men, several of them glaring at Andreas. Kasandonis waved them to rigid quiet once more.

"Then, my young hawk"—he made an effort to speak lightly—"would you banish me from Crete, as well?"

"I stand by my words," Andreas said.

Kasandonis sat stiff and perplexed as if he were trying to understand the reason for the provocation.

"Is it the wine speaking, Andreas? If it is the wine, we will forget what you said. I will not take offense."

"Are you deaf?" Andreas cried. "If you cannot remember, I will say it again! Turks, Franks, Venetians and their bastards should be driven from Crete!"

Now there was no restraining the men, who burst into indignant clamor. Several moved threateningly around the fire toward Andreas. A stone whistled by his temple. Mitsos, trying desperately to clear his sodden senses, took a stand beside Andreas, fumbling for the pistol in his belt.

"Damn you all, stop!" Kasandonis shouted. "This is my affair!"

Slowly, reluctantly, the men grew still. Kasandonis rose and walked to Andreas.

"All right," he said hoarsely. "When you have sobered, we will settle our accounts."

"I am sober now!"

"You are drunk now and God knows what else," Kasandonis said scornfully. "Not so drunk you do not know what you are saying, but too drunk to fight. Morning will be soon enough."

He turned and walked away from the fire into the outer circle of darkness. The men moved somberly and quickly to their beds, speaking in grim, hushed tones. Mitsos and Andreas were left alone beside the fire.

"Move out of the light!" Mitsos whispered uneasily. "You make a clear target and someone may decide to save Kasandonis the trouble of killing you!"

Andreas walked slowly toward his pallet by the rocks, Mitsos stumbling along beside him.

"Andreas, you were not fair," Mitsos slurred the words. "He may be only half Cretan, but he risks his life for Crete like us all. Let me go to him and tell him you're . . ."

"Too late for that," Andreas said. "We have to fight now."

Through the long hours of that night, staring toward the embers of the fire that cast up trailings of smoke, images formed and then dispersed. He saw strings of dried tomatoes on the walls of his father's house; tiny, flickering candles of icons; the first, steaming chunk of lamb hacked from a carcass on the spit celebrating his twelfth birthday, sprinkled with salt and handed to him; the furry, bleating heat of ewes crowding against his knees to be milked; the shy, smiling faces of village girls; the soothing voices of women as they baked; the rain-bleached cross above his mother's grave.

Sometime before dawn he became sick, whether from the raki or because of disgust and shame at what he had done, he did not know. He crawled away from his sleeping brother on his hands and knees like an animal and by a bush spewed out his belly. When he returned weakly to his pallet, his mouth sour and his tongue coated, from some crag a wild cock crowed, driving away the lingering shades of night.

In the first glimmering of dawn, men rose morose and silent. From the pallet beside Andreas, Mitsos raised his head, his eyes bloodshot and his cheeks drawn.

Kasandonis appeared, dressed and booted as he had been the night before, almost as if he had been waiting for the dawn sitting just outside the circle of fire.

"Do you want to pick seconds, Kasandonis?" one of the men asked quietly.

"Andreas and I will settle this alone," Kasandonis said.

Once again the chieftain was seeking to minimize his humiliation, spare Andreas having his comrades witness any beating or defeat. That gesture served to intensify his shame.

He started from the camp, Kasandonis following a few feet behind him, branches and twigs snapping and crackling under their boots. They came to the spring, water flowing from the clefts in the rocks to a small, clear pool. In the thick foliage of trees surrounding the clearing, Andreas caught a glimpse of the small, downy heads of birds, watchful and waiting. He turned slowly to face the chieftain.

"Goddam you for a fool, boy!" Kasandonis said grimly. "I

give you every chance and you spit them back in my face! You were drunk and poisoned with envy because your father left me in command. It is only because I might have felt the same at your age that I don't kill you. But I am going to give you a beating that will disable you for days! That may help curb your impudent and offensive tongue!"

Andreas shook his head slowly. A curious calm descended upon him, a conviction that honor could only be redeemed by his death. He reached to the belt at his waist and drew out his long-bladed dagger.

Kasandonis pounded his fist in fury against his thigh.

"You traitorous mongrel!" he cried. "Your arrogance and brashness will cost you your life! By God, you better put that away!"

The tempo of the flow of water in the pool had altered, hissing in shrill warning as it plunged from the spring.

"You think it was the wine that loosened my tongue," Andreas said quietly. "That I envy you because you are captain. Those things mean nothing to me. What matters between us, the reason we must fight, is Voula."

Kasandonis stared at Andreas in shock.

"What do you have to do with my Voula, you bastard?" he cried hoarsely.

"From the time we were children, she has been mine." Andreas felt the words burn his lips. "Betrothals and pledges made with you mean nothing. The only way to stop me claiming her is to kill me."

A searing outrage swept the chieftain's body. His black eyes shone with a strange, scorching heat. He whipped out his own dagger. The birds in the trees erupted in shrill, flurried cries.

Kasandonis charged, swinging his dagger like a scythe. Andreas parried his blow. Once, twice, three times, metal rang against metal, the impact driving them apart.

For a moment they both stood poised. Andreas watched the chieftain's arm and hand tighten about the dagger preparing another thrust. Some terror and force to survive stirred in him.

Leaping closer, Kasandonis feinted and stabbed and Andreas dodged, the dagger missing his throat by inches. Kasandonis whirled swiftly and thrust again, Andreas avoiding his blow by a narrow margin once more.

Slashing and parrying, stabbing and dodging, the battle went on, their boots pounding the earth, matting and crushing brush and leaves. Andreas defended himself, making no effort to attack.

"Are you coward as well as fool!" Kasandonis cried. "Fight, you deceiving bastard, fight!"

The words barely out of his mouth, he charged again. Retreating before him, Andreas stumbled, lost his balance, Kasandonis on him in a flash. He was driven to the ground, the chieftain straddling his fallen body, dagger poised above his heart. Andreas saw the peak of the mountain limned against the sky, braced himself for death, his final thought a cry of love to Voula.

"I should kill you now!" Kasandonis groaned. "But Crete cries for mercy! Swear never to utter Voula's name again and I'll let you live to kill Turks!"

That moment of faltering, that instant of reprieve, allowed Andreas to roll aside, tumbling Kasandonis to his knees. Both men leaped like cats to their feet.

"You had your chance!" Kasandonis roared. "God forgive me, I must kill you now!"

He charged again. At the last minute, rejecting escape, Andreas turned to meet him, raising his dagger to parry the thrust. Their bodies slammed together. Driven backwards, Andreas felt his knife wrenched from his palm. Before him, Kasandonis gasped, his dagger dropping from his stunned hand. His fingers, like slow and sluggish snails crawled to his chest, fumbling at the blade of Andreas' dagger impaled above his heart.

His mouth formed the shape of a scream, but no sound

came from his lips. Watching in horror, Andreas saw life drain from his face, flesh and blood dissolving eerily, leaving a frail, sheer shell.

Kasandonis dropped to his knees, swayed there stiffly for an instant, light from his eyes fading through gaps between his lids. A final spasm of breath flew like an arrow past his teeth. Then he plummeted forward, his body striking a tremor through the earth.

A strange sound came from the crags of the mountain, a wind sweeping along the ravines, wailing down the canyons, a churning of rock and earth that Andreas knew was the soul of Crete mourning.

Overwhelmed by the enormity of what he had done, he stood numbed and helpless, making no effort to flee, his face turned away from the body of Kasandonis.

After a while a group of men from the camp came to the spring. When they saw the chieftain's body they cried out in shock and grief. A man cursed Andreas, a second spit in his face, a third struck him a blow across the cheek. Andreas accepted the blow and watched the man unsheathe his sword. Mitsos leaped between them, wrestled the man away, and saved his life. In that moment he did not care.

Their shock and anger passed into sorrow. They gently wrapped the body of Kasandonis in a cape, crossing themselves, murmuring a soft litany of prayers for the dead and asking mercy for their own souls.

They bound Andreas to the pommel of his saddle and three grim Cretans led him up the mountain to the cave. Descending into the dark catacombs, into the weird light of torches once more, passing the stunned faces of men and women of the clan, Andreas did not speak. Later, when he heard a woman scream, a terrible cry that echoed like the wail of some stricken bird through the cave, he knew it was Voula.

He was led into a chamber where his father lay on a pallet beside a fire, his injured leg and thigh raised so the red, swollen wound drained pus into a pan. Kyriakos waited for him to speak but Andreas could not confess. He could not explain the tangled sequence of events that caused the chieftain's death.

"Crete! Crete!" his father mourned. "What a hundred Turks were not able to do to you, unhappy island, my own flesh has done! In madness, envy, rage, he has murdered one of your heroes! Forgive me the moment I took his mother in my arms and seeded him!"

When the Council of Elders ruled that he be banished from the clan and the cave, set loose in the mountains to live and die alone, the hand and heart of every Cretan as well as Turk against him, remembering his father's grief, he bore that condemnation and accepted it as just.

Driven from the cave into the wild, craggy mountains, all that had been familiar and endearing suddenly alien and sinister because the holy spirit of Crete abandoned him, a new, terrible strength subdued his pain and remorse. In this time of his soul's surrender, he still loved Voula, had sealed the bond he felt to her by the blood of another man. If he were spared, able to survive though he deserved nothing but to die, she might, in time, come to understand what he had done was because he loved her so much. Perhaps, by God's mercy, she might even someday find it in her heart to forgive him and let him offer her his love once more.

For the grave was colder and more silent than the cave and sorrow needed the consolation of a warm and living heart.

CHAPTER
TWELVE

From the beginning of the rebellion in the spring of 1821 to the late summer of that first year, the monk Papalikos was daily reinforced in his conviction that the men who had assumed leadership of the revolt were scoundrels and fools, traitors and fops, eloquent only in deception, dedicated above all to ambition and greed. When he had left the monastery and abandoned the ineffectual Brothers who feared their own shadows, he had entered another cankered order, influenced by power instead of the canons of timid faith.

Money ruled the councils of the chiefs. With money any fool could buy himself a band of soldiers and indulge his adoration for titles. He who could pay ten men became a "captain." Double that number in his service and he became a "colonel." And any buffoon who could afford to pay and arm a hundred men became a "general." All across Greece in those first months of the revolt, stable hands and petty bourgeois were strutting like decorated donkeys proclaiming their right to command.

What about dedicated, outspoken patriots like himself? Unable to afford more than a handful of stalwarts who rode with him despite his inability to pay them regularly, he had been forced to endure one slight and insult after another, his warnings and strategy ridiculed, his advice rejected. Any idiot could see that the initial Greek victories were triumphs of surprise. As the Turks recovered and mustered the vast resources of their Empire, they would invade Greece with powerful armies. The only natural line of defense the Greeks had, their mountains, had to be secured with strong detachments of troops to thwart the enemy's progress. But various primates and captains, more concerned with political maneuvering than with waging war, held their armed bands close to the towns and councils as a warning to the other chiefs.

Time and time again his help had been scorned, his life menaced so he had to flee. He had been driven from Patras and from Kalamata by men not fit to wipe his boots. Who were these self-appointed leaders? Petrobey Mavromichalis, that Maniat dandy strutting like a peacock in his finery, ruler of a wasteland of lizards and stones, conqueror of a city that laid down its arms without resistance. And the swaggering brigand Kolokotronis, clumsy figure with his brawny, bull neck, coarse face, imagining himself the reincarnation of some ancient Greek hero in his pretentious headpiece, shouting, blustering, flourishing his sword. How much better for all of Greece if he had lost his life when his ragtail army was dispersed and beaten by the Turkish cavalry at Karitena! But his failure had been rewarded, he had survived, reassembled a force, managed a small victory of some kind or another at Valtetzion and now, with the other captains, ringed the hills of central Peloponnesus, laying siege to the rich, opulent Turkish fortress of Tripolitza. From all over the Peloponnesus, bloated, swollen Turks had fled with their harems and their gold to take refuge behind those walls. And, he, Papalikos, was being denied his rightful share of those Croesus-treasuries when the city fell!

By God, he had sworn a holy oath that when he achieved his proper place, he would see the scoundrels chained and

dragged before a tribunal of justice. Petrobey and Kolokotronis would be the first to feel his righteous wrath but there
would be ample nooses to include that capon Patriarch Germanos and a dozen of his bishops and primates like Zaimis,
Poniropoulos and Kanakaris!

As if those swine were not enough, every month of that
summer saw more self-appointed liberators scurrying into
the country. Barely a week after an assembly at Kaltetzi
monastery in June proclaimed Petrobey Mavromichalis
Commander-in-Chief of the armies of Greece, Demetrios
Ipsilantis arrived in Greece from Trieste, to be greeted by
the barnyard with extravagant joy and named at once their
generalissimo by those primates jealous of Petrobey's power.

If ever a man's appearance decried the imposing title, it
was the insignificant visage and puny stature of Ipsilantis.
Small as a gnome, skeletal-skulled, stiff and pretentious as if
he did not need to squat and shit like mortals, he was attended by a retinue of slavish clods whose sole ability was
their talent for fawning and flattery. Only a few weeks after
his arrival, word was received that the army his brother,
Alexander, had led into the Danubian provinces was totally
destroyed, the prince in frantic flight! These were the men
who aspired to lead Greece! Both boobs should have been
gelded and set to herding sheep on some rocky islet.

Meanwhile, whatever successes the Greeks were achiev-
ing had been gained by the people themselves and by small
bands of klephts and armatoli. Mustering among the olive
trees or in the foothills of the mountains, they had harassed
and driven the Turks to barricade themselves in towns and
fortresses. While they achieved victories, armed often with
more scythes and pitchforks than guns, the leaders and nobles apportioned power and titles amongst themselves. Some
even preached mediation and mercy, ignoring the holy cru-
sade God had decreed against the Mussulmen minions of
Satan!

For the Turk was a wild and murderous beast that had to be exterminated! From the Sultan to the most menial hod carrier, they were all responsible for murder and rapine! Had they not butchered tens of thousands of helpless Christians in the streets of Constantinople after the outbreak of the revolt in Greece? Had they not sold off thousands more into slavery? After the brilliant attack of the Psariot fireship on the Mussulman frigate at Erissos in June (for nights after he heard news of that conflagration, his dreams seethed with visions of God's sacred fire!) the enraged Turks had scourged the Christian town of Kydonies on the Asia Minor coast. Kydonies had sought to remain neutral but the barbarians had sparked an incident and sent in Turkish troops. Of the 30,000 inhabitants of that defenseless town, only a scant 5,000 souls managed to flee aboard the brigs of the Greek fleet that came bravely into that harbor to evacuate those they could. The remaining men and youths were butchered, the women, girls and younger boys (after being forcibly circumcised by the mullahs) were carried off to the slave markets of Constantinople to serve the brutal lusts of the rich. When he thought of the tender, innocent beauty of those Christian women and children defiled by the Turkish dogs, his throat burned with a craving for vengeance!

Yet, instead of fulfilling his destiny by leading a triumphant Greek army, once again hearing rumors that his enemies among the chiefs and captains were sending assassins to kill him, he had fled into the mountains of Arcadia, taking refuge in a small, isolated mountain village.

When he had first ridden into the village of Liatos with his band of a half-dozen men, they had ordered the two score of villagers into the square. Papalikos addressed them, requisitioning lodgings and provisions from them in the name of the Society of Friends and the freedom forces of Greece. There was some whining among the villagers about bands of klephts who had already decimated their scanty supplies of food. Papalikos had called harshly for silence and when one burly farmer persisted in grumbling loudly about thieves masquerading as revolutionaries, he opened the rascal's impudent head to the bone with the butt of his pistol.

As the man thrashed howling in the dust of the street, clutching his bloodied skull, the remaining villagers fell mute. Yet several of the women stared at the monk with a strange intensity, their pulses quickened by the violence and the blood. He noticed one of them, a lithe, handsome woman in her early thirties, an animal vigor evident through her tattered skirt and blouse. Even as he felt repelled by her unkempt black hair hanging in oily strands across her breasts and by an unwashed coarseness to her cheeks, there was something about her sullen eyes and hungry mouth that sparked an excitement in his belly.

A pair of children clung to her skirts, a small boy of about five and a girl of ten or eleven. The boy resembled a hundred grimy village urchins but the girl was a little beauty, an exquisite, miniature sun-haired nymph with lissome arms and satiny bare legs.

"You!" he called gruffly to the woman. "Come here!"

For an instant she seemed uncertain whether he meant her. When he pointed to her again, she stepped uneasily forward, the boy clutching her skirt, the girl following a step behind. Mother and children stared at the man still moaning on the ground.

"Is your husband here?" Papalikos motioned to the males among the villagers, trying to assess which of them might be the girl's father. Aside from a few beardless youths, most of them were ugly, withered old goats, their chins stained with tobacco.

"He's not here." She spoke for the first time, her voice surly, frightened, yet defiant. "He's gone to fight up North with the captains."

"Has he gone to fight, woman?" Papalikos smirked at his

men. "Or has he fled to get away from your unwashed stink?"

His men snickered and a few old crones cackled with derision. The woman lashed them with a scornful glance. He stared again with a curious unrest at the lovely golden child.

"I'll stay in your house," he said brusquely to the woman. "Go and get it ready." He motioned to the villagers. "My men will pick houses in which to stay. God pity your poor bones if you don't extend yourselves and make them welcome. And get this bloody wretch out of my sight."

In the next week, quartered in the woman's one-room house, he came to despise her litter and stink. If it were not for the girl who bloomed like a rare, exotic flower in a dunghill, he would have moved to one of the other houses. But he delighted in the child's presence, her slender, golden legs flashing as she moved about the room. When she laughed he was reminded of the song of a bird.

He saw they were provided with ample food requisitioned from other villagers. As if they were being fed sufficiently for the first time, mother and children ate ravenously. When they had finished eating and the girl sought to leave the house to play, he tried to find ways to keep her beside him.

"Eat a little more, darling," he would say gently. "Have another serving of mutton. It will make your slim arms and legs strong and bring more bloom to your pretty cheeks."

"She has had enough," the mother grumbled. "You don't leave anything on the table for her brother or me. All goes for that child."

He struck his fist on the table in fury.

"Shut your mouth, bitch!" he roared. "I am sickened by your stench and your vomitous complexion! Go and wash before I rip your greasy locks out by their roots!"

Trailing hostility and fear, the woman hurried from the house. He drew the trembling girl into the nest of his arms.

"Don't be frightened, my child," he said soothingly. "Brother Papalikos would never hurt his little darling." Gently, as one would touch a dove or a pullet, he stroked her throat, caressed the shell-like lobes of her tiny ears, rubbing his fingers slowly between the silken strands of her hair, feeling a strange, reverential adoration for her beauty.

His men brought them logs taken from other houses in the village and each evening, as the noose of twilight garroted the day, he had the woman build a blazing fire against the chill of the descending night. He sat cross-legged on the hearth, staring moodily into the flames. Behind him he heard the rustlings and whisperings of the mother and children undressing for bed in the corner behind a curtain the woman had strung from a cord. In the sinuous flames he had a tremulous vision of the girl naked, golden hair tumbled about her delicate shoulders, her belly glowing like the moon, sloping to the chaste, untainted bud and tiny petals nestled between her legs. Then, as the mother's churlish voice rose in some strident reproof, the vision of the girl wavered and was lost. He felt an impatient loss and rage.

When he lay down before the fire to sleep, stretching out his arms and long legs, turning his eyes away from the glowing logs, dark dreams came like ravens with portents and warnings. He knew he had to resist any mercy or gentleness that might fasten upon his heart. They were lures of the demons who sought to deflect him from his mission. Evil could only be destroyed by men who rejected tenderness and love.

From the anonymous seed and nameless womb that had spawned him, abandoning him as a swaddling baby before the door of the monastery, he understood cruelty and evil. In the lonely years of his childhood among the musty odors of the cloisters and the rancid stench of old monks, he was quickly weaned from the fallacy of goodness and the illusion of affection.

Growing into young manhood, he came to comprehend

that among weaker mortals a game was played in which the human soul sought to evade and hide from itself, claiming that evil thoughts, evil words and evil deeds were contrary to God's will. He scorned such evasions, as he rejected the long hours of futile, mumbled prayers, fashioning instead a militant theology and creed of his own.

Many centuries and aeons before, in an ancient time when the angels had been false to their orders, God had cast them from his side and bitterly abandoned the earth, whose first humans had failed him, as well. In his renunciation, demons from the dark regions vested their reign, the satanic and unholy flourished.

That was the life on earth for sorrowing centuries until the angels who had been cast out by the Lord gathered in penance. By their remorseful, savage prayers they scattered sharp-toothed dragon's seedlings across the earth. Hidden in the wilderness and in scrublands, on the switches of shrubs and in the foliage of trees, the virulent seedlings grew to messianic infants. In a hundred habitations, houses, farms, sheepfolds and cloisters, they matured into a lean, hard host, unsoftened by love, unweakened by compassion, their resolute mission to repossess the earth and redeem the angels for the Lord.

Now, the monk knew himself to be one of those seedlings of the banished angels. Many nights he heard them hissing and counseling him in the recesses of his heart, tempering his soul by gusts of their burning breath. They strengthened his arm and fortified his spirit so he might join his nameless brothers and by their concerted effort return the mountains, rivers and valleys to the illumination of God.

To achieve that holy purpose, evil had to be cauterized by evil, fire hurled against fire, wickedness used in assaulting wickedness. The minions of the devil had to be scourged by apostles willing to exceed their ferocity, use whatever means the end decreed.

In this way, though they might die in battle like mortals,

they would live like princelings in heaven, companions
through eternity with the Lord Jehovah, the Almighty, the
All-powerful King of Kings.

Each day that he lost waiting in the village, his men
idling away their time when they should be fighting and
killing Turks, he fretted in fury. His temper grew surly and
knife-edged and the villagers, men, women and even dogs,
scurried fearfully from his heavy-booted path. He thrashed
a farmer he felt had stared at him impudently and nearly
pulled out the beard of an elder who dared complain to him
about the conduct of his men.

"I put a boot in his skinny ass and sent him flying!" he
ranted to his companions. "These squids don't understand
what it is like for fighting men to sit here rotting among
potherds and hags with our pistols silent and our knives
sheathed!"

Yet it was not the enforced inactivity alone that tormented him. He knew the small girl had something to do
with his distress. She had become a temptation that burned
his body and his eyes.

With a curious terror he came to understand that it was
not lust he felt for her. That simple craving he could have
accepted and found some way to satisfy. In her innocent
and trusting presence, his limbs turned to water, his strong
hands trembled, his cravings faded into devotion. She
turned his thoughts away from the clangor and bloodcall of
war to prayer and meditation. For the first time in his life,
like an adder in his body, eating at his entrails, he felt the
tender hatchings of love.

Meanwhile, the mother, subduing her churlish and
unwashed demeanor, labored to please him. She bathed and
washed her hair until it was glistening and clean. She
scrubbed her ears, cheeks and hands until they glowed.
She mended her frocks, prepared food he might find sa-

vory, and even began cleaning the litter in the house. Still he had no desire to touch her.

There was a night he had returned from hours of riding in the mountains. He gave his weary horse into the care of a youth with orders to rub him down and feed him. When he entered the house, the mother and children seemed asleep, the curtain drawn across their corner of the room.

The fire had begun to subside and he added several more logs. He sat down on the hearth, the tingling heat of the flames dispersing the chill and dampness in his limbs. He started to remove his boots and heard a movement behind him. The woman stood there in her nightgown, barefooted, her hair brushed back carefully, the strands tied with a strip of ribbon.

"Let me take them off for you," she said softly.

When he grunted in answer she bent and tugged at the boots, removing first one and then the other.

"I sent the children to my neighbor's house tonight," she said, her voice shaken and low. She stood a moment beside the hearth and then sat down slowly on a low bench to one side. She drew her bare feet under the hem of her cotton gown and put her hands together nervously in her lap. They sat in silence while he stared into the flames.

"You're a man," she said. "'But it is different being a woman. From the beginning it is that way. My father would celebrate his sons and mourn his daughters." She paused as if waiting for him to look at her. When he did not turn his head, she went on. "Until she finds a man to marry, all other women are her enemies, think she is a whore. After she marries, if she becomes pregnant, it does not mean her husband loves her. She fights to raise her children, grows hard, gives up hope she will ever find tenderness and love."

"I am tired, woman," he said impatiently. "Quit your babbling and say what you want to say."

"The first day in the square, when you looked at me . . ." Her voice trailed off into the hissing of the flames. "I thought . . . I thought you wanted me. I was dirty as a pig and you were right to be disgusted. But I have washed and scrubbed now, made myself clean and neat . . ."

"Do you think I came to this dung-heap of a village for a woman?" he said harshly. "The land is torn by war, a great, rich city is under siege, there are enemies who should be slain. I have more important things to do than satisfy the itchings of every bitch in heat!"

She rocked slowly back and forth, one hand rising from her lap to her breast, her fingers tugging feebly at the fabric of the gown above her heart.

"I would not feel this way if you were not so close, if you were not in this house," she said. "But when I hear your boots at the door, my heart trembles. At night I cannot sleep because I know you are in the darkness only a few feet away. I swear to God I only want you to love me a little, make me feel like a woman once more."

"My horse carries me on his back all day and does not ask for love!" he cried. "What are you doing for me that you should ask for love?"

"I can help you," she said, her voice desperate and tight. "I have heard you talking to your men of the troops you could recruit and arm if you had money. I can help you get that money."

"Your dowry?" he mocked her. "Two pigs, a pot and a bolt of poor cloth? Maybe your husband is a nobleman and you know where his fortune is hidden."

She rose from the bench, started toward the corner and then turned back to him, her face tremulous and pale.

"I'm telling you God's truth about the money," she said. "It is not my husband who has a fortune hidden, but someone else."

The room was silent except for the snapping and crackling of the fire. He heard a sound from the corner as if the children were there and one of them had stirred restlessly in sleep.

"Who is it?" he asked quietly.

She stared at him, her breasts rising under her gown with the tumult of her breathing. He motioned her down and she came swiftly, gratefully, to sit close beside him on the hearth, squeezing her shoulder and thigh against his body. He braced himself to touch flesh he did not desire.

"You are a warm and juicy woman," he said with an effort at gentleness. "From the first day in the square, I saw you were a morsel to please a man's taste."

He raised his hand slowly from his knees and put the palm to her belly. When he fluttered his long fingers, they pressed into the doughy mound of her breast. She closed her eyes and uttered a small whimper. He resisted an impulse to send the bitch sprawling with a blow.

"Who has the money?"

"There is a woodcutter named Nostos," she spoke quickly, her eyes staring at his mouth. "He lives alone a few miles further up the mountain. Everyone knows he is wealthy, treasure inherited from his father and grandfather, who were brigands. They say he has a fortune hidden in that house."

"Who says?" he asked sharply.

"The people in the village . . ."

"People spread rumors like dung! If you make me waste my time . . ."

"No, my dearest!" she cried. "I'm telling you the truth! Ask anyone in the village! They'll tell you it's the truth!"

He nodded slowly.

"All right," he said. "I believe you and will not ask anyone else. And you are never to mention you told me anything about this woodcutter or his money. Do you understand?"

She shook her head mutely. Then she leaned hard against him and he was assailed by the stench of her body, rank odors of oil, moist, hairy clefts and sweat smothering a faint scent of soap. As she rolled over against his knees, he caught a glimpse of her naked thighs and felt a singe of heat in his loins.

"I love you!" she whispered. "I love you!"

As she burrowed into his arms he looked toward the corner. When he turned to the woman he pulled roughly at her gown, tugging it above her thighs, parting her legs, determined to mount her as quickly and ruthlessly as he could, needing to wound and humiliate her because she was so wretched a substitute for the body he really longed to possess.

The following morning, trembling with an eagerness he could barely control, he ascended the rough, unaccommodating terrain of the mountain above the village. Although he had taken directions from the woman as to the location of the woodcutter's house, there wasn't any visible trail through the tangled brush and scrub, the bare rocks and stony slopes on which the hooves of his horse slipped and stumbled.

"The bitch has sent me to hell!" he cried angrily. "When I get back I'll tear the ears from her head!"

He searched all day, growing more furious with each passing hour. When it appeared he would not find the house before dark and would have to make camp on the mountain, a thin trace of smoke became visible against the descending twilight. Moving quickly toward the faint trail that seemed to come from the core of the mountain, he came upon the small house built in such a way that the mountain almost totally camouflaged its roof and walls. If it had not been for the circumstances of the smoke and the waning light, he might have passed within a few feet of the house without discovering it. As he rode into the narrow clearing, he caught a flicker of movement at one of the tiny windows, light glinting on the metallic barrel of a musket.

"I am a friend!" he cried. "I am a Greek and a friend!"

A long moment passed without any response from the house. He held the reins high before him so the woodcutter could see he held no weapon. His horse pawed the earth restlessly and he felt the breath of death at his cheeks. Then the heavy oak door of the house opened a fraction and a musket appeared in the slit.

"Who are you?" the man called in a harsh voice, fear and suspicion carving each word. "What do you want?"

"I am a friend."

"I have no friends."

"I am a captain in the army of free Greece."

"There is no fighting here! Don't lie! What do you want?"

"A detachment of Turks has been reported in these mountains," Papalikos said. "I am scouting to report on their whereabouts for the troops that follow behind me."

The door opened wider and the short, squat figure of the woodcutter became visible. Papalikos walked his horse forward slowly.

"That's close enough!" the man called. The barrel of the musket trembled. Papalikos paused and raised his hands, spreading his fingers to expose his palms.

"I can understand your mistrust, my friend," he said. "I would be concerned, as well, if Turks were creeping around my house."

"There haven't been any Turks in these mountains for years." The woodcutter spoke with apprehension. "What do the devils want up here now?"

"What does any cursed Turk want?" Papalikos said gravely. "Mischief and mayhem, robbery and murder." He made his cross fervently. "I began to grow frightened myself at the prospect of spending the night alone in the dark. By God's grace I stumbled upon your house. Could you let me have a bite of food and a corner where I might spend the night?"

The man stared at him uneasily.

"This is a poor house," he said. "I barely have enough for my own needs."

"God will bless you, my friend, for whatever you can spare."

The man muttered something under his breath. "You can come inside, I suppose," he said grudgingly. "But no funny business, hear? I can handle this musket like a marksman."

"Gladly, my friend!" Papalikos said. "My thoughts now are directed only to some warmth and rest." He dismounted and tied the horse's reins to a tree. The woodcutter stepped back and opened the door. The monk stooped from his tall height and entered the house.

The interior resembled the simple unadorned rooms of peasants and farmers all over Greece. A rough wooden table, a few ragged wicker chairs, a narrow fireplace with a fragment of log glowing beneath a pot, a pallet of straw and twigs in the corner.

When Papalikos saw the man clearly for the first time, he marked the ugly, scowling visage of a beast who trusted no one, small, crafty eyes like windows on a brain that seethed with fear and hate.

"Are you carrying a pistol?" the man held the musket tensely.

Papalikos parted his cape and carefully drew the pistol from his belt. Holding it by the barrel he offered it with a smile. The woodcutter stuck it into his own belt and then placed the musket on the hooks against the wall.

"You can have the gun back in the morning," he said gruffly. "A man living alone has to be careful, you understand?"

"Of course," Papalikos said gravely.

From the small pot hanging over the log, the man ladled broth into a pair of wooden bowls. He brought them to the table with a small loaf of rough-grained brown bread.

"This is all I can offer," he said. "This is a poor house. I told you that."

"This will be fine." Papalikos made his voice hearty. "And to show that I am not a total beggar, I have something to add to our meal, as well." From a cord at his waist he raised a wine flask and placed it on the table beside the broth and bread.

"We'll drink to victory against the bloody Turks." Papalikos pushed the flask across the table. The man stared at it, his tongue coming from his mouth to lick his lips.

"You drink first," he said. He blinked his cunning eyes. "You're the guest."

The monk raised the uncorked spout to his mouth and tossing back his head, drank a long, fervent swallow, feeling the pungent juices streaming into the parched riverbed of his belly.

"Arrrrrggghhh!" he cried, pausing finally to get his breath. "The blood of the grape!" He wiped his mouth with the back of his hand, grinning as he handed the woodcutter the flask. The man raised the spout hungrily to his own lips.

They ate the broth and bread and finished the flask of wine within a half hour. Papalikos tossed it against the wall with a sigh.

"A shame! A bloody shame!" he said mournfully. "The whole evening before us, a chance to talk of the war and of life and not a drop left." He peered entreatingly across the table at the woodcutter. "You're sure you don't have a flask or small jug stored here someplace, one you might have forgotten?"

The man stared at Papalikos, caught between avarice and thirst.

"There may be a small jug around someplace," he muttered. "One I have been saving for the holidays, to have a drink or so when I am feeling lonely and wretched."

He rose from the table and began a charade of stooping and searching, walking from one corner of the room to another alcove. Papalikos watched his clumsy deception with contempt and a growing rage.

The man moved into the shadows at the far end of the

room. There was the sound of a cabinet door being opened and the woodcutter released a satisfied grunt.

"Found one!" he said.

"Good for you, my friend!" Papalikos said. "A man never knows when a party will be his last, so it is wise to keep celebrating as long as possible."

Within the space of another hour's drinking, they finished the second flask. The woodcutter grew slightly drunk, his eyes becoming bloodshot, spittle and wine dribbling from the corners of his mouth. He grew sullen and uneasy, staring with perplexity at Papalikos.

"What did the people in the village tell you about me?" he muttered.

Papalikos shook the empty flask.

"There's no more wine," he said. He reached across the table and placed his fingers gently on the woodcutter's wrist. "Get some more wine, my friend."

"No more wine!" The man pulled roughly away from the monk's fingers. "There's no more wine!"

"Are you sure?"

"I'm sure!"

"Perhaps you've misplaced another flash you were saving for the holidays," Papalikos said softly. He had to control himself to keep from leaping on the swine at once. "Why don't you look again?"

"There's no more wine!" the man cried impatiently. "This is a poor man's house! There isn't any more! I told you!"

Papalikos rose slowly from the table and started toward the shadows in the rear of the room. The man twisted in his chair watching him.

"Where are you going?" the man shouted. "I told you there wasn't any more!"

Papalikos paused before the cabinet. Even before he opened the door he could smell the tangy scents of wine, olives and cheese that came from crocks on the shelves. He brought down another flask and started back to the table.

The woodcutter had risen and stared at him angrily.

"What the hell do you think you're doing!" he shouted. "I told you there wasn't . . ."

Something in the monk's face cut off his breath. He fumbled for the pistol in his belt. With a few swift strides, Papalikos crossed the distance between them. He tore the pistol from the man's hand and then struck him a short, hard blow across his temple. The woodcutter shuddered and dropped to his knees. He crouched there, swaying slightly, trying to gather his shattered senses. Papalikos drew back his booted foot and kicked him in the belly, a terrible blow that sent the man tumbling in a tangle of arms and legs against the wall.

The monk drew up a chair a few feet away from where the woodcutter lay and sat down. He held the flask of wine and from time to time raised the spout to his mouth. The woodcutter moaned, rubbing his belly, now and then gagging with a hoarse croak.

"You are really a beauty," Papalikos said. "I never expected when I came looking for you I would find anyone so stingy and cheap, a worthless lickspittle, undeserving to live." He shook his head grimly. "Yes, destiny has brought us together."

"Please . . ." the man mumbled. "Please . . ."

"Don't waste your breath," Papalikos said. "You are a useless and wretched shit and in a few moments I am going to kill you."

The woodcutter gasped for breath. "Kill me! Why?" His eyes filled with tears. "Because I lied about the wine? My God, why?"

"Not because of the wine," Papalikos said. "Oh, I bet you'd spread a table now fit for a king. You'd bring it all out gladly now. But it is too late. That is not why I am going to

kill you. I am going to kill you because the armies of free
Greece require the money you have hidden."

"I don't have any money!" the man wailed. "Who told you
I had money? The swine in the village? They are jealous of
me because I won't have anything to do with them. They
lied! I have nothing!"

"You'll draw your last breath on that lie!" Papalikos
snarled. "You niggardly pig! You'll claim you have no money
as you sputter your last, stupid breath!"

He rose from his chair and started menacingly toward the
wall. The woodcutter pressed back fearfully, making an
effort to swallow, only a dry rattle sounding from his throat.

"I have saved a little money!" he gasped. "Years of scrimp-
ing and saving for my old age. Maybe I could give you
part of it for the armies of Greece. I have been meaning to
contribute from the time I heard of the war!"

"I have come to collect your contribution," Papalikos said.
"Every bloody pound you own! All of it! God help you if
you hold back a penny!"

"All of it!" the man wailed. "All of it! In God's name, have
mercy!"

"All of it!" Papalikos roared, and almost above the man he
raised his foot as if he were going to kick him again. Tears
of terror streamed down the man's cheeks and he bleated like
a sheep. Then he pushed himself away from the wall and
crawled on his hands and knees toward the pallet of straw.
Moaning and crying he pushed the pallet aside and exposed
a trap in the floor. He raised the cover of the trap and burrowed his fingers into the dirt below.

"God have mercy! God have mercy!" he cried as he dug.
"You think I live like this because I enjoy poverty? I can't
help myself! It's a sickness. You don't know how many times
I've dug this up, determined to spend some of it, buy a few
things I've wanted for almost sixty years. But I cannot bear
to part with it. Just to own it gives me reason to live. To look

at it, run my fingers over it, touch it to my cheek and lips, that's my only joy, my only love!"

"Dig faster!" Papalikos felt his excitement growing as the mound of dirt excavated from the pit grew thicker.

"I can't help myself!" the man babbled. "Do you think I like being a miser, a pinchfist?" He clawed wildly at the dirt, scattering it across the floor of the house. "I can't help myself! It's a sickness! You've got to understand!"

Bending into the pit, his cheek almost on the floor, he slowly drew out a leathern bag that he raised as if it were a holy relic excavated from the tomb of some saint. He brushed the dirt from it carefully and placed it gingerly on the floor beside him. Then he bent and brought up another bag that he cleaned in the same way. In a few moments there were four bags on the floor.

Papalikos bent and raised one of the bags. Even before he had untied the cord he knew by the weight and by some talismanic prescience what it contained. When he saw the thick mass of sparkling golden nuggets, he loosed a harsh, jubilant shout.

"Gold!" he cried. "A king's ransom in gold! A sultan's treasure! God be praised! I never expected this!"

Swiftly, he examined each of the bags. They all contained gold. He spilled the contents of one of the bags on the floor, spreading the nuggets into a glittering circle. The walls and ceiling of the shabby room seemed to take on a translucent sparkle.

The woodcutter remained on his knees, watching him with sorrow and resignation, his hands clasped across his belly.

"You should be pleased!" Papalikos said fervently. "Man, you will make possible the destruction of thousands of Turks! You should be proud! That is an infinitely more noble climax to your life than living like a groundhog in the mountain, worrying and fretting about your hoard!"

"Kill me . . ." the man whispered. "I don't want to live

now . . ." In the passageway to death his face grew mummified as the skull of a corpse, his eyes sunken into hollow sockets, a pallor mantling his cheeks.

"Yes, I will kill you!" Papalikos cried, his voice trembling. "You have fulfilled your destiny! Like the seed and the spore dropped by mosses and ferns to breed new life, you have been born to this holy purpose, lived to achieve this sacred moment! A great Turkish fortress waits for us! Because of you, my men and I will be there! For that reason I pledge I will bury you as a soldier is buried, coins for the ferryman of Hades placed upon your eyes, a musket fired over your grave, and my prayer for your soul into the safekeeping of the Lord!"

He moved closer to the man, holding the pistol against his chest for a clean, swift bullet into the heart. In the final moment of his life, the miser turned his head slowly to stare at the treasure, his face cleansed and innocent of avarice and sorrow, images and events relinquished and forgotten before the gilded, golden vision he would carry with him into the dark of eternity.

Papalikos chiseled a grave out of the lime and stone of the mountain and buried the woodcutter as he had promised. He placed coins on his eyes for the ferryman of Hades, anointed his temples with dabs of oil and wrapped him in a blanket for a shroud. He fired the musket over his bier and commended his soul into the holy vineyard of the Lord.

Then he mounted his horse and rode down the slopes, the saddlebags swollen with their golden booty, resting like stones against his legs. While he rode he prayed in homage to the Deity who moved in strange and mysterious ways. For all that had happened, he knew, was a blessing and a covenant the Lord had placed upon him.

Of all the remote villages the monk might have chosen, who but God directed his steps toward that small, insignificant hamlet? There he had languished, faith draining from him like water from a broken cistern, until, like the terrible visions of St. Anthony in the wilderness, the demons had tempted him toward tenderness and love by the bewitching beauty of the golden child. But he had resisted, yea, he had fought the temptation and, as a benediction, the Lord loosened the tongue of the carnal woman in whose house he had lodged. Then, the greatest miracle of all, that of tens of thousands of rumors about treasures with which these villages all over Greece abounded, this rumor led him to the miser who all of his life had hoarded his gold awaiting the monk's ordained arrival.

"Thou art mighty, O my God!" he cried.

He pressed his knees against the heavy bags of gold. With this fortune he would be able to recruit a thousand men, provide them provisions and arms for a year, lead them into battle, a vengeful and terrible host that would smite and destroy the wicked and impenitent enemies of the Lord!

"By fire and by sword in Thy name, O my God!" he roared.

He galloped into the village, dogs and chickens scattering before his horse's pounding hooves. He paused only long enough to assemble his men, fill their flasks with fresh water and their packs with bread, dried meat and cheese before starting on their way. As they passed the house where he had lodged, the woman came to stand silently in the doorway. They stared at one another as if they were strangers.

At the outskirts of the village, from behind the great, scarred trunk of a plane tree, the small, golden-haired girl appeared. In a short frock, barelegged and barefooted, she ran for a few moments alongside his horse and then with a sweet, beguiling smile tossed him a single pink rose.

He caught the flower and at once scented the girl in its fragrance, felt the satin of her flesh in the petals that he touched to his lips. Like a man waking from a dream, he looked back one last time at the receding figure of the child.

Then he crushed the flower in his palm, threw it away without another glance and spurred his horse forward, a prince of the Lord, riding toward the plain of Tripoli and the fortress of Tripolitza.

CHAPTER
THIRTEEN

That summer, camped with the bands of irregulars that comprised the Greek army in the mountains circling the cold and naked plain of the fortress of Tripolitza, Xanthos began the writing of his history. By oil lantern in the late evening, owls hooting at him from the hidden foliage, he assessed the months since the start of the revolt, analyzing and probing, seeking parallels between the Greek tribes that emerged from the Dark Ages of antiquity and the Greeks who rose from the grim centuries of Moslem bondage. While he understood the men of Kolokotronis and the other Greek captains were not Achaeans, some portion of blood might have flowed to them from those warrior-kings who fought tyranny at Marathon, Thermopylae and Plataea. And if the events were not totally similar, like the Greeks at Troy many years and years before, once again camped about a great city, the descendants of those Greeks sought to seize wealth, to win glory and immortal fame.

Yet, while Thucydides watched the progress of the war he recorded from exile in a neutral land, Xanthos faced the hazardous task of writing the beginnings of a history during the turmoil and tension of a siege. His duties on the staff of Kolokotronis, seeing to supplies, writing letters and dis-

patches, sifting and filtering information about the fortress
from spies or from Greeks who had escaped from within the
city, occupied most of his waking hours. By these gleanings,
however, the Greek captains had full knowledge of the
strength of the fortification and the number of the defenders.

Tripolitza (even the name connoted to Xanthos secluded
seraglios, eunuchs and veiled, exotic concubines), headquarters of Turkish provincial government in southern
Greece, residence of the Pashas of the Morea for generations, was reputed to be one of the wealthiest cities in all of
the Sultan's Empire. That wealth and power were enclosed
in the shabby, cluttered city bulwarked by a wall of stone
two miles in circuit and fourteen feet high, with a number
of small towers and demibastions on which cannons were
mounted. The lower part of the rampart was six feet thick,
the upper part about three, leaving at a height of nine feet
from the ground a narrow gunner's platform along the inside of the parapet. Within the walls, at its western extrem-
ity, stood a citadel armored with bombproof casemates.

The ordnance of the fortress consisted of about thirty
pieces of cannon, mostly of small caliber, planted on the
ramparts and served by a company of gunners from Constantinople. The city had once contained a population of
about 15,000 of whom 7,000 were Greek, 1,000 Jews, and
the remainder, Moslems. By the end of July, the third
month of the siege, the Greeks had fled except for some
wealthier merchants being held by the Turks as hostages. In
their place had poured in the refugee Moslems of Mistra,
Bardounia, Leondari and Fanari, and some thousands of
others who managed to flee the sieges taking place around
Nauplion, Navarino and Monemvasia. The Greeks had allowed these refugees to enter Tripolitza, adopting a strategy
similar to that of the Spartan general Lysander, who, determined to blockade Athens by land and by sea during the
Peloponnesian War, offered every Athenian in the cities he
captured safe-conduct to Athens or death. Since famine

would be his weapon, the more people the city had to feed, the better.

By July, the population of Tripolitza had swollen to somewhere between 25,000 and 30,000 men, women and children, of whom perhaps 9,000 carried arms. The most dangerous contingent of the defenders during the first weeks of the siege was the Turkish cavalry, numbering about 2,000 horse, able to raid swiftly outside the walls. There was also a corps of about 1,500 Albanian mercenaries, sent by Khurshid Pasha from his camp before Jannina. These were hard, seasoned warriors who practiced the barbaric rite of severing the head and right hand of an enemy killed in battle. After a skirmish between some of these Albanians and a patrol of Greeks early in the siege, Xanthos would never forget the half-dozen mutilated Greek bodies on the field. Their leader, the Mongol-souled Elmas Bey (Kolokotronis had fought against him before and called him the most savage and ruthless enemy he had ever met) was reputed to have been among those beasts who had the Greek hero Athanasios Diakos spitted and roasted at the battle of Alamana in April.

Surrounding the plain of Tripoli and the fortress of Tripolitza, the troops of Greeks occupied the mountains of Maenalion, Parthenius and Artemision, their camps pitched high on the slopes whose upper reaches were forested thickly with oak and maple, yew and cypress, silver fir and pine.

The largest contingent of these troops, an aggregation of volunteers from Rumelia and Epirus, were the 8,000 men commanded by Prince Demetrios Ipsilantis, arrived in Greece in June from Trieste, claiming that because his brother, Prince Alexander, was also chief of the Society of Friends, Demetrios was entitled to act as his brother's viceroy, commander of all the forces of the revolution in Greece. (An extravagant pretension, Kolokotronis growled to Xanthos, in view of his brother's failure and defeat in his invasion of the Danubian provinces.) But, rightly or not, Prince Demetrios was believed to have the support of Tsar Alexander I of Russia, the harbinger of 40,000 Russian bayonets that would, at an appropriate time, sweep into Greece to aid the insurgents. Even rumors of such massive assistance made Ipsilantis honored and warmly welcomed by many soldiers, some captains and some primates who flocked to his banner. Since his force was the largest, and because he had the loyalty of many of the men, the other captains grudgingly played a charade of obedience before him.

There was the force of Kolokotronis, of which Xanthos was a part, numbering about 2,000 men mustered slowly and trained painstakingly after the defeat and rout of their original corps at Karitena. They had won several skirmishes and one battle against the Turks since that defeat but Karitena still rankled in the heart of the chieftain and he had sworn to have that loss revenged.

In the mountains not far from the breastworks of Kolokotronis, Petrobey Mavromichalis was encamped with some 3,000 Maniats including his son Elias and his brother, the valiant Kyriakulis. These fierce fighters from across the Taygetus mountains in the south, spent the hours in wrestling and mock duels, endlessly polishing and cleaning their weapons, much as their Spartan progenitors prepared for battle against the Persians more than two thousand years earlier.

Archbishop Germanos, credited with having raised the initial banner of the revolt at the monastery of Aghia Lavra in March, commanded a corps of 2,000 citizens from Patras. If they were not the strongest or best-trained detachment among the besiegers, the Archbishop made certain they were the most zealously serviced by liturgies and prayers.

In contrast to the religious aura that canopied the Archbishop's camp, there was the scummed cantonment of the barbaric monk Papalikos. One of the first Greeks to appear before Tripolitza, his harangues had so aggravated some of the other captains that an assassination attempt had been made on his life. He had fled, Xanthos glad to see him depart. Then, at the end of July he had come marching back to the encampment, commanding approximately 1,000 cut-throats that the veteran sergeant, Balalas, swore to Xanthos looked as if they might have been recruited from a mad-house or prison. Soon after their arrival, there were midnight raids against some of the neighboring Greek settlements, livestock stolen and women molested. Although Ipsilantis issued an edict threatening severe punishment for such trans-gressions, the raiders had not been found, although many suspected who they might be.

There was even a woman among the captains, the Spet-ziot corsair Bouboulina, whose renown as a buccaneer (the Turks called her that epithet, while the Greeks acclaimed her a heroine) made her name feared by Moslems through-out the Aegean. Leaving her ships guarding the water approaches to the besieged city of Nauplion, east of Tripolitza, she had traveled overland with a detachment of seamen to join the siege.

Finally, there were more than a score of groups of various klephts and armatoli, bands of a dozen to half a hundred men, drawn by the lure of wealth within the city. They kept to themselves, denied any other captain their allegiance, and thought more of spoils, Xanthos feared, than of freedom.

After the first few months of fighting, the Greeks had swept the Peloponnesus free of Moslems except for Tripo-litza, Nauplion, Navarino and Monemvasia, and the citadels of Patras and Methone, all of which were under siege. Their strategy was an ancient tactic used by armies for centuries, the legions of Hunger and Famine, commanded by "General Bread." The blockading forces formed a circle or noose about the besieged enclave, preventing them from breaking out or relief supplies being brought in. The aim was to de-

moralize the defenders, weaken them, forcing them to surrender or grow too weak to resist a strong, concerted attack.

Through the early part of the summer, the siege of
Tripolitza proved the most difficult and ineffective of any of
the surrounded citadels or towns because the Greeks could
not prevent the Moslem cavalry from foraging outside the
walls in search of provisions. But, as the months passed, the
villages and fields about the fortress stripped of the last
ounces of grain, the cavalry began longer, more desperate
expeditions in search of supplies. Once they left the plain,
however, the Greeks harassed them, trapping them in
defiles, ambushing them in passes. Greater damage might
have been wreaked upon these raiders had the Greeks been
bolder, but the memory of the carnage at Karitena rendered
many a soldier timid. Kolokotronis tried earnestly to dispel
their superstition and terror about the invincibility of cavalry.

"Why should you despair because we have no cavalry and
the enemy has hundreds of mounts?" he cried. "A thousand
cavalry, after all, are only the same number of men. Has a
Greek ever died in battle because he was bitten or kicked by
a horse? Men on the ground stand more solidly on their feet
than cavalrymen, who are suspended precariously in the air,
at the whim and mercy of some confounded and eccentric
beast! They not only have to worry about fighting but about
falling off! With our feet on solid earth, we can aim our muskets better and deliver harder blows with our swords. We
are much more likely to hit what we aim at. We can take advantage of every rock or tree while the horseman cannot
take cover!"

He would wink at them, his mouth curved in a wry, sardonic smile.

"Remember, my Palikars," he said. "The only advantage
cavalry has over good, courageous infantry is they may find
it easier and safer to run away!"

In more solitary councils with Xanthos as they worked

over dispatches and letters, Kolokotronis spoke of other fears.

"It is not individual courage which is lacking among our men," he said gravely. "But what the English and French call esprit de corps, the spirit of the corps, that confidence and comradeship which long discipline and a tradition of service give to the soldier."

He cited the siege of Navarino in the southwestern Peloponnesus, when among the thousand Greeks surrounding the town, the majority began to leave just before Easter to spend the holidays back in their villages.

"Can you imagine such folly in an English or French army?" Kolokotronis said angrily. "Despite the pleadings and warnings of their leaders, the men felt they had every right to celebrate with their families. After the holidays the oafs would return to resume the blockade."

"Well, on the day of the feast," the chieftain went on grimly, "a scant fifty or so men remained holding the breastworks around the town, another twenty guarding the outposts in the surrounding hills. The fools at the breastworks, to make matters worse, celebrated by drinking, dancing and firing their pistols. The Turks, understanding the ways Greeks celebrate, heard the sparse pistol shots, understood what had happened and made a determined sally from the town. The Greeks at the breastworks were being overwhelmed and on the verge of fleeing when the outpost guards came running and shooting from the hills. Only by God's grace did the Turks, thinking the whole affair a scheme to lure them from the town, retreat in panic. So narrowly was a disaster averted as a result of the devilish Greek incapacity for discipline!"

Sometimes, in the evenings, the sun setting across the crags and ridges of the mountains, crimsoning the dark-green peaks of trees, glowing on the stone ramparts of the fortress so that it assumed the shimmering luster of some mystical, legendary castle, Xanthos recorded the sights and sounds of the encampment. Around him men built their tiny campfires, putting makeshift kettles on to boil water, shaking in coffee they had ground by pounding the beans on a stone with the butt of their pistols. The scents of sizzling meat trailed across the shadows and there was the excited, expectant laughter of men before a meal.

At moments such as those, Xanthos felt himself an old campaigner, a veteran of battle, waiting once again for fighting to commence. He also felt the majesty of a vast dream moving slowly but inexorably to fruition. An age of slavery was ending, he wrote with fervor, and an age of freedom was being born for Greece. He spoke of his excitement to Balalas.

"Do you understand, Balalas, the grand destiny all of us here are sharing, you and I, the captains and the men? We are making history!"

The veteran, crouched on his haunches, broiling a piece of pork impaled on a stick over a fire, grunted.

"I am about to eat now," he said. "That is more important to me than history."

"You cannot mean that!"

Balalas grinned, raising himself slightly to point toward the bastion down on the plain.

"There is Tripolitza. Here are we. Starve them out and we beat them. If they break through or supplies reach them, we lose. We could be camped here for another year. Those are the things I think of."

"But the overall strategy!" Xanthos said impatiently. "The direction of the war, the mission we have to bring liberty again to this land that once fostered liberty. Surely you understand that?"

"My mission is to stay alive," Balalas said. "To accomplish that much I have to kill Turks, who, in order to stay alive, have to kill me. If that butcher's dance helps fulfill your grand design, that's fine."

"You are a splendid soldier and my good friend"—Xanthos shook his head in exasperation—"but you have no imagination."

Balalas raised the smoking fragment of pork to his nostrils, sniffing in anticipation.

"Imagination is for captains and princes," he said. "For historians and teachers. I have this chunk of meat, ready to drop into my belly. Later, I will smoke my pipe and then sleep. Those things are all clods like me know or need to know."

He bit into the savory, charred pork and uttered a fervent grunt of pleasure.

That was in the early summer of the siege. Later, as the summer wore on, Xanthos wondered if Balalas might not be right, that strategies and grand designs were unimportant beside the simple rituals of a soldier's day. The best moments were those Xanthos spent sitting among the men, sharing the warm dalliances of eating, laughing, listening to them talk of their villages and farms and families.

"I have this son, see, and his eyes are like two olives, you know, the great black ones from Kalamata."

"I wonder what my wife has planted in our garden this summer? Last year the squash grew large as melons and I told her to be sure to plant more this time."

"My father-in-law was a Samian and wanted to be buried at sea. So when he died, I poured a cup of water over his grave."

The grimmest, most disheartening parts of his day came to be the hours Xanthos attended and transcribed the endless debates in the meetings of the captains and the primates, the bickerings that marked the sessions of the Senate, the pompous ceremonies at the headquarters of Prince Ipsilantis. How much of the spoils should be allocated to the national treasury for the war, how much to the Church, how much to the captains and, finally, to the men? What should the terms of surrender include? How should the lands owned by the wealthy Moslems be divided? What should the strategy of battle be if a relief force of Turks came to the aid of the fortress?

Days running into dismal weeks, Xanthos felt his initial enthusiasm dissipated before the snarling feuds. He came unhappily to understand how much suspicion, malfeasance, greed, intrigue, jealousy and vanity were rampant in the leaders. He saw them in a harsher, disenchanted light.

Prince Ipsilantis, small, frail, almost totally hairless, an unimposing figure lounging in his chair as if it were a throne, beckoning magnanimously to orderlies and retainers. He was obviously an honorable, well-intentioned man but one disabled in his effort to command and evoke loyalty by an icy and haughty vanity and arrogance.

"You may approach us, Captain . . ."

"We will be pleased to take your suggestion under consideration at the proper time."

"We will be resting at that hour and unable to grant such an audience."

The bearded, nervous Archbishop Germanos, a cleric who seemed to wish to exchange Turkish despotism for an Orthodox tyranny of his own, spinning theological webs of demagoguery out of his fertile brain as a spider spins his lair to ensnare flies.

Petrobey Mavromichalis, elected leader of the Senate, the venerable commander who had impressed Xanthos during the assault on Kalamata, become querulous now about challenges and infringements upon his authority, uncertain of his ability to co-ordinate a larger theater of war than the Mani, seeking the advice of less scrupulous men who assembled under his mantle of unblemished reputation and respected ancestry.

There was the obese, rancid-tongued Bouboulina, tougher and craftier than most men, her venality apparent to everyone each time she uttered a word from the puckered figs of her lips.

The vengeful monk Papalikos, like some infectious disease, fusing every meeting by his tirades that their sacred mission was not merely to defeat but "to exterminate the hellish Turks, those horse-leeches of Christian blood!"

Even Kolokotronis, who could not abide the bitter rantings of the monk and who could usually be depended on to find the sense within a debate, seemed to Xanthos somehow changed. Seething to raze this central and most important fortress of the Peloponnesus, the shame of the defeat at Karitena like a dagger in his side, the endless debates bringing out some wolfish and intolerant strain in his nature, he appeared driven by crosswinds of anger. Undoubtedly the most qualified soldier of them all, he could not understand why they denied him his rightful position.

Reading Thucydides one night before sleeping, Xanthos came upon a passage he had read before but had forgotten, the historian writing of the agony of war between the Greeks, more than two thousand years earlier, on this same land:

> And so there fell upon the cities on account of revolutions, many grievous calamities, such as happen and will always happen while human nature is the same . . . for war, which robs men of the easy supply of their daily wants, is a rough schoolmaster and creates in most people a temper that matches their condition . . . And war is not the only reason for men's deeds becoming brutal, it twists their words, reckless audacity come to be regarded as courageous loyalty to party, prudent hesitation as specious cowardice, moderation as a cloak for unmanly weakness, and to be clever in everything was to do naught in anything . . .

> The cause of all these evils was the desire to rule which greed and ambition inspire, and, also, springing

from them that ardour which belongs to men who once
have become engaged in factious rivalry.

Indeed, men do not hesitate, when they seek to
avenge themselves upon others, to abrogate in advance
the common principles observed in such cases . . .
those principles upon which depends every man's own
hope of salvation should he himself be overtaken by
misfortune.

Xanthos pushed the book aside and wearily closed his
eyes, the light of the campfires glowing even through the
lids. A cold presentiment fastened about his heart, and, for a
long time, in spite of his exhaustion, he could not sleep.

At the beginning of August, word came to the Greeks at
Tripolitza of the surrender of one of the other besieged
fortresses, Monemvasia, to the insurgents. The rattling of
musketry and the wild shouts of joy echoing from crag to
crag among the Greeks must have filled the Turks inside the
walls of the city with foreboding. To vent their anger and
terror, perhaps to disprove that their own eventual fate had
moved a step closer, the guns from the ramparts of the fortress erupted quick spurts of flame, rolling clouds of soiled
smoke from the walls, thundering harmlessly through the
canyons and passes.

The mighty rock of Monemvasia, set in the ocean like a
mountainous anvil, could have remained impregnable except for starvation that forced the besieged to surrender.

Despite the fact that the blockade of the fortress had
been carried out for more than four months at the expense
and by the effort of the Greeks of that region, when capitu-
lation seemed inevitable, the Turks of the fortress, hoping
for more generous and humane terms from Ipsilantis,
requested a representative from his headquarters. Ipsilantis
sent a member of his council to take possession of Monem-

vasia in his name and guarantee the safety of the inhabitants.

The Turks, by these promises, relinquished their weapons and were allowed to retain some personal property. The representative of the prince made arrangements for them to be sailed to Asia Minor aboard several Spetziot vessels. But a number of the Greek soldiers who had taken part in the siege, angry at being denied what they felt to be their rightful share of the spoils, opposed the departure of the Turks. They killed several of the Moslems and plundered their property.

When the details of the surrender and departure of the Turks were conveyed to Ipsilantis, the truce violation was obscured and attributed to the actions of a few malcontents. The prince was not made aware, Xanthos knew, that only the fact that most of the Moslems had already embarked on the ships and their captains set sail at once prevented a general massacre.

That first week in August, still another leader appeared in the camp before Tripolitza. The Phanariot Alexander Mavrokordatos, from a distinguished family, had been in France when he heard of the outbreak of the revolt. Partly at his expense and by the contribution of wealthy friends, he loaded a brig with arms and ammunition and sailed for Greece.

When Xanthos saw him briefly in the camp, Mavrokordatos appeared a man in his late thirties, with a fine olive complexion and jet black hair hanging in ringlets about his face, above large mustachios and bright, black eyes. His extreme politeness and continual smile convinced many of the captains that he was a silly, shallow fop. But Xanthos felt an undeniable quality of strength in the man, a keen mind and a sharp wit. He thought this might be the leader to unify the bickering of the captains and the primates, giving a more coherent direction to the conduct of the war. But

Mavrokordatos, apparently sensing quickly that little could be achieved by a newcomer in the intrigues and clamor of the council, asked for and received a commission to leave for Missolonghi, in order to co-ordinate the resistance in that important town.

Shortly after the departure of Mavrokordatos, another of the besieged fortresses, Navarino, surrendered to the Greeks. Once again, hearing of the imminence of surrender, Ipsilantis sent a deputy Xanthos knew as an honest bungler. As at Monemvasia, under a promise of safety, the Turks of Navarino relinquished their weapons and some of their money and jewels, the Greeks agreeing to transport them to Egypt or Tunis.

In the reports received at Tripolitza it was unclear what had agitated the Greek soldiers. Perhaps they had determined they would not be denied the spoils their comrades had lost at Monemvasia. An argument about the method in which the Moslem females were being searched served as the pretext they needed. Fighting erupted and more than six hundred Turkish men, women and children were massacred.

At a meeting of the council in the headquarters of Ipsilantis, convened to discuss the events at Navarino, the prince denounced the massacre.

"This action against my orders was unspeakable!" His shrill voice quivered with outrage. "I have come here to lend the name of my family and the prestige of my office to our venture but I am mocked when our own countrymen behave like barbarians. We are not savages, gentlemen, but Hellenes, inheritors of a distinguished tradition. Our pretenses to self-government are mocked in the courts of Europe by such an episode and my own integrity and honor is besmirched!"

Kolokotronis was the first of the other captains to rise and speak.

"If we kill after promising safety," Kolokotronis said, "we

stiffen the resistance of all other Mussulmen. God forgive me, there has been too much barbarism against the Greeks, not only since the beginning of the revolt, but for centuries, for me to weep for Turkish blood. But from military expediency, an episode like Navarino makes our labor here more difficult. Why should the Turks in Tripolitza surrender when they believe they will be slaughtered anyway?"

The monk Papalikos rose in agitation to his feet.

"This is a war of extermination, Your Highness!" the monk cried. "It will be to our eternal shame, even before those not yet born, if we do not wreak total vengeance on the slayers of our sons and brothers! The initial error is in entering any negotiation with these infidels! Let us remember that the army of Mohammed II, camped before Constantinople in those last days of Byzantium, was promised a three-day sack of the city. The scurviest of Anatolian riffraff had his chance to despoil churches, kill or violate Christians, sell those who survived into slavery. Chaos, brutality and license prevailed. The Church of Saint Mary came to be known as the 'Church of Blood' because of the blood that streamed past it in rivers flowing towards the Golden Horn! That barbarism must be revenged! Mercy is not a word the cursed Mussulmen understand! Fire and the sword are their religion and by fire and the sword must they be scourged!"

"All those depredations Brother Papalikos speaks of are only too true," the sonorous tones of Archbishop Germanos resonated through the air, "but I question whether any purpose is served by senseless slaughter. We might consider mercy to those heathens willing to lay down their arms. In this way we demonstrate our superior capacity for compassion. But our Christian Lord, may His name be forever blessed, says nothing about extending leniency to the possessions of the heathens. Did not His enemies allow Him only a simple rag on His back when He rode into Jerusalem for that infamous trial and crucifixion . . . ? So we must consider that, and must understand the cost of this war and the

cost of replenishing the empty coffers of our churches demands that every last vestige of value be extracted from
these unrepentant Mussulmen . . ."

No man could predict what the future would hold,
Xanthos thought grimly as he listened to the rumbling, con-
tentious arguments, but at moments like these, hints of disaster and calamity came like a tainted wind.

Several times in the weeks that followed, contingents of
the Turkish cavalry made desperate efforts to break the lines
of siege. Finding all the surrounding countryside stripped
and barren of any provisions, they came into the foothills to
breach the breastworks. Each time a heavy fire from the
Greek positions drove them back. Finally, with the rations
of the inhabitants reduced once more so they would barely
be able to sustain strength and life, Mehemet Selik ordered
the Turkish cavalry to attack the Greek positions in force,
seeking to cut their way through the lines of siege.

Shortly after dawn, the shadowed earth still suspended in
the stillness of the night, the Turkish cavalry came galloping
from the fortress, brandishing their yataghans and shrieking
their war cries to Allah. From an ominous, imposing mass as
they poured out the gates, scattering as they raced across
the plain, they spread out before the foothills in long charging lines, four and five horses deep.

The sentries had alerted the Greeks, muskets fired from
crag to crag as a signal, and from their camps the men
rushed to the breastworks.

Roused by the first alarm, Xanthos watched from a higher
plateau as the Turks lashed their horses up the slopes. The
fury and desperation of their charge brought them
perilously close to the breastworks. But, just short of the
fortifications, the horses began to slip and stumble on the
steep, stony terrain. They fell backward on their hind-
quarters, thrashed and kicked, sending up clouds of brush
and stones. The men were hurled from their saddles, crushed

and trampled by the horses as they rolled together down the incline. The Greeks left the breastworks and raced down behind them, pausing from time to time to pour a furious fire into the disordered horde.

Seeing the tumbling horses and falling men, hearing the cries of panic and terror, and the wails of despair echoing from the canyons and defiles about him, it seemed to Xanthos that the mountain heaved at the death and destruction on its slopes, rumbling with a volcano's brawl and storm.

In the end, unable to sustain the losses and the decimating fire, leaving the slopes strewn with dead and wounded horses and men, the remnants of the attackers retreated to the fortress, pursued to the edge of the plain by the hot, vengeful Greeks. As the horses pounded through the gates, the cannons on the ramparts hurled out a burst of futile fire. While in the ring of mountains that circled the plain the Greeks roared in jubilation and triumph.

Later, Xanthos walked along the slopes with Kolokotronis. The earth had a fearful look and a deathly smell. As far as the eye could see, the carcasses of horses and the bodies of men glistened like a weird, stunted harvest.

Teams of soldiers stripped the Turkish bodies of weapons and clothing and dragged them by ropes into heaps to be burned. From time to time shots rang out as wounded horses were put to rest.

The chieftain paused above a fallen horse whose flanks steamed with sweat and whose groin was drenched with blood. As his shadow fell across it, the animal whinnied in pain, turning up the whites of its eyes. Kolokotronis cried out softly in pity, pulled out his pistol and held it a foot from the animal's temple. When the bullet rammed home, the horse wrenched in a final spasm and then lay still.

They walked on. Kolokotronis stopped again over the body of a Turkish trooper, face turned toward the sky. A dark, young Anatolian visage, thick black hair and black brows curling above his open eyes. His full, crimson lips were parted slightly, revealing a row of small, white teeth.

"Look, teacher, how young this one is," Kolokotronis said quietly. "No more than twenty-two or twenty-three. Look how the shot has frozen the heart that a few hours ago beat with fear and hope and anticipation of victory. How could his father and mother have known when they celebrated his birth that he would die so young, on the slope of a mountain, overlooking the fortress he sought to defend? I think in this moment of their grief, because he will never see his homeland again, never know the joy of his children playing about him. Now he is no longer my enemy, simply a fallen soldier on a field where we fought."

Yet, contravening that instant of compassion, Kolokotronis walked forward to a crag and stared down at the fortress. The wind rustling the plume of his helmet, his face hardened in passion and resolution, it seemed to Xanthos he resembled a vengeful, implacable scourge who lived only to conquer and destroy.

With the last efforts of the Turkish cavalry to break the siege thwarted, the inhabitants of Tripolitza grew more despondent and desperate. Night and day dolorous wails and laments sounded from within the walls. The last mangy cats and dogs were eaten, stems and roots devoured. Families were reduced to existing for several days on a little meal mixed with a few drops of water, often eaten unbaked because fuel was almost gone. Robbery and murder became rampant as men sought to keep alive. When the thieves and murderers were caught, Mehemet Selik ordered them hanged and hardly a day passed without at least a score of bodies hanging from the trees in the central square. Finally, there were reports the Albanian mercenaries threatened mutiny unless the horses of the cavalry were slaughtered for food.

"That will provide relief for only a little while," Balalas told Xanthos grimly. "With so many thousands of people to feed, that horseflesh won't last long."

At the beginning of September, a new army appeared in the mountains where the Greeks camped. They were hundreds of ragged beggars, driven from the towns under siege, almost as ravenous as the occupants of the fortress, carrying slings, scythes, clubs and daggers strapped to the end of long poles. They came under cover of darkness and in the morning swarmed like locusts in a grove or clearing, waiting for the fall of the fortress. In vain did Kolokotronis send squads of soldiers to drive them off the mountain. Scattered once, they would quickly assemble again, an ominous and malignant host.

Finally, the chieftain had a dozen of the beggars caught and dragged into the Greek camp. They were stripped, and tied to the trunks of trees while burly soldiers lashed them with leather belts. Howling and screaming as their backs were spurred with raw, bloody welts, they were finally cut down, driven from the camp as a baleful warning to their companions.

"I doubt it will scare them off," Kolokotronis said to Xanthos. "The bone-poor devils have always lived on the edge of starving under the Turks. Now they have heard the wealth and riches of pashas are to be divided here. Every man who managed a scrap of loot at Navarino has returned to his village or settlement boasting it is ten times as much to make his feat ten times more impressive. Tripolitza is bigger by far and wealthier many times over than Navarino. Anticipation has driven them berserk with greed." The chieftain smiled wryly. "If the captains assembled here are tormented by visions of that wealth, who can blame those poor wretches?"

"But they are totally undisciplined," Xanthos said. "And cannot be counted on to follow orders."

Kolokotronis nodded.

"When the time comes to enter the city," he said, "we will set up a cordon of soldiers to keep them out."

During this time when the horses were being slaughtered and eaten inside the fortress, an unnatural trade developed between the besiegers and the besieged. Xanthos did not hear of it until Balalas told him how, each evening as darkness fell, a procession of Greeks carrying baskets of provisions, moved stealthily from the mountains down the path to the plain and to one of the gates of the fortress. In a few moments the gate was opened and Turks met them in hasty, furtive negotiations.

"They are selling the Turks food," Balalas said.

"In the name of God, why?" Xanthos asked. "The siege is to starve the Moslems into surrender! Why then sell them food?"

"Not to all of them," Balalas said contemptuously. "Only to the wealthier Turks. And at extravagant prices. I have heard a loaf of bread brings a string of pearls."

"Who is responsible?"

"Who knows?" Balalas shrugged. "Men trading for themselves or acting for their captains. They think in this way to cheat those who are waiting for the city to fall and gain the spoils at that time."

The trading went on, more and more blatant and bold, until it seemed that each night scores of men were on the move, crowds of them bargaining heatedly at every gate of the fortress. Kolokotronis did not mention the bartering to Xanthos, but a certain seething impatience marked his words. He joined Petrobey in proposing to Ipsilantis an immediate assault on the fortress.

Prince Ipsilantis vacillated, made indecisive by the advice of many of the other captains, feeling a few more days might weaken the inhabitants further and prevent any more of the Greek soldiers being killed than was necessary.

"We must concern ourselves with the lives of the men

under my command, Captain," Ipsilantis spoke with a pa-
tronizing haughtiness, as if he alone, Xanthos thought, were
civilized enough to consider the cost in human life.

"If we concern ourselves with life, Excellency," Kolokotronis said, and Xanthos could hear the anger trembling in
his voice, "perhaps it is better to put an end to the starving.
Make them our final terms for surrender. If they refuse, we
assault and win the fortress. Then we can see the women
and children inside fed. Each day and week we delay, hundreds and then thousands will die."

"We will take your suggestion into consideration,"
Ipsilantis said. "We are, at the moment, preparing a final
draft of the terms of surrender for the Turkish leaders in the
fortress."

"When will the terms be delivered to them?"

"As soon as we feel they properly reflect our conditions,"
Ipsilantis said.

"Time is important, Excellency," Kolokotronis said
sharply. "This is not some European court where men
debate the modes and ritual of surrender. This is war . . ."

The prince flushed and his lips quivered.

"Captain, you forget yourself!" He spoke shrilly and indignantly.

Petrobey interposed himself between them, motioning
for Kolokotronis to show restraint.

"Your Excellency," he said soothingly. "Let me make a
compromise proposal. Since there is no longer any fear of
the Mussulman cavalry, let us break our mountain camps
and move down to new positions on the plain. If the Turks
see us closing the ring more tightly, it might make them
more amenable to negotiations and surrender. Meanwhile, if
they or the Albanians venture out, we might counterattack
and storm the bastion."

Ipsilantis agreed and with a perfunctory motion of his
hand indicated the audience was over. Kolokotronis and Petrobey left the headquarters, Xanthos following close

behind. He could surmise from the angry brace of the chieftain's shoulders, how close he had come to a storm.

The order to break camp was received by shouts of acclamation, and all that day and the following day the procession of mules plodded down the mountains to the plain. The Maniat corps of Petrobey and the men of Kolokotronis were the first to move, taking up places opposite the southern wall, where they set to work at once throwing up an embankment of earth against any attack from the fort. The Albanian mercenaries remained dangerous and precautions had to be taken if they decided to charge in an effort to cut their way out. In the space behind the embankment, went up the rows of barracks, roofed in with osier and oleander boughs.

The Turkish sentries on the walls stared down at them less than four hundred yards away, but whether they were weakened by hunger or simply resigned, they did not shout or fire upon them. The cannons on the ramparts remained silent, as well, leading to speculation that ammunition for that ordnance was in short supply or totally used up.

By midday on September 27, the Greek lines formed a tight noose of earthworks around the fortress. That same afternoon the surrender terms were carried to Mehemet Solik. The Greeks demanded the Turks relinquish their arms and, as an indemnity, be required to pay forty million piasters, that being, according to the captains who fixed the sum, approximately the cost of the war including the provisions and pay of the men from the outbreak. If these terms were met, the Turks would be given safe passage from the fortress.

Mehemet Selik refused indignantly. The sum was impossible to meet. The Turks offered a counterproposal. They would relinquish the whole of the property within the town, renounce all rights to the land and retain only sufficient means to enable them to reach a port on the coast of Asia Minor. They would not, however, give up their arms and they also insisted on occupying the pass over Mount

Parthenius, between Tripolitza and the Argive plain, until their women and children had crossed in safety.

These terms the Greeks rejected flatly. If the Turkish regiments occupied Parthenius, they would have the means to march on to Nauplion and join the garrison there. Nauplion still held a line open to the sea from which they received supplies of provisions and arms. The Greek captains had not labored six months in reducing Tripolitza to allow the besieged to reach another fortress.

With negotiations at a standstill, Kolokotronis and Petrobey again urged an assault on the fortress. Prince Ipsilantis, once more halfheartedly agreeing on the expediency of attack, found himself strongly counseled by captains and primates for an additional delay. Perhaps some of these leaders were sincere, Xanthos thought, but others must have anticipated an even richer bounty in barter during the days ahead as hunger among the Turks grew worse. This was not the siege of Tripolitza, Xanthos wrote sadly in his journal, it was the marketplace of Tripolitza.

The day following the breakdown of the negotiations for surrender, a courier came to Kolokotronis under a flag of truce with a message from Elmas Bey, commander of the Albanian mercenaries, asking to parley. Kolokotronis sent a troop of men to escort the leader back to their camp. In a short while the troop returned with the Albanian commander riding one of their horses.

As he reined his horse and leaped down to the ground, his short, stocky body presented an appearance of litheness and great strength. Bristling with sword, dagger and pistols, he swaggered to the plane tree where Kolokotronis waited arrayed fully in battle dress of his own. Xanthos stood a few feet away, a pen and sheaf of paper in his hands.

As the legendary mercenary reached them, seeing him at close range for the first time, Xanthos marveled at the battlefield of his face, a mass of blemishes, cuts and scabs. As if

Elmas Bey counted any battle fruitless if he did not gain a fresh scar to mark a wound.

"Well, Kolokotronis," Elmas Bey said, his voice rumbling from the disfigured lips. "Haven't seen you since Vostitza."

"You look well fed, Elmas Bey," Kolokotronis said. "The rest of the inhabitants of Tripolitza may be hungry but you don't appear to be lacking food."

Elmas Bey laughed loudly.

"Fighting men need their nourishment," he said wryly. "We take it from whoever has it. Let the useless sots scrounge for bones."

Kolokotronis motioned him to a bench and sat down on another one nearby. The Albanian hunched his trunk forward and motioned toward Xanthos, who had seated himself, as well.

"I asked for a private parley. Who is he?"

"A scribe," Kolokotronis said. "To record our conversation, making sure there is no misunderstanding about what has been spoken between us."

Elmas Bey sneered, a cold baring of his teeth.

"All this stuff about armies of liberation," he said. "Scribes and dispatches and councils of captains. You've changed, but I haven't."

"Fools never do," Kolokotronis said quietly.

Elmas Bey's huge head stiffened, his eyes sparking like flint from steel. A quiver of fear swept Xanthos as he felt the merciless, malignant force of the man. Then the Albanian relaxed.

"Still quick to cut with words, eh?" he said.

"And you . . . still quick with the knife?" Kolokotronis asked coldly. "I remember the way you and your men mutilated the corpses of our fallen Greeks." The chieftain spoke tensely as if the recollection had stirred his fury.

"We were being pursued." Elmas Bey shrugged. "You know that mutilated corpses always slow the pursuers down." He bobbed his head in a parody of deference. "I apologize, Captain, if we offended the Greek obsession for proper burial of their dead."

A slight wind rose, trembling the leaves of the plane tree. As if sensing the significance of the meeting, crowds of silent and watchful soldiers had gathered some distance away.

Seeing the two men poised against one another, Xanthos marked the contrasts between them. The Albanian, so obviously bred to war, skilled in the slow and fast kill, scornful of subtleties and words. Kolokotronis, a fighter directed by mystic, intuitive flashes, ranging far with brooding insights, a shrewd judge of others, a patriot who execrated war but who was intoxicated by it, as well.

"Well, Elmas Bey," Kolokotronis said quietly. "You haven't asked to parley so we could reminisce about old battles. What do you have to say?"

"Perhaps a swig of wine would salivate my tongue," Elmas Bey said with a sardonic smile. "No food, of course, because that would violate the siege, but a little wine."

Kolokotronis called to a man to bring wine. Elmas Bey took the flask greedily and threw back his head for a long, thirsty swallow.

"God, that's good!" he said when he regained his breath. He held the flask loosely between his knees, stroking the neck gently with his fingers.

"Well, I think it won't be long now," he said. "Their bellies and bones are beginning to rattle. No place in there for fighting men anymore."

"Yes, we'll be inside the walls soon," Kolokotronis said.

"Understand me, Kolokotronis," Elmas Bey said, and all mockery and taunting left his voice that became hard and sharp as a sword. "We will not wait, my men and me, for starvation to weaken us. If an agreement is not reached between us today, I return to make plans for us to cut our way out of that death-hole."

"You won't get through us alive."

"Some of us will!" Elmas Bey cried. As his voice rose, the watching, attentive soldiers stirred and muttered, a few pushing closer, their fingers near their guns. Elmas Bey swept them with a look of fearless contempt. He turned back to Kolokotronis. "And we may do more damage than you think. Your men are conscripts, peasants with guns, farmers with swords. A charge by professionals might cut through them like a lance through a field of wheat. Better than dying like pigs inside. If my men go down in battle, they'll take along as many Greeks as they can. You're an old campaigner and you know what I am saying is true."

Kolokotronis nodded slowly.

"But why fight unless we have to?" Elmas Bey went on. "Better carry our lives and our possessions away. What you do to the Turks in the city is no concern of ours. We hired to fight and starvation annuls the rules. Give us safekeeping through your lines. We'll head north and arrange for shipping to get us home. Maybe join Ali Pasha against Khurshid."

"What are your conditions?" Kolokotronis asked.

"Our arms and our money! Not one sword or gun or piaster do we give up! Touch us, and you have a battle to the death!"

"What if we grant you safe exit from the fortress," Kolokotronis said, "let you pass through the mountains to go home, how do we know you won't join the Turks against us again?"

"How do we know you won't promise safe passage and then decide to attack us, maybe ambush us somewhere along the way?"

"You have our word."

"Your word!" Elmas Bey laughed harshly. "The same word you gave the Mussulmen at Navarino? God, you Greeks are generous!"

"I was not at Navarino," Kolokotronis said quietly. "You have my word this time. Not because I wouldn't like to kill you, but because it is more expedient to get you out of the way."

Elmas Bey stared at him for a long, piercing moment and then nodded. "I accept your word," he said. "You'll give your life to keep it. And I give you my word that my men and me will never enlist in Turkish service again. I don't like the way they smell, anyway."

"Good," Kolotronis said. "Now, all that remains is that you understand I am not alone in command here. I will submit your proposal to the council, and tell them I have given you my word. I do not think they will be fools enough to vote against our treaty or against me."

The Albanian rose to his feet.

"As to their being fools," he said. "You'd be better to take away their captaincies, put some baggage on their backs and use them as asses." He smirked. "They are such unselfish gallants. You should see the activity each night at the gates. As long as a jewel remains in the fortress, my men and me will eat. That's what the longing for liberty does to you Greeks."

Kolokotronis was silent, cut by the words. The Albanian grinned and walked toward the waiting troop. He mounted his horse, then reined round and returned to the tree.

"One last word," he said, and his stocky, armored figure loomed huge and black against the sky. "Make sure none of those scurvy captains decide they want to be heroes." He looked at Xanthos. "Scribe!" He spit the word. "Write that warning from Elmas Bey and write it clear!"

He spurred his horse to rejoin the escort. The soldiers who had been watching opened a path just wide enough for horse and man to pass, his stirruped and booted legs brushing their bodies. He rode through them without looking down, savage and unafraid.

"That is the end of Tripolitza," Kolokotronis said. and Xanthos sensed the jubilation in his voice.

"They have no loyalty to the men who paid them to fight?" Xanthos asked.

"They are mercenaries," Kolokotronis said. "No loyalty to God or man, only to themselves."

He motioned urgently to Xanthos.

"Now we will draft a strong letter to be sent to Ipsilantis and the captains, making sure they understand the consequences if a few fools start a war of their own with Elmas Bey. That band will need as much killing as a pack of crazed she-bears, and will take a Greek army with them to Hades!"

Late that evening Xanthos walked away from the camp into the darkness. Below him he could see the ramparts of Tripolitza, the watchfires on the citadel. In the mountains that surrounded the plain, the campfires of the besiegers gleamed like the torches of some vengeful host.

That is the end of Tripolitza, the chieftain said. Yet what would happen when the fortress fell? Would they narrowly avert disaster like Monemvasia or suffer their enemies to a destruction like Navarino? How dearly might the Turks sell their lives and how many good Greek soldiers would die?

He knew the Turks as a cruel and barbarous people. Their ferocity and bloodthirstiness had been evidenced countless times from the fall of Constantinople, through the centuries of slavery, to the massacre at Kydonies. If one returned them treatment in kind, they did not deserve mercy. Yet Xanthos knew that cruelty and barbarism existed in all races and religions. Far back in Greek history, there were instances recorded of such savagery.

On the very morning of Salamis, the battle in which the Athenians, sticking to liberty, as Herodotus wrote, saved Greek independence from the Persians, Themistocles, wishing to insure victory for their side, offered three human sacrifices to Dionysus, "Eater of raw flesh." They were three young prisoners of great beauty, nephews of the Great King himself, magnificently attired and adorned with jewels. And Themistocles slew them with his own hand, on the flagship, in the presence of the whole fleet, not as an act of reprisal but as a solemn consecration.

For the sake of his people and his land, Xanthos wished them to achieve freedom as a boon for their centuries of suffering and their willingness to die for its sake. Yet he could not help hoping this freedom might be realized without the loss of their humanity.

Despite the evidence of selfishness and greed, there were the good intentions and the honor of Ipsilantis, the pledges of the captains that they would not allow a repetition of the atrocities of Navarino, the respect with which their men regarded Kolokotronis and Petrobey. These might permit a generosity of spirit, a mercy toward the besieged even as they conquered, that would, at the time of victory, contain the spores of more glorious triumphs still to come.

Now, in the darkness of the night, suspended between the peaks of the mountain and the fortress, Xanthos prayed that redemption might be true.

CHAPTER
FOURTEEN

I

At the end of September, the sixth month of the siege of Tripolitza, the weather turned hot and stifling, the midday sun burning down like fire. Suffering with the rest of the soldiers, Xanthos sweltered behind the entrenchments on the plain, his throat parched and his nose dry, his head throbbing and the blistering air sucking the moisture from his body. Men crawled beneath any oasis of shelter they could find, while around them plants shriveled and the petals of flowers turned brown and withered.

If the heat consumed the besiegers, the suffering of the inhabitants of the fortress, almost out of water as well as food, was a greater agony. All day the gaunt, emaciated figures of men and women could be seen on the ramparts, staring hopelessly at the camps of the Greeks and at the mountains beyond, the passes that were the roads to freedom. In the shimmering waves of heat, the air pulsed and vibrated so that even the walls of the fortress seemed to be swaying and unsteady.

The night brought scant relief. The heat, carrying into the darkness, seemed to drink the moon so that it receded into a pale, eerie mist.

The only food entering the fortress were the provisions sold to the inhabitants by the Greeks. That trading went on with increasing quantities of bread and fruit bartered. Every evening the long lines of Greeks carrying food wended their way to the various gates, where they were met by scores of Turks, servants of the wealthy Moslems trafficking for their masters, soldiers bargaining for their captains, eunuchs negotiating for the women of the harems, all of them desperate to trade jewels or money for a crust of bread or a scrap of meat. Back in the camps, men boasted openly of the prizes they were accumulating, inflaming the envy of others, making them eager to join the bartering.

Prince Ipsilantis issued repeated warnings about the illegal traffic, threatening severe punishment to the offenders. Few paid any attention to these warnings because the exchanges had become so widespread that whole regiments, the captains included, were profiting from the trade.

The crafty Bouboulina proved the most ingenious at reaping plunder. Astride a great ornamented horse, displaying a flag of truce and attended by retainers who could speak Turkish and act as interpreters, leading donkeys with large panniers hanging at their sides, she boldly paraded into Tripolitza. Gaining entrance to the harems because of her sex, she assured the terrified concubines she would issue them certificates of protection from the Greek soldiers in return for the jewels in their coffers. They pushed their treasures gratefully upon her, pleading for her to take the gilded, turquoise bracelets and necklaces, the pearl tiaras and coronets, the jade and emerald earrings. When her donkeys emerged from the gates late in the afternoon, bearing the heavily loaded panniers in which she carried her immense booty, the troops in the camps raised their fists and muskets to the sky, shouting in frustration and rage at still another provocation designed to cheat them.

"I have seen some ugly things in war," Balalas said to

Xanthos as they prepared to bed down on their pallets. "The brutality of men when their blood is up. But there is a bitterness in the men here because they feel gulled and rooked at the stealing of their spoils, unlike any fury I have ever known."

"What do you think will happen, Balalas, when we enter the fortress?"

"I don't know, teacher," the Maniat said grimly. "But when the storm breaks, commands, pleas, prayers . . . I am afraid nothing will stop it from eating us all."

The first days of October and the searing heat continued to blaze down on the plain, the camps and the fortress. The atmosphere hung deadly and smothering, a blistered silence full of foreboding. Rumors that plague had broken out within the fortress lashed the Greek camps with terror. In confirmation of those ominous tidings, spirals of black smoke rose from the burial grounds outside the walls of the town, the stench of burning flesh carried on the scorched, tainted air. Every man dreaded the pestilence bringing chills and fever, convulsions and gruesome death to scourge an army or a city. But not a Greek fled from his place, because greater than the terror of the plague, he feared withdrawing from Tripolitza without booty and spoils.

A number of the hungry, miserable wretches from the fortress, unable to afford the bartering for food, fled from its gates at night, pleading with the Greeks to be allowed to surrender in return for a crust of bread. They were often driven back to the fortress, where the Turks refused to allow them to re-enter. They huddled outside the walls, under the unshielded fury of the sun, growing weaker until they ceased to wail and shriek.

In the camp of Kolokotronis a few of these refugees were allowed entrance but they were herded together roughly and penned in a compound to the rear. From them Kolokotronis and his staff learned that the last of the horsemeat had been eaten, that except for the provisions to be traded from the Greeks, starvation had begun.

On the third of October, a report stormed the camp that a strong Turkish fleet under Kara Ali, the Capitan-pasha, bearing massive quantities of food and arms to relieve the siege of Tripolitza, had been sighted off Patras. The combined Greek fleet of Spetziot, Hydriote and Psariot ships was too far away to make any effort to obstruct them.

The Greek captains gathered in an emergency meeting of the council and the Senate and urged on Ipsilantis that he take personal command of a force to march and deter this threat.

Xanthos was not sure if the reports about the Moslem fleet were accurate or whether the threat was cannily contrived to get Ipsilantis away from the camps. Whatever the reasons each of the captains might have had, their unified agitation and combined pleas alarmed Ipsilantis and he made plans hastily to march north with a detachment of 1,500 men.

At dawn on the fifth of October, the prince's corps was barely out of sight through the northern mountain passes when the traffic before the fortress bloomed into a full-scale bazaar. All pretense to secrecy or concealment was abandoned and some of the captains even set up tents and flimsy booths to protect them from the blistering sun. The long lines of hungry, desperate Turks filed from the fortress, bartering their possessions, weapons and money for whatever scraps of food the Greeks wished to give them in return.

All morning and into the early afternoon, the trading went on, a blatant, shameless spectacle of an army demoralized by greed. Arguments broke out in the camps when some officers sought to restrain their men from joining the trade, and it seemed to Xanthos that the eventuality Kolokotronis and Petrobey had warned Ipsilantis about had indeed come to pass. The Greek army seemed less inclined to fight and more obsessed with commerce.

To remove himself from the sight of the teeming, trading frenzy, Xanthos retired to a small grove in the foothills, some hundreds of yards behind the entrenchments, making entries in his journal beneath the shade of a tree.

Sometime in the middle of the afternoon, the strident, raucous shouts and cries from the direction of the plain were suddenly submerged in an outburst of gunfire. By the time Xanthos had risen and hastened back to the entrenchments, the plain had become a noisy, clamorous and disordered battlefield. From a cook in the nearly deserted camp Xanthos learned that the corps of Kolokotronis and the Maniats of Petrobey had attacked the fortress. One instant the plain before the city was a thriving marketplace and then, without warning, breaking from their camps, several thousand Greeks charged forward. One contingent sped toward the Argos tower, where the walls could be scaled because of the rough, projecting stones, and another group dashed toward the gates from which the Turks emerged. While many of the traders still bartered in the tents and booths, the attackers had scaled the walls, overpowered the sentries, and dangled ropes down for their comrades. At the gate a short, fierce battle had been joined, the Turks trying furiously and ineffectively to close the iron-barred portals.

As the Greeks and Turks at the booths and tents became aware of what was happening, they drew weapons and attacked one another. Some Turks fought desperately, others fled toward the mountains, Greeks dashing after them to cut them down.

Meanwhile, the other corps of Greeks, hearing the tumult and shooting from the area of the plain and the south wall, rushed to join the assault. From the earthworks Xanthos saw the men of Archbishop Germanos launch an attack against the east wall, the horde of Papalikos moving in a mass on the Patras tower. Bouboulina on her ornamented charger led a group of sailors toward the southern gate, which had been breached in the first charge. The scene became one of stunned and reinless disorder, less an organized assault by an army than a series of chaotic charges.

Perplexed and rattled by the swiftness of what had transpired, uncertain whether the attack had been ordered or the men were simply bursting free on their own, Xanthos joined a score of soldiers who had been guarding the prisoners in the compounds. Hearing the firing they abandoned their charges and rushed forward to join the attack.

Xanthos ran across the plain with these men, passing the tumbled and overturned booths and tents. There were bodies of dead Greeks and dead and dying Turks, some still clutching parcels of bread and fruit.

When they passed through the shattered gates into the city, they were hurled into bedlam. At the far end of the narrow street, a mass of Turkish servants and harem girls, long, black hair flowing from beneath their veils, had descended from the houses and buildings, shrieking and waving the certificates of protection signed by Bouboulina and some of the other captains. The Greek soldiers, maddened by months of frustration, enraged by the treachery of the captains, saw those papers as reminders of that betrayal. They stabbed and shot without mercy or restraint. Xanthos saw men run through, women's throats cut, bodies kicked and tossed aside, trampled by others trying to flee and by the onslaught of the Greeks. And from the streets beyond the one where he stood, a brutal aberrant roar covered the city.

Unable to move against the milling, hysterical mob, killers and victims crammed tightly together, some of the Greeks dashed into the alcoves of houses, battering open the outer doors with the butts of their muskets. Frantic to escape the carnage of the street, Xanthos followed several of the soldiers into one of the larger dwellings. He saw them kill a servant, the man on his knees whimpering for mercy as they cut him down. They ran forward through the salon to the stairwall, where a robed Turk clasping a yataghan sought to bar their way.

For a few moments, crying to Allah and the Prophet, swinging the yataghan in a wild arc, he held them at bay. Then they overwhelmed him, one soldier piercing him through the abdomen with his sword. As he dropped the yataghan, a shriek bursting from his lips, another soldier stabbed him in the chest, tumbling him down the stairs, to sprawl in a heap at the base. The soldiers rushed up the stairs.

Xanthos stood staring at the man's body until an outcry of screams sent him hurrying up the stairs. On the upper landing he saw a woman come running from a room into the hall, a Greek at her heels. Snaring her by the hair, he jerked back her head and reaching around her swiftly cut her throat, so sharp and deep a slash that blood spurted like a geyser from her neck. He dropped her body and ran into another room.

Xanthos cried a plea to the men, beseeching them to mercy, his words muffled in the noisy din as they tore at furnishings, overturning cupboards and chests in their mad search. They came angrily from the rooms, cursing at their meager loot, a few silken garments and a silver frame, shoving him violently aside as they raced down the stairs, leaping across the body sprawled at the bottom.

In another room, Xanthos found two dead children, boys of about six or seven. The older child seemed pinned to the floor on his belly, hands and arms extended and feet and legs spread wide. Between the bony, winged blades of his upper back was a deep, blood-soaked gash.

The younger child hung over the edge of the bed, head dangling limply, arms hanging down. The shirt had been ripped from his shoulders and the nape of his small, frail neck gleamed like the soft, downy throat of a bird.

For a long time Xanthos sat on a bench in the hallway, his gaze drawn back time and time again to the body of the woman on the floor. The roaring from the street outside which seemed to go on and on, finally diminished and receded until he could distinguish a solitary shriek and a single scream. He heard his heart then, beating in futility and fear.

After a while he rose and opened the doors to a terrace. and stepped outside. He was assailed at once by the brutal heat of the sun. The street below was strewn with the bodies of the slain, men and women tossed in gutter and doorway like deadwood and wastements. The crowd that had not been slain had been dispersed, driven deeper into the city. From the distance he could hear that gruesome roar of murder and death. To the north, above the minarets of a mosque, black smoke surged into the sky. In the hot, breathless air, the thick, cloying stench of blood reminded him of the battlefield at Karitena.

On the street below a small girl appeared, her arm drenched in blood, running and howling in pain and terror. After she had disappeared, several jubilant Greek soldiers passed, one carrying a small chest full of silver coins, some falling over the rim to the ground, a man behind stooping clumsily and happily to pick them up.

Xanthos considered finding Kolokotronis or Petrobey, hoping they might issue and enforce orders for the slaughter to cease. Yet he stood there, his legs reluctant to move, his hands clasping the railing. He stifled a strange impulse to scream.

Grateful he did not have to enter the house again, he crossed from the terrace to an adjoining one, descended a stairway to the street. He began walking up one passageway and down another, every corridor containing dead and stripped bodies. When someone still alive uttered a moan or a plea, he bent to offer aid, often nothing more effectual than to place his water flask for a moment to their lips, wetting the caked, black tongues, or flailing his arms and shrieking to scatter the multitudes of black flies swarming over the congealing puddles of blood. After a while, one ghastly street resembling another, kites and ravens and hawks wheeling and screaming above his head in the sky, he lost direction, wandered aimlessly, circling so that he passed the same dangling, mutilated body several times. Or are they different bodies, he thought with despair, and I can no longer tell them apart?

If the streets were corridors of grisly specters because of the bodies of the dead, they were still rendered more hideous for the living. He saw a boy trying to flee his captors, caught, clubbed and stabbed to death. An old woman's naked body, bony, fleshless ribs and withered teats, dragged along the street by a rope about her throat until she strangled. On a balcony above he saw a baby snatched from its crazed mother, impaled on a soldier's sword, and then tossed like a melon or a piece of garbage to the street.

Sometimes, he could not see the torture, only hear the victim's screams from some courtyard or house. Once, in an effort to intervene and aid a family being attacked, he was kicked and driven off.

By late afternoon, wearied and sickened, Xanthos huddled in a doorway as a motley procession of ragged Greeks, the beggars from the mountains, who must have entered the city on the heels of the soldiers, passed in a screeching mob. On a rough and crude wooden cross they held high above their heads, they had crucified a bearded Turk, the man's palms and feet pierced by nails, and, on his head, wedged so tightly into his flesh that blood ran down his cheeks, a crown of thorns.

A scarlet twilight settled a steaming mist over the roofs and terraces and latticed windows. The sun recoiled, the sky darkened, and a dry, cankerous wind disseminated a poison of smells. The tumult from the distance came to Xanthos in a fierce scraping and roaring, as if the city were not set in a landlocked plain but at the edge of a stormy sea whose breakers pounded sharp and jagged rocks.

A score of soldiers burdened Xanthos with a spate of rumors. The Turks in the central citadel were still resisting and Kolokotronis and Petrobey led the attack against that inner bastion. Archbishop Germanos proclaimed his acceptance of the city's surrender in the name of the Holy Orthodox Church and called for the forcible baptism of Moslem children. Papalikos had set up his headquarters in a Moslem nobleman's palace, whose ramparts he decorated with a hundred severed Turkish heads. And all over the city, inexhaustible and relentless, the slaughter, pillaging and looting went on, Greeks often fighting with one another over the slaves and the spoils.

A new terror was added to the shambles. A Maniat told Xanthos that packs of gaunt, ravenous dogs had entered the city under cover of darkness. The months of siege and the stripping of the countryside had starved them, as well, and smelling the abundance of flesh and blood, they came to forage among the dead. From some dark street, a baying and snarling would break out as they tore over a body.

Seeking a sanctuary from the fearful dogs and from the terrors, compounded by darkness, Xanthos asked the Maniat where he might find a place of safety. The soldier pointed him in the direction of one of the larger houses some streets to the south, whose courtyard was being used, he said, as a haven for wounded Greek soldiers and as a depot for the distribution of food.

His body numbed and exhausted, Xanthos hurried through the streets, guiding himself by the stars that emerged from time to time, a frail linking of light, in the smoking vault of night.

The day he had passed seemed a hallucination and a horror beyond belief. He thought of ancient curses and omens, calamities and disasters, conquerors sowing the sites of destroyed cities with salt, the vengeance of armies from the time of bloody Troy. He sought precedents to help him accept what was taking place, prevent him believing he had gone mad before the shock and enormity of the things he had seen over the span of a few hours in the doomed city. In that moment, passing a doorway, he heard a plaintive whimper.

Resisting a fear that urged him to go on, he peered uneasily into the shadows.

"Who is it?" he asked.

The whimper came again, shaken with terror.

He stretched out his hand, his fingers touching the cloth of some covering, and a huddled form beneath it that flinched away. He knew a Turkish woman or child would not understand words of reassurance, so he stroked the cloth, slowly, soothingly, feeling the body trembling.

Stepping closer he made out the small form of what he took to be a child. He fumbled and found the cover was a cape, located the hood and drew it gently down. In the streaked light from the stars falling faintly across the doorway, he saw the head of a girl.

Even in her trembling and terror he was aware she was beautiful as a doll, a pale, small face with delicate bones and large, dark Shulamitish eyes. Her hair was twined in long thick plaits. She appeared no more than fifteen or sixteen and he pitied her rampant fear.

"I won't hurt you," he said softly, relying on the tone rather than the words.

Her pores exuded a sweat of dread, until something in his gentleness reassured her.

"Come with me," he said, and made a slow, stiff effort to raise her. "We'll find a place, God willing, where you'll be safe."

He drew her into the circle of his arm, surprised at how

tiny and slender she was. He was reminded of his Chryseis and thought that his helpless role as witness to horror had been redeemed because he had been given this frail young Turkish girl to save.

They walked through the streets, slowly at first, her steps hesitant and faltering as if she did not yet fully trust him, then more quickly as his fear passed to her. Every shadow and darkened nook along the way became more ominous to him because she was now his charge.

At the end of the following street he saw the walls of a courtyard, a few Greek soldiers entering and leaving. He hurried toward the gate, stopped before a couple of soldiers just inside.

"I am a Greek," Xanthos said excitedly. "Xanthos, the scribe, on the staff of Kolokotronis."

"I believe you, scribe," the soldier said. "If you were a Turkish pig, you'd be hiding or dead." He stared at the cape. "What do you have there?"

"A Moslem child," Xanthos said earnestly. "A frightened girl I am trying to save."

"I believe that too, scribe," the soldier sneered. "If you're looking for a dark corner to taste that Turkish fruit, go back under the trees. They're only some wounded men there and I don't think they'll bother you."

As Xanthos and the girl moved on, the soldier spoke to his companion and both men broke into raucous laughter.

The courtyard was lit by a score of torches planted on stakes. The flames reflected across the facade of an imposing house that had been gutted, the door torn from its hinges, the windows empty and dark. In the center of the courtyard was a fountain ornamented by a dolphin whose dry snout hung suspended in the air. At one corner of the wall there were several fires built, kettles of some broth or soup hanging from sticks above them, and a couple of dozen men, sitting or standing as they ate. At the opposite end of the courtyard was a row of lemon trees.

Xanthos led the girl toward the shelter of the trees. Passing the wounded men, a dozen or so with rude slings about their necks and arms or bloodied bandages about their heads, he was startled to see Balalas among them. The veteran was lying on his side beneath one of the trees, one arm straight and stiff along his leg, the other holding his smoking pipe, the bowl glowing like a small red eye. Xanthos led the girl to stand above him. Balalas looked up and when he recognized Xanthos, he took the pipe from between his teeth and shook his head with a faint smile.

"You keep coming back from the dead, teacher."

"As often as you do!" Xanthos said. He was delighted for the presence of the old campaigner. He peered closer at his face, saw the flesh discolored and drained of the man's copper vigor and strength. A wide strip of rag was bound about his waist, portions smeared with stains of dried blood. "How badly are you hurt?"

"A pistol ball in my side," Balalas said quietly. "Burns like hell from time to time but I'll be all right." He stared at the lumpy cape. "What have you got there, teacher? Don't tell me you're looting like the rest of the bloody army?"

Xanthos lowered the hood of the cape slightly to expose the girl's dark head and slim shoulders. She gazed at them with dark, nervous eyes, a flutter of quickened breathing raising her small, scant breasts. She looked at Xanthos, managed to free one hand from the cape and made a silent, imploring motion with her fingers to her mouth.

Balalas fumbled beside him and brought up a few dried figs and a thin slice of cake sticky with honey. She cried out softly when she saw them, took them and began to eat, her white teeth rending the figs with tiny and ravenous bites.

"A thousand men would murder you for her, teacher," Balalas said grimly.

"I found her in a doorway nearby," Xanthos said. "A marvel how she has escaped harm this long." He looked beseechingly at the Maniat. "Will you help me save her, Balalas? So many are being butchered, so many dead. If you help me, maybe we can save this one child!"

"A pullet in the middle of a pack of wolves," Balalas said somberly, "but I'll do what I can. I sent for a couple of wagons to take us out of this graveyard and back to a camp in the mountains. They'll be here early in the morning and I'll get the drivers to let you both ride with us."

A soldier from the group eating at the kettles, had approached the area of wounded men. He was a chunky-bodied, shaggy-haired and unkempt man, a bandolier slung across his ragged shirt, the long bone handle of a knife thrust in his belt. As he bent furtively toward one of the wounded men, Balalas caught sight of him.

"What are you doing there, buzzard?" Balalas shouted harshly, and Xanthos could tell the pain the cry caused him. "Get back to your garbage!"

The man stared grimly at them but did not speak. He moved a few steps in a curious lurching gait, his heavy head thrust forward, long arms swinging apelike at his side. When he came closer, Xanthos discerned the hunchbacked swelling above the ridge of his shoulder and then, at some ugliness and evil in the man's face, he moved nervously to shield the girl from his gaze.

"One of the monk's black spawn!" Balalas spit, his hand releasing the butt of a pistol in his belt. "Seeing if there was anything he could steal off the wounded! Bastards!" He drew a deep, hard breath. "They almost got us into a full-scale war today. Elmas Bey and his Albanians had barricaded themselves in his palace, meaning to keep the treaty unless we broke it. Papalikos and his men were all for going in after them. We should have let the scum go ahead, but good men would have died, as well. The captain cracked a few skulls to convince them. That's how I got this wound. One of the bastards, a Greek, mind you, shot me! I got a knife into his belly afterward, but . . ."

"You are lucky to be alive," Xanthos said.

"God help us, we got them out!" Balalas said fervently. "All fifteen hundred of them, swords and guns at the ready, watchful as a pack of wolves. They should be at Trikorpha now, Niketaras ready to start them north for the Gulf first thing in the morning." A low growl emerged from his throat. "They are lucky to get away from this hell. There is murder here, not war, and madness and greed. I'm sick of it all!" A tremor of some uncommon fear touched his tight-fleshed cheeks. "There is plague here too," he said with revulsion. "I've seen the rotting bodies they haven't burned. In the end Tripolitza will become a graveyard for the Greeks, as well as the Turks. Maybe it's what we deserve."

He made a slow and painful effort to move.

"I'm tired now, teacher," he said wearily. "Too much jabber for a wounded man. Let's get some sleep. Keep the girl close to us so we can hang an eye on her."

He turned his head away. Xanthos motioned the girl to lie down. When she curled into a cramped little bundle beside them, he draped the folds of the cape about her. Then he lay down himself.

In the next few moments of silence, one of the wounded men nearby groaned. Another whispered something to console him.

"I tell you, Balalas," Xanthos said quietly. "The cruelties I have seen today, the torture and the brutality . . . I am convinced butchers are butchers whether they are Turks who massacre Greeks at Kydonies or Greeks who massacre Turks at Tripolitza."

He twisted on his side, staring toward the sky in the distance, a crimson reflection of flames.

"There is no victory for us, however just our cause," he said, "if we do not overcome the temptation to hatred. I could never raise my hand in hate to kill another human being. If we do not show mercy even toward our enemies, how do we differ from the animals?"

Conscious suddenly that the Maniat was not listening to

him, that he had slipped into sleep, Xanthos fell silent. He watched the torches planted on long stakes around the courtyard begin to burn low, a few fading into smoldering red cores of glowing ash. He heard the coming and going of small groups of noisy, excited men, the snarling of dogs from some dark street not too far away, and, from time to time, a sporadic burst of gunfire carried across the night.

He heard the girl moving, sliding her body lightly along the ground. She came to rest closer beside him, her shoulder pressed timidly against his arm, seeking warmth and reassurance. He reached out and gently touched her cheek, feeling her skin flawless and soft beneath his fingers. Once again he thought of Chryseis and he cried quietly then with homesickness and longing for his island and his love.

Despite his exhaustion, he could not sleep. The dreadful sights of the day, a lifetime of horror, would not leave his thoughts. And he knew that the plunderings and slaughter were still going on in other parts of the city. In addition, the stench of the air grew stronger with each hour, reeking odors of raw blood and putrid flesh. Grateful for the warmth of the girl, he waited tensely for the dawn.

When the first purple blemishes of daylight appeared at the peaks of the surrounding mountains, he heard the rumble and creak of wagons entering the courtyard. He sat up quickly and, as if she too had been sleepless, the girl raised her head.

The shadowed figures of men, apparitions in the gloom, descended from the wagons, calming the donkeys that were tense and jittery in the foul air. The men moved among the wounded, hurriedly raising them to be loaded on the wagons. One of the wounded men moaned as they bumped him. Xanthos reached down beside him to shake the arm of Balalas gently.

"Balalas," he said. "The wagons are here."

The soldiers came to the wounded man nearest to them,

bent and heaved him up as he cried out for them to be careful.

Xanthos shook the Maniat again.

"Balalas," he said urgently. "Come on, old friend, it's time for us to move out."

With a sudden dread, he bent closer to Balalas. In the gloomy, sodden light of the grisly dawn, he saw the flinted hardness of the Maniat's cheeks, his face rigid and unmoving as stone.

As if she understood what had happened, the girl knelt beside Xanthos, her tiny fingers clutching his arm.

"Is Balalas ready?" One of the soldiers asked.

"He's dead," Xanthos said.

The soldier moved on. Xanthos remained on his knees beside the Maniat. He reached out to touch his face, his throat, his chest and sturdy arms in a senseless, frantic stroking and rubbing. He felt the anguish of the day and night join his grief at that moment.

Balalas was dead. The valorous veteran of countless battles, formidable as a hill-bred lion, had died, not as Ajax prayed to the gods for death, in daylight, but silently in darkness, only a solitary friend and a Moslem girl as his companions.

The two soldiers completed loading the wagons, anxious to be on their way. Except for Xanthos and the girl, the courtyard was empty, the men about the kettles having left during the night.

"We can't leave Balalas like this," Xanthos said to one of the soldiers. "Can we take a few minutes to bury him?"

The soldier spit on the ground.

"You must be crazy," he said harshly. "The whole blasted city is littered with unburied bodies. If we don't get out of this stink soon, we'll join them." He waved the other soldier to the second wagon and moved to mount to his own seat.

Xanthos followed him, his grief for Balalas submerged in his fear for the girl.

"Can we come with you?"

"My orders are to carry only the wounded."

"Balalas wanted you to take us."

"Balalas is dead."

"In God's name, have mercy!"

The soldier pulled impatiently at the reins.

"There's no room in the wagons anyway," he said. "You can tag along in back if you like. If you fall behind, I won't wait for you."

He struck the reins sharply across the flanks of the donkey and the wagon jolted forward.

Xanthos hurried back to the girl, wrapping the cape about her shoulders. As he raised the hood over her hair, he saw her eyes, large and black, staring at him with a strange devotion.

He bent one last time beside the body of the veteran, making his cross and murmuring a low, quick prayer. He took the Maniat's weapons, the dagger and the pistol, slipped them into his belt. He mantled Balalas with a blanket, wrapping it tightly around his head. He rose and from a branch of the lemon tree above them he gathered a handful of petals and leaves that he scattered across the body.

He motioned urgently to the girl and they started to the gate as the second wagon rolled through the portals. On the threshold of the courtyard, Xanthos looked back a final time. A murmur of wind touched the branches and leaves of the trees. The dawn, a streaking of scarlet and purple clouds, painted the stone of the fountain, gilding the dolphin, tinting the canopy and ledges. A burial catafalque worthy of a pagan king, he thought with a flicker of solace.

They emerged into the narrow street, the girl's sandal-clad feet running to keep pace with his longer, quicker stride.

Away from the small refuge of the courtyard, hurled into the city once more, seeing the grotesque forms of bodies as if they floated in the mist, fear and the sweat of fear came to him again. The wagons ahead were lost to their sight but the wheels echoed in rumblings back to them. He hurried the girl on so they would not fall too far behind.

They had gone only the length of a street, his head bent because the unbearable stench made it painful to breath, when a shadow separating from the pillar, lunged upon him. A fierce blow struck him across the temple, stunning his senses, driving him to his knees. The girl tangled in the cape and fell, a muffled shriek rising from beneath the cloth.

Swaying on his knees, Xanthos saw the hunchback. The man leaped to loom above him, mist flashing on a knife. When the blade split and severed the flesh of his shoulder, he screamed. Tearing the knife free, the hunchback struck again, scraping the bone and ripping the flesh of his cheek. He sprawled backwards on the street, his arms flung out, a wind blast of pain and terror gusting in his blood. The hunchback straddled him, grabbed him by the hair, baring his throat for a final thrust.

In that moment the girl scampered to flee, cape whipping off like a severed black wing. The hunchback bounded off Xanthos, snaring her in a swift and crooked leap. Beating savagely at her head with his fist, he dragged her frail body across the stones. Then they were lost to sight in the mist but through the hissing and bubbling of his blood, Xanthos could hear the dull, thudding hammer of the blows.

He did not know how long he groveled there. There were the grunts and groans of the hunchback, like the wild ruttings of some beast, but no sound from the girl and he knew she was dead. He made an effort to rise, whimpering and moaning, slipping on the gore that formed a puddle beneath him. He felt the blood flowing from his body, emptying his veins, his life draining out. Then I will die too, he thought, my history unwritten, my Chryseis unloved.

The hunchback emerged from the shadows, huge, twisted body bobbing up and down. In Xanthos then, surpassing pain, terror and the squall of his blood surged a hate so intense it bred a trenchant strength. Twisting his body, fingers clawing for the pistol in his belt, he tugged it free.

"Gold," he whispered. "Gold."

Ready to flee, the hunchback paused.

"Help me," Xanthos cried softly. "I'll give you my gold."

As the hunchback swooped again upon him, knife raised once more, Xanthos flung up the pistol, the long barrel almost touching the shocked eyes. He pulled the trigger, a burst jarring his flesh.

The hunchback's face shattered and he flew backwards. Landing on the stone of the street, his heavy body whipped and flopped in a thrashing, headless frenzy. Then his misshapen trunk lay still.

As if the bullet had also extinguished his life, Xanthos tumbled into darkness.

II

A high, narrow window set in rough stone. A patch of open sky beyond that aperture, sometimes blue tracked by the filament of clouds, again night-black etched by fragments of an aloof moon. Around him he heard the tolling of bells, the braying of donkeys, the creak of a mill wheel, the chanting of voices. Closer, a white stub of candle, the flame curling and wavering at the summons of the wind.

Xanthos recalled these impressions woven into the threads of a web that enmeshed him. While, on a proscenium before them all, a face floated in and out of his vision, features indistinguishable but attached to the ministrations of gentle hands, drawing the coverlet to his throat, bathing his stiff and aching body, feeding him with a voice wheedling and coaxing as that of a playmate from his childhood.

"Honey and a tonic, Brother, for feasting and healing."

Then the face within the nimbus haze broke free, becoming clear and well defined. A head with white hair, sparse across a rolling forehead, thick white brows over eyes of an innocent and beguiling blue, cheeks high boned and flushed like fruit, a bountiful brush of silvery beard.

The countenance smiled, so compelling and engaging a salutation that Xanthos made an effort to respond. The muscles of his face strained in vigorous refusal but some sign of the exertion must have been visible.

"Wonderful!" the monk cried, his voice as convivial as his smile. "God bless us! Wonderful!"

"Who are you?" Xanthos asked. His tongue slurred the words as if speech, like smiling, were a faculty he had not used in a long time.

"I am Brother Apostolos," the monk said. "But, in honesty,

I must tell you that a number of the members of our order here call me Brother Foolish, because, you see, I am short on sense." As if the confession tickled him, he burst into genial laughter. When he regained his breath, he said, "And this is the monastery of Aghios Vasilios in the mountains near Kalavryta."

Xanthos wished to ask how he had gotten to the monastery but the few words he uttered had exhausted him. The monk seemed to understand.

"You have been ill, very ill," he said. "Oh, when they brought you in, the abbot, the Brothers, no one thought you would live. You had lost so much blood and your wounds were terrible! God bless us, you survived!" He beamed at Xanthos, arched his gaze to the ceiling of the cell and made his cross in a flurried motion of his hand, up, down and touching both shoulders.

"The war?" Xanthos asked.

"Oh yes, the war!" The monk's thick brows hinged forward, and he frowned. "The war goes on. They are fighting here and there. Some victories and some defeats . . . oh yes, the war. And the plague."

Xanthos' lips formed the dreaded word.

"Yes, the plague!" the monk whispered. "Terrible . . . terrible, they say thousands are dying." He commiserated briefly. "But I cannot do anything about those poor souls. You are my charge. And you are getting better. Soon, now, you will be able to get up."

"How long have I been here?"

Brother Apostolos stroked his silvery beard.

"They brought you . . . I think, yes, I believe six weeks ago, or was it seven?"

The bells he recalled from his dreams tolled and echoed through the small stone cell. The monk rose quickly to his feet. He was short, round-shouldered, with pale and stubby fingers.

"I must go to prayers," he said. "His reverence, the abbot,

does not tolerate our absence for any reason. I will be gone only a little while and then I will bring you something to eat."

"Honey and a tonic, for feasting and healing," Xanthos said.

"Wonderful!" Brother Apostolos cried. "God bless us! Wonderful! See how they have helped?"

He hurried to the doorway, pausing at the threshold to wave Xanthos a fleeting, consolatory farewell.

In the days that followed, Xanthos felt better and, rising from his bed, was able to go outside. He was still weak and unsteady on his feet, unable yet to raise the arm where his shoulder had been wounded. Brother Apostolos aided him in walking slowly back and forth along the upper terrace of the cloisters. Sometimes he sat for a while on one of the rough benches, absorbing the fading warmth of the winter sun. In the courtyard below, the robed figures of the monks went about their tasks, gardening, working the mill wheel, feeding the tethered donkeys. When the bells of the monastery rang, they left their work and moved into the chapel for prayers.

Then for a little while Xanthos sat alone in the silence of the cloisters. Across the tiled roofs of the monastery buildings, beyond the bell tower that loomed like the rampart of a citadel in the sky, he saw the range of peaks that looked down on Tripolitza. He thought of Balalas, Kolokotronis, Niketaras, the captains and the men. The disorder of those weeks of siege, the carnage of the assault, seemed, in these serene, unflurried surroundings, obscured as if they were events he had experienced years before. Only the young Turkish girl and the hunchback scourged his memory.

The other monks rarely spoke to him or to one another, going about their duties silently engrossed in their thoughts. When they passed him, sitting or walking, they thrust their heads lower into their cowls, murmuring some inaudible greeting. But Xanthos was never lonely, because Brother Apostolos was with him often.

"A smell of snow in the air today," he said to Xanthos one morning as they sat on the bench together.

"Does much snow fall here?"

"Not until late December," the monk said. "Sometimes we get a heavy snowfall then. For a while the earth seems mantled in a purity that suggests all our insalubrious sins have been cleansed." He paused, his eyes sparkling. "Isn't that a lovely phrase?"

"Poetic and lovely," Xanthos said.

"It belongs to Brother Mathon," the monk said, and sighed. "I don't really mean to steal them but I can't think of any original ones myself. And Brother Mathon devises such splendid thoughts, even his reverence is impressed." He whistled softly in admiration of any feat that could impress the abbot. "If I could think of such fine phrases," he said, "I would probably have to add the sin of pride to my other sins. Not that those are significant, because opportunities here are limited." He looked around warily and lowered his voice. "My biggest affliction is gluttony. Sometimes a little sweet red wine I'm not supposed to have or a parcel of rabbit stew. One gets weary of mountain greens, you know, makes one's stomach thorny and dry."

Suddenly, as if he had just thought of something, his cheeks flushed brighter and he leaned nearer to Xanthos.

"Sometimes there are important sins," he said in a low, exhilarated voice. "Like the attachment some years ago of one of our older Brothers to a young novitiate." He faltered, struggling between the urge to continue and some mandate of caution. "I better stop," he said ruefully. "His reverence has warned me about gossip. But I do love it so, especially the scandals."

Sometimes in the late evening, when Xanthos was restless and could not sleep, shivering because the rawness of the

December nights seeped into his stone cell, he walked along the terrace that was splashed in the glow of an unblinking moon and descended the steps to enter the church.

In the damp, gloomy sanctuary, empty at that hour and lit only by a few flickering candles, amid the scents of incense, he knelt and prayed. Among the artifacts the monks revered as devotional and precious, the sacred icons and the mosaics fashioned in piety centuries before, he did not invoke the Father of Mercies for himself but for his struggling people and for the land they sought to free. But, for whatever the reason, perhaps because his heart was weary and his spirit afflicted, he felt himself an unworthy petitioner, his profligate prayer remaining earthbound and mute.

On a morning when he and Brother Apostolos walked together further from the enclosure of the cloisters than Xanthos had ever gone before, passing a building separated by a graveyard from the main part of the monastery, he heard the unmistakable sound of children's voices. He looked in surprise at Brother Apostolos.

"Oh yes, there are children here," the monk said. "We have about thirty boys, children whose parents are fighting or missing, and who have been sent here for safety."

"How old are they?"

The monk struck his cheek several times as he pondered.

"Eight or ten, I think, perhaps up to fourteen or fifteen."

"I had told you, Brother, that I was a teacher on Zante," Xanthos said. "If it would not disrupt the routine of the monastery, I would be glad to teach the children a few classes. The sums of arithmetic and some geography. That would provide a way for me to be of some use until I am strong enough to return to my duties."

"God bless us!" the monk cried. "I will implore the abbot right away, but I am sure his reverence will be delighted! The Brothers have been teaching the children church history and the Scriptures, but none of them could teach arithmetic and geography! Wonderful!"

He started for the main buildings and then turned back.

"Do you think, Brother," he said, his eyes earnest and pleading, "that if I promised to sit well behind the children, not moving or uttering a sound, that you might allow me to join the class?"

"I would be honored to have you, Brother," Xanthos said.

Brother Apostolos released a fervent, thankful sigh. He rushed away then to seek the abbot's consent, his ragged cassock flapping about his bare feet in their patched and mended sandals.

Each morning in the days that followed, Xanthos gathered with the children in one of the rooms of the cloisters or on one of the terraces. He taught them to add and subtract and spoke of oceans and continents across the world. There were times during those days when it seemed to him he taught in a classroom on his island of Zante once more. Closing his eyes for a few moments while a student recited, he envisioned opening them to see the lovely countenance of Chryseis.

The most diligent and attentive participant in the class was Brother Apostolos. Although he never spoke, remaining as inconspicuous as he could, he attended zealously on every word Xanthos or the students uttered. If a student recited well, the monk brightened in triumph, while if a student faltered or could not answer, the monk shared his ignominy and distress.

There was a morning in middle December when they had begun their class for the day inside the cloisters because a dark, seething mass of clouds hung overhead. Then a wind rose and the clouds scattered, the sun breaking free, the firmament gleaming crisp and blue. Xanthos moved the class to the terrace, sunlight and the brisk air bringing smudges of color to the children's cheeks.

In the course of their lessons that morning, he mentioned the war and the children grew tense and excited. Two of the older boys jumped up, racing about the terrace, grimacing and snarling, swinging their arms as if they brandished swords at one another. The mock duel sparked grim memories in Xanthos and with his voice trembling, he called for them to stop.

"But we are practicing to kill Turks, teacher," one of the boys said earnestly. "They are our enemies and we must kill them!"

"The Turkish fathers and brothers are enemies of your fathers and brothers now," Xanthos said, "but a day may come when they will not be your enemies, a day when hate and violence will be superfluous on the road of your lives."

In the moments that followed, he tried to tell them of the elegies that lingered in his heart. The glory of their ancient, hallowed race; poets and kings whose deaths were rituals for noble resurrections; men's valor against invading hosts; the depredations of these same men against their brothers. He spoke of the rage and sorrow of a nation's decline and the despairing centuries of bondage; freedom banished and chained for so long but surviving from generation to generation, knotted, obstinate and persevering as the olive tree that flourishes among the stones.

He warned them of the evils of ignorance, the malignance of power, the corrosions of greed, envy, vanity, ambition; the eviscerations of war, throttling mercy and compassion, despoiling men's dreams so they became the gutted shipwrecks of nightmares.

Suddenly he became aware the children were not listening to him. Before their restless, inattentive faces, his voice grew irresolute. What he sought to explain was unexplainable to them. Yet he could not stop chattering, could not cease trying to make them understand, his tone shriller, his words flogging the wind.

At that moment, beyond the children, he saw the hand of

Brother Apostolos raised in a timorous wave for his attention, the first time in all the classes that the monk ventured to speak. Without waiting for Xanthos to acknowledge him, Brother Apostolos pointed slowly and warily to the railing of the terrace, where a solitary and downy thrush perched on a narrow ledge.

"Teacher, please hush," the monk said gently. "Let us listen to the thrush."

As the children turned to look at the bird, Xanthos heard the fluent, tremulous and iridescent melody rising in clear, cherished tones from the bird's throat and tiny beak.

The sweet and haunting song was a medley of vast journeys; flights above rocks and the crests of trees; over groves and orchards and the temple ruins; shadows of wings reflected in island-strewn seas; soarings by the lamp-vigils and candle-flakings of the stars; leapings through the storm and tempest; into the wild and honey gardens of the sun.

The children listened transfixed and silent, and in his battered spirit Xanthos divined the dream. The words, the books, the descriptions, the efforts to unravel and explain, all were fossils of the vision, the babble of sullen, sightless men.

The thrush was Greece, its song an unfoldment of the lovely, eternal and inextinguishable land.

The thrush was Greece . . . he knew by the grateful and consoling tears of his soul. And he would hush so they might listen.

EPILOGUE

The Greek War of Independence lasted almost ten years. For most of that time, the fighting was limited to the Peloponnesus, a few mountainous regions of northern Greece and Crete, and to the engagements of the Greek fleet at sea. But the brutality and ferocity of the struggle matched that of any global conflict. That the Greeks were not always in agreement on the course of the war was proven by the two civil wars that were fought during the revolution, and that once, three assemblies convened at the same time in different parts of Greece, each one claiming to have been lawfully granted the authority to represent the people.

If any single element united the Greeks during the ten years, it was their suffering. The community of Kydonies was destroyed in 1821, men massacred and women and children sold into slavery in the thriving markets of the Ottoman Empire. The island of Chios suffered the same fate in 1822 (to become the subject of the painting by Delacroix, *Massacre at Chios*), the island of Psara in 1824; and there were massacres of thousands of Cretans that same year, and the fall and massacre of the Greeks at Missolonghi in 1826 (where Lord Byron, lover of the Greek spirit, had died of

disease in 1824). In 1825, the dreaded Ibrahim Pasha, son of
Mehemet Ali of Egypt, vassal and ally to the Sultan, in-
vaded the Peloponnesus with a strong force of Egyptians
and for the next five years burned and devastated that land.
But the Greeks made a few cruel entries of their own, nota-
bly the massacre of Turks at Tripolitza.

When it seemed that Ibrahim Pasha would reconquer
those final areas of Greece still remaining free, a muddled
or deliberate misinterpretation of orders from the Admiralty
by an English admiral named Codrington, who was sympathetic to the Greeks, produced, at Navarino, one of the great
sea battles in history, where a fleet of English, French and
Russian ships sank a fleet of almost eighty Egyptian and
Turkish warships. By this irredeemable defeat, the Turks
were denied any ultimate victory, although Ibrahim Pasha
continued to ravage the land for several more years.

When the Egyptians and Turks were finally driven from
the Peloponnesus, among the bounties won by the Greeks
were a devastating famine, widespread disease, strife and
rampant jealousy among factions of her leaders, and the
humiliation of having the Great Powers so apportion her
boundaries that only 800,000 Greeks lived within the new
free Greece while 2,500,000 still dwelt in unliberated terri-
tories. Among the areas excluded from the Greek state were
the Ionian islands, Thessaly, Macedonia, western Thrace, a
part of Epirus and the eastern Aegean islands. Also excluded
was the island of Crete. By that culpable decision, Cretans
obtained only the freedom to fight and die for an additional
seventy-five years before they gained their independence.
Finally, to exercise some control over the volatile Greeks,
the Great Powers installed a foreign king, Otho, son of King
Ludwig of Bavaria, to rule the new Greek state.

For any novelist or historian writing of Greece, the province of what is fictional or mythic and that of what is fac-
tual, are often inextricably meshed. The sense of place and
of time is so immersed in a vision and memory of the past,

that all events are somehow obscured in what the humanist-scientist Loren Eiseley has called the "necromantic centuries."

One heroic fact about that small, mountainous and tragic country comes stunningly clear. From the time of the Persian invasions, through centuries of Roman and Ottoman rule, through two world wars, two Balkan wars, an Italian invasion, and German occupation in World War II among the most brutal imposed on any conquered land in history, she has managed to endure and survive. Even in recent times, after World War II, she suffered famine, a fearful civil war, and a series of military coups from which she has just emerged, free once more.

Perhaps an answer to the method of that survival is provided by the poet and novelist Nikos Kazantzakis, the greatest of the modern Greeks.

"The Greek Race has always been, and still is, the race which possesses the great and dangerous prerogative of performing miracles. Just like the powerful, long enduring races, the Greek race may reach the depth of the chasm, and exactly there, at the most critical instant, where the weaker are destroyed, it fashions the miracle. It mobilizes all of its qualities and in one stroke soars up, without intermediate pause, to the summit of salvation. This abrupt surge, toward the heights, unexpected by logic, is called, 'miracle.'"

HARRY MARK PETRAKIS
Dune Acres, Indiana
1976

GLOSSARY

AGA	Turkish military chief
AGORA	Marketplace
ARCHON	Greek of the upper class. (Also PRIMATE.)
ARMATOLOS	Greek militiaman retained by Turks to protect the roads against the klepht bands
BEY	Turkish dignitary, ruler
BISMILLAH	"In the name of Allah" Turkish battle cry
BRULOT	Fire-ship
CAÏQUE	Small fishing boat
CAPITAN-PASHA	Lord High Admiral of the Turkish fleet
CAPOTE	Greek peasant's cape
CHAROS	Death, and the ferryman of Death (also CHARON)
CHIBOUK	Long-stemmed pipe
DERVISH	Moslem monk, sometimes practicing whirling, howling as a religious act

FUSTANELLA	White, pleated kilt worn by Greek peasants
GIAGIA	Grandmother
GIASOU	Hello, how are you?
GLENDI	Feast, celebration
INFIDEL	Derogatory term for unbeliever
JANIZARY	(pl. JANIZARIES) Turkish mercenaries conscripted at first from Christian families by taking the elder son
KAFENEION	Coffeehouse-tavern
KHARAJ	Head-tax required of every non-Moslem subject of the Sultan to avoid beheading
KLEPHT	Greek guerrilla fighter, mountain dweller
KOUMBAROS	Best man, godfather of one's child
MANTINADES	Rhymed, song-poems
MOREA	Peloponnesus
MULLAH	Turkish priest, teacher
MUSSULMAN	Turk. (Also, MOSLEM, OTTOMAN.)
PALIKAR	Warrior
PARNASSUS	Mountain in central Greece.
PASHA	Turkish ruler of a province or pashalik
PHANARIOT	Greek from the Phanar or Lighthouse Section of Constantinople
RAYAH	Human cattle
RHYMADORI	Balladeer, folk singer
SERAGLIO	Turkish palace, sometimes harem quarters
SERASKER	Turkish commander. (Also KAIMAKAM, VOIVODE.)
STREMA	About a quarter acre of land
SUBLIME PORTE	Seat of Turkish Government, palace of Sultan Mahmud II

SULTAN	Ruler of the Turkish Empire; in 1821, Sultan Mahmud II
TAYGETUS	Mountain of the Mani
TURKOCRETANS	Cretan apostates who accepted Moslem faith
VIZIER	Turkish administrator
VRAKES	Cretan, baggy breeches
YATAGHAN	Long, curved sword